LEGACY OF THE LOST

ATLANTIS LEGACY, BOOK 1

LINDSEY FAIRLEIGH

RUBUS PRESS

Editing by Katherine Shaw
www.katherinedshaw.com/

Cover by We Got You Covered
www.wegotyoucoveredbookdesign.com/

ISBN: 978-1949485141

MORE BOOKS BY LINDSEY FAIRLEIGH

ATLANTIS LEGACY

Sacrifice of the Sinners

Legacy of the Lost

Fate of the Fallen

ECHO TRILOGY

Echo in Time

Resonance

Time Anomaly

Dissonance

Ricochet Through Time

KAT DUBOIS CHRONICLES

Ink Witch

Outcast

Underground

Soul Eater

Judgement

Afterlife

THE ENDING SERIES

The Ending Beginnings: Omnibus Edition

After The Ending

Into The Fire

Out Of The Ashes

Before The Dawn

World Before

For more information on Lindsey and her books:

www.lindseyfairleigh.com

Join Lindsey's mailing list to stay up to date on releases

AND to get a FREE copy of *Sacrifice of the Sinners.*

www.lindseyfairleigh.com/sacrifice

For all who are afraid
but do it anyway.

"Get down!" Fiona shouted, her voice ricocheting off the cavern walls.

I reacted without thinking, dropping to my belly and making myself as flat as possible. An arrow whizzed past my right ear as I pressed my cheek against cool, rough stone.

On the very edge of my vision, I could see Fiona laying a few feet behind me, one hand covering the back of her ducked head, the other beneath her, clutching the Staff of Osiris. A horde of black-robed goons was pouring out through the gleaming, golden exit of the tomb we'd just raided, some hundred paces beyond Fiona. The sound of their footfall thundered up the cave, echoing off the walls, growing ever louder.

I rolled onto my left side, pulling the pistol from the holster strapped to my thigh. Curling upward, I aimed the gun over Fiona's auburn ponytail, targeting our pursuers.

Two bowmen fanned out from the head of the horde and settled into firing stances near the cavern walls. We were maybe forty yards from reaching the mouth of the cave. With them firing on us, we would never make it out alive.

Sweat coated my palms, but my grip on the gun remained steady. Just three rounds left. I had to make each shot count.

I squeezed the trigger. The explosive crack of gunfire was magnified by the stone surrounding us, making my ears ring.

My aim was true, and the bullet struck the nearest bowman in the shoulder. He spun around, black robes flaring out, and landed face-first on the cavern floor. His comrades swarmed over him, but thankfully, none paused to retrieve his bow. The action must not have been programmed into them.

Shifting my aim to the right, I focused on the other bowman, nearest the tomb, and pulled the trigger.

"Shit!" I hissed as the bowman ducked behind a massive stalagmite. But I didn't lower my gun. I had one round left. I couldn't miss. If I did, we were dead.

I inhaled deeply, held my breath, and waited. Seconds passed. My pulse hammered in my ears. The horde drew ever closer.

The bowman finally peeked out from behind the stalagmite, and I didn't hesitate. I squeezed the trigger, blinking reflexively.

In that fraction of a second, the bullet struck the bowman in the abdomen. He stumbled back a few paces, then dropped to his knees and keeled over.

I watched him for a moment, making sure he was really down. Belly shots were tricky. But thankfully, he didn't move again.

Blowing out my breath, I shoved my pistol back into its holster and rolled onto my belly. The horde was halfway to us. We were running out of time.

"Let's go!" I yelled to Fiona, scrambling up to my feet.

As I lurched into a dead sprint, I could hear Fiona's boots slapping stone right behind me.

The mouth of the cave, a bright beacon just ahead, beckoned us onward. Our pursuers were close on our heels, but daylight— safety—was mere paces away.

I spared the quickest glance over my shoulder, the corner of my mouth raising in a faint smirk. They were too far behind us; they couldn't possibly catch us, now.

When I returned my attention to the way ahead, my eyes widened. The mouth of the cave opened to a sheer cliff high above the glittering Nile.

I skidded to a halt, barely stopping myself from hurtling over the precipice. I thrust out my arm, sucking in a breath to warn Fiona to stop.

"It's the only way!" she shouted, ramming into my arm and grabbing on with her free hand.

I screamed as she yanked me over the edge, and down, down, down we fell . . .

"Cora?" Fingers touched my shoulder through the cotton of my T-shirt. Real fingers, not virtual ones.

Startled, I jumped out of my chair, tripping over the stocky pit bull lying at my feet. I stumbled into the desk off to the right, the cord of the virtual reality headset pulling tight between me and the console, and the jerky motion yanked the headset clean off my head. I lunged to the side, barely catching the headset by the cord before it crashed onto the hardwood floor.

Roused from her slumber, my dog Tila ambled past me, snorting derisively. She settled down near the dormant fireplace in the patch of rare March sunlight filtering in through the window, shooting me a baleful glance for the unwelcome disruption.

"Fio!" I said, voice raised, fingers fumbling with the VR headset to angle the microphone toward my mouth. "I'll be right back. Hang on . . ." I tucked the headset under my arm, pressed the button on the back of my interactive gloves that would withdraw me from the game, and turned around to face the intruder.

Emerging from the virtual world was always a disorienting

experience—for anybody. But for me, the jarring transition verged on painful. In the virtual world, I could be whoever I wanted to be. Go wherever I wanted to go. In there, I could have adventures that felt almost real. But out here, in the real world, simply leaving the house for a quick trip to the grocery store felt like a life-and-death excursion.

Out here, I had to face the truth of my pathetic existence: for the rest of my life, I would never really go anywhere, and I would never really *do* anything. I was twenty-six going on ninety, a prisoner of my own body. Of my own mind.

Emi stood behind the discarded desk chair, petite and poised, hands upraised and expression appeasing. "Sorry, Cora," she said, angling her head to the side. Her long, sleek braid slipped over her shoulder, and the light from the desk lamp lent a golden gleam to the gray streaks in her black hair. "I shouldn't have touched you—I know," she said, "but I couldn't get your attention, and—"

I raised my eyebrows. Emi knew better than anyone how dangerous a simple touch could be to me. It could trigger an *episode*. An attack. It could leave me bedridden, trembling as I fought to break free from the prison of my own mind. I pressed my lips together, thinking she'd better have a good reason for playing fast and loose with my sanity.

I grabbed the pair of discarded gloves off the desk and tugged them on, covering my hands and forearms with the thinnest, softest leather. They were custom made by a glover in Italy, a guy my mom found years ago during one of her trips. I had a pair for every season, plus a few dozen extra. My "episodes" were triggered by skin-to-skin contact, but cotton and other knits had proven to be an unreliable barrier. Latex, rubber, and pleather worked well to prevent an episode, but they made my hands sweat like crazy. So, leather it was.

"You have a package," Emi told me. If that was her excuse

for risking touching me, it wasn't nearly good enough. Unless . . .

A surge of excitement made me all too eager to forgive and forget. Emi had been careless, but no real harm had been done, after all. And I had a new toy to try out—a full-body virtual reality suit meant to translate the sensations from the virtual world into the real one. It was the latest, greatest gadget on the gamer scene, and I couldn't wait to get my hands on it.

"Where is it?" I asked, giving the bedroom a quick scan. The box would be large. Hard to miss.

Emi stepped to the side, rolling my abandoned chair out of the way right along with her to reveal the brown box resting on the foot of the four-poster bed. It was smaller than I'd been expecting—barely larger than the standard shoebox, but not nearly large enough to contain a whole VR suit. Had they only sent part of it?

I started toward the bed, but my steps faltered. The box didn't bear the tell-tale logo of *Techtopia*; the massive online tech retailer didn't miss a chance to advertise, which meant no box ever left their vast warehouses without their logo stamped on all sides. *This* box, however, was dented and battered, with no identifying markers other than a hand-scrawled address and foreign-looking postage markings on the top. This was definitely *not* a package from *Techtopia*.

Frozen in place, I furrowed my brow. I glanced at Emi, then back at the box.

My name—Cora Blackthorn—had been written hastily on the top in black permanent marker, along with the rest of the address for Blackthorn Manor. But that didn't make the hand-writing any less recognizable.

The writing was my mom's.

The small surge of excitement from moments ago melted, warping into dread. The unsettling sensation pooled in my belly, leaden and sickening.

The only other time my mom had ever sent me a package while she was away on an expedition, she hadn't expected to return home. She had sent me the package because she'd wanted the invaluable artifacts within to have a chance to make it to safety, even if she couldn't. I hadn't seen or heard a thing from her for nearly two months after receiving the package. I was twelve, at the time, and I thought mom was dead. I mourned her.

When she finally surfaced, more than a little worse for wear, I gave her the silent treatment for another two months, hoping my cold shoulder would force her to rethink her constant need to gallivant around the globe in search of adventure. Hoping she would, for once, choose me.

And it had worked. She'd stayed home. For a little while.

I stared at the package on the bed. How long would I have to wait for her, this time? Another two months? A year?

Forever?

"Emi . . ." I looked at my mom's best friend, my chin trembling. "When was the last time you talked to my mom?"

Emi and her son, Raiden, had lived in the hill house on the edge of our estate, Blackthorn Manor, for as long as I could remember. She and my mom were incredibly close, often fighting like sisters. Emi was a second mother to me, caring for me when my mom was away. Sometimes she seemed more like a mother than my own mom. It wasn't unheard of for my mom to call Emi when she was away, but not call me. But it was unheard of for Emi not to share word of the call.

Emi's dark eyes glistened with unshed tears. I could understand now why she'd risked touching me to get my attention. She hadn't been careless, at all; she'd been afraid. Afraid of what was in the box. Afraid of what the box meant.

I had a feeling I wouldn't be rejoining Fiona in the game anytime soon.

Emi gripped her onyx braid with slender fingers until her knuckles blanched. She shook her head. "I haven't spoken to

Diana since her call a couple weeks ago," she said. "You know how she is—always so bad about checking in."

I had spoken to her then, too. Weeks ago. She'd been in Brazil, hopped up on the adrenaline of a promising lead, certain she was days away from discovering *Z*, the lost city made famous by Col. Percy Fawcett's obsession and resulting disappearance in the 1920s.

My mouth went dry, and I swallowed roughly. What if that brief phone conversation was the last time I ever heard my mom's voice?

"Be careful," I'd said for what had felt like the millionth time over the last two and a half decades.

My mom's response had been the same as ever. *"Always."*

I cleared my throat, eyes glued to the package. "What's in it?" I asked, fully aware that Emi couldn't possibly know, because the box remained unopened.

Emi moved closer to the bed and reached out, skimming her fingertips along the top of the box. Her eyes met mine, and she gulped. "Only one way to find out."

Fighting through the paralyzing fear, I moved closer to the bed and, gripping the carved wooden post, sat on the edge. I released the bedpost and reached for the package, hands trembling.

Out of the corner of my eye, I could see Emi gripping the top of the chairback tightly, her delicate fingers digging into the cushioned leather.

I moved the box to my lap and started picking at a corner of the packing tape. Despite being roughly the size of a shoebox, the package was light—lighter than it would have been had it actually contained shoes, even sandals.

"Here," Emi said, drawing my gaze as she plucked a pair of scissors from the ceramic utensil cup on my desk.

Emi held the scissors out for me.

"Thanks," I said, accepting them.

I hesitated for a few seconds, scissors opened wide and one pointed blade poised over the seam of the package. I licked my lips. Maybe there was nothing to fear. Maybe this was just a souvenir. Just some trinket.

My gut told me that wasn't the case.

I pressed the blade against the packing tape, sinking it into the seam. The adhesive strip resisted for a moment, then gave with a gentle *pop*. Breath held, I slid the scissors along the length of the package, then cut the tape along the sides.

I exhaled slowly, then drew in another breath as I slid my thumbs into the opening and lifted the flaps.

The box was filled to the brim with wadded-up newspaper. I took out a ball of newspaper and unfurled the sheet. The words printed on the page weren't in English. The language was easy enough for me to identify—Italian, one of the three foreign languages I'd mastered during my homeschooled studies. I was also fluent in Spanish and Arabic, and I was currently working on a fourth language—Gaeilge—courtesy of Fiona, who got a kick out of my butchered pronunciations of her native, tongue-twisting vocabulary. It's amazing the skills you can master when you have no place to go and nothing but time on your hands.

I balled up the sheet of newspaper and tossed it onto the floor, then closed the box so I could see the postage mark.

Rome. Shipped out eleven days ago.

Anything could've happened to my mom in that span of time.

"What was she doing in Italy?" I wondered aloud, glancing at Emi.

This was supposed to have been a South America trip. A few months in the Amazon rainforest. Back by the end of March.

Emi's grip on her braid tightened, and she shook her head. "I don't know," she said, a haunted cast to her eyes.

I stared at her for a moment longer, trying to decipher her expression. Small but mighty, Emi was always cool composure and unshakable nerves—no doubt a result of the shadowed military past she shared with my mom. But she was shaken now, and seeing her like this frightened me almost more than the arrival of the package itself.

"Well," I said, turning my attention back to the box, "what did you send me, Mom?"

I pulled out sheet after sheet of crinkled-up newspaper, opening up each to ensure it was nothing more than filler. During my careful unpacking, I unearthed two newspaper-wrapped bundles; one the size of a baseball, though much lighter, the other small enough to fit in my closed fist. I set them beside me on the bed and continued the search.

At the very bottom of the box, I found a receipt, folded in half, and then folded in half again. There was handwriting on the back, the thick black ink easily visible through the thin paper.

"It's a note," I told Emi as I unfolded the receipt. Once again, my mom's distinctive semi-cursive handwriting was unmistakable. "It's from her."

"What does it say?" Emi asked, stepping closer. She eased down onto the foot of the bed, craning her neck to see the words.

"Cora," I read aloud, *"I screwed up."* My heart lurched and my voice failed, and I had to clear my throat in order to keep reading. *"I'm so sorry. These should help. You won't have to live in fear anymore. I wish I'd figured this out sooner. Everything could have been so much easier for you. Better late than never, I hope. I'm sorry, sweetie. I love you."*

When I finished reading, I closed my eyes, fighting the telltale sting of tears. My nostrils flared as I attempted to regulate my breathing. I clenched my teeth and opened my eyes, staring at the note but not really seeing it.

"May I?" Emi said, reaching for the slip of paper.

Numbly, I handed the receipt to her, then picked up the smaller of the newspaper-wrapped bundles. It was the heavier of the two, but by no means heavy. The majority of the bulk was paper, and unwrapping it seemed to take forever. But finally, I reached the core.

It was a necklace. An antique one, by the looks of it. The links of the gold chain were heavier than was fashionable for women's jewelry these days. A golden, teardrop-shaped pendant hung from the chain, about the size of a silver dollar. Delicate, intricate designs had been etched into the metal surrounding the smooth, round stone set into the center of the pendant. The stone was the color of yellow amber but devoid of any imperfection, and it had a strange, incandescent quality.

"It's beautiful," Emi said, her voice hushed.

I nodded. "And ancient."

It wasn't that the necklace looked old or worn or anything like that; rather, it appeared to be in pristine condition. But it *felt* old. I couldn't explain it, but instinct told me this pendant was older than anything I'd ever touched before.

"Here," I said, handing the necklace to Emi. "Take a look."

When she took it, I reached for the second bundle.

"That's interesting," Emi said, holding the pendant on the palm of her hand and letting the chain dangle.

"Hm?"

"Look," Emi said, angling her palm toward me so I had a good view of the pendant. "It must be some kind of a mood stone."

It took me a moment to register her meaning. But then I saw it. The stone was no longer amber; it was clear, devoid of all color.

I frowned. "Weird," I said, returning my attention to the second bundle as I unwrapped it.

The final layer of newspaper pulled away, and an orb as smooth as glass settled in my palm. It was filled with some sort of liquid, more viscous and far lighter than water, cut through by ribbons of glittering, gleaming turquoise that slowly shifted and swirled, ever-changing and never stopping. I was either looking at the world's most hypnotizing paper weight, or something else. I was leaning toward *something else.*

It started with just a tickle in my mind. The buzz of invisible mosquitos. It grew louder, until whispers filled my ears. Thousands of voices. Too many to distinguish one from another. Too many to ignore.

My mind suddenly felt fuzzy, my eyelids heavy. The room tilted to the side, then started to spin and darken as the voices grew louder and louder.

An episode. I was having an episode, I realized distantly. This one felt different. Strange. But it had to be an episode. It was the only explanation my hazy mind could come up with.

I thought I could hear Emi, but she was too far away. Her words were drowned out by the mass of voices, all shouting to be heard.

I was grateful for the darkness closing in around me. It promised peace. Quiet.

And thankfully, it delivered.

[3]

I woke in a daze, mind groggy and memory jumbled.

"Cora?" It was Emi. "Are you awake?"

It took some effort, but I managed to crack my eyelids open. One look at the brass and bronze light fixture on the ceiling, and I knew I was lying on my bed, stretched out on top of the comforter, from the feel of it.

I blinked, then opened my eyes wider and really looked around.

Tila lay stretched out beside me, a none-too-dainty snore rumbling the mattress with every inhale. Emi was perched on the edge of the bed near my right hip, her upper body angled toward me, close but not touching. She was cradling the glass orb in one hand, absentmindedly rubbing her thumb against the smooth surface.

"What happened?" I asked, then coughed gently to clear my throat.

Emi frowned, her eyes shifting from me to the glassy orb and back. "I was just about to ask you the same thing," she said softly.

Groaning, I propped myself up on my elbows, my stare

fixing on the orb. It was empty, looking like nothing more than clear glass Christmas tree ornament.

"It's empty," I commented.

Emi's brow furrowed. "There was something in it?"

I looked from the orb to Emi and back. "Yeah, the blue swirly stuff . . ."

"Oh." Emi frowned. "I didn't see that."

It was my turn to frown. Had I imagined the swirling ribbons of blue? Had it been a hallucination, just an early symptom of the mounting episode?

"So, was that an *episode*?" Emi asked, the concern in her voice palpable.

I swallowed roughly, finding the implications that touching the orb had caused an episode extremely disturbing. Up until this point in my life, the debilitating effects of my condition—the hallucinations, seizures, and on occasion, loss of consciousness —had only reared their ugly heads when I'd had *human* contact. Skin-to-skin, for the most part. Animals were a safe zone.

But if touching *things* was going to start triggering episodes now, I might as well just seal myself off in a bubble. No food or water, thanks. If I couldn't touch any*thing* anymore, I wouldn't want to live that long, anyway.

"It felt kind of like one," I admitted reluctantly. Speaking the words out loud made the horrific implications seem that much more real. That much more threatening. What would trigger an episode next? Tila? My computer? The VR headset? A glass of water? The *air*?

I let my elbows slide out from behind me and dropped back down to the bed, exhaling in a huff. After a second thought, the few days it would take me to perish in that bubble would be too long to wait. Better to just end it now.

The worst part of it was that my mom wasn't even here to talk me down. If the package and its ominous note were anything to go by, it looked like my worst fear about her was coming true. She might never return.

The tears that had threatened earlier were closer now, making my eyes sting and my chin tremble. Sure, my mom was gone half the time, but she was still the most important person in my life, and I couldn't imagine her being gone for good. Being gone forever.

I rolled onto my side, away from Emi and curled into the fetal position, knees tucked against my chest. I'd never been a fan of putting my misery on display. I was damn good at sucking it up, and my stiff upper lip had been perfected a long time ago. Both my mom and Emi tried so hard to make me feel normal— each in her own way—and I never wanted them to know just how far short they'd fallen.

As I moved, something metallic slid out of the V of my T-shirt and landed in front of me on the comforter. It was the necklace my mom had sent. Emi must have put it around my neck while I'd been unconscious.

I raised one hand and curled my fingers around the pendant, enclosing it in my fist. The stone felt warm against my skin and, somehow, strangely comforting.

The bed shifted as Emi stood. "I found the number for the shop where the receipt came from," she said softly. "No answer, but I'll keep trying." I heard a dull *clink* as, I assumed, she set the orb on the nightstand. "Get some rest," she said. "I'll let you know if I hear anything."

Her footsteps were soft, quiet. Barely audible. The sound of the door's hinges creaked once. Twice. And then she was gone. I was alone.

I squeezed my eyes shut and, chest shuddering, gave in to the tears.

Sitting at my desk, I fingered the pendant hanging from a chain around my neck and stared out the window, watching the rippling sea.

Well, technically it's a *sound*, an ocean inlet too large to be a bay, too wide to be a fjord, and too deep to be a bight. It's East Sound, to be exact, not to be confused with West Sound on one side of the island or Rosario Strait on the other. I knew this—had a brain packed full of useless, obscure knowledge—because I had no life. Because this place *was* my life. This place, along with my mom and Emi—and Raiden, once upon a time—were my whole world.

I'd only stepped foot outside of the San Juan Islands a few times. This archipelago was my home, Orcas Island my safe haven. Unlike Raiden and the other kids who'd grown up on Orcas and the surrounding islands, I hadn't taken the interisland ferry to Friday Harbor on neighboring San Juan Island to attend school past a single, disastrous week of kindergarten.

Sometimes, on weekdays when my mom was home, the two of us would head into town for ice cream and some light shopping. The town of Eastsound was next to dead on weekday mornings, especially mid-week, when tourist traffic was nil. Only the shopkeepers posed any kind of a threat to my tenuous sanity, but they knew me—the Blackthorn girl—and rumors abounded about what ailed me. I was sick, or insane, or both. They knew enough to keep their distance, which was all I needed.

Those were my favorite days.

And if my mom never returned, those days would be a thing of the past.

My mom wasn't all right. The package pretty much guaranteed it.

Emi had spent the afternoon tracking down my mom, or trying to. She'd managed to get a hold of the shop owner, but the woman on the phone had claimed she didn't remember my mom coming in. Emi also called just about every governmental organization, both US and Italian, but everyone told her the same thing: they couldn't help.

Apparently, there was no record of my mom entering Italy, let alone leaving Brazil. There was nothing for any agency, foreign or domestic, to use as a starting point in the search for her. No way for anyone to help. We'd been advised to file a missing person's report with our local law enforcement agency. Fat lot of good that would do.

Swallowing the growing lump in my throat, I focused on a distant ferry gliding across the water's silvery surface. For minutes, I watched the ferry, following its slow, steady path, until the mounting fear and frustration dimmed into the background of my mind and I had better control over my emotions. Ominous looking clouds were rolling in from the east, coloring parts of the water a duller, darker gray. A storm was moving in. The swells would be high tonight.

Movement caught my eye in the yard below, out near the edge of the grounds, where the subtly manicured landscaping met up with the sandstone bluff that dropped straight into the sea. It was Raiden, Emi's son, picking up the branches that had fallen during the previous night's storm and piling them in a wheelbarrow. He limped slightly each time he took a step.

I rose from the chair and moved around the desk to stand near the window.

Raiden had been my best friend, once. My only friend. But that was years ago. Now, he was practically a stranger. He barely resembled the boy who I explored the wooded grounds with as a child. The boy who I taught to hold his breath underwater, despite being a few years younger than him. The boy who helped me build Fort Blackthorn from driftwood on the beach. The boy who had always been able to make me smile, even during the bleakest of times.

I was three years behind Raiden in age, and he joined the Army straight out of high school, even against his mom's protests. As a teenager, he'd been eager to make a difference, to fight the good fight. He had wanted to change the world, but it seemed to me that the world had changed him.

Raiden had always been a big, solid kid, taking after his father, I supposed, though I had never met the man. Emi's husband was Hawaiian, allegedly, and must have been huge to make Raiden dwarf his mother the way he did. Raiden was even bigger now than he'd been when he left. Stronger, and harder.

But it was the changes inside Raiden that seemed most drastic to me. He left the islands a boisterous, fun-loving young man, filled to the brim with confidence and ambition, ready to right the world's wrongs. He returned subdued and somber, the light in his eyes dimmed by whatever he had seen *out there*. By whatever he had done. Things I could only imagine.

Raiden had been back for a few months, but I more or less avoided him now. He was more dangerous to me than Emi or my mom, my mind ready to fill in the unknown with all manner of horrors should contact between us trigger an episode. The horrifying hallucinations I experienced when I bumped into him in the kitchen shortly after his return had left me bedridden for a solid week. I didn't want to experience that again. Once had been enough. More than.

But even in his seemingly damaged state, I envied Raiden. He'd made it out. He'd had adventures. If *his* mom went missing in Rome, *he* would have gone after her. He would have been able to find her if she was still alive—to save her—and he would have been able to avenge her if the worst had happened. He was everything I wanted to be . . . and everything I never would be.

Bile rising in my throat, I hugged my middle and turned away from the window. It was pointless to pine for such things.

My gaze landed on the receipt that had been tucked beneath all of the wadded-up newspaper pages in the package. It was sitting on my desk in front of my laptop, flipped over to the back, displaying the note from my mom.

I narrowed my eyes. Just because I wasn't as outwardly capable as Raiden didn't mean I was completely useless. Maybe I could track down my mom—save her if she needed saving—*in my own way.*

I walked around the corner of the desk and settled in the chair. I opened my laptop and flipped the note over to reveal the receipt side. I typed the address at the top of the receipt into the internet browser's search bar, then clicked on the map of Rome that popped up with the location of the address marked by a yellow star. Maybe the shop owner didn't remember my mom, but somebody else might—maybe another worker or shopper or just a passerby. Or maybe a street camera had captured her leaving.

It was time to unleash my inner Veronica Mars and get to sleuthing.

I scanned the map, noting the various landmarks surrounding the location. The receipt had been printed in a shop near Vatican City, just northeast of the tiny sovereign nation in what the map informed me was the Prati neighborhood of Rome. The shop appeared to be a convenience store of some kind, but didn't have a phone number listed. No matter. Emi had already found the number. I could get it from her.

I pursed my lips and repeatedly tapped the nail of my index finger on the keyboard.

After a long, thoughtful moment, I turned my attention back to the receipt. Assuming it was a genuine receipt from a purchase my mom had actually made and not just some scrap paper she'd fished out of the garbage, she had physically been in the shop at 10:19 the morning of the same day the package had been post-marked, and she had purchased four things: a box, a newspaper, a bottle of water, and a lemon. The total had come to just under eleven Euro, and she'd paid cash. Useless details, at first glance, but I couldn't help thinking there was more to it.

I blew out a breath and ran my fingers through my hair. It was longer than usual, the dark brown waves reaching well past my shoulders, and it was starting to drive me crazy.

I twisted my hair up into a bun that I secured with the tie I'd been wearing around my wrist. I pinched my bottom lip, my gaze drifting above the computer screen to the window behind the desk. The ferry I'd been watching earlier was long gone, and a seagull was swooping lazily over the bay, just beyond the bluff at the edge of the yard.

"What happened to you, Mom?" I asked, the question barely audible.

How long after mailing the package had she gone MIA? Had someone been chasing her? Had she been injured? Was she an unconscious Jane Doe lying in a hospital bed somewhere in Rome? Or was she awake, but suffering from amnesia? Or was she in a ditch somewhere? Or face-down in a river? Had she been abducted? Was she being held prisoner? Was she being tortured?

Was she even still alive?

The sun set while I considered all of the horrifying, mind-numbing possibilities, and the view through the window faded to a deep, inky darkness. After a while, all I could see was a ghostly reflection of myself sitting at the desk in the dim bedroom.

Sighing, I reached across the desk to pull the chain dangling from the antique banker's lamp sitting near the corner. The halogen bulb flared to life, the brightness momentarily making me squint, and I angled the lamp's green glass shade downward so the direct light would be out of my eyes.

I shut the sleeping laptop and picked up the receipt, turning it over to reveal my mom's message, once more. I moved the thin paper into the pool of light from the desk lamp. My mom's words were the same as ever, but I still felt like I barely understood their meaning.

I screwed up.

So she'd made a mistake of some kind. What, exactly? And, when?

I'm so sorry. These should help.

Somehow, the necklace and orb were supposed to rectify her mistake. But what had she "screwed up" in the first place? And how could two such seemingly random objects help with *anything*?

I shook my head, not even close to understanding.

You won't have to live in fear anymore.

. . .

Because of the necklace and the orb? Was my fear—my *condition*—the mistake? Was *I* the mistake?

I wish I'd figured this out sooner. Everything could have been so much easier for you. Better late than never, I hope.

"What are you talking about?" I wondered aloud. The more times I read her words, the less sense they made.

I'm sorry, sweetie. I love you.

My eyes burned as I read my mom's final words. It sounded like a goodbye.

Absently, I rubbed my thumb over a faint brownish smudge near the corner of the receipt.

Much to my surprise, the smudge appeared to darken under the friction rather than clear away.

I squeezed my eyes shut, thinking I'd been staring at the receipt for too long. So long that I was starting to see things. But when I opened them again, not only was the smudge still there, it was definitely darker. And if I wasn't mistaken, it was looking more like two smudges than one.

I moved the receipt closer to the lamp's bulb and leaned in.

The smudges not only darkened the longer the thin paper remained near the bulb. They *grew*.

Into letters. Into words. Into a hidden message.

"The lemon," I mouthed, eyes widening as I sat up straighter. "Of course!"

It had been right there in front of my face the whole time; I'd just been too blind to see it. My mom had bought a box, a newspaper, a bottle of water, and a lemon. She must have used the juice from the lemon to create a rudimentary invisible ink, hidden until enough heat brought whatever else she'd written to light.

I waited not-so-patiently as the blurred letters became darker and more defined. As the hidden message became clearer.

And then I blinked, and I could make sense of it—a message meant for my eyes, and my eyes alone. A single line. A *clue*.

Light will be thrown on the origin of man and his history.

I read and reread the line, over and over. It was a quote from Darwin's *On the Origin of Species*.

A slow grin spread across my face. My mom wouldn't have included a hidden message if she wasn't still out there. If there wasn't still hope. If she didn't want me to find her.

And thanks to that message, I knew exactly what she wanted me to do.

[5]

After that brief, abysmal stint of kindergarten when I was a kid, my mom had pulled me out of public school, opting instead to home school me right here in Blackthorn Manor. Emi had helped out in the math and science departments, her particular specialties. They'd been an excellent teaching team, finding ways to make learning feel like an adventure, an endless quest for knowledge. In fact, they'd been so good that I hadn't understood why Raiden was constantly complaining about his classes and homework. *All* of my work was homework. And I'd loved it.

My mom's specialty was history, of course. And languages. And, oddly enough for someone who wasn't even remotely religious, she knew *a ton* about religion, especially the Judeo-Christian family. I never really understood that.

All of my studies had been interdisciplinary, with history at the core of almost every project. When tasked with creating a model of the solar system, I also learned about the lives and times of the pioneering astronomers who'd honed our understanding of the universe over the millennia, as well as the rich Greco-Roman mythology behind the Western names of the various celestial bodies. When studying the Golden Ratio, I was tasked with photographing as many examples of it in nature as I could find on our property, as well as learning about the pyramids of Egypt and Euclid, Fibonacci, and Da Vinci, who'd all incorporated the Golden Ratio into their work. And during the year I spent executing a series of Mendelian pea plant experiments in the greenhouse, I also worked through an interactive digital simulation of Darwinian evolution and read *On the Origin of Species*.

Though that had been my first time reading the entirety of *Origin*, it hadn't been my first exposure to Charles Darwin's groundbreaking foundational work. My mom was a big fan of *Old Charlie*, as she called him, and as far back as I could remember, she'd been pulling quotes from *Origin* to qualify any myriad of topics or explain away the mysteries of backward thinking over the span of human history.

"Light will be thrown on the origin of man and his history."

That particular line had been one of her personal favorites. Once, she even used it to justify why my education was so history-heavy. The one and only time I complained about it, whining that studying the past was pointless—I blame emerging teen angst— my mom had relied on *Old Charlie* to set me straight.

I was twelve at the time, and we were in the library, deciphering the symbols on a 300-year-old nautical chart.

"Do you know what the light is?" she had asked me after reciting the line.

I had rolled my eyes, possibly even going so far as to groan. "I bet you're going to tell me."

"Knowledge, Cora," had been her response. "Curiosity. The search for truth—*that* is the light." Her words were laced with gentle vehemence, the blue of her irises alight with quiet intensity. "We must always keep searching, seeking the light, or we risk falling into the darkness."

Unable to resist, I had asked her what was in the darkness.

She had looked away, her gaze growing distant and filling with ghosts. "Monsters," she had whispered, that single, hushed word laden with more fear than any scream or shout.

I never asked her about the things in the darkness again. They scared my mom, the bravest person I knew; that was enough for me to want to stay far, far away.

I wasn't sure I could keep my distance any longer.

Armed with the receipt from Rome and the cryptic message my mom had hidden in invisible ink on the back, I rolled the chair away from the desk and stood. I grabbed my gloves, quickly pulling them on up to my elbows. I didn't usually wear them when I was alone, but after that latest episode, I figured I couldn't be too careful. Emi was in the house, after all—she'd long ago taken to staying in the guest bedroom three doors down from mine when my mom was away.

Tila, dozing on the foot of the bed, roused at my movement and raised her head, watching me with interest.

"Come on," I told her, moving closer to the bed to scratch behind her short, floppy ears. "It's time for an adventure."

She inhaled deeply, sighed as she exhaled, and stood, getting in a good, long stretch before lazily slipping off the bed. She shook her head, her ears making a clapping noise, and looked at me.

I patted the outside of my thigh, and she fell in step behind me. Dog at my heels, I crossed the room, eased the bedroom door open, and slipped out into the dark hallway. As quietly as possible, I made my way along the corridor that led to the library deep within the heart of the old mansion. The discovery of my mom's hidden message was still so fresh, I wanted to keep it to myself just a little bit longer.

Blackthorn Manor was huge and old, or at least old by

Pacific Northwest standards. It was built in 1906 by my great-great-grandfather, a prominent shipbuilder of the time, and the century-old teak flooring creaked and groaned with each footfall, no matter how softly I stepped.

There was nothing gothic about the nautical-themed mansion, but I felt in need of a long nightgown and a flickering candle as I crept along the dark hallway, ghostly memories lurking in every crack and corner. It almost felt as though my mom were there with me, guiding me toward whatever it was she wanted me to find.

I slid open one panel of the library's enormous, teak pocket doors, slipped into the cavernous room and waited for Tila to join me, then turned and closed us in. The heavy darkness was punctured by the exterior lights shining through the maritime stained-glass window on the far side of the library, the patches of light tinted amber and blue from the colored pieces of glass. The pipes of a massive, two-story organ climbed up the walls to either side of the decorative window, the brass gleaming silver and gold in the filtered light. Two spiral staircases connected the main floor to the mezzanine, one on either side of the room.

I'd spent more time here in the Blackthorn library than I had in the virtual world—which was really saying something—and I knew the layout of the room better than the back of my hand. I cut a path through the center of the library, angling slightly to the right to circumvent the four-foot-tall armillary sphere my mom had added ten years ago.

Some people redecorated by changing up the curtains or paint color or by purchasing some art, but not my mom; she redecorated by hunting down antique astronomical instruments and other historical artifacts to put on display. She'd collected so many pieces during her seemingly endless string of expeditions over the years that Blackthorn Manor was as much a museum as it was a home.

I made a sharp left just past the armillary sphere to avoid the senet table and accompanying pair of armchairs, then made a beeline for my mom's desk. It was a beastly thing of brass and carved walnut. It had been custom-built for the house, and so far as I knew, had never been moved from its place beneath the stained-glass window.

When I reached the desk, I pulled the cord on the small Tiffany lamp set in the corner, lighting the library with the lamp's muted glow. The surface of the desk was as sparse and pristine as ever, not a paper in sight and not an antique accessory out of place.

"Stay here," I told Tila, patting her muscular cheek.

She sat, head cocking to the side.

"Good girl," I said, turning away from both dog and desk.

I headed for the spiral staircase on the left side of the library. Hand on the brass railing, I carefully made my way up to the mezzanine. I'd made a full 360 by the time I reached the top.

I didn't pause as I stepped foot onto the mezzanine. I followed the railing around to the far end of the library, toward the two bookcases that housed my mom's most prized volumes. Her copy of *Origin* was among the books stored there.

As I stopped in front of the bookcases, the light was almost too faint to read the titles on the spines. Almost, but not quite.

I found the leather-bound edition of *Origin* near the center of a shelf just below eye-level. When I pulled the book free, I peeked at the top before even cracking it open. The ribbon marked a page near the beginning, in the exact place the line from my mom's hidden message should be.

My heart beat a little faster, and my hands trembled. In mere moments, I would find out whatever it was my mom wanted to tell me but had been afraid to write directly.

I slid the nail of my index finger between the two pages separated by the ribbon and opened the book.

A single word was scrawled in pencil in the outer margin on

the left-hand page, beside the quoted line. Or rather, a name: *Hypatia*.

I blew out a breath. I hadn't reached the endpoint of this mystery, just a stop along the way. Apparently, my mom had set up a secret scavenger hunt meant just for me, and there was no saying how long the hunt would take or what the purpose would end up being.

There were better ways for me to be spending my time, like trying to figure out what happened to her in Rome, rather than following a path she'd laid out before she'd even left. Before she'd gone missing.

I blinked, lips parting and eyes opening wide.

If my mom had set this up *before* her trip, then she'd known it might end badly. Hell, she'd expected it to. What, exactly, had she gotten herself into? And moreover, what did she think I could do about it from here? Something, evidently, but *what*?

Motivation refreshed, I shelved the book and rushed back to the spiral staircase. I raced down the steps, hand gripping the brass railing tightly. When I reached the bottom, I headed straight for the Classics section on the other side of the room, near the opposite spiral staircase, Tila falling in step close behind me.

Hypatia was an ancient Roman Neoplatonist scholar who'd lived in Alexandria during the fourth and fifth centuries, this side of zero. She'd been a brilliant mathematician, philosopher, and astronomer, going so far as to teach and even advise prominent Alexandrian men, something that was extremely uncommon for women of her era. Unfortunately, Hypatia had been caught up in a period of religious and political turmoil and had been murdered by a Christian mob for her pagan beliefs. She'd become a martyr to philosophy, and many centuries after her death, she'd been turned into a feminist icon.

My mom viewed Hypatia with the same sort of reverence Catholics viewed the Virgin Mary. As I skimmed the book spines, searching for any volume of Hypatia's work, I recalled the deep sadness that had shown in my mom's eyes as she expressed what a pity it had been that none of Hypatia's writings had survived the centuries.

Which explained why I wasn't currently having any luck finding anything authored by the ancient scholar on the bookshelf. There wasn't anything to find.

"Moron," I admonished, shaking my head as I turned away from the bookcase.

I followed the wall of books away from my mom's desk, seeking out the biography section six or seven bookcases down. I wasn't looking for something written *by* Hypatia, but *about* her. I had no idea what I would find in the collection. Biography was one of my least favorite genres, and I was entirely unfamiliar with the books lining these shelves.

When I reached the section, I slowed my search, taking my time to read each and every title. I didn't know if I was seeking a book about Hypatia exclusively, so as I skimmed the spines, I looked for any sign that the book might either be about Hypatia, or even just reference her. To complicate matters, the books were organized by author, not subject matter, which didn't help me at all. My frustration mounted with each successive shelf.

"Come on," I muttered. "Where is it?"

Second shelf from the bottom, five books from the left. *Hypatia*, written by someone with the last name of Kingsley. The volume was bound in black leather with gold writing. The book was far from new, the black finish on the spine was worn, peeling in some places to reveal the leather's warm brown hue.

I felt a spike of excitement the moment I spotted it. I was one step closer to figuring this all out.

I reached for the book, curling a fingertip over the top of its spine, and slowly pulled the volume toward me. It tilted out maybe a third of the way, but then it stopped, seeming to be stuck.

Brow furrowing, I gripped the spine of the book and tugged.

There was a faint click from somewhere within the wall behind the bookcase.

Tila stood, a low growl rumbling in her barrel chest.

A moment later, the entire bookcase sank into the wall, then swung away from me with the soft creak and groan of shifting wood, revealing a passage. A *secret* passage.

"Wow," I whispered, mind frantically processing what I'd found.

There was a genuine, honest-to-God secret passage right here in Blackthorn Manor. In *my own* home. It had been right under my nose my entire life.

I was utterly flabbergasted. It seemed crazy and impossible, like something straight out of one of my video games. Then again, the house had been built by a man who'd thought including a massive pipe organ was a logical design element for a home library, so maybe I should've expected something like this.

I shot a quick glance over my shoulder, taking in the comforting familiarity of the library, then took a deep breath and stepped into the passage. Into the unknown.

6

A wall sconce lit up as I entered the tunnel, startling me. I sucked in a breath and backed up a step.

Unruffled, Tila continued on, nose to the ground as she sniffed the floor of the shallow landing.

The light appeared to be on the newer side, but the teak floor in here was dull and worn, as though it had been tread upon day after day for a hundred years with minimal upkeep. Beyond the landing, a narrow set of stairs descended, steeper than anything that would meet modern building codes. Whatever lay beyond the foot of the stairs was shrouded in darkness.

I frowned, wondering just how many times my mom had walked down these stairs. How long had she been hiding this from me? *Why* had she been hiding it?

Tila paused at the edge of the landing and raised her head, her ears perked up as she looked back at me. She seemed to be saying, *"Are we doing this, or what?"*

"Yeah, yeah, I'm coming," I muttered, waving her on.

The stocky pit bull turned her attention back to the stairs and started down, her tail wagging back and forth with each successive step.

Heart hammering in my chest, I followed my dog. I placed one hand on the wall to steady myself as I descended the steep staircase, counting the steps as I went. I reached twenty around the halfway point.

There were twenty steps in the grand staircase just between the first and second floors of Blackthorn Manor. It seemed safe to assume that *this* staircase descended well below ground level. The odd part was that the house didn't have a basement, at least not one that I knew about—so where was the passage leading me? *What* was under the house?

My pace increased. Whatever was down here, it must have been an original feature to Blackthorn Manor, perhaps used by my mom, but not created by her. The passage had to have been commissioned by my extravagant great-great-grandfather to have been built between the walls during the original construction of the house.

By the time I reached the bottom step, the temperature had dropped at least ten degrees. A little too cool for comfort in my T-shirt and leggings, even with the gloves. The chill gave rise to goosebumps on my arms, but it wasn't quite cold enough for me to see my breath. This was subterranean cold—a constant, low-grade cold that flavored the air and permeated the walls. I was definitely underground.

The moment my foot touched the floor at the base of the stairs, more lights flickered on, these lining either side of the passageway in sconces of glass and brass fit into recesses in the wall. Tila hadn't triggered the sensor, which meant it must have been targeting motion higher up.

I paused to take in my new surroundings. The floor and walls were brick, and the chill quickly seeped in through my socks. The brick continued overhead in an arch to form the ceiling.

Tila had already reached the end of the passage. She was sniffing the crack at the bottom of a reinforced stainless-steel door, tail wagging half-heartedly. The striking newness of the door looked totally out of place next to the aged brick.

This was all so bizarre, and once again I had the sense that I'd left the realm of reality and had stepped into one of my games. Was I dreaming? I didn't think so, but then, that was what I usually thought when I was dreaming.

Swallowing roughly, I continued onward. Dream or not, I wanted to find out what was beyond the door.

When I was barely three steps away, an eight-inch square of steel slid open in the center of the door at chest height, revealing a shiny, black screen. I could see myself reflected in the surface, my eyes wide and hair wild.

I froze, head tilting to the side and eyes narrowing as I stared at the door's new feature. Cautiously, I moved closer, bending down a bit to get a better look.

Sensing my excitement, Tila raised her head, focusing on me and dancing in place. A whiny groan emanated from her barrel chest.

"I don't know what's behind this door, either, T," I told her, patting her head.

She sat, her attention returning to the door. Her tail continued to wag, making a swishing sound on the brick floor.

All of a sudden, the outline of a hand glowed neon green on the screen.

"State your name," a disembodied female voice ordered from somewhere overhead.

I straightened, looking up at the ceiling. A small, inconspicuous speaker and camera were set near the apex of the archway overhead. I'd missed them before, my focus entirely on the door.

"State your name," the voice repeated. It was pleasant enough, and almost imperceptibly artificial.

"Cora," I said, but when my voice came out weaker than expected, I cleared my throat. Taking a deep breath, I repeated, "Cora. Cora Blackthorn."

"Welcome, Cora," the voice said. "You are approved."

My eyebrows rose, and I glanced down at Tila. She was standing again, her tail no longer wagging.

"Please place your hand on the screen to verify your identity," the voice instructed.

Brow furrowing, I shifted my focus from my dog up to the camera and speaker overhead, then down to the screen on the door. I moved closer and raised my hand, tugging off my glove by the fingertips. I hesitated for just a fraction of a second before pressing my palm to the screen and positioning my hand so it fit within the five-fingered outline.

The screen flared bright green, quick as the flash of a camera, then faded to black.

Tila went completely still, ears perked up as she listened to something I couldn't hear.

A moment later, there was a loud clanging sound, followed by the hiss of air being released, and the door swung outward. As it opened, hanging Tiffany lamp chandeliers lit up within the room beyond, illuminating the space in a warm, welcoming light.

My eyes opened wide, and my lips parted. "What *is* this place?" I wondered aloud, slowly scanning the space.

It was like the love child of an alchemist's laboratory and an archaeologist's study. The brick of the passageway behind me continued into the secret room, the arched ceiling widening to a Catalan vault with a set of pillars dropping down to support the arches every five or six feet. From my vantage point, it looked like the room extended back a good twenty to twenty-five yards.

Rectangular wooden tables filled the spaces between the pillars, running the length of the room. Some were laden with antique brass or glass scientific instruments, others with enormous leather tomes propped up on bookstands, left open to some seemingly random page. Others, still, displayed complex equipment that looked like it would have belonged in some of the most modern, high-tech labs around.

An aisle ran down the center of the space between the two sets of pillars and their aligning tables, with another aisle on the outer sides of the pillars on either side of the room. The walls running parallel to the pillars were lined with towering bookcases, each with its own attached ladder. Books of all sizes and colors filled the shelves, sitting beside manuscript boxes—some utilitarian, some ornate—and thin glass cases containing single sheets of papyrus, parchment, and amate.

There was a sense of stillness about the place, of absolute quiet, despite the gentle hum of the bulbs in the chandeliers hanging over head. It was the heavy quiet that comes from solitude and isolation. From secrecy.

Tila trotted in ahead of me, disrupting that stillness, and proceeded to sniff *everything*.

Slowly, eyes scanning this way and that to take in as much as possible, I followed her in. I made my way down the central aisle, afraid to touch anything.

My mom had always been a fan of hands-on history— must've been the archaeologist in her—but I often struggled with the fear of destroying what could never be replaced. That was the nice thing about video games. Nothing was real. Nothing was permanent, not even death. There was always the chance for a do-over. For a second chance.

A desk at the far end of the room beckoned me onward. It was an antique executive desk made of some dark wood, the type you'd have found in a nineteenth century banker's office, with three sets of drawers running up each side. An out-of-place looking ergonomic desk chair was all that stood between me and the desk.

Papers were stacked into a messy pile on the left side of the desk, topped with my mom's leather-bound journal, its thin leather band wrapped around the covers, holding in place the loose papers tucked away between the pages. The right side of the desk was cluttered with a small Tiffany lamp, a pen jar, stacks of unused sticky notes in a rainbow of colors, and a wireless computer mouse. And I could just see the corner of a laptop keyboard peeking around the back of the chair.

The spartan organization of the desk in the library was nowhere to be seen. I'd long thought it odd that my mom's desk clashed so severely with her sometimes frenetic, often chaotic personality. Now I knew why. That desk was a decoy; this one was the real thing.

I picked up the journal first. It was the only familiar thing in this unfamiliar place.

I'd caught my mom scouring the leather-bound book's pages time and time again, though I'd never managed more than a cursory stolen glance. She was always quick to snap the cover shut and tuck the journal out of sight as soon as she realized my attention had turned her way. She rarely wrote anything new in the journal, at least not that I witnessed, and when she did touch pen to the paper bound within, she did so with the utmost thought and care.

I unwound the leather cord from around the covers and licked my lips, feeling like I was breaking some sacred promise by even touching the precious book. But if I was ever going to find out what happened to my mom—what exactly she had gotten herself into and what had led her on her ill-fated detour to Italy—I would find it between these covers. After all, she was the one who had led me down here in the first place.

The trio of ceramic beads at the end of the journal's leather cord dropped to the desk, landing on the laptop's touchpad with just enough pressure to wake the computer. The screen lit up, and I glanced at it.

I sucked in a sharp breath.

I was looking at a picture of my mom captured by the computer's built-in camera, with video controls near the bottom of the screen. She was sitting right here, at this desk. In this chair.

I stood there, frozen in place, eyes locked on the screen. On my mom's face.

Without breaking my stare with the computer screen, I pulled the chair away from the desk and sat, exactly where my mom had been sitting when she recorded the cued video. I hugged the all-but-forgotten journal to my chest with my left hand as I reached for the mouse with my right. I inhaled deeply, then held my breath. And pressed play.

There was a millisecond delay, and then my mom came to life right before my eyes. She smiled, but even as her lips curved, a darkness—part sadness, part something else—filled her azure gaze.

"Hey, Cora Borealis," she said, her eyes meeting mine. It was almost like she was really there on the other side of the screen, and hearing her favorite nickname for me—hearing it spoken in her voice—made my heart ache.

My chin quivered, and I swallowed roughly.

"I'm sure you're confused," she said, "but I'm glad you found the study. I should have brought you down here years ago, but . . ." She sighed, averting her gaze and shaking her head ruefully. "It's hard to explain."

"Try," I said.

Another sigh. "You're special, Cora." My mom raised her eyes to the camera. "More special than you could ever guess." She smiled again, less sadness to it this time. "And I'm not just saying this because I'm your mom and you're my baby girl." She paused for a moment, seeming to consider her words. "You're different from other people. You're not—" She hesitated, frowning. "Well, you know you're my special science baby, right?"

Out of habit, I nodded, leaning in a little.

When I was a young girl and would ask about my dad, my mom would tell me I was her "special science baby" and that unlike all the other kids, I was unique because I didn't have a father. At least, not in the traditional sense. As I grew older, she explained that I was a product of in vitro fertilization—a test tube baby—a child she had wanted so badly that she had relied on advanced science to bring me into her life. She explained that my father had been an anonymous donor selected purely based on his desirable genetics to contribute his DNA to the IVF procedure.

"It's a little more complicated than that," my mom said on the computer screen. "I carried you in my womb, but you weren't the standard IVF baby because, well . . ." Again, she hesitated, closing her eyes. "Because you're not mine, Cora." Her eyelids raised, unshed tears turning the blue of her irises more brilliant than ever. "You're not even human."

"*What*?" I blurted. My chest heaved with each breath, and I slowly scooted the chair backward, shaking my head. This was a joke, it had to be. A cruel, sick, twisted joke.

"You were found in a preserved embryonic state," she continued. "So far as we know, you are the last remaining member of an ancient, advanced species of hominids who came to this planet seeking refuge thousands of years before the dawn of human civilization."

I balked, my jaw dropping and eyes bulging. First, she told me I wasn't hers. Then, I wasn't even human. Now, she was claiming I was an *alien*?

"And I don't think your condition is an illness, but a gift native to your species." She pressed her lips together, tears sneaking over the brim of her eyelids and streaking down her cheeks. She hastily swiped the tears away. "I've always thought that, but I didn't know how to help you. I probably should have told you a long time ago—Emi's been on me about this for years —but the longer I carried this secret, the harder it became to admit the truth."

I felt like I'd been punched in the gut. Not just my mom, but Emi was in on it, too?

"I know I'm taking the coward's way out, telling you like

this." My mom inhaled and exhaled deeply, focus drifting away from the camera. "I don't know, maybe I should go upstairs right now and tell you all of this in person, but . . ." She raised her left hand, chewing on her thumbnail. "I have nothing to show you—nothing to *help* you." She bowed her head, shaking it weakly. "Not yet, anyway."

I clenched my jaw. My mom hadn't gone upstairs. She hadn't come to my room and confessed any of this to me in person. And for the briefest moment, I hated her for doing this to me.

"I hope you never see this," my mom said quietly. A moment later, she cleared her throat and straightened her shoulders, seeming to regain some of her composure. Her focus returned to the camera. "Helping you—that's the whole point of this expedition to Brazil. I'm looking for guidance from your people, or at least, from the last remnants of your people. From the things they left behind. There's a device that should help you control your gift—I've seen one, once, but it's impossible to get to. But . . . I think I know where to find another one."

I shook my head ever so slowly. She was serious. Dead serious. Subconsciously, the fingers of my right hand sought out the pendant with its odd, color-changing stone hanging from the chain around my neck. I couldn't help but wonder if the necklace was the device she was talking about.

"You'll find a full explanation of everything I've gathered about you and your people and their origins in my journal. I just . . ." She took a deep breath, her eyes seeming to search the camera. "I thought you deserved to hear the truth from me . . . just in case I don't make it back."

I laughed hollowly, chest tight and throat constricting. This was crazy. Pure insanity.

My mom leaned in suddenly, resting her elbows on the desk, and her expression darkened. "Listen very carefully, Cora," she said. "I don't know if you'll believe any of what I just told you, but that doesn't matter right now. If you're watching this video, then I've been caught."

I straightened, eyes narrowing. I shoved all of the craziness she'd just dumped on me into the back of my mind. *This* was what I'd been searching for. Now, more than ever, I wanted to find my mom. I *needed* to find her.

"If they figure out what I've done," she said, "if they learn about you, they'll come after you." Her stare intensified. "You cannot let them capture you, Cora. They want to use you. To dissect you. To destroy you. If you get even the slightest suspicion that you're being watched, run. Run as far and as fast as you can. I will do everything I possibly can to help you." The complete and utter conviction in her voice frightened me. "So long as I still breathe," she said, "I will find a way back to you, and I *will* protect you."

I was gripping the pendant so hard that the edges dug painfully into my palm, even through the thin leather of the gloves. "Protect me from *who*?"

"I hope this isn't goodbye," she continued, "but if it is, know one thing—I love you, Cora. I feel so honored to have been a part of your life, and I will carry you in my heart until the very end." She smiled one last time, and closed her eyes, releasing a string of tears that streamed down both cheeks.

When she reopened her eyes, the blue of her irises seemed to have dimmed. "Remember to read the journal. It's all explained in there." She kissed her fingers, then touched them to the camera, and then the screen went black.

Behind me, someone cleared their throat.

I nearly jumped out of my skin. I sprang out of the chair and spun around, my mom's journal still clutched to my chest.

Emi stood in the center aisle a dozen or so paces into the room, her hands clasped before her and her mouth pinched.

Tila ducked under one of the long tables to reach her, tail wagging and nose sniffing.

"So, Diana finally told you," Emi said, ignoring the dog. She raised one eyebrow pointedly and added, "Not the way I would've gone about it, but I'm glad it's done."

Bummed, Tila let out her patented groan-whine, then sat, her eyes glued to Emi.

I opened my mouth, then shut it again when I found I had no words. Instead, I simply shook my head.

Emi's expression softened, her eyes filling with compassion. "It sounds crazy, I know, but—"

"What?" I said, voice layered with disbelief. "*What* do you know, Emi? What do you know about me? About my mom?" I waited for her to answer—to confirm or deny the things my mom had said in the video—but she said nothing. I took a step toward her. "Please, Emi. Tell me what you know."

She stared at me for a long moment. "I—it's complicated, Cora."

"No," I said, shaking my head with more force. Hurt and betrayal mixed together within me, resulting in a surprising emotion—anger. "It's simple, Emi. You lied to me. My whole life—" I clenched my jaw, barely holding in the sudden, simmering rage. I breathed in and out through my nose, staring hard. Accusing. "Did you know what my mom was really doing?" I asked. "Did you know where she was going? Did you lie to me about all of that, too?"

Emi returned my stare, her lips pressed into a thin, flat line. Her lack of denial was admittance enough.

"Do you know what happened to her?" My voice had taken on a hard edge I'd never heard from myself before. "Do you know who 'they' are?"

Emi nodded. "The Custodes Veritatis."

"The *guardians of the truth*?" I said, translating the Latin aloud.

Again, Emi nodded. "It's a secret organization whose sole

task is keeping the world from finding out about the Atlanteans."
At my blank stare, Emi clarified, "The *aliens*."

My brow furrowed. I could hardly believe that Emi was
confirming my mom's crazy story.

"Diana and I were members," Emi explained. "It's where we
met."

"So, you weren't in the military?" The sense of betrayal I felt
sharpened my words.

Emi shook her head. "Read it," she said, glancing down at
the journal clutched to my chest. "I'm sure Diana explains everything in there far better than I will."

"I'd rather hear it from you," I said. I wasn't sure I'd ever
been mad at Emi. But now, the anger roared through my veins,
burning away two and a half decades of complacency. Of ignorance. Of misplaced trust.

I gave Emi seconds—eons—to respond. When she finally
did, her words were beyond disappointing. "Read the journal,
Cora. After that, I'll answer any questions you have—and I'm
sure you'll have many. Just read it, first."

I blew out a breath and shook my head. "Thanks for nothing,"
I muttered as I brushed past Emi, the exposed skin of my arm
skimming against hers. Normally, the brief contact would have
triggered an episode, but I hardly noticed the lack of one, now.
My thoughts were too disordered, and I was too pissed off to care.

Tila's nails clicked on the brick floor as she followed
behind me.

Closing in on the reinforced door, I picked up the pace, full-
on running by the time I reached the stairs.

First my mom, and then Emi—with all of the secrets and lies,
I didn't know what to think anymore. Reality wasn't making any
sense, and I could no longer count on the people I had trusted my
whole life.

I fled to my bedroom, Tila close on my heels. I slammed the

door behind me and leaned my back against it, sinking down to the floor as I stared ahead at nothing.

Tila danced in place for a moment, but quickly sensed that my mood wasn't playful and fell still. She lay down on the floor beside me, resting her heavy head on my thigh.

Idly, I scratched her along her neck. This morning everything had been normal. My life had been shitty, but at least it had been predictable. Familiar. Known.

Now, I didn't recognize the world around me.

I didn't recognize the home I grew up in or the people who raised me.

I didn't even recognize *me*.

7

Cora,

I hope you never read this. I really do. I've made so, so many mistakes where you are concerned. I just wanted to give you a normal life. I wanted to be the loving mother you deserved. I wanted to keep you safe—from them. From the world. I wanted so many things for you, ordinary things, but now I realize that you were never meant for ordinary. You're destined to be extraordinary.

Emi and I have long suspected there's more to you than we can see or detect, but it wasn't until last week, when I attempted to enroll you in kindergarten, that we realized just how different you are. How much <u>more</u> you are—and how much more you deserve from us. I just wanted to give you a chance to be a kid, at least for a little while. You've only been around the two of us and Raiden for so long, and in a few years, once you're older and understand your birthright, well . . . I wanted to give you some fond memories to look back on. I wanted you to remember what it felt like to be one of us.

But I'm getting ahead of myself. Let me start at the begin-

ning. My name—my real name—is Diana Crane, and this is the story of how I became your mother.

I suppose it all began when I was eighteen years old and they first started recruiting me. I was enrolled at Oxford, a London orphan armed with a full-ride scholarship and a passion for the past. I was smart and ambitious, and coupled with my lack of familial ties, this made me a prime candidate. A professor of mine, one of their recruiters, picked me out and submitted my name without my knowledge. Once I was approved as a recruit, again, without my knowledge, I was offered a position on a top-notch excavation in the Egyptian Delta run by the Vatican, along with a full scholarship for the experience. How could I turn that down? It was the definition of too good to be true.

The grooming began that summer, during the excavation. I still didn't know anything about them—I didn't even know they existed. But they planted the seed that would one day make me desire to join them. I finished the summer believing there was only one path forward, only one way to fulfill my dreams to become the greatest archaeologist of my time, and by the end of fall term, I'd been accepted to the Pontifical Gregorian University in Rome, where I would be guaranteed access to some of the best excavations and most exclusive artifacts, and where I would learn under some of the most renowned archaeologists, classicists, and historians in the world.

I joined a small cohort of enthusiastic students, all specializing in different disciplines. Emi was one of those students. We did everything together. We even lived together. We became a family. It was everything I'd ever wanted, and I loved every minute of it. I would rather have died than give it up. Which was exactly what they wanted, what they'd been waiting for. I was in too deep. I couldn't go back to who I'd been before—a nobody with no one. Once they knew they had me, they revealed themselves to me, and I officially became one of them.

They're called the Custodes Veritatis—Guardians of the

Truth—or simply "the Order" by those of us on the inside. Though the name sounds mundane, their purpose is anything but. They are an elite secret order under direct Papal authority with the sole directive to guard one specific truth—to hoard it from the rest of the world. Because if the world found out, the Catholic Church, along with all of the world's religions, would be seen as they really are—bearers of lies. And in the wake of the revelation of that terrible truth, civilization would crumble.

We aren't alone in the universe, and we don't need a space program to find extraterrestrial life. It's already here. It's been here for thousands of years, before humans ever even considered the possibility of life existing elsewhere in the universe. Before we were even aware of the universe, at all.

We don't know where they came from or why they came here, to earth. According to legend, their home world was destroyed, and they had to flee. Earth was already populated by a species of hominids similar enough that they could blend in, so they sought refuge here, where they could hide in plain sight, longing for their broken world. A world called Atlantis. At least, that's what legend says.

What happened to the Atlanteans after they arrived is the real mystery – they built two massive labyrinths, and then they vanished. We have a few Atlantean artifacts of theirs, but the objects are so technologically advanced that we have no idea what they actually are, let alone how to use them.

Maybe those higher up in the Order know more about the Atlanteans, but neither Emi nor I ever made it beyond middle management. The Liber Veritatis is said to hold all of the knowledge gained by the Order over the centuries, with each Primicerius adding to it during his reign, but the book was lost decades ago. We know so little about the Atlanteans, but then, we don't need to know much beyond the fact that they exist. That simple truth alone is enough to shatter our understanding of our place in the universe.

As an initiate in the Order, I was trained to believe I was protecting the world. Chaos and disorder would wash away the refinements of civilization should the truth ever get out. My education in Rome went beyond academics. I was trained to fight. Trained to protect myself and the mission, no matter the cost. Trained to kill. Trained to die.

For nearly a decade, I drank the Kool-Aid. I may have had moments where I struggled to fall in line, but in the end, I always ended up dutifully following orders. The repercussions of not doing so were too terrifying. The Order didn't respond well to treachery. Part of me doubted what we were doing, especially when I saw the brutal violence the Order was capable of, but another, stronger, more desperate part of me truly believed that what we were doing was right. For the good of humanity, and all that. I needed to believe it, because I needed the Order. I didn't have anything else.

But one day, that all changed—the day you came into my life. You were such a tiny thing then, an embryo visible only through the lens of a microscope, your DNA almost human, but varied in the slightest, strangest of ways. You see, you'd been preserved in a miniature cryogenic stasis pod that fit easily in the palm of my hand. It was one of the Order's most prized artifacts, dated at over ten thousand years old, though it had only been in the Order's possession since it was discovered by Percy Fawcett in Brazil in 1925.

As one of the Order's science prodigies, Emi was the one to discover the stasis pod's true purpose and the nature of the embryo contained within. Genetically, the life form's DNA was a close enough match to human that Emi and her team believed it would be compatible with a human surrogate mother. This was a few years after the world's first successful IVF birth, and as soon as the leader of the Order realized there was a way to bring a real, live Atlantean into the world, he leapt at the chance. Not even the Pope's direct order not to use IVF could stop the Prim-

icerius. He was too desperate for the chance to study you. To learn from you. To use you.

It was fairly common for Order members to develop an obsession with the Atlanteans. I was no different. The Atlanteans were all I could think about. I wanted—needed—to know more about them. I was excited about the prospect of an Atlantean child being born to a human woman, and I wanted to be that woman. The child would be alone, like I'd always been alone. I could be its family. I could raise it. Learn from it. And unlike my beloved Order, I wouldn't simply want to use the child—I would love the child, with all my heart.

The Atlantean embryo was scheduled to be implanted into the surrogate mother's uterus in three months' time. That gave me plenty of time to work on Emi, to convince her to swap out the embryo and instead implant the Atlantean child within my womb. She was resistant, at first, but I played on her fears for her young son, and gradually she warmed to the idea. Even so, I couldn't get her to commit. I'd all but given up, when we received word of an attack on the Primicerius—the leader of our order was fine, but several members of his guard had been killed. One of those men was Emi's husband, Kai.

Kai's death triggered something within Emi, and two weeks before the implantation procedure was scheduled to take place, she came to me in the middle of the night, eyes red and swollen from crying and lack of sleep. She wanted out—she wanted her son out—and she wanted me to help them escape. To run with them. She knew the only way to get me to abandon the Order would be to offer me something bigger, something I wanted more. So, she offered to do the procedure on me. Then I wouldn't have any choice but to leave.

I didn't hesitate, not even for a second. Emi procured a second, human embryo, and the night before the implantation procedure was scheduled to happen, we swapped the embryos, implanting the Atlantean child within my uterus. I still have *nightmares about the other child—the poor human child—what his or her life must be like, growing up a ward of the Order, and as the Order's greatest disappointment. But it had to be done. I had to save you.*

The scheduled procedure happened as planned, and while the Order's attention was focused on the chosen surrogate, I feigned illness, resting in bed to give the Atlantean embryo as good of a chance to take hold as possible. It was touch and go there for a few days, and after a full day of spotting about a week in, I was sure we were going to fail. But we didn't. The embryo implanted successfully. And nourished by my body, it started to grow. You started to grow.

Now, we faced our largest hurdle—escape. Much like with a violent street gang, few people ever made it out of the Custodes Veritatis alive. Once you were in, you were in it for life. You couldn't retire out; you either died serving the Order, ran and hid, or were executed for betraying it. But I had a way out. An older gentleman had been sniffing around my excavations for years. He was good—very subtle, very sneaky, very smart. His name was George Blackthorn, and he only approached me once. He hinted at knowing about the Order and suggested that there were others who knew the truth—others who would be willing to share more of that truth with me than the Custodes Veritatis had during my years with them. He fed me just enough information to make me want more.

By the time I was carrying you, I'd been secretly communicating with George for two years. He'd heard enough from me to read between the lines—to know of my growing discontent with the Order and their brutal ways, and that I stayed not just for the chance to continue to study the Atlanteans, but for the sense of belonging I felt in the Order. He'd offered a safe place, should I ever find myself in need of somewhere to hide. A place to call home. No strings, save for one—bring him one of the Atlantean artifacts.

It took months to devise and plan our escape, and the execution was fraught with peril. But when Emi, Raiden, and I finally showed up on George's doorstep after a grueling week-long, back-and-forth journey halfway across the globe to his family home on Orcas Island, Blackthorn Manor, I brought him something far better than any artifact. I brought him you.

I assumed the identity of George's niece, Diana Blackthorn. George was something of a recluse, and he was old enough that none of the Island's residents remembered he'd been an only child. Nobody suspected a thing. It was perfect. I just wish he'd been in better health. He passed away shortly before you were born.

Your gestation took longer than was normal for a human child, both baffling and intriguing Emi to no end. At times, I was terrified of you, especially near the beginning. But as the months passed and my belly grew, I came to love you, deeply. After a little over a year, I delivered a healthy, happy baby girl, indistinguishable from an ordinary human child. You were so tiny, so helpless. You were all alone in the world, the last of your kind, so far as we knew, and you had no idea about any of it. You were an orphan in every sense of the word. I vowed, while first holding you in my arms, to make sure you never felt the loneliness I'd felt growing up. Even if that meant hiding your true nature not just from the world, but from yourself.

After your birth, your growth and development seemed relatively normal. Emi tested your reflexes and responses regularly, and while you always tested slightly ahead of the curve for your age and were capable of deep emotional insight beyond that of most adults, it was nothing astounding. For all intents and purposes, you were human. So, I raised you as such.

Which brings us to the disaster of this past week. Initially, when the kindergarten teacher told me how distraught you were during the first day of school, I thought it was just separation anxiety. You had never been away from me before. Your reaction didn't seem all that abnormal. But the second day was worse. On the third day, I stayed to observe, but my presence only seemed to intensify the problem. I took you home at lunch, and you screamed as I carried you to the car, like my touch was hurting you . . . until you gave in to exhaustion and passed out cold. Something about that setting, about being around so many other people, triggered something within you.

Later that day, when you were settled in your bed, sound asleep, the teacher called the house and told me she suspected you might be somewhere on the Autism spectrum, based on the way physical contact seemed to set you off. She gave me the names and phone numbers of a few child psychologists who specialized in diagnosing such disorders and advised that I homeschool you until your underlying "mental condition" could be identified.

Your underlying mental condition. It's almost laughable. A person can raise a wolf as a dog, but it's still a wolf. Its brain is still wired differently from the dog's, and no matter how the wolf is raised or trained, that wiring will always win out in the end. You aren't autistic, and you don't have any underlying conditions, mental or otherwise. There is nothing wrong with you, beyond the simple truth: you aren't human.

Whatever latent sensory or psychic abilities are hardwired into your brain have been awakened, and now, even the slightest touch sends you into what Emi calls a "psychic overload"—the sensory input seems to get stuck in a mental feedback loop, like when a microphone gets too close to a speaker, until your mind is overloaded and you lose consciousness.

It happens because you aren't human. You may look human. You may even act human. But you're not human, no matter how hard I tried to blind myself to the truth. After the trauma my blindness caused you this past week, I've finally come to grips with the reality of your existence. You are so much more— capable of sensing things beyond that of a human—and I've done you a massive disservice by ignoring your true, glorious nature.

But you're still my baby. I carried you within me for over a year. We may not share any DNA, but my blood flowed through your veins before you developed your own, and after you were born, I nourished you with milk from my body. In my heart, you're my flesh and blood. You're my daughter, and nothing will ever change that. I owe it to you to find out more about your species . . . more about your true potential and the remarkable insight you were born with. I owe it to you to give you the quality of life you deserve, not the sheltered, isolated existence you'll otherwise be doomed to live.

Thanks to George, I have the means to embark on private expeditions to try to uncover everything I can about you and your people. He invested the Blackthorn fortune wisely, and it's more than tripled since his death.

I will not rest until I have the answers I'm looking for. Until Emi and I can find a way to improve your quality of life. You're such a lively, adventurous child; it breaks my heart to think that you'll be trapped in Blackthorn Manor all your life, afraid of the world simply because your mind processes more sensory input than ours do.

You are my daughter, Cora, and you will have the chance to be the remarkable woman you're meant to be. I look forward to the day when I can watch you step into your own. When I can see you blossom into the beautiful being trapped within your frightened mind. When you can shed your fear and finally, truly live.

[8]

I hugged my mom's journal to my chest as I scooted lower in the bed, staring up at the ceiling, thoughts spinning. First the video, and now this book—my mom was crazy. Delusional. She'd lost her mind, clearly, but *when*? How had I not noticed her slide into insanity?

I rolled onto my side, absently stroking Tila's flank. The windows were dark, the outside world looking like a deep, yawning blackness.

Was this why Emi had wanted me to read the journal before talking to her? Had she wanted me to see the full depths of my mom's delusions?

I inhaled deeply, exhaling a heavy sigh, and closed my eyes. I would talk to her in the morning, once I'd had a chance to read through the rest of the madness my mom had scribbled on the journal's pages. I just needed to rest my eyes for a few minutes, then I would get back to reading . . .

I wake slowly, but as my mind becomes more alert and the memory of the overwhelming terror returns, my eyes pop open.

"Mommy!" I yell, bolting upright in bed. I hug JoJo, my stuffed T-rex, to my chest so tightly that his squishy body is practically bent in two.

My bedroom door bursts open, and my mom rushes in. "Oh sweetheart, I'm so sorry," she says, slowing as she approaches the bed. "I just stepped out for a minute. I wanted to be here when you woke."

I toss JoJo aside and hold my arms out to her. I need a mommy hug so bad right now, it hurts.

My mom hesitates, just for a second.

I whimper, reaching for her.

She sits on the bed and wraps her arms around me, but the comfort I seek evades me. The deluge of fear and worry is instantaneous. It pours into me, filling me up and drowning out everything else.

I cling to my mom, sobbing as agonizing tremors and spasms wrack my body. Images flash through my mind—my mom and Emi, running, fighting. I can't make sense of them.

A scream builds in my chest. It claws its way up my throat and erupts from my mouth, raw and piercing. Breath after breath, the scream renews. I can't stop it.

Until, finally, my muscles cramp up and body goes rigid, and darkness blots out the world.

I float in that darkness for what feels like eons. I'm not a little girl anymore. I'm me, now—twenty-six years old and wise to the dangers of the world. I know what made five-year-old me scream. I know not to touch people anymore.

In a blink, the darkness is gone, and I'm somewhere else. Somewhen else.

I'm sitting at a kid-sized drawing table in a doctor's office. At least, I think it's a doctor's office. It's weird, because there's no exam table, and the floor is carpet, and the doctor isn't wearing a white coat and she doesn't have a stethoscope hanging around her neck. A rainbow of crayons is scattered on the table around the drawing I'm working on. It's of my mom and me, the day we left school forever.

The doctor is kneeling on the floor a few feet away, watching me draw.

I finish the curly cues that are my mom's hair, then set down the brown crayon and pick up the red one.

"That's very good, Cora," the doctor says. "You're a very talented artist. Do you draw often at home?"

I glance at her, my shoulders bunching up. "I draw some-times," I say, then return to my drawing.

The doctor moves closer. "What are those, Cora?" she asks. "What are you drawing on your mom?"

"Fear," I whisper. "Spikes of fear."

"Is that what your mom feels like to you—like she's covered in spikes of fear?"

I nod.

"And do you actually feel the spikes poking you?"

My crayon stills, and I nod again, eyes glued to the drawing. I can still remember the feeling of the fear stabbing into me.

"I see," she says. "And when is the first time you noticed the spikes?"

I add smaller spikes to the drawing of my mom and shrug. "They used to be smaller . . . and softer," I say. "They used to just tickle, like feathers."

"I see," she says again. She reaches out, her hand hovering near the edge of my drawing. "Tell me, Cora, what do I feel like?" Her hand covers mine, and my entire body shudders as a jolt of agonizing sadness zips up my arm. I see flashes of images in my mind.

A girl with no hair.

The doctor sitting beside a hospital bed.

A bunch of daffodils lying on a grave marker.

I jerk my hand out from under hers so quickly that I fall out of my chair, but the tremors don't stop. The images—the sadness and pain—don't stop. I curl into a ball on the floor and hug my knees to my chest. The darkness is already creeping in at the edges of my consciousness. I wish it would hurry up.

"Cora?" The doctor says.

My teeth chatter, and my body shakes. My eyes are closed, but I can sense the doctor moving closer. The sadness swells as she nears, the pain overwhelming me.

The darkness is so close now. I reach for it. Welcome it. Embrace it.

I sigh, my body already relaxing as the darkness carries me away.

Again, I float in that peaceful darkness, aware of the present but reflecting on the past, on the forgotten memories resurfacing from the deepest recesses of my mind.

Without warning, I'm sucked into another moment from my childhood. Another visit with a specialist. Another suppressed traumatic memory. I skip through moment after moment, like flipping through channels on a TV. I relive the experience of seeing dozens of experts, from psychologists to psychics, neurologists to shamans. I haven't thought about that period of whirlwind trips off the island for years; it's a blur to me, a hazy point in my memory, clouded by the trauma of pain and the frequent loss of consciousness as we tried to get a handle on what my mom and Emi called my "condition."

The moments flash past, faster and faster, and I lose track of where one ends and the next begins. The shift from memory to memory is dizzying, and I feel mental whiplash settling in. Until, suddenly, it stops.

I'm in the library, hiding under my mom's desk, reading The Voyage of the Dawn Treader. *The late afternoon light filters through the stained-glass window, making blue and orange shapes on the pages of my book.*

Hushed voices drift into the library, and I stop reading and tilt my head to the side, listening. It's my mom and Emi, talking quietly as they make their way up the hallway leading to the library. I can't tell what they're saying, but I can hear their footsteps now that I'm listening for them.

Grinning, I close my book and curl up deeper into the recess under the desk so they won't be able to see me. When they get close enough, I'm planning to jump out and surprise them.

". . . need to stop," Emi says, her words becoming discernable as they enter the library. "It's not fair to her. She thinks there's something wrong with her."

"I hear you, Em, I really do," my mom says, "but we're close. I can feel it. I've been emailing with a Yogi who says he's seen these kinds of episodes afflict those who unlock siddhi powers prematurely—"

"Diana," Emi says, voice raised slightly. They're maybe halfway to the desk, now.

I can feel my grin wilting on my lips. They're talking about me. About my condition. About what's wrong with me.

"I've done some research into the siddhis," my mom says. She's much closer. Almost to the desk. "Here, look at this book— some of the powers it describes sound just like what Cora has been—"

"Diana," Emi repeats, even louder, "stop!"

They're standing on the other side of the desk—so close that I'm afraid they'll hear my shallow breaths, my pounding heart. I hug the book to my chest, making myself as small as I possibly can.

"Listen to yourself," Emi says. "You're grasping at straws and getting nowhere."

They fall silent for a moment, and I hold my breath.

"I get that you need to feel like you're doing something to help her," Emi continues. "I get it, Diana, I really do. But this isn't helping her. It's helping you." After another long moment of silence, she adds, "But it's hurting Cora."

My mom makes a sobbing sound that crushes my heart. "I

don't know what else to do." She makes that sound again, and tears well in my eyes. "How am I supposed to help my little girl, Em? How am I supposed to comfort her when I can't even touch her? I can't just leave her like this. I have to do something . . ."

"I know," Emi says. "I know. I'm not saying we stop trying to help her. I'm saying we go about it another way . . . a way that leaves Cora out of it. She's only eight years old. There's a good chance she'll forget most of what's happened so far."

My mom clears her throat. "So, what do you suggest?"

"The Atlanteans couldn't have survived to become the advanced species we know they were if they'd been as debilitated by their innate gifts as Cora is," Emi says. "They must have come up with some way to regulate the sensory input."

"Some way—like what?" my mom asks.

"Honestly, I don't know," Emi admits. "The best analogy I can come up with for what Cora is experiencing is like when a human stares directly into the sun without eye protection—only now, the whole sky is the sun, and Cora can't go outside without being blinded."

"So, you're saying we need to find the Atlantean equivalent of psychic sunglasses," my mom says. Her voice sounds more distant, like she's walking away from the desk.

Emi laughs softly, dryly. "Yeah, Diana, that's exactly what I'm saying."

9

I woke with a gasp, heart hammering in my chest, and sat bolt upright. It took my sleep-addled mind seconds to register Tila growling and scratching at my bedroom door. Her hackles were raised, the short fur fluffing her shoulder blades and forming a ridge that ran the length of her spine.

I shot a quick glance at the clock on the nightstand. It was half past midnight; I couldn't have been asleep for more than thirty minutes, an hour at the most.

Trembling, I moved painstakingly slowly, slipping my legs over the edge of the mattress. Just as my toes touched the cold hardwood, my mom's journal slid off my lap and onto the floor, landing in the pool of golden light from the lamp on the night-stand. The noise seemed as loud as a gong in my adrenaline-fueled state of hyperawareness.

I stared at the journal, my thoughts returning to the insanity my mom had written on the first few pages. To the things she'd written *about me*. Her story—it was impossible. Science Fiction. Not real. It couldn't be. *I* couldn't be something else. Something alien. Something *other*.

But then I thought of the strange trip down memory lane I'd

just taken in my dreams, of the long-suppressed memories that had resurfaced, and I wasn't so sure. In that last memory, it had been pretty obvious that both Emi and my mom believed I was one of these *Atlanteans*.

An explosive crack made me jump. A gunshot. Inside the house.

Tila was no longer growling. She was now emitting a string of barks laced with a vicious snarl that set my teeth on edge and reverberated in my bones.

I stood beside the bed, immobilized by fear. I was so scared, I could barely draw in a shaky breath.

Someone was in the house. An intruder.

. . . if they figure out what I've done—if they learn about you, they'll come after you . . .

Had my mom predicted this? Was it *them*? Was it the Order—the Custodes Veritatis—if the Order was even a real thing? Was this linked to my mom's disappearance? Or was it possible that her going missing weeks before our remote estate was broken into was just a crazy coincidence?

Two more quick crack of gunfire made me flinch. I could hear shouting and what sounded like muffled grunts.

Another couple gunshots in quick succession, and the house fell silent.

With a disgruntled whine, Tila turned away from the door and trotted across the room, back toward me. She circled around me, hackles still raised as she sniffed at my legs, intermittently emitting something that sounded like a cross between a low growl and a whine.

Was it over? I couldn't hear anything happening out there. All I could hear was Tila, along with my own hammering heartbeat and raspy breaths.

I counted to sixty, silently mouthing the numbers, then ever so slowly, slid my foot forward over the smooth teak floor. It took me at least a minute to make it to the bedroom door, and another thirty seconds to work up the nerve to reach for the doorknob. Just as my fingers closed around the handle, it started to turn.

I pulled my hand away from the doorknob like I'd been burned, and backed up a step. But as the door started to inch open, I froze.

Relief flooded me when I saw the face peeking in through the crack. Raiden.

His jaw was tensed, his brows drawn together, and his eyes were opened wide, alert. The left side of his face was spattered with blood, and he was holding a black handgun positioned down by his thigh. He lifted his free hand, holding a finger up to his lips telling me to be quiet, then raised his eyebrows. He was asking if I understood.

I swallowed roughly and nodded.

Raiden opened the door just enough that he could slip into the room, then eased it shut. "You need to hide," he said, his voice the faintest whisper as Tila widened her orbit to include us both.

I understood his words, but I could no longer get my feet to move. Terror had fused them to the floor.

"Now, Cora," Raiden hissed, curling the fingers of one hand around my arm, just above my elbow, his palm flush against my bare skin.

Raiden's hand. On my arm. He was *touching* me. His skin on mine.

My eyes bulged, my stare locking on his hand. But before I could pull free, he tightened his hold. I couldn't get away.

And yet, there was no pain. No terrifying hallucinations. No vertigo, no pounding headache, and no hint of the darkness creeping in on the edges of consciousness. Just Raiden, staring down at me, his features taut with worry.

The spike of panic slowly decreased, and I fell still under Raiden's touch. My chest heaved with each too-quick breath, but I could feel my heart rate already slowing as the receded, coherent thought returned. Raiden was here, but his mom wasn't.

"What about Emi?" I asked, voice hushed.

"Who do you think sent me up here?" Raiden whispered and gave another tug on my arm, pulling my thoughts back to the very real and present danger.

I let him lead me across the room toward the bed. With his help, I eased down to the floor on my belly and, feet first, slid underneath the bed's wooden frame. At the last second, I reached for my mom's journal and dragged it under the bed with me.

Raiden held a hand down in the gap between the floor and the bedframe, fingers splayed wide as if to say, *"Stay here."*

Fine with me. In the virtual world, I might have been all about the fight, but here in the real world, I was a run-and-hide kind of girl.

From the middle of the floor, Tila watched me curiously, head cocking to the side. She took a step toward me, then paused, looking from me to Raiden as he silently crossed the room, heading for the closed door.

If she followed him, I had no doubt that she would resume the growling and door-scratching routine. Whoever was still in the house was sure to hear that and head straight for us.

I snapped my fingers twice, signaling for her to come to me.

She didn't budge.

I snapped again, hissing, "Come here, Tila, *now*," as firmly as I could without raising my voice above a whisper.

She stared at the door for a moment longer, chuffed, and then padded toward the bed.

"Come on," I whispered.

She chuffed one more time, then dropped to her belly and

crawled under the bedframe, coming to rest beside me. Her presence had always had a calming effect on me, and even now, scared as I was, I felt a little better having her next to me.

I shifted the journal out from under my arm and eased it shut, carefully wrapping the leather cord around its cover to hold it closed, then laid my head down, resting my cheek on the worn leather. Strangely, it made me feel closer to my mom, almost like she was there with me, at least in spirit. She would've been a stand-and-fight kind of girl. Not a doubt in my mind.

Despite everything I'd learned about her in the past few hours, thinking of her courage brought a tiny smile to my lips.

From my limited vantage point, I watched Raiden's bare feet as he closed in on the bedroom door. For such a large man, his ability to move in near silence over the house's creaky old floors was incredibly impressive.

The door was shut, and Raiden flattened himself back-first against the wall beside the door frame like he expected bad guys to burst through the door at any moment. He became absolutely, completely still.

My already racing heart gave a frightened skip, and my body started to shake as a second wave of adrenaline flooded my system. Sweat gathered on the back of my neck and under my arms. I pressed my palms against the floorboards, and closed my eyes, focusing on taking deep, even breaths.

Sensing my mounting panic, Tila nestled closer. She tucked her face in the crook of my neck, her breaths tickling the hairs that had escaped from my loose, messy bun.

At the sounds of a scuffle coming from some other part of the house, I sucked in a breath.

There was only one other person in the house, only one other resident of the estate to fend off intruders—Emi.

My fingernails dug into the teak floor as my fingers formed claws. Emi sparred regularly with my mom, and they were both highly skilled fighters. I had always thought it was a leftover of their military days, but now I knew better. They'd never been in the military. At least, not in any traditional military.

Emi had been teaching me a discipline she called "pankration" since I was eight or nine, but my mastery of the grapple-heavy form of martial arts was hindered by my inability to touch anyone. I dabbled in knife throwing and sparring with a wooden staff, but mostly Emi and I just did Tai Chi together. It kept me in decent shape, and helped me concentrate and center myself, but that was about it. I knew she could take care of herself—between Emi and my mom, Emi was the better fighter—but she was quite petite, and she was no spring chicken. If the intruder was young, skilled, and even average in size, then she might not have the upper hand.

Raiden's thoughts must have gone to the same place as mine, because he reached for the doorknob, like he was intending to go help his mom. As he twisted the knob, the sounds of the scuffle died out, and he froze.

My whole body tensed. Vivid images of Emi lying on the floor, body bloody and broken, flashed through my mind. I would never forgive myself if my last words to her had been spoken in anger. I feared the worst, and my gut twisted into knots, making me feel nauseated.

Footsteps. I could hear them, faint but audible, like someone was trying to move as quietly as Raiden, but not quite managing. They were on this floor, slowly moving down the hallway in the direction of my bedroom. And from the sound of the footsteps, there was more than one person.

Beside me, Tila tensed up, her stocky body becoming a hard bundle of coiled muscle and barely restrained power.

Ever so slowly, Raiden pulled his hand back from the doorknob.

The footsteps paused, and I heard the distinctive creak of the door to the empty bedroom beside mine being pushed open. The room was used for storage and entered so rarely that nobody ever bothered to oil the hinges.

After what sounded like a cursory search of the room next door, the footsteps continued up the hallway. Toward my bedroom.

Tila scurried out from under the bed before I could stop her. She ran to the door, her nails scraping on the hardwood floor. The hairs along her spine were raised, once more, and a deep, menacing growl rumbled in her chest.

"Tila!" I whispered, snapping my fingers.

She glanced at me, but turned back to the door, too deep into guard-dog mode. A moment later, she lunged at the door, a string of baritone barks warning the intruders to stay away.

Raiden scooped Tila up, wrapping his free arm around her middle. He held her tightly, even as she struggled to get free, limbs flailing and teeth snapping. He sidestepped away from the door a heartbeat before a burst of automatic gunfire cut through the wood, the bullets splintering the floorboards mere feet from where I was laying.

I stared at the shredded hardwood for a fraction of a second, then scurried back farther under the bed. In the moment of quiet following the gunfire, my whole body trembled, and my heart-beat thundered in my ears. I sucked in a shaky breath, holding the air in my lungs.

The intruders were just outside. Would they fire again? Or would they burst into the room, guns blazing?

Raiden didn't wait to find out. He tossed Tila off to the side, swapped gun hands, and reached for the doorknob. In one quick jerk, he yanked the door open.

I couldn't see much from under the bed, just two sets of black combat boots, one set notably smaller than the other, like it belonged to a woman.

My view was obscured further as Tila lunged at the intruders, a dark, snarling blur of fur and fury. The smaller pair of boots disappeared, pushed deeper into the hallway by the powerful dog.

The *pop* of gunfire made me jump, and I whacked the back of my head against the bottom of the bed.

A heartbeat later, the larger intruder dropped his rifle on the floor, then fell to his knees and toppled onto his side. His fingers twitched a few times, and then he was still.

There was a small bullet hole in his brow, dead center between his sightless eyes. Eyes that stared straight at me. His irises were pale, contrasting with his darker skin, though whether they were blue, green, or even gray, I couldn't tell in the dim lighting.

Raiden stepped out into the hallway, where the struggle continued between my dog and the other intruder.

I knew my attention should have been locked on Raiden, on the remaining threat in the hallway, but I couldn't look away from the dead man's eyes. His lifeless stare entranced me. Who was he, and why had he come here? My mom's words whispered through my mind, and I couldn't suppress the sickening suspicion that this man—these people—had broken into my home looking for *me*.

Two quick gunshots broke my stare with the dead man. I sucked in a breath, and my eyes locked on the doorway. I couldn't see Raiden or Tila or the other intruder out in the hallway—just darkness, deep and deafening. I didn't know who had fired, and nothing else mattered. The rest of the world faded away, and all of existence narrowed down to that patch of darkness.

A body thudded onto the floor out of sight, an arm flopping into the doorway a fraction of a second later. It was small and gloved. Not Raiden's, I realized, relief flooding my body.

I watched Tila pad out of the darkness and back into the bedroom, her hackles still raised. She was panting, her tongue lolling out to one side, and the patch of white fur spanning from chin to chest was stained crimson. She trotted toward the bed, stopping and turning around when she reached it. Still panting, she stretched out on the floor, head raised and ears alert. She was resting, but she was ready to attack again, if necessary.

Raiden was still out in the hallway. Or, at least, I thought he was. I wanted to ask him if it was over, but I didn't seem to be able to take in enough air to speak. My lungs worked in tiny, frantic movements, making my breaths quick and shallow.

I waited under the bed, paralyzed by terror, for what felt like ages. In time, my breathing slowed, and I was left feeling cold and numb, distant and withdrawn. It was as though I'd witnessed the whole deadly struggle through a television screen.

I started at the sound of hushed voices out in the hallway. The arm stretching halfway across the doorway disappeared suddenly, dragged out of the dim patch of light from the lamp on the bedside table, and my eyes locked onto the pair of feet that appeared in its place. They were bare and small, feminine and familiar.

They were Emi's feet.

Some of the tension humming through my body eased, relaxing my muscles, just a little. Emi was fine. Whatever else had happened while I was hiding under the bed, at least she was okay.

Emi walked into the room, closely followed by Raiden. From under the bed, I watched her pick her way around the body on the floor. "Where's Cora?"

"Under there," Raiden said, passing his mom and heading for the bed. He stopped beside Tila, and a moment later, his hand appeared in the gap between the floor and the bedframe, partially blocking my view of his mom's feet. "You can come out, Cora," he said. "It's safe, now."

Robotically, I scooted forward and out from under the bed. I avoided Raiden's proffered hand and reached for the bedpost, using it to help me stand. My legs felt shaky, and I couldn't stop staring at Emi.

She stood in the center of the room, a shotgun gripped in one hand and her buttercup-yellow silk pajamas spattered with blood. Her braid was slightly mussed, and her cheeks were flushed, but she looked fine. Clearly, she'd fought the intruders, just as I'd feared, and clearly it had been a brutal, bloody battle. But it was just as clear that she'd come out on top. Little Emi. Gentle, brilliant, ruthless Emi.

I hugged my mom's journal to my chest, clinging to the tangible feel of it. Nothing was making any sense anymore. It was like I'd stepped into someone else's life. Like I was in a video game. Was this what shock felt like? Was I in shock?

Ever so slowly, I started to shake my head. Or maybe I wasn't in shock. Maybe I was dreaming. That made more sense. The package, the secret passage and hidden study, my mom's video and the journal, the break in—it was all part of a strangely vivid, twisted dream.

Raiden looked from me to Emi and back. "She's in shock," he said to his mom. "We should—"

"There's no time," Emi said, cutting him off. She took a deep breath, then set the shotgun on the mattress before turning away from both Raiden and me and heading for the closet. She switched on the closet light and pulled the door open, disappearing within for a moment before reemerging with a duffel bag. She crossed the room, heading for the bed, and set the bag on the mussed comforter, unzipping it and running her hands along the inside to open it more fully.

"You need to pack," she said, raising her gaze to meet mine and planting her hands on her hips. "Now, Cora."

"What?" I was still shaking my head. Still not understanding a single thing that had happened tonight. Still not sure any of this was real. "Why?"

"Because," Emi said, "This was only the first wave."

Instinctively, my focus shifted to the dead man on the floor near her feet. Bloody pieces of skull and hair and brain were spattered on the floor and walls beyond him.

"Now that the Order knows about you," Emi said, "more will come."

I looked at her. The Order. So, it was them—and as insane as it sounded, they had come here looking for me.

"Did you read it?" Emi asked, glancing at the journal.

I gulped and nodded, not bothering to mention I'd only read the first part.

"Good," she said. "Then you're up to speed on the situation."

"How—" Again, I shook my head. "This isn't a dream?"

"No," Emi said, eyes locking with mine. Her face was a mask of sympathy. "I'm so sorry, Cora. I wish there was more time to help you understand, but the Order is ruthless and relentless. More *will* come for you," she said. "And they won't stop until they have you."

10

Besides the countless trips to the dozens of experts my mom consulted those first few years after my condition became apparent, I could count the number of times I had stepped foot off the San Juan Islands on one hand. My mom hadn't ever taken me out when I was little, before my condition became obvious. I never understood why. Until now.

She was afraid. Of being found. Of losing me. Of losing everything.

The first time I ever left the safe familiarity of the islands, I was five. It was the week after my dismal stint in kindergarten, and I could clearly remember my mom telling me it was time for me to see a real city. She took me to Bellingham—not exactly a *big* city, but to me it was enormous.

During that first trip, we visited her "friend"—a child psychologist, I now realized after reliving the experience in my dreams—and took a driving tour of the city. I remembered feeling overwhelmed by the sheer volume of buildings and people, but thankfully we remained within the safety of the car the whole time, only getting out to grab lunch at a tiny cafe on the waterfront. We even stayed in the car on the ferry.

The flurry of appointments and consultations over the next three years took me to the mainland every month or two. But after those stopped, I remained on Orcas for years.

The next time I left the islands, I was twelve and deep into my studies of the history of Washington State. I had just learned about the Great Seattle Fire of 1889 that led to the city getting a complete facelift—a literal lift, with the street level being raised over 20 feet—and little twelve-year-old me wanted to see the remains of the old city, now called Underground Seattle, with all my heart. I hounded my mom non-stop with pleas to go on a tour until she relented. Seattle had overwhelmed me so much that we never even made it to the tour.

The next and final time I left the islands, it was for a three-day backpacking trip through Mt. Rainier National Park with Raiden and his Eagle Scout troop. Emi and my mom had gone as chaperones, and I'd been allowed to tag along. I was thirteen at the time, having the time of my life, absorbing the natural splendor of the park and interacting with a group of some of the most genuinely kind boys around. They were a few years older, and they had all seemed to go out of their way to make me feel welcome and included.

Well, I had *been having* the time of my life, up until the morning of day three, when one of the boys caught me alone after a trip to the bathroom—no harm intended—and made the mistake of grabbing my hand. The touch triggered an episode, and I was knocked unconscious for a solid two hours. Even though it was an accident and the boy truly didn't mean to hurt me, Emi and my mom were outraged. But it was Raiden's reaction that surprised me the most. I still didn't know exactly what happened, other than that he broke the troop's zero-tolerance violence policy and was not only kicked off the troop, but banned from Eagle Scouts completely.

That episode was the first I had experienced out of sight from my mom, Emi, or Raiden since that initial visit to the child psychologist. Once we returned home and a sense of safety and security settled in, I could remember—vividly—the moment I realized that I could never leave . . . could never have a normal life. That was the moment I accepted my fate as a prisoner of my own mind. That was also when I became obsessive about wearing gloves.

Another thirteen years passed without me leaving the San Juan Islands. Thirteen years of acceptance. Of complacency. Of going through the motions.

That was all about to change.

Now, I didn't have a choice. I had to leave Blackthorn Manor —had to leave my beloved islands, my safe haven. My life depended on it. Even so, I was just as terrified of leaving this place as I was of the people who'd invaded it. Of the people who were driving me away.

I was just grateful that I didn't have to run alone. Raiden was coming with me. Emi had already filled him in on the gist of the situation while I was packing, glossing over my supposed alien origins with a vague explanation about genetic testing and me being a "coveted asset" of the Order's, so he would be prepared for what we were up against. Emi, however, was dead set on staying behind—with Tila—planting diversions and misdirections before catching up with us in a few days.

"You're sure she'll be all right?" I asked Raiden as we loaded our bags onto our boat, the *Argo*. The thirty-five-foot Pursuit Drummond Island Runner was made more for island cruising and casual fish trolling than quick getaways, but we had to make do with what we had.

Raiden tossed his duffel bag onto the *Argo's* deck, then took mine and tossed it in, too. "She can take care of herself," he said, repeating a variation of the assurances both he and his mom had already given me. A million other questions spun around in my mind, but I'd been fixated on that one since Emi announced her intention to remain behind. That question didn't require me to acknowledge the things I wasn't ready to face, yet.

"But—"

"We don't have time for this, Cora." Raiden turned to face me, raising his hands like he was about to grab my shoulders but stopping himself short when I flinched. Now that the danger was less imminent, it seemed easier for him to remember that I was a no-touch zone.

He took a deep breath, balling his hands into fists, and crossed his arms over his chest. "My mother will be fine. She'll be safe and sound in the hill house, where she'll be able to monitor the Blackthorn Manor for any activity. Besides, she'll have Tila to keep her safe," he added. "The only person you should be worrying about right now is yourself."

I jutted my lower jaw forward. There was no condescension in his voice, just matter-of-fact this-is-how-it-is. Emi was strong, capable. I was weak, needing to be protected. These were facts, plain and simple. I knew it—I accepted it—but I hated it.

Raiden gestured to the boat. "Now, can we please get moving?"

I nodded, not trusting my voice not to wobble. After tightening the shoulder straps of my backpack and pulling up the faux-fur-lined hood of my black, waterproof parka, I stepped closer to the boat, placing my gloved hands on top of the boat's fiberglass side and kicking my leg over, just as I'd done a thousand times before.

For years, the *Argo* had given me an illusion of freedom. One of the beautiful things about the San Juan Islands was that there were so many little islands, many of which were uninhabited, rife for fishing and exploring. Those islands had made my tiny world feel a little bigger. Now that I was facing leaving my sheltered existence behind, I could see that sense of freedom for what it had really been all along—an illusion.

While Raiden untied the boat's mooring lines, I moved our bags off to one side of the deck, arranging them on top of some unstowed fishing gear. The full moon peeking through the clouds provided plenty of light to work under.

The strap of Raiden's duffel bag caught on the four-pronged tip of Emi's fishing spear, and I had to crouch down to unsnag the strap. Once I was satisfied with the arrangement of our bags, I set about folding up the boat's canvas cover.

The *Argo* rocked as Raiden boarded, and I glanced up, meeting his eyes for the briefest moment. "Ready?" he asked.

Feeling like a deer caught in the headlights, I nodded. That nod was the single biggest lie I had ever told.

After a quick return nod, Raiden headed for the helm, starting the boat with the turn of a key. The engine rumbled to life beneath my feet, and I moved to the stern to sit on the bench seat.

Once we were out of the tiny marina and cutting across Cascade Bay, skipping over the larger swells, Raiden killed all of the boat's lights. The sky was partially overcast, the clouds blotting out the stars, but the moon was full, leaving us plenty of light to navigate the familiar waters. The frigid March wind burned my nostrils, and the icy sea spray felt like razorblades on my cheeks. I hunched my shoulders, hugging myself to hold in my body heat.

Slowly, something that resembled calm returned to me, and my thoughts circled back to one of the night's significant, if not urgent, happenings—Raiden had touched me. Full contact. Skin-to-skin.

Raiden had *touched* me, and *nothing* had happened.

No dizzy spell. No flashes of deranged hallucinations. No loss of consciousness. Absolutely, blissfully nothing. Just like nothing had happened when I'd brushed arms with Emi, earlier. Skin-to-skin contact with another person without repercussions —that hadn't happened in as far back as I could remember. Once could be a fluke, but multiple times—that was huge, even in the face of all the craziness of the night.

Was it possible that I was finally growing out of my miserable affliction?

Or was it something else?

My thoughts turned to the pendant hanging heavy around my neck. Was this *its* doing?

In her note, my mom had said the pendant and orb should help, that they would make it so I wouldn't have to live in fear anymore. I couldn't help but cling to the last shreds of skepticism, but with the intruders, and Emi backing my mom's story, and me touching people without ill effects—was I experiencing evidence of the truth of my mom's wild claims? And if the Order was real and the necklace really did help me, were the other things she'd written true, too? The things about her past? The things about *me*?

I could feel myself beginning to accept it. Could feel my brain fitting together the pieces of evidence to transform what seemed impossible to not just possible, but probable. My sense of self-identity was tenuous, at best. I was a house of cards—one more blow, and I would collapse in on myself. The person my twenty-six years of limited life experience had shaped me into would cease to be.

We were almost to the tip of the island when Raiden killed the *Argo's* engine, snapping me out of my thoughts and back to reality.

The boat slowed, bobbing in the swells as it drifted. I stared at Raiden's moonlit form. He was absolutely still, his head cocked to the side like he was listening for something.

I stood, feet spread wide and knees bent to steady myself against the boat's unpredictable motion. "What is it?" I asked, joining Raiden at the helm.

"An engine," he said grimly.

I tilted my head to the side, eyes narrowing as I, too, listened. It took me a moment, but my ears finally picked up the rumble over the whooshing of my breaths and the thud-thump of my racing heartbeat.

"How did you hear that?" I asked. The sound was so faint. There was no way he could have noticed it over the roar of our own engine.

"I saw the lights of a boat," he said. "Coming out of Buck Bay."

I turned, glancing back at the bay we'd passed barely a minute ago. "I don't see anything."

"I know, that's what worries me," he said. "The other boat turned its lights off . . ."

"Oh." A chill crept up my spine. I could still hear the sound of another boat's engine. And unless my ears were playing tricks on me, it was growing louder.

Raiden turned the key in the ignition, and the *Argo* roared to life. In seconds, we were hurtling through the night at top speed, the sound of our engine thunderous in my ears.

But it wasn't loud enough to drown out the explosive *crack* that instinct told me could only be one thing.

I stared back in the direction of Buck Bay, fingers gripping the edge of the dash and eyes opened as wide as they could go. "Was that a gun?"

"Yeah," Raiden said, taking a step back to make room for me at the helm. "Take the wheel."

I did so without hesitation, splitting my attention between scanning the glimmering, inky water ahead and watching Raiden make his way to the stern. Having a task to focus on kept the mounting panic at bay.

Raiden drew a pistol that had been hidden somewhere inside his coat and planted a knee on the back bench, taking aim. For seconds, he held his position, steady against the drop and lurch of the boat as it raced over the water. Those seconds felt like an eternity.

Until, finally, the crack of not-so-far-off gunfire came again.

In an instant, Raiden adjusted his aim and fired. Three quick shots—*pop, pop, pop*. The sound was deafening.

I faced forward, opening my mouth wide in an attempt to clear the ringing from my ears. In the back of my mind, I thought I should probably have been freaking out right about now. But I wasn't. I felt calm. Alert. Focused. All of my questions and concerns drifted into the background, and I was absolutely and completely present.

We were nearing Obstruction Pass, the narrow passageway between Obstruction Island and the southernmost tip of this half of Orcas Island.

I kept peeking over my shoulder, searching the darkness for some visible sign of the other boat, but it remained a phantom trailing behind us, the only evidence of its existence the periodic crack of gunfire. Each shot was a little louder than the last. Our pursuers were gaining on us, and I ducked a little lower with each successive shot fired our way.

And then, between one heartbeat and the next, I could see the boat. It appeared ghostly in the darkness, a mere trick of the eye. But it grew clearer and clearer as it closed the distance to the *Argo*.

"A waste of ammunition," Raiden said over the roar of the engine, returning to the helm. "At least they know we're armed. Should keep them from getting too close."

I nodded, like I had any clue about shootout tactics, and moved out of the way, letting Raiden retake the helm. I pointed to a dark land mass up ahead. It was Deer Point, a shallow, rocky section of Orcas Island's shore, relatively hazardous for a boat if one didn't know to avoid it. A hail-Mary plan was forming in my mind. I didn't know where it had come from. It was like someone else was feeding me the idea.

"What if we drove them into the rocks?" I said, voice raised and heart hammering.

I couldn't make out Raiden's expression clearly, but I could see well enough in the moonlight to tell that he was frowning.

Crack. Crack. Crack.

I ducked, my grip on the stabilizing bar white-knuckled. The leather of my gloves creaked against the metal. "What other options do we have?" I shouted.

Raiden didn't reply with any bright ideas, but he also didn't seem convinced.

But then, he couldn't see the plan that had formed in my mind. Even if he could've seen it, he probably would've given it a big thumbs down. It sounded crazy, even to me. But the urge to try was growing within me, becoming overwhelming. It was like my brain had switched over to believing I was in the virtual world and this was all a game. The constant fear I lived with every day evaporated, leaving me feeling strong and capable. Or, at least, stupidly brave.

"I have a plan. Just get us close to Deer Point," I told Raiden. "Trust me."

He stared at me for a long moment. Then, surprising the hell out of me, he nodded.

Adrenaline surged within my veins, making my heart beat even faster and my senses sharpen. I was really going to do this.

Trying not to stumble, I made my way back to the stern. I dropped down on one knee by the bags, shifting them out of the way so I could reach the fishing gear underneath. I leaned back a little, counterbalancing as Raiden steered the boat toward Deer Point. After a moment of searching, I plucked Emi's four-pronged fishing spear out of the jumble of gear and regained my feet.

"What's the plan?" Raiden called from the helm.

I glanced up, noting that we were heading almost straight for the deadly rocks lurking beneath the water at Deer Point, then looked back at Raiden and gave him a thumbs up. I could hardly tell him I didn't really know *what* I was doing, just that something within me was driving me to take action. It almost felt like I was being possessed by some other entity, like I wasn't even in control.

I shed my bulky parka, dropping it on the deck near our bags, then lifted my left boot onto the bench seat and focused on the boat trailing us.

It had altered its course as well and was maybe forty yards back and closing in fast—way too close for comfort. It would be on us in minutes.

I counted four silhouettes, dark and menacing in the moonlight. No matter how easily Raiden had taken out the two intruders trying to get into my bedroom, I didn't think the odds would be in our favor should this vessel overtake us out here on the water.

Compelled by some internal driving force, I hoisted the fishing spear up over my shoulder, holding it in my right hand like I'd seen Olympic athletes do with javelins in the summer games. I was grateful for my gloves; the leather made my grip solid, unhindered by my sweaty palms. I extended my left arm out before me, pointing at the other boat.

The frigid sea air whipped and snapped the fabric of my T-shirt, biting into my flesh. I ignored the sting and honed in on the shadowy outline of the driver, barely twenty yards away. I aimed for him, and waited. We were still a little too far from Deer Point. I wouldn't get more than one shot at this. I just had to wait a few more seconds—

Another gunshot cracked through the night. I felt the bullet whiz past my neck, searing my skin as it rustled the tiny, misbehaving hairs that had snuck free from my ponytail. I felt it, but I didn't flinch. Inside, I was screaming. Outside, I was calm personified.

I focused. I drew in a deep breath. And on my exhale, I launched the spear.

It vanished from sight almost the instant it left my fingertips, swallowed up by the night.

Two more gunshots were fired our way.

The sound shattered my calm, and this time, I ducked. I dropped down to the deck on hands and knees, barely peeking over the stern of the boat.

Without warning, Raiden spun the wheel sharply to the right, jerking the *Argo's* bow away from the rapidly approaching shore. The stern skittered out, hopping over our own wake, and I lost my balance, falling onto my hip.

By the time I regained my knees and was looking out at the other boat again, the driver was nowhere to be seen. The three other occupants scrambled for the helm as their boat rocketed toward the rocky shore.

The other boat turned sharply, veering away from the underwater hazard.

I crossed my fingers and held my breath, hoping their course correction had come too late.

Seconds later, the other boat exploded into a ball of fire, like something straight out of a blockbuster movie.

Reflexively, I raised a hand to shield my eyes from the brilliant glow. I stared for a moment longer, then turned and sat on the deck of the boat, completely stunned. It had worked. My crazy, stupidly brave plan had worked. I'd done it.

I felt the boat turn slightly, then slow as Raiden set us on a course to pass safely through Rosario Strait, between Blakely and Cypress Islands.

A moment later, Raiden abandoned the helm to make his way to the stern. He crouched before me, planting one knee on the deck and handing me my discarded coat. "How the hell did you do that?"

"I . . ." I shook my head, looking at him but not really seeing him, and hugged the coat to my chest. The shock was back, and it had returned with a vengeance.

How *had* I done it?

I swallowed roughly, then confessed the truth. "I don't know."

11

By the time we reached the mainland and docked the boat at the Anacortes Marina, I was chilled to the bone. It didn't matter that I'd been nice and bundled up for the majority of the hour-long boat trip. My cheeks were numb from the frigid sea spray, and my nose felt like a snotsicle. With his stiff shoulders and reddened face, Raiden didn't look like he was faring much better.

We tied off the boat in silence, moving robotically. We both wanted to get out of the damp, early morning chill and into the warmth of the waiting car that was always parked in the marina's parking lot. Our boat slip was covered by a corrugated metal roof, so we left the *Argo's* canvas cover off and, hoisting the straps of our bags onto our shoulders, hightailed it to the car.

Since I first discovered the secret passage in Blackthorn Manor, events had been pushing me deeper and deeper into a state of shock. Now, I was in a daze.

I thought I should've felt something—anything—after causing the other boat to crash. Nobody could have survived that explosion. And I had made it happen. I had *killed* people. Just hours after watching Raiden do the same in my home. In my bedroom. I should've felt horror or guilt or remorse. I should have felt *something*. But I didn't.

Remotely, I wondered if that made me just a little bit of a psychopath—and was that even possible, to be a little bit of a psychopath, or was psychopathy an all-or-nothing deal? Regardless, even considering that possibility should have frightened me. There were so many feelings I *should* have been having, but in their place, I felt a whole lot of nothing.

I told myself the combination of the drop in adrenaline after such an extreme rush and the cold sea air must have muddled my mind. Not much emotion was getting through at the moment. That had to be it.

As we passed through the security gate leading from the dock to the parking lot, I gave myself ninety-to-ten odds of falling asleep within ten minutes of being on the road. I'd always been a motion sleeper, and in my current state, I was in prime condition to zonk right out. At least then I wouldn't have to think about why I wasn't feeling anything anymore.

The car, a slate-gray Lexus sedan, was parked right where it was supposed to be, in spot number eighteen. The parking spot came with the boat slip, and as such, shared the same number.

We tossed our bags into the trunk of the sedan, then climbed into the car, Raiden driving and me in the passenger seat. I didn't technically know how to drive a car, so the arrangement was pretty much a given. Virtual driving didn't count. And at the moment, I was grateful for my vehicular inadequacy.

I fiddled with the car's climate control system while Raiden guided us onto the main drag cutting through the flat, sprawling marina town. Once the heated seats were warmed up, the air from the vents was nice and toasty, and we were pulling onto the highway, I settled back into my seat and stared out the window. I could already feel my heavy eyelids drifting shut.

"How are you doing, Cora?" Raiden asked, cutting through a few layers of the sleepy haze settling over me.

Blinking, I turned my head without lifting it from the head-rest and looked at him.

His profile was strong, his expression stoic. Until he glanced at me, and I spotted the concern wrinkling his brow and intensi-fying his stare.

"I don't know. I feel . . ." I shrugged, then frowned, picking at a hangnail on my thumb. How could I tell him I felt nothing? "I don't know," I repeated. "Is that weird?"

Raiden grunted softly. "Nah. You've been through a lot. 'I don't know' sounds just about right." After a moment, he added. "But it won't last, Cora, so let me know when 'I don't know' turns into something else, okay?"

I looked down at my hands and nodded. I was an expert at hiding my feelings, a skill born of not wanting my pain and lone-liness to infect those around me. Raiden had always been the one person who could get me to open up. But he'd been gone for nearly a decade, and his visits home had been few and far between, his phone calls—to me, at least—dwindling from weekly to almost nonexistent after *that* visit. The one I didn't like to think about. After everything, I wasn't sure our connec-tion remained intact.

"You might as well get some rest," Raiden said. "We'll be driving for a while."

Again, I nodded. I lodged my elbow on the armrest jutting out of the door and rested my cheek on my palm. "Where are we headed, anyway?"

If it was anybody other than him behind the wheel—or my mom or Emi—I would have been a lot more diligent about figuring out where I was being taken. But no matter the distance that had developed between us over the past decade, Raiden was still *Raiden*. Still the boy I'd grown up with. If I couldn't put my life in his hands, what was the point of living at all?

"To a safe house in Seattle," he told me.

Mention of the "big city" made my heart skip a beat—not in

a good way. Seattle was so ginormous, with such tall buildings blocking so much of the sky and so many people rushing about. It was a lot—too much for a recluse like me. At least my beloved Puget Sound would be nearby; I hoped that would help to ease the choking agoraphobia and claustrophobia I could already feel chipping away at the numbing cocoon of shock.

Even with the promise of Seattle lurking ahead, within minutes, the motion of the car combatted the mounting tension and lulled me back into a sleepy daze. Eyelids droopy, I stared out the window. Sleep was so close I could taste it.

I barely registered the word "NORTH" on the sign hanging over the I-5 on-ramp as we made our way onto the freeway. Seattle was *south* of Anacortes by a solid eighty miles. Confusion disrupted the lure of sleep and some clarity returned to my mind.

Lazily, I turned my head toward Raiden. "We're going north?"

"Just covering our trail," he said, not taking his eyes from the road.

I stared at him for a few seconds longer, but when it was clear that he didn't intend to explain further, I frowned and returned to looking out the window. I was too tired to think, and too numb to care much at all.

Within seconds, my eyelids were drooping. Within minutes, I was out.

12

The next time I opened my eyes, Raiden was pulling our car into a parking spot in a moderately crowded lot. The sky was starting to lighten, though the sun had yet to peek over the hills. A quick glance at the dash told me forty minutes had passed since I'd last looked at the clock.

Sitting up straighter, I blinked and looked around; the parking lot was enormous. At the sound of a muffled roar, I leaned closer to the windshield and looked up into the sky. An airplane was flying close overhead, nose angled upward as it climbed ever higher. It was a hell of a lot bigger than the seaplanes I was used to seeing.

I cast another quick look around, my mind finally making sense of things. We were in an airport parking lot.

I turned my attention to Raiden. "Are we *flying* to Seattle?" I'd never been to an airport before, let alone ridden on a plane— at least, not in real life—and my stomach knotted at the prospect.

Raiden pulled the keys from the ignition and shook his head. "Just exchanging cars so we're harder to follow." He offered me a tight smile. His usually warm, brown irises had dulled and darkened, and his eyelids were rimmed with red. He looked as exhausted as I felt, his tired eyes lingering on my face. "Come on," he said, nodding toward his door. He pushed the door open and climbed out of the car.

After a few seconds, I followed.

Toting our bags, we left the Lexus behind and crossed the lot, heading for a long building at the far edge of the mass of parked cars. We passed a sign proclaiming BELLINGHAM INTERNATIONAL AIRPORT. So, we were in Bellingham.

I glanced up at the sky once more, noting the position of the soon-to-be-rising sun over my left shoulder, and reoriented where I was on the map in my head.

I followed Raiden into the airport through a set of huge sliding glass doors, eyes opened wide and taking in everything. He made an immediate left once we were inside, veering away from the ticket counters—I recognized them from the movies— and heading for the car rental kiosks instead.

"Wait here," he said, dropping his duffel bag onto the floor by a string of four interconnected chairs that had been bolted to the ground.

I placed my duffel bag beside his and sat, holding my backpack on my lap and hugging it to my chest. All of my most important possessions were in there. Strangely enough, the most valuable to me were things that hadn't been in my possession twenty-four hours earlier—the strange orb and my mom's journal.

I looked around, eyes taking in everything. It was all new to me. There were so many people. So many threats to my sanity. I felt small and too big at the same time. Like everyone was staring at me. Like I didn't belong.

I wished I had my phone, so I could pull it out and hide within a game. But that wasn't an option, right now. I'd left my phone behind, as directed by Raiden. Apparently, it was too much of a tracking risk. So, as I waited, hugging my backpack more tightly, I watched the activity all around me.

It had been ages since I'd seen so many people all in one place. It wasn't as busy as I would've expected—not like airports in the movies, which always seemed jam-packed with people—but then I wondered if that was due to the early hour. Did things like time of day matter in an airport when the whole point was to connect travelers to other places with other times of day?

Suitcases with wheels seemed to be the norm, filling the brightly lit, cavernous space with a dull buzzing sound. I could smell coffee, which sounded amazing, but I couldn't see any kind of cafe or restaurant. All of the service people looked to be airline employees or security personnel, not baristas or wait staff. I wasn't even sure if cafes were a standard feature in airports. I couldn't recall seeing them in any movies.

My stomach rumbled, triggered by the coffee-centric line of thinking. When was the last time I ate anything? Breakfast, yesterday, I realized. *Before* the package.

My stomach rumbled again, louder this time. As amazing as a real breakfast with eggs and bacon and toast or maybe even pancakes sounded, I would have settled for pretty much anything at this point.

On a whim, I turned my backpack around and unzipped the smaller front pouch. Any time I left the house, Emi was big on making sure I had three things: a coat, a bottle of water, and a snack. I crossed the first two fingers of my left hand, hoping that this time was no different.

The faintest smile touched my lips when I saw the six granola bars tucked into the pouch, right next to a bottle of water. "Thanks, Emi," I whispered, pulling one of the granola bars free.

I scarfed it down in three bites, then took out the bottle of water and twisted off the cap, gulping down nearly half in one go.

As I lowered the bottle, I spotted Raiden heading back toward me, a set of keys and a tri-folded bundle of paper in his hand.

"Ready?" he asked as he drew near.

I nodded and stood, resetting the straps of my backpack on my shoulders.

Raiden bent over to pick up his bags, transferring the paperwork into his backpack and putting the new car keys in his jeans pocket. He arranged the straps of his backpack and both of our duffel bags on his broad shoulders, and in no time, we were heading back toward the automatic doors. They slid open as we approached, letting in the chilly morning air.

Raiden looked this way and that, his eyes constantly moving as he led the way across the road toward a separate, smaller parking lot. He was on high alert, and it was making me paranoid. I couldn't shake the feeling that we were being followed. It made my skin crawl and the hairs on the back of my neck stand on end.

Thankfully, my mostly empty belly provided a much-needed distraction. "Can we get something to eat?" I asked, hunching my shoulders and slipping my hands into my pockets. Now that I'd had a chance to warm up from the boat trip, the morning chill felt downright freezing.

"We'll get something on the road," Raiden said, his strides long and quick. With my shorter legs, I practically had to jog to keep up with him.

"Something like McDonalds?" I asked, perking up a bit.

I'd never actually visited the golden arches myself—there were no McDonalds in the San Juan Islands and my mom was anti-fast food—but Raiden had long since made a habit of bringing back a bag whenever he returned from the mainland. I'd come to associate the greasy, addictive fast food with him visiting.

"Yeah, sure," Raiden said, chuckling softly. His laugh startled me.

I frowned, brow furrowing. It took me a moment to figure

out why: this was the first time I'd heard him laugh since he'd
returned from the military. My frown deepened.

"Unless you want something else?" Raiden said as we
entered the rental lot, and I realized his eyes were on me.

I glanced at him, forcing a smile. "No. McDonalds is
perfect." My smile turned genuine. "Besides, I've never had their
breakfast, and it always looks so good on the commercials."

My comment earned me another chuckle from Raiden, plus
an amused headshake. Two for two. I was on a roll.

"I think this is us," Raiden said, slowing his pace as we
neared a cluster of SUVs. He retrieved the car keys from his
pocket and pressed a button on the key fob.

The tail lights on a compact white SUV two cars away
blinked twice. A Toyota RAV4, according to the back of the car,
and a newer model, from the looks of it. If the plan was to blend
in, Raiden had chosen well. Even on Orcas I saw these things all
over the place.

We loaded our bags into the backseat, then ourselves into the
front. In no time, I was comfy in the passenger seat, butt warmed
to perfection and a bag of greasy goodness resting on my lap. I'd
let Raiden order for me, having no idea what I might like. The
smell of fried food and coffee filled the car, leaving me feeling a
surreal sense of contentment. If it weren't for the mad men
chasing us, this could've been the beginning of an amazing road
tripping adventure, the likes of which I'd only seen in the movies.

I sighed, wishing things were that simple.

"Are we going to eat that food or are did you just want to
soak in the smell?" Raiden asked, shooting me a sidelong glance.

My stomach grumbled, and I flashed him an apologetic
smile. A big guy like him—with biceps the size of my thighs—
was probably even hungrier than I was.

"Sorry," I said, opening the bag and digging in to the toasty
contents. I handed him random things—what looked like a fried

potato patty and a "McMuffin" according to the wrapper, which I knew from TV commercials was a breakfast sandwich. "Is that all right?" I asked. "There's other stuff, if you want—"

"This is fine, for now," Raiden said around a mouthful of fried potatoes. "Thanks."

"Mmhmm," I murmured, reaching into the bag to pull out a fried potato patty of my very own. I sniffed it—it smelled amazing, like French fries, only more fried—then glanced at Raiden. "What is this thing, anyway?"

"Hash browns," he mumbled, stuffing the remainder of his own hash browns into his mouth. Oh yeah, he was hungry.

I took a tentative bite. It was unlike any kind of hash browns I'd ever eaten, and my mouth exploded with the flavor of salty, golden-fried potatoes. "Oh my God . . ." I swallowed and took another, larger bite. "It's so good!" I said, talking with my mouth full and not caring at all.

That earned me chuckle number three.

I looked at Raiden, a stupid, close-mouthed grin plastered across my face as I chewed. For a moment, I felt normal. We were just two people on a road trip, sharing a breakfast and shooting the shit. Nobody was chasing us. We weren't killers. I wasn't an alien. I wasn't *me*. It had to be one of the single greatest moments of my life.

"What?" Raiden said. He grabbed a napkin from the center console and swiped the side of his face self-consciously.

"Nothing," I told him, contentedly settling back into my seat to finish my meal.

It had taken a full shake-up of pretty much my entire world to shove me out of my existence as an island-bound hermit, but strangely, I wasn't as upset by everything that had happened over the past day and night as I should have been. And I was pretty sure I wasn't still in shock. At least, not as deep in shock as I'd been. Maybe running for my life and having to kill to survive was as close to normal as it would ever get for me, and maybe that was all right.

Or, maybe this was just another phase of shock. I didn't know. And, at the moment, I didn't care.

I decided to just go with it. To pretend. This taste of normal was more than I had ever hoped for. For now, it was enough.

When the food was gone and we were left with just our Styrofoam cups of coffee, Raiden tossed the paper bag stuffed full of wrappers and greasy napkins into the backseat.

"Can you grab the rental papers from my bag?" he asked. "They should go in the glove box."

"Yeah, sure." I turned in my seat and reached for Raiden's backpack. I unzipped the front pouch and pulled the papers from the rental agency free. Facing forward again, I opened the glove box and unfolded the papers, eyes subconsciously skimming the information typed into the fields on the form. And froze.

It was wrong. It was all wrong. The name, the address—everything—was wrong.

I looked at Raiden. "Who's *Michael Greer*?" I asked, emphasizing the name. Clearly it was meant to be Raiden. But that wasn't his name. It wasn't even close.

Raiden reached across the center console and snatched the papers out of my hands, shoving them into the glove box and slamming it shut. "He's nobody," he said. "Just a remnant from another life." *From before*, he meant. From his time in the military. "We'll get you some alternative documentation once we're in Seattle. It'll make it easier for us to move around unnoticed."

Some *alternative documentation*.

I wasn't sure what shocked me more—that Raiden had a false ID legitimate enough that he could use it to rent a car, or that we needed to rent a car under a false name, at all. That we'd had to ditch our car. That I would need a false ID of my own. That our situation was too dangerous for me even to have brought my cell phone, in case someone tapped my line or was tracking my cell. That people were chasing us. That we were on the run. That I'd watched Raiden kill people. That *I'd* killed people.

That my mom's wild claims weren't all that wild, after all. That they were, quite possibly, true.

There was no fooling myself anymore. This was no normal road trip.

I turned to stare out the window, lips pressed firmly together to keep my chin from trembling.

There was nothing *normal* about our situation. About my life.

And part of me was afraid that there never would be again.

13

Pieces of my life that used to make sense simply didn't anymore. I spent the car ride from Bellingham to Seattle staring out the window, thinking about how much had changed overnight. And wondering how much still might change, depending on how deep I wanted to dive into the rabbit hole opened up by my mom's journal.

I was *other*. Alien or something else. I wasn't human. I may have started to accept my new reality, but I certainly hadn't processed it, let alone internalized it.

But there was no avoiding one simple fact: from the moment I first donned the necklace with its strange, antique pendant that seemed to glow in a certain light, my condition had ceased to be an issue. Numerous times, I'd come into contact with both Raiden and Emi, and not once had that contact triggered one of my trademark, debilitating episodes. There hadn't been any hallucinatory visions. No petit mal seizures. No losses of consciousness.

Touch was suddenly, shockingly benign.

Logic told me the necklace was somehow protecting me— that it was the "Atlantean sunglasses" my mom and Emi had been talking about in that long-suppressed memory. But *what* was it protecting me from? Psychic powers? Clearly, that was my mom's theory, and Emi seemed to be on board with it, but I wasn't so sure.

In my mind, belief in psychic powers required belief in such supernatural things as gods and monsters. In magic. I wasn't remotely prepared to take the leap into the world of belief. Of faith. I wasn't even sure that was something I was capable of doing.

As the tall buildings of Seattle came into view, peeking over the treed hills and shorter buildings of the city's northern outskirts, I turned my head to look at Raiden. Neither of us had said much in the hour and half we'd been on the freeway. I wondered if his thoughts were as twisted and tangled as my own.

"Hey, Raiden?" I said, my voice cutting through the silence.

Raiden grunted, his eyes flicking away from the road and toward me for a fraction of a second.

"Do you believe in God?" I asked.

I didn't. Or, at least, I thought I didn't. I'd never really considered the idea of the deity—or deities, depending on who you talked to—as portrayed by the world's many religions with much seriousness. I supposed that was the result of being raised by my mom and Emi, one a secular humanist, the other an atheist and biologist.

Raiden was quiet for a long moment, considering my question. "I believe in humans," he said eventually, echoing the philosophy we'd both been raised with.

"What about aliens?" I asked.

He shrugged, amusement tilting the corner of his mouth upward. "Why not?"

I chewed on the inside of my cheek. "Even though there's no real proof?"

Raiden inhaled and exhaled deeply. "That we know of . . . yet," he said. "Besides, after everything I've seen, I know that believing something just because it's easier or less scary than the alternative—or because it's what we've been told our whole lives is true—is way more dangerous than being open to unexpected or undesirable possibilities."

He fell silent again, and I thought he was done, but after a moment, he continued on. "The way I see it is this: God and religion—that's all, for the most part, based on hearsay. On he-said, she-said, my-mom's-cousin's-friend word-of-mouth claims. It's about feeling. About believing without evidence or reason."

I frowned, considering his words.

"But the idea that there's life out there, on some distant planet—that's based on logic. On statistical probability. On science. It's a belief based on facts, even if the proof isn't there."

"Yet," I added, a small smile tensing my lips.

Raiden tilted his head in a slight sideways nod. After a few seconds, he turned the question back onto me. "What about you? Where do you lie on the gods-and-aliens spectrum?"

I returned to chewing on the inside of my cheek, untangling parts of the messy thoughts filling my head. "I don't know," I finally admitted.

If we'd had this conversation yesterday, I would have said I believed in aliens for sure, but not so much in God and that kind of thing. Today, belief in aliens carried implications that were far too heavy for comfort. God was easier. But then, that was kind of the whole point of everything he'd just said.

Intrigued by the depth of Raiden's response, I looked at him sidelong, tilting my head to the side, just a little, and studied his profile.

Raiden was handsome, I supposed, in an unconventional way. His tanned features were bolder than those favored by photographers and Hollywood alike. I'd had a crush on him at various stages throughout my life, but as I grew older and more introspective, I attributed my feelings to the fact that I hadn't had much interaction with any other boys. Now, I wasn't so sure about that. The distance that had grown between us allowed me to view him from a new, somewhat objective lens. He was strong and capable, thoughtful and smart.

And wounded. It was clear that his past haunted him, but that only added to his intrigue. To his allure. I felt drawn to him.

Heat suffused my cheeks as I felt a growing desire to *touch* him. With my hands. No gloves. Full-on, skin-to-skin contact. For the first time ever, such a thing was possible. That realization deepened my blush, making my neck and cheeks burn hotter.

"What?" Raiden said, glancing at me for longer this time.

I froze, feeling like I'd been caught doing something naughty. In a sense, I had. "I—" I bowed my head, neck and cheeks flaming, and returned to staring out the passenger-side window. "Nothing." I cleared my throat. "Sorry."

"Hm," Raiden murmured. He was letting it go, thank God. Or, thank *something*.

I shoved the feelings—the desire—into a deep, dark corner of my mind. I was terrified of getting my hopes up, then having them dashed away when the inevitable happened. When touch would, once again, trigger an episode. When this remission from my condition—or psychic powers, or whatever it was—showed itself for what it truly was. A fluke. Better not to get too attached to impossible possibilities.

I stared out the window, excitement tempered by the self-imposed reality check. The blush was long gone, replaced by dull disappointment. By acceptance.

It would be better this way, in the long run.

Maybe five minutes later, we exited the freeway. It wasn't much longer until Raiden slowed the car and pulled over to park against the curb.

"We're here," he announced, exhaustion lending a monotone quality to his voice.

I leaned closer to the window, ducking my head to get a better look. We'd parked in front of a five-story, seventies-era apartment building—our safe house. Or rather, our safe apartment. It didn't look like much, but then, maybe that was the point.

———

I sat on the edge of the queen bed tucked away in the apartment's lone bedroom, my fingers clutching my mom's journal. I'd been holding it on my lap since taking it out of my backpack. A solid ten minutes had passed.

I was intending to continue the journey into my mom's past, but I just couldn't bring myself to unwind the leather cord and open the book. The temptation to read more was strong, but the fear of doing so was stronger. The fear of what other shocking revelations might be hidden on those pages.

With shaking hands, I set the journal on the nightstand, next to my discarded gloves, and scooted back on the bed to lay down on top of the quilt. I curled up on my side and squeezed my eyelids shut, blocking the journal from view. I was exhausted, tired beyond the point of being able to sleep. I felt wired. Alert, but fuzzy-brained. Confused.

I focused on my pulse thrumming in my neck, on the rhythmic beating of my heart, on the gentle whoosh of air in and out of my lungs. I concentrated on my physical body, isolating each set of muscles, starting with those in my face and working down to my feet, not moving on to the next area until the current one was completely relaxed.

The apartment smelled funny, like the ghosts of cigarette smoke, dirty socks, and wet dog. I wondered if the odor was an apartment thing, or just something unique to *this* unit. I'd never been in an apartment before, and I wasn't sure what I'd been expecting, but it wasn't this. Apartments on TV and in movies were always jam-packed with furniture and décor. With signs that people lived in them. This place was sterile, furnished by a few odd pieces of utilitarian furniture and not much else. The walls were bare. The kitchen counters empty. There wasn't even a television.

From the other room, I could hear Raiden talking—to Emi, I could only assume. Like me, he'd left his personal cell phone behind, but he'd brought a burner phone in its place, a pre-pay cell phone he'd programmed with a single number—that of another burner phone held by his mom. Less traceable, he'd explained. Not *un*traceable, just *less*.

I honed in on Raiden's voice, lowered but still audible, preferring it to the chaos of my own thoughts.

"That's not the point," Raiden said, then paused. I assumed he was listening to whatever his mom was saying on the other end of the line. "No, *you're* not hearing me, Mom." His voice was still hushed, but there was a hard edge to it. He was upset. "You should have told me *before*."

I wondered what the issue was. What had Emi not told him that was setting him off? About the Custodes Veritatis? She'd filled him in about that before we left Blackthorn Manor. Or had she finally told him about the Atlanteans? Had she finally confessed the truth about *me*?

"I get that, Mom, I really do," he said, "but if I'd known they were hunting us, I never would have left to—" His words cut off, and he was quiet for a long moment. "Yeah, no, I get it. You're right. You made the right call." He blew out a breath. "I just wish —" He paused, not to listen, I didn't think, but to collect his thoughts. "I wish I'd known. I would've stayed." His tone had softened, his mood calming. "I could've helped."

I imagined I was in his place, talking to my mom on the phone. What would I say to her? Would I yell? Would I cry? Would I demand answers? An explanation? A reason for all of the lies? Would I confess to the horrible things I'd seen—I'd done—just to stay alive? Or would I be so relieved to hear her voice that I would forget about everything else?

"I'm not sure," Raiden said. "Stay here for a day or two, at least until I get Cora's alternative documentation squared away."

The pull of sleep was too strong, and now that the heat had faded from Raiden's voice, his words were growing distant to my ears. To my mind.

"No, I know," he said. "We can't stay here. We have to keep moving."

Remotely, I registered that he was talking about me, now.

But the distance between my mind and Raiden's voice grew, until his words were a far-off, muffled hum and blessed sleep drowned out the world.

[14]

I'm eleven years old, sitting at the big desk in the library with my mom. We're both studying a map spread out atop the desk. Our shoulders are close, but we're careful not to touch. Not touching is automatic by now. It's like blinking, or breathing.

The map is an ancient thing, the parchment yellowed by age and the edges frayed. It's a centuries-old copy of Philip Bauche's 1737 map showing Antarctica divided into two islands.

"And see this here," my mom says, pointing to a space of ocean between two land masses. "This is where Bauche claimed that Antarctica was broken into two islands rather than one large land mass."

I look at my mom. "Is it broken into two islands?"

She shakes her head. "Not today. But, the Transantarctic Mountains—the mountain range dividing the continent into East and West Antarctica—suggest that Antarctica is the product of two islands colliding a very long time ago."

"Kind of like India and the Himalayas?" I ask.

"Exactly," my mom says, flashing me a brilliant smile. "The curious part, though, is wondering if Bauche knew Antarctica used to be two separate land masses—or was he just guessing?"

I frown, studying the map once more. It's so detailed. So calculated. So precise. There's no sense of uncertainty about it. "It doesn't look like he was guessing," I say.

*"My thoughts exactly," my mom says. "Which leads to the next question—*how *did he know about the two islands?"*

I straighten and shrug. "Maybe he saw them on another map?"

My mom stares at me for a moment, then sits up straighter and starts to laugh as she shakes her head. "We'll find a way to make it safe for you to get out there one day, Cora," she says. "You're going to make one hell of an archaeologist."

Abruptly, the scene shifts.

I'm no longer in the library at Blackthorn Manor, but in a cavernous room twenty times the size of the library. The walls are white, the high, arched ceiling supported by polished metal beams. I've never been here before, at least, not that I can recall, but there's a sense of familiarity about the place.

And I'm no longer sitting beside my mom. I'm sitting at a hexagonal table in the center of the room, a severe looking middle-aged woman in the next chair over. Her skin is pale, almost translucent, and her hair is a deep blue-black. Her features are fine, sharp almost, and I think she might even be beautiful if she smiled. I don't recognize the woman, but just like the room, there's something familiar about her. I have the strangest feeling that I know her—that I know her well*—though I can't put a name to her face. I know, in my gut, that she rarely smiles.*

"Your progress has surpassed all of my expectations," she says, placing a closed fist on the table, fingers down.

Though I can understand the meaning of her words, I still recognize them as some unfamiliar language, the vowels and consonants fitting together in strange, new ways to my ears. When she uncurls her fingers and moves her hand away, a small, golden disk remains on the table, the metal set with a perfectly rounded, perfectly clear stone roughly the size of my thumbnail. It's a pendant, and it's for me. And it means something. Something huge.

My eyes widen, and my lips part in surprise. I reach for the offering, but hesitate before touching it. I look from the pendant to the woman, half expecting her to laugh in my face and take it back.

"You've earned it," she says, her lips softening, if not fully curving into a smile. "Report to Genetec in the morning to begin the enhancement process. You're going to make one hell of an Amazon."

The scene shifts again.

I'm seventeen years old, standing in the foyer of Blackthorn Manor, shoulder leaned against the open door as I watch the driver tote my mom's bags out to his town car. My mom is heading to Morocco, where she'll assemble a team for an underwater "exploration"—her code word for an unofficial, undocumented, and highly illegal excavation—of the coastal areas along the Strait of Gibraltar.

My mom comes tromping down the stairs, one last messenger bag strapped across her body. "Thanks for watching my bags," she says as she approaches me. Her eyes shift to the driver, and she lowers her voice to say, "Nobody can be trusted . . ." She winks.

I snort a laugh and roll my eyes. Her paranoid mistrust has become a long-running inside joke.

My mom stands in front of me and reaches for the end of my braid—the closest she can get to touching me without risking triggering an episode. Her blue eyes are alight with hope. "It's still not too late for you to join me, Cora-bora . . ."

I force a smile, though I know it must look strained, and shake my head. "I'd just get in the way." I avert my gaze to the Persian rug covering the teak floor of the entryway, eyes tracing the maroon and gold design, heart brimming with shame.

We planned this expedition together. It was supposed to be my first real adventure. We ordered what practically amounted to an entire new wardrobe of leather clothing—my armor, as my mom called it. And so many pairs of gloves.

But fear slowly crept in, chiseling away at my excitement, and I became convinced that no amount of preparation or precaution could safeguard my sanity. I officially chickened out a few nights ago.

I know my mom had been holding out hope that I would come around. But now, I watch that hope drain out of her, dimming her eyes and turning down the corners of her mouth, until all that remains is disappointment. In me.

She inhales deeply, exhaling in a sigh. "Well, there's always next time . . ."

Once again, the scene shifts.

I'm sitting on my thinking rock, a bench-shaped boulder teetering on the edge of the bluff. It's a five-minute walk from Blackthorn Manor through the woods to get here, and the trees block the house from view, giving this spot an illusion of seclusion. I come here when I feel like I need to get away. When I'm here, perched on the boulder, looking out at the mass of blue-gray water, I can pretend that I'm somewhere else. Someone else. At least, for a little while.

I hear quiet footsteps on the well-worn trail behind me. I don't turn around. I already know who it is.

"Can I join you?" Raiden asks.

"It's a free country," I say, curling my legs up so I can hug my knees to my chest. I rest my chin on top of my knees and take a deep breath. I suppose it's a free country because of people like him, but I'm not willing to voice that thought, not after all of the spiteful things I said to him earlier.

Raiden climbs onto the boulder and sits, leaving about a hand's width between us. He rests his forearms on his upraised knees, letting his hands hang over his sneakers. "It's not you," he says, his deep voice soft, almost apologetic.

I roll my eyes and laugh bitterly. It's funny his words are the same used so often in the movies when people break up. We aren't a couple or anything like that—never have been, and never will be—but I love him, all the same. He's my other half, even if I'm not his. And now he's leaving, again. Reenlisting. Some elite force, or something, and I'm terrified that the next time he leaves will be the last.

I hate him for leaving me, again.

"I was never good at school—at books and computers and all that stuff, not like you—but I'm good at this," Raiden says. "These past four years, I feel like I've actually been able to make a difference in the world . . . like I matter."

My chin trembles, and my eyes sting with unshed tears. I choke on the words, "You matter to me," and clear my throat instead of speaking.

Raiden is quiet for a long moment, but in time, he inhales deeply, and I know he's about to say more. "I need it, Cora—that feeling."

The tears spill over the brims of my eyes, and I hastily swipe them from my cheeks. "Great," I say, voice thick with emotion. "I'm happy for you."

"Bullshit," Raiden says. I can feel his eyes on me, but I refuse to look at him. "What do you want me to do, Cora?" There's heat in his voice now. My reaction is hurting him. "Tell me what you want me to do—right here, right now—and I'll do it. Do you want me to stay?"

I scoff and shake my head. Like I would ever tell him to stay. Like I could ever—ever—do that to him, when leaving was all I'd ever wanted. I stand, slide down the backside of the boulder, and wipe off my butt. "Go," I say as I walk away. "Just go."

Leave me behind, I don't say.

The scene shifts, once more.

I'm standing at the mouth of a massive ice cave, watching a half-dozen women in tight, black suits reminiscent of diving wetsuits stream into a sleek submarine. Another group of people follow the women, some male, some female, clothed in what looks like refined, white hazmat suits, the hoods and masks draped down their backs, exposing their faces. Everyone has pale, almost translucent skin and high, pronounced cheekbones, though hair color varies from the lightest blond to sapphire blue to the blackest black.

There's something off about these people, but I can't quite put my finger on it. They're all slightly too pale or slightly too tall or slightly too fine-boned or slightly too something.

"You're disappointed I didn't select you for this mission," a woman says from beside me.

I look at her, recognizing her as the woman who gave me the pendant. Interest sparkles in her gray eyes as she stares at me.

This is a test. This, right here, right now. How I behave will determine my future.

If I'm petulant, if I show her that I only care about myself, about my advancement in the rank of Amazons, I'll be stuck in our frozen city for who-knows-how-long. But if I show her I'm willing to do whatever is best for our people—even if that means remaining behind while others go out and explore this new, wild world—then I'll prove to her that I can put the needs of our people before my own.

"It's fine," I say, blanking my expression and returning my focus to the submarine.

Everyone is on board the submarine now, and I'm desperate to join them.

"If I can best serve our people here, then this is where I belong," I say. I lie. I just hope she believes me.

"Indeed," the woman says. "Besides, there's always next time."

I fight the urge to smile. Even so, the corner of my mouth rises, just a little. Next time, I won't be left behind. I'll make damn sure of that.

———

I woke slowly, rolling onto my back and staring up at the ceiling. It had a strange, lumpy texture, and I wondered if this was what I'd heard called a "popcorn ceiling" on the home renovation shows I sometimes watched in the middle of the night when I couldn't sleep. Late afternoon light streamed in through the narrow cracks in the vertical blinds, drawing amber stripes across the ceiling.

Another string of strange, vivid dreams had plagued my sleep. Some of the dreams were memories from my past, but they'd been broken up by scenes from what felt like an alternate reality. Those other dreams had felt just as real—just as much like memories—only they weren't *my* memories. It left me feeling fractured, like there was a disconnect within my mind.

But across that disconnect, a single thought echoed through my mind, a remnant from the dreams: *I won't be left behind.*

Twenty-six years of hiding had been more than enough for me. I wouldn't do it anymore. I was ready to take my future into my own hands. I was ready to take action. No more next times. *This* was the time. It was now or never.

I had a plan. I knew what I was going to do. I felt brave. Determined. And not remotely afraid.

It was like I was channeling that alternate me from the dreams, the one who wasn't real. The one who was strong and bold. Who was capable. Who never let fear hold her back. The one who *could be* real, if I let her be.

I would retrace my mom's steps until I discovered what happened to her. Dead or alive, I would find her.

I'd been left behind too many times before. Not this time.

[15]

"Here," Raiden said, holding his open hand out in front of my face so I could see it. There was a single, tiny blue pill resting on his palm. "Take this."

I sat up a little, momentarily raising my head from its place of safety between my knees to cast a sidelong glance at Raiden. The faux-leather airport seat creaked as I moved. I put up mental blinders, doing my best to ignore the hoard of people swarming all around us. SeaTac Airport made the Bellingham Airport look like a child's toy.

I was light-headed, my heart hammering in my chest, my breaths quick and shallow. I held in the words, "I don't think I can do this," for the umpteenth time. This whole run-off-to-Rome, track-down-my-mom thing had been my idea in the first place. I couldn't back out now. We were at the airport—at the gate—minutes away from boarding.

I eyed the pill in Raiden's hand, thinking it looked a hell of a lot like a Valium, but trying not to get my hopes up. "What is it?" I asked.

I'd tried countless medications over the years in a vain attempt to get a handle on my condition; brain chemistry being the special butterfly that it is, some didn't work on me at all, while others seemed to have an exaggerated effect. Valium—diazepam—fell into the latter category.

"Valium," Raiden told me.

"Oh, thank God," I said, reaching for the pill without hesitation. I was wearing one of my thinner pairs of gloves, despite the apparent state of remission my condition had gone into—better safe than sorry—and deftly picked up the pill with my leather-covered thumb and forefinger.

I hadn't taken any form of sedative in years, preferring avoidance over medication when it came to managing my condition. But right now, after having survived *airport security*—I shuddered simply remembering the terror I'd felt while watching the guy in front of me get pulled out of line for a pat down—I wasn't about to turn down a happy pill. Just the idea of having some stranger's hands roaming all over me . . .

I popped the pill into my mouth and swallowed it dry.

"Here," Raiden said, unscrewing the cap on a bottle of water and handing it to me.

I remotely recalled making a pit stop in a little convenience shop en route from the hell that was passing through security to the slightly lesser hell that was waiting at the gate. Raiden must have picked up the bottle of water there. The whole airport experience was sort of a blur. An endless, hellish blur.

I accepted the bottle of water and took a swig. "Thanks," I said, gulping down a little more, then holding my hand out for the cap.

I twisted the cap onto the bottle, grateful that in a half hour I would be feeling pretty damn good. I took a deep breath, letting the air out slowly. I just had to keep it together until then.

Raiden nodded, leaning forward to rest his elbows on his knees. He stared ahead, his eyes slowly scanning our surroundings. Our backs were to a wall of glass, the runway and an endless string of airplanes visible on the other side. But there were hundreds—thousands—of people on *this* side of the glass. So many potential threats.

There was no reason for the people who were after us to suspect we'd gone to the airport; Raiden had taken every precaution to ensure we weren't being watched and hadn't been followed. *But* considering this was the main international hub in the area and the most likely place to hop on a plane and hitch a ride out of the country to, oh say, my mom's last known whereabouts, it wasn't outside the realm of possibility that *they* might have someone posted here as a precaution.

I could understand why Raiden was being extra watchful. Guessing we might be here, at this very gate, wouldn't take a huge mental leap.

I sat back in my seat, focusing on Raiden. It made ignoring the thousands of people crammed into the terminal all around us just a teensy bit easier.

He had a prescription for Valium. I couldn't help but wonder why, though I wasn't about to ask. Mental health could be a touchy subject, and I didn't want to be rude. It had to be because of the war—or was it *wars*? I knew he had spent the majority of his time abroad in the Middle East, so I could only imagine the things he had seen.

Raiden's slow scan of the terminal turned his face away from me.

When I first brought it up two days ago, Raiden hadn't exactly been excited about my plan to head to Rome to search for my mom, but swaying him hadn't been all that hard. I figured he was just glad we were getting out of Dodge. The Order was looking for us *here*. It made sense for us to get ourselves *elsewhere*.

A voice came on through the overhead speakers, announcing that it was time to begin priority boarding. The last few tickets available had been in business class, so we'd been forced to dig into our cash-on-hand for the splurge. We were operating strictly cash-only, now, credit and debit cards being way too traceable. It was a pain to deplete our resources so quickly, but Raiden assured me we could get more money once we were in Rome.

Hearing the call to board, Raiden and I stood, hoisted our backpacks onto our shoulders, and left the crowd of waiting passengers to join the line of several dozen people already formed at the gate. I felt like all eyes were on us, and it took a concerted effort not to glance around suspiciously.

Thankfully, nobody jumped us while we were boarding, and we found our seats easily enough. I took window, Raiden took aisle. I felt safer knowing I only had to worry about brushing up against his arm rather than spending the whole flight avoiding anyone who moved up and down the aisle.

I sat stiffly in my seat, seatbelt buckled and backpack stashed under the seat in front of me. I fidgeted with my boarding pass and forged passport while I watched the remaining passengers shuffle onto the plane and slowly funnel down the two aisles.

"Nervous?" Raiden asked. I could feel his gaze skimming the side of my face.

A thready laugh bubbled up my throat. "Uh huh," I said without looking at him.

This would be my first ever flight, and I had no idea what to expect. Like the majority of my knowledge about the world, everything I knew about airplanes came from TV, movies, and video games, and a good chunk of my source material included some pretty serious issues—hijackings, malfunctions, or full-on crashes. In my head, I knew airplanes were a relatively safe mode of travel, but my vast second-hand experience made me *feel* like our odds of dying on this plane were somewhere around fifty-fifty.

"The flight's the least of our worries," Raiden said.

I looked at him, lips pressed together. "Thanks, Raiden. Super helpful."

He frowned slightly, then shrugged and settled back into his seat, elbows on the armrests and hands clasped over his abdomen. He rested his head against his seat back, looking to all the world like a man in repose.

But I could see the tension in his jaw. The focus in his gaze as he watched the other passengers. He studied each and every one of them as they boarded.

Inhaling and exhaling deeply, I turned my attention to the window. To the cart on the ground delivering bags to the plane. Our duffel bags were down there, somewhere. I'd shuffled some things around, making sure all of the essentials were in my backpack, but it still felt strange to be separated from my things, just trusting that the bag would make its way halfway across the world and meet me in Rome.

It felt even stranger to be separated from Tila. Emi had dropped her off at the doggy ranch the morning after Raiden and I fled the island, where she would remain until my return. For six years, she'd been my constant companion, lending me her sturdy strength and support. And snuggles—her snuggles were probably one of the main things that kept me sane through my no-human-contact life sentence. Leaving her behind felt like leaving behind a vital part of me. I was the tin man without his heart, the cowardly lion without his courage. I was fractured, far from whole.

I glanced down at my passport, flipping the cover open. My picture stared back at me, but that was about all there was of me on the identifying page. I had a new name. A new date of birth. A new everything. I was a new *me*: Sarah Summers. At least, I was on paper.

I returned to staring out the window, trying to convince myself that this new identity would provide a fresh start. I could break free of the weaknesses that had held me back for so long. The name was an homage to one of my all-time favorite TV shows, *Buffy the Vampire Slayer,* where the main character was named Buffy Summers, played by actress Sarah Michelle Gellar.

I'd picked the name hoping it would help me to be strong and brave, confident and competent, like Buffy, herself.

I could be someone who never let herself be left behind. Not anymore.

As the plane pulled away from the gate and taxied to the runway, I clutched my knees and repeated a series of affirmations in my head.

I am strong and brave. I am someone who won't be left behind.

I repeated this as the plane accelerated and as the wheels lifted off from the ground. I repeated it, over and over, until I actually started to believe it.

The plane climbed higher. The flight attendants performed what was clearly a well-rehearsed show, explaining the plane's safety mechanisms and what to do in the case of an emergency. The captain's voice came on over the plane's intercom system, announcing that we would be reaching cruising altitude soon. And still, I repeated the affirmations in my head.

I am strong and brave. I am someone who won't be left behind.

"How are you feeling?" Raiden asked.

Shaken out of my semi-meditative state, I looked at him. "I —" I stopped myself before I could blurt out the thirteen words repeating in an endless loop in my mind.

I cleared my throat, taking a mental assessment of myself. I hadn't thought about the other people on the plane in a while, not since take off, at least. And the fact that I was in a metal tube, hurtling through the air, didn't seem to be bothering me one bit.

"I feel all right," I told him. Clearly, the drug was working. "I'm scared, though," I added, surprising myself with the admittance. Oh yeah, the drug was definitely working. My usual MO was more of a feelings-hider than a feelings-sharer. There were fewer pitying looks that way.

Raiden nodded, more to himself than to me. "Makes sense,"

he said, expression open and kind, not a hint of judgment or pity in sight. "A lot of firsts . . ."

I shook my head. "It's not that—not flying or heading out to experience the big, wild world that scares me." I frowned, looking down at my hands as my fingers fidgeted with the metal clasp on the seat belt. "I just—I finally feel like I'm waking up . . . like I'm able to really live, and I'm afraid it'll all disappear. I'm afraid I'll go back to the way I was, and I don't want to. I don't want to be that girl anymore . . . so isolated and lonely. So afraid of everything."

I ventured a sideways glance at Raiden, laughing under my breath. "So, I guess I'm afraid of being afraid."

Raiden met my hesitant stare, nothing but kindness and understanding in his warm, brown eyes. "Acknowledging fear is half the battle," he said, voice unusually soft. "You can only face your fears once you've admitted to yourself that they exist. Once you've accepted them."

I laughed, once again shaking my head, my gaze landing on the journal tucked into the pocket on the back of the seat in front of me. "Easier said than done."

Raiden grunted in agreement, his stare returning to the seat ahead, as well.

Maybe the affirmations were working, because I was suddenly struck by a bout of bravery. Or maybe it was just that my inhibitions were muted by the Valium. Either way, as I stared at the journal, I inhaled deeply, only holding my breath for a moment before saying, "I'm scared of what's in here, too." I reached out and skimmed my fingertips over the top of the journal.

"Oh?" Raiden said.

I pulled the journal free from the pocket and looked at him.

"What's in there?" he asked.

"The truth," I said, handing him the leather-bound book. "Have a look for yourself."

16

I'm sitting in a classroom of some sort, in the far back-right corner, my position giving me a good view of row after row of stainless-steel desks. There are exactly sixty-three desks, set up in nine columns.

Kids fill the desks. Or teenagers, maybe. They fall somewhere in the brief, awkward window between child and teen. A quick glance down at my underdeveloped body tells me I count among them.

The room is all sterile white and silver. No color. The wall on my left is lined with two rows of bookshelves atop a long string of cabinets that reaches from the back of the room to the front, maybe forty or fifty feet. The wall on the right is one long mirror, broken only near the center with a sliding door that remains shut unless opened by an instructor.

I've been here before. Many times, though I can't recall any specific memories. But I feel a general sense of familiarity. And I know things.

I know that instructors stand on the other side of the mirror-wall, watching us. Assessing us. I know that my position in the back-right corner of the room marks me as the best among my cohort—the strongest, smartest, healthiest, and most capable. I know that the desks are often cleared out to make room for other, more physical tasks besides reading, writing, and written assessments.

And I know that the test I'm about to take will determine my future. What I do. Where I do it. Who I do it alongside. This group, like the others before us, will split up after today, each of us separated into new groups based on the training we will need to successfully carry out our duties as workers.

I glance at the wall of mirrors. We've been in here for hours —five or six, maybe—sitting, waiting. My stomach has been rumbling for the past hour. Though the clock has been removed from the front wall, I know it's well past the time of our usual lunch break. I have to go to the bathroom, but I can hold it. I'm not willing to risk my future based on a little discomfort.

Unless—is this the test? To see who cracks first? Or who holds out longest?

I narrow my eyes, carefully considering the purpose of such a test. To measure obedience, perhaps? Or maybe even willpower?

I return to staring ahead and wonder what action might be viewed favorably during such a test, and what might be considered failure. There are only two options: do nothing, or do something.

I look to my left, scanning the faces of the six students seated in my row. None move save to blink or to breathe. So far as I can tell, the same goes for the rest of the kids in the room.

My lip curls. My gut tells me their blind obedience is a weakness. Whether it's fear or determination that paralyzes them, they all look the same to me—pathetic. If this is what passing looks like, I'd rather fail. I'm not interested in any work assignment that requires such blind obedience, anyway.

I place my hands flat on my desk, then push my chair back and stand. I can see some of the other kids watching me out of the corner of their eye. But still, none move.

I give the room one final scan, then march over to the door and reach for the thumbprint scanner in the wall to the right. I've never used it myself, and I hold my breath, half expecting nothing to happen. We were told to wait. To sit and wait and not talk. Not move.

The door slides open. The hallway beyond is dark compared to the bright light in the classroom, and it takes my eyes a few seconds to adjust.

Almost immediately, I know I've made a mistake. I've failed.

A woman stands before me, not one of the usual instructors. She's young, but her stern expression makes her seem ancient. And terrifying. She's wearing a black, form-fitting suit and carries a long, golden staff. A name forms in my mind: Demeter.

Demeter holds a position of power, a position that comes with an important title. Others stand along the wall of glass to either side of her, dressed in looser fitting clothing in varying shades of gray, but Demeter's domineering presence makes them all seem to disappear.

"Mother," I say, addressing Demeter by her official title as I bow my head. It's a relief to be staring down at the floor rather than into her steel-gray eyes. I hold that position, thoughts spinning. I made the wrong choice. I should have been patient like the others.

"I knew you were different," Demeter says. I can't tell if she means "different" in a good way, or in a bad way.

My brow furrows, and I'm glad my face is angled down toward the floor. I hate the idea of her seeing my confusion. My fear.

"Persephone," she says. "Come." She turns away from me and, in a few steps, her boots move out of my line of sight.

I stand there, frozen, thoughts spinning out of control. Instinct takes over, and a moment later I straighten and rush after her. I can feel the eyes of the other adults on me, but I'm too focused on catching up with Demeter to register any of their faces save for one—Hades. His presence makes me almost as nervous as Demeter's does.

He stands farther down the hallway, his shoulder leaned against the wall and his arms crossed over his chest. He exchanges a look with Demeter as she passes him. The look holds layers of meaning, every single one a mystery to me. When his focus shifts to me, the corner of his mouth rises almost imperceptibly. He nods his head as I pass. The gesture feels almost respectful.

I am more confused than ever.

I follow Demeter through the maze of hallways that make up Sector C. When she reaches the door leading out of the sector, I stop, hanging back several paces. I'm already standing closer to the exit than is allowed. I consider backing up, but my shoes feel glued to the floor.

Demeter presses her thumb to the scanner, and the door slides open. She passes through the short airlock to the second door and presses her thumb to a second scanner. That door opens, too.

I can't stop staring. I've never left Sector C, and I've only ever seen into the airlock. Everything beyond is a mystery to me. Sure, all the kids have theories about what lies beyond. "Outside" we call it. It's a place of limitless wonder and endless possibilities, at least in our imaginations.

I'm disappointed to see that, in reality, "outside" is just another hallway, no different from those within Sector C.

Demeter pauses in the new hallway, turning just enough that she can peer back at me over her shoulder. "Come along, Persephone. There's something I would like to show you."

Numbly, my right foot moves forward, then my left. I take another step, and another, my body taking over while my mind races, attempting to figure out what's happening.

Demeter leads me through a warren of new passageways and doorways marked with various numbers and letters, until finally, we reach the widest doorway I've ever seen. A word is painted on the dull metal in huge, blocky white letters. It's in some strange, foreign language made up of strange, foreign symbols, but my mind translates the word to "COMMAND."

The door glides open as Demeter approaches it.

My steps slow when I see what lies beyond.

The space is enormous—dwarfing the classroom where I've spent so much of my life. Even the cafeteria seems tiny in comparison. I gawk as I step through the doorway, eyes finding the ceiling high above, then dropping to a massive thing in the center of the room. It's made up of huge, golden rings, the largest taller than the ceilings I'm used to. There are seven rings in total, each fitting one within the others.

People dressed in white from neck to toe move around the thing, touching it here or there. More people stand near the walls, fingers pushing buttons and sliding across light-up screens atop the desks scattered about the periphery of the cavernous space.

Demeter crosses the room, and I follow, taking it all in as I trail behind her. I notice people pausing what they're doing to glance at her, then stopping completely when they notice me. They stare at us. At me.

A layer of cold sweat forms on my palms and on the back of my neck. I wipe my hands on my pants.

"Prepare the gephyra for a trip to Atlantis," Demeter orders as she passes the mass of golden rings.

Beyond it, there's a broad, circular basin in the floor, filled with what appear to be tiny metal beads. Beyond that, the floor drops off, and the ledge is blocked by a three-barred steel railing.

Demeter skirts the basin and continues on toward the railing, where she stops, waiting on me.

I follow, doing my best to ignore all of the unwanted attention. When I reach Demeter, I grip the top bar of the railing.

The floor drops off here, and there's a whole other floor below us, with dozens of desks, all covered in an amalgam of screens, lights, dials, and buttons. There are more people down there, dressed much like the ones up here, except their clothing is navy-blue rather than white. The far wall ahead appears to be some sort of a video screen. Bright, pale lines stream out from the center of the screen toward the edges. I've never seen anything like it. I've never seen anything like any *of it.*

I stare down at the people working at the desks on the floor below. They're all so busy, just like the people up here. Everyone seems so confident and moves with such purpose. All I can think is that I want to be like them. I want to work here, dressed in all white or all blue, and I hope, desperately, that Demeter has brought me here to show me a glimpse of my future.

"Watch," *Demeter says, redirecting my attention toward the video screen on the wall. The lines are slowly shortening.*

An alarm sounds, a series of three low, drawn-out tones that seems to come from everywhere and from nowhere at once, filling up the vast space.

My body tenses, and I tighten my grip on the railing, preparing for the lurch.

As expected, a few seconds later, the floor shudders, and I'm thrust forward into the railing.

It's nothing new. The alarm, followed by the lurch, happens twice a day: once just before breakfast, then again right after dinner. No wonder my stomach is gurgling with hunger pains; I've missed both lunch and dinner, now.

Ahead, the lines on the video screen disappear, giving way to a complex and endless array of single points of light.

"Tell me, Persephone," *Demeter says,* "Where are we?"

I look at her, frowning. I'm not sure I understand the question, let alone have an adequate answer. I recall the word on the last door we passed through and venture a guess, "Command?"

A slight smile touches Demeter's thin lips, like my answer amuses her. "*True enough,*" *she says.* "*But where is 'Command'? Where is Sector C? Where are all of the sectors?*" *She raises her arm, sweeping it out to the side to encompass the cavernous room and beyond.* "*Where is all of this?*"

I feel a little more comfortable now that I know what she's looking for. "*Tartarus,*" *I tell her.*

She nods. "*And what is 'Tartarus'?*"

"*I—*" *My eyebrows draw together, and I search her eyes. Now, I really don't understand the question.*

Tartarus is the world. It is existence. It's the things around us that can be touched and felt. It's everything.

I shake my head. "*I don't know.*"

Demeter sniffs and looks away, focusing on the screen. Clearly, my answer—or lack thereof—displeases her.

I, too, look at the screen, though I'm really watching Demeter out of the corner of my eye. "*I'm sorry,*" *I say softly. I can only hope that my ignorance doesn't ruin my chances of working here—outside.*

"*Why?*" *she says, letting out a lone, dry laugh.* "*Your ignorance is no fault of your own; it is ours.*" *She turns away from the railing and starts back across the room.* "*Come, Persephone,*" *she says, stopping beside the broad, circular basin.* "*Let me show you the truth.*"

I follow, my curiosity far outweighing my unease.

Demeter touches the tip of her index finger to the amber stone in the pendant hanging around her neck, tracing the outer edge of the stone. Much to my surprise, the color drains from the stone, and it starts to glow with a brilliant white light. Not a second later, channels light up running the length of her suit, from fingertips to collar and down to the soles of her boots, glowing the same, brilliant white.

Demeter waves her hands over the edge of the basin, and the tiny metal beads shift and swirl. Slowly, they rise up, forming a single, person-sized blob that hovers over the center of the basin.

"The Tartarus is a ship," Demeter says, "carrying our people across the universe."

As she speaks, beads drain away from the blob and scatter throughout the air surrounding the larger, shrinking shape. They form into clusters, some swirling spirals, others loose spheres, others amorphous clouds. As the blob gradually transforms, becoming more defined, the beads surrounding it begin to glow in muted variations of every color imaginable.

The now fist-sized blob elongates and takes on a smooth, almost conical shape with small, sharp protrusions along the surface spread out at regular intervals. The cone is broken up by sections that spin in opposite directions around a common axis. There are fourteen sections, and in the back of my mind, I realize it's no coincidence that there are also fourteen sectors. This blob —this ship—*is the Tartarus.*

Demeter extends her right hand, slowly swiping it to the side. With her motion, the ship begins to move.

"The Tartarus travels among the galaxies and stars," she says, "carrying us to our new home, a planet we call 'Atlantis.'" As she speaks, the ship draws closer to one of the little spiral clusters.

The spiral grows in size, sucking in beads from the remaining clusters, but the Tartarus remains the same. The spiral cluster gives way to a series of orbs rotating around a massive, glowing mass of yellow light. The orbs continue to grow, one by one moving off to the periphery before disappearing, their beads being absorbed by another orb, until only one remains. It's blue with patches of green and brown, and is marbled all over with white. It hovers over the center of the basin, dwarfing the Tartarus as the ship draws ever nearer.

"Atlantis," Demeter says, voice filled with reverie.

The Tartarus makes a full rotation around the planet, shrinking as it moves closer to the surface. The planet grows, metal beads melting away as it becomes too big for the basin.

Soon, there is only a slightly curved, lumpy surface arching over the basin. The Tartarus slowly descends, finally coming to rest on the surface of the planet.

An opening forms on one end of the ship, and a ramp extends down to the surface of Atlantis. I watch, entranced, as miniature people march down the ramp and walk out onto the uneven surface beyond.

I don't fully comprehend what I'm looking at, and yet, I can't look away. Puzzle pieces rearrange within my mind as my understanding of the world collapses and reforms into a new shape. Into a much grander shape. The Tartarus—a ship—is just one tiny part of it. Within Sector C, we dreamed of "outside"—but none of us had any idea that this is what's out there.

I want to see more. I want to see everything.

When I look at Demeter, I have no doubt that the hunger I feel shines in my eyes.

She grins. "Good." She flings her hand over the basin, and the metal beads lose all color and shape, dropping back into the hole. "Come," she says, turning and making her way around the basin.

I follow, but pause when I see that the thing made up of those huge, golden rings has changed. It's now a glowing sphere of flickering, golden light. It's twice the height of any person, and just as wide.

I gape.

"Come," Demeter repeats, heading straight for the sphere.

I gulp, taking stumbling steps to catch up with her. I can feel waves of heat and static radiating off the sphere, growing more intense the closer I get.

Demeter stops mere steps from it, and I come to stand at her side. So close, the energy radiating from the sphere is so intense it's almost overwhelming.

"Isn't it glorious?" Demeter says, gray eyes reflecting the golden light.

"What is it?" I ask. I can't help myself. I've always had a curious nature, but Demeter has awakened something within me by showing me just how little I understand of our existence. My desire to learn has morphed into a ferocious beast starved for knowledge. For understanding. For experience.

"A gephyra," Demeter says. She glances at me sidelong and holds up a hand, palm up and completely flat. "When active, like it is now, it opens a gateway connecting two distant points," she says, bringing the tips of her thumb and forefinger together, "bending the very fabric of reality."

I can't even begin to comprehend what she's telling me, but I nod and say, "Oh," anyway.

"Do you want to try it out?" She looks at me head-on, now.

I nod robotically. I'm terrified, but there's nothing I want more than to see what's on the other side of the gateway created by the gephyra. "Where—" I clear my throat. "Where does it lead to?"

Demeter's eyes sparkle with secrets. "Why, to Atlantis, of course."

My heart skips a beat, or three. I swallow roughly, though my mouth is suddenly so dry that swallowing does little good.

Demeter takes a step toward the gateway, and I follow, moving closer to the unknown. "Are you afraid?" she asks.

I nod. I was afraid to leave Sector C, but now I'll be leaving the Tartarus completely. I've never been more afraid in my entire life.

"Do you want to turn back?" she asks.

I look at Demeter, fear of something worse than the unknown widening my eyes and tightening my chest—fear of standing still. Fear of stagnation. Fear of never knowing more . . . of never seeing what's out there.

A tiny smile touches Demeter's lips, and she extends her hand toward the mass of heat and light just out of arm's reach. "After you."

17

I stared out the little, oval window, thinking about the dream. This was the second time I'd dreamed I was this other woman— Persephone, as she'd been called in the dream—and once again, the dream hadn't felt so much like a fantasy, but like a memory.

Like so much in my life these days, the premise seemed like something out of one of my video games, and I wondered if that was the source. I'd played so many games over the years that it wasn't impossible to think I'd forgotten about one.

The setting—a spaceship traveling across the universe—and the mythological context—a spin on the ancient Greek Persephone myth, with some Atlantis mystery thrown into the mix— all seemed like excellent video game source material. People would eat that premise up. *I* would eat that up. And maybe I had . . .

I leaned into the forgotten-game theory. It was a lot more pleasant than some of the other options dancing around in my mind, like that I was reliving a past—alien—life or that I was experiencing a full-on mental break. The past few days had been *a lot*, and not just by my sheltered standards. By *anyone's* standards.

My mom had gone missing. I'd been attacked in my own home and forced to run for my life. I'd killed people. Oh, and the coup de grace had to be finding the video from my mom in which she claimed I wasn't even human. It would've been a big couple of days even for someone as adventurous as my mom.

Maybe these dreams of being Persephone were my mind's way of dealing with all of the insanity. Persephone had an inner strength I couldn't even dream of having. Or maybe that I could *only* ever dream of having. Maybe that was the point.

A mental fracture. A new *alter*-ego. A better version of myself, capable of dealing with the things I couldn't handle.

At the sound of a soft snore coming from my left, I turned my face away from the window to glance at Raiden. He was asleep, finally. It was a good thing and brought the tiniest smile to my lips. I was pretty sure he hadn't slept more than a few hours total since leaving Orcas, and we would both need him to be well-rested and have his wits about him when we reached Rome. I didn't know a damn thing about international travel—or any kind of travel, for that matter—and I was especially clueless when it came to evading people. This was all him.

The journal was back in its place in the seat pocket in front of me, as was a small, orange prescription bottle along with a bottle of water. I considered reaching for the pill bottle, thinking another Valium might be just what I needed to relax enough to snooze through the rest of the flight, but I didn't feel anxious or stressed out. There was no hint of panic sneaking around the edges of my mind.

I felt *good*. Calm. Confused by the dream, but not really disturbed. More curious than anything. It was as though I could feel Persephone's strength of will reinforcing my own, like her resolve to step through the gateway created by the gephyra had settled into me, lending me a hearty dose of resolve, too.

Like her, I was still afraid. There was no guessing what I would find in Rome. But I was determined to face that fear head-on, to shove it aside and keep on walking. Keep on searching. My mom was out there somewhere, waiting for me to find her. She might not have been aware that she was waiting for me, but she was waiting for me. And I wouldn't let her down. Besides, she owed me some answers.

Leaning forward, I reached for the pre-pay not-so-smart phone Raiden had bought me the other day while out arranging my forged travel documents. It could make calls, text, and had a camera, and it was loaded up with a few classic games, like *Snake*. I flipped the phone open to check the time on the small display screen. There were still six hours left of the flight.

Snapping the phone shut, I tucked it back into the seatback pocket and pulled out my mom's journal. Raiden had rewrapped the leather cord tightly around the cover, and as I unwound it, I couldn't help but wonder what he'd thought of the things written within . . . of the things written about me.

I pulled off my leather gloves and tucked them into the seatback pocket, then opened the journal's worn leather cover and flipped through the thick pages, searching for the place where I'd left off.

I look forward to the day when I can watch you step into your own. When I can see you blossom into the beautiful being trapped within your frightened mind. When you can shed your fear and finally, truly live.

I turned the page. The next page was titled *Kelsey Schmidt – Child Psychologist*, followed by a date that landed roughly one week after my third—and last—day of kindergarten. On the page, my mom had summarized what happened during the session and recorded Dr. Schmidt's assessment—inconclusive— as well as made some additional notes of her own.

The fronts and backs of the next dozen or so pages were filled with more of the same, from consultations with far more specialists than I had actually visited. A bold line had been drawn under the final summary, under which my mom had written:

Em is right – it's time to change directions. We've been looking for help in all the wrong places. Humanity can't help Cora, but maybe her own people can. The Atlanteans must have left behind more than what the Order has locked away. I just have to find it . . .

A pencil sketch filled up the next page. It was a symbol—a thick, dark band nearly encircling a lighter but equally thick upside-down triangle, with only a minimal gap midway up the right side of the circle. In the center of the triangle, a floating eye stared out from the page, above which three ornate crowns had been drawn, one stacked atop the other, cutting through the top line of the triangle. It reminded me of the Eye of Providence-based Illuminati symbol, cherished by so many conspiracy theorists. It was like that symbol, but different. More.

As I stared at the symbol, the meaning behind the triple crown surfaced from the depths of my memory: the pope. The triple crown was a standard element of the pope's insignia, usually sitting atop a pair of crossed keys, one silver, one gold, wrapped together by a crimson cord. It was such an important symbol that it was on Vatican City's flag.

The shapes took on new meaning, and I realized that this wasn't just a symbol; it was a monogram. The circle and triangle were really the letters C and V—for *Custodes Veritatis*.

Intrigued, I turned the page. On the back, my mom had written out a bulleted history of the Custodes Veritatis. I skimmed over the list. The timeline traced the Order's origins back to ancient Egypt, nearly two thousand years before the life of Jesus and well over two millennia before the foundation of the Catholic Church. According to my mom's notes, the Order hadn't been founded by the Catholic Church, but adopted into it sometime during the eleventh century, shortly before the First Crusade. Now, *that* was interesting.

I shifted my attention to the next page, where my mom had written a list of GPS coordinates. Two neat columns of coordinates filled the page. Some were written in pencil, some in ink, both blue and black, as though the list had been added to over time.

I turned the page. The list continued onto the back.

The next page was titled ATLANTEAN ALPHABET and it was filled with two columns of symbols. There were thirty, total, and they reminded me of the ancient Greek alphabet, but with some more ancient, Eastern characteristics. There was a strange sense of familiarity about them, but their meaning remained a mystery to me. As it was to my mom, apparently; the page was littered with question marks.

I turned the page to a two-page spread. The paper was covered in a tangle of lines, some thinner, some thicker, some zigzagging, some straight, often crisscrossing over one another. There was no discernable pattern, at least, not one that I could make out. It reminded me a bit of the maps in some of my video games—the kind that were revealed bit by bit as the avatar made their way through the virtual world. But if it was some kind of map, there were no labels, leaving me with no frame of reference. It might as well not have been there at all.

After that, there were a few pages of sketches of various objects, including a glassy sphere I recognized all too well—it was currently wrapped in a sweatshirt and stuffed into the bottom of my backpack—as well as the pendant tucked away under my T-shirt. There was also a disk that reminded me of a sand dollar, labeled *EMBRYONIC STASIS POD,* and a rod of some kind, sketched from several different angles to capture the intricate designs carved along its length.

I turned the page, and froze. An androgynous human figure had been drawn on both pages, the front view on the left and the back on the right. It was headless, and lines ran down the length of the figure, along the arms, neck, and legs in a pattern I couldn't possibly recognize.

And yet, I did recognize it. In my dreams, Demeter had been wearing a tight-fitting suit marked with the same exact pattern running the length of it, the lines glowing with a brilliant, white light.

I stared at the drawing, lips parted and eyes searching as my thoughts spun. I flipped back a page, taking a second look at the sketches of the rod. I recognized it, too—and though Demeter's had been longer, the length of a staff rather than a ruler, the resemblance was too similar to dismiss.

How was this possible? How had I dreamed of objects drawn in my mom's journal *before* ever seeing the drawings? It went beyond the realm of coincidence, diving deep into the abyss of things I had been trying not to consider. Hell, I didn't know *how* to consider what something like this might mean.

"Cocktail?" a female flight attendant asked from the aisle.

I jumped, instinctively clutching the journal to my chest. My heart hammered against my sternum, and I stared at the woman with wide, unblinking eyes. "What?"

She flashed me an apologetic smile, clearly used to catching people off guard. "Would you like a cocktail?"

"Uh . . ."

"We also have wine, beer, soda, water, juice, coffee, tea, and hot cocoa."

The options were too much for my overloaded brain, and for several seconds, I simply stared at the flight attendant. She had the patience of a saint.

Raiden snorted awake beside me, causing another little jump. Blinking, he looked first at me, then at the flight attendant.

She shifted her attention to him. "Something to drink, sir?"

"Coffee," he said, voice gruff. "Two cups, please."

"Vodka," I said, finally finding my voice. I settled the journal on my lap. "And orange juice, please."

I copied Raiden, unlatching the tray table from the seatback in front of me while the flight attendant poured his coffees. She handed him two steaming cups of Joe, along with a small pouch of accoutrements like cream and sugar, then plucked a miniature bottle of vodka from a drawer in her cart, glanced at me, stare-assessing, then pulled out a second bottle. Apparently, I looked like I needed it. She poured juice from a carton into a plastic cup already loaded with ice, then handed it all to me.

"Dinner service will begin shortly," the flight attendant informed us. "The menu is on the card in the seatback pocket in front of you." She flashed me a tight smile. Apparently, her saintly patience wasn't endless. Next time, she wanted us to be ready.

I returned her smile and nodded. "We'll be sure to take a look," I promised, already unscrewing the cap on one of the little plastic bottles.

Her gaze slid past me, and she wheeled her beverage cart farther down the aisle. "Cocktail?"

I poured as much vodka into the cup of orange juice as it would hold, then brought the bottle up to my lips and tossed back that half-inch that remained. I coughed as the splash of liquor burned down my throat.

Raiden watched me as he sipped from his first cup of coffee black, the plastic-wrapped pack of accoutrements untouched on his tray table.

I took a gulp of the screwdriver, swallowed, then took another.

"You doing all right?" Raiden asked.

I froze, cup to my lips. "Yep," I said before taking another sip. I set the drink down on the tray table, tapping the sweating plastic with the nails of my index fingers.

He was still staring at me.

I cleared my throat. "How'd you sleep?" I asked, glancing at him sidelong.

"Fine," he said, though he didn't sound happy about it. He took a swig of steaming coffee, not the least bit deterred by the heat, then another.

I was getting the impression that he didn't intend to fall asleep again—that he hadn't intended to fall asleep at all and was more than a little miffed about it. I wondered if it was hesitancy at letting his guard down on the plane that was making him reticent to sleep or if it was something else, but I didn't want to intrude. I kept my wondering to myself.

Raiden chugged the remainder of his first cup of coffee and stacked the second in the empty cup, then raised his tray table, locking it back in place. He stuffed his little pouch of coffee things into the seatback pocket and unbuckled his seatbelt.

"Mind if I set this here for a sec?" he asked, placing his double-stacked cup of coffee on my tray near the edge.

I shook my head. "Go ahead."

"Thanks," he said, then stood. "I'll be right back."

I watched him walk up the aisle and slip into the bathroom. Once he was out of sight, I uncapped the second mini bottle and poured the vodka into my drink. I stirred the precariously full drink with my finger, then carefully lifted it to my mouth to sip. I had to choke down the barely diluted vodka.

With another throat clearing, I set the drink down and shifted the journal from my lap to the tray table, in front of the cups. I quickly turned the page, not wanting to stare at the sketch of the suit Demeter had been wearing in my dream. The implications were too unsettling. Out of sight, out of mind. At least, for a little while.

The heading on the next page read: *PERCY FAWCETT.* I tried to study the bulleted notes filling the page, but my attention kept wandering to Raiden's empty seat. He would be back soon. And now that we were both awake, there would be talking. About the journal. About aliens. About *me.* How could there not be?

I'd given him the journal, but I'd fallen asleep shortly after. I had no clue how far he'd made it into the thing, let alone how he'd reacted.

Though my eyes skimmed over the letters on the page, the words written there didn't mean a damn thing to my preoccupied mind. My thoughts raced, swerving and veering off course, constantly circling back to the same questions: *What did he think of what he read? Was it new information to him? Or had he known about me all along?* I wanted to think that at least one person in my life wasn't a liar.

I reread the heading on the page: *PERCY FAWCETT.*

"You finding anything useful in there?" Raiden asked as he eased back into his seat. He buckled his seatbelt. "I didn't make it past the journal entries at the beginning. Not that it wasn't interesting," he said, raising his eyebrows for emphasis. "But it just didn't feel right . . . reading through it without you."

I looked at him, eyes unblinking.

He studied my face, his shrewd gaze scrutinizing. "Do you believe it?" His eyes flicked down to the book lying open on the tray table, then returned to my face. "What she wrote in there . . . about you?"

I gulped, staring at the seatback in front of me. I could already feel the tears welling in my eyes. I nodded. "Did you know?" I asked, not looking at him. I couldn't. I was terrified of seeing the truth written across his face.

"Did I *know*?" Raiden said, clearly taken aback. "Are you serious, Cora?" He lowered his voice to an outraged whisper and leaned in closer to me. "Are you seriously asking me if I knew you were an alien and what—lied to you your whole life? You really think I could have done that to you?"

His affront caught me off guard, and I looked at him. The hurt in his eyes was genuine. Hurt I'd put there by doubting him.

"You know me, Cora," Raiden said. He was so close that I could smell the coffee scenting his breath. "Have I ever lied to you?" His eyes searched mine. "Ever?"

"I—" I shook my head, flustered by both his reaction and his close proximity. "I don't—how would I know?" A hysteria-tinged laugh bubbled up from my throat. "How would I know, Raiden? How? My mom and Emi—"

"Lied to me, too," he said. He sat back in his seat. "Did you think about that?"

I opened my mouth, but found I didn't know what to say, so I pressed my lips together, once more.

Raiden inhaled and exhaled deeply. "If I'd known, Cora— about you, about the danger you were in—I never would have left." His stare was hard, reinforced by the conviction lacing through his voice. "Never."

My eyes stung, the tears returning with a vengeance. I swallowed roughly, nostrils flaring with each breath as I tried, desperately, not to cry.

"I wish I hadn't, you know," Raiden said quietly, staring ahead. "I wish I'd listened to you—to what you didn't say." He took a deep breath. "I wish I'd stayed."

But he hadn't. Raiden had come home with a Purple Heart and a pronounced limp, but other than that, I didn't know much about what had ended his military service. I hadn't wanted to intrude, let alone pry—after how we'd left things all those years ago, I wasn't sure he even wanted to talk to me about *anything*. But now I could see that keeping my distance as I'd been doing was more about hiding from my shame than about being considerate of Raiden. I suddenly felt like the most self-centered asshole in the world.

I took a shaky breath, looking at him, but averting my gaze before I spoke. "I'm sorry, Raiden," I said softly. "About how I've been since you got home, I mean. I didn't know how to—" The words caught in my throat, and I shrugged one shoulder. "I was so mad at you for so long, and I was so scared that you would never come back, and then you were back, and I didn't know what to say to you . . . so I just didn't say anything at all, and—"

Raiden nudged my shoulder with his, and the unexpected contact froze my tongue. "Don't worry about it," he said, just the faintest edge of hurt in his voice. "I understand. I really do. You and me—we're good."

I glanced at him, not quite believing him. "Cross your heart?"

The corner of his mouth lifted in a half-smile. "Hope to die," he said, completing the exchange just as he'd done thousands of times when we were kids. It had never sounded sinister then.

It did now.

18

I finished reading the final lines of writing within the journal and slowly raised my head, setting the book down on top of my closed laptop on the tray table. I looked at Raiden, excitement making my breaths come faster.

Raiden peered at me without changing his arms-crossed, tough-guy pose. He didn't even move his head. "What is it?"

"I think I know where my mom went," I told him. "In Rome, I mean." I placed my hand palm-down on the open journal, covering the floorplan my mom had drawn of the Order's headquarters, located underground beneath the Apostolic Palace in Vatican City. It was all right here, a million tiny clues pointing me in a single direction.

Raiden looked at me, one eyebrow raised.

"There's a vault under the Vatican," I explained. "It's where the Custodes—" I paused, shooting a quick, paranoid glance over the back of my seat. "Where *they* stored this"—I fished the pendant out from the neck of my T-shirt by the chain—"along with the crystal orb and a few other artifacts." I figured those were still in the vault, probably too large for my mom to grab and run, as she must have done with the pendant and orb.

I curled my fingers around the pendant, enclosing it in my fist. "Whatever my mom found in South America must have made her think I needed these. She must've already known these were in the vault from her time with the Order, so she went back there to get them." I tapped my mom's final page of notes with the tip of my index finger. "If we're going to find her, I think we need to start in that vault."

Raiden narrowed his eyes, the corners of his mouth angling downward. "But she sent you the pendant and the orb, so obviously she made it out of the vault. We won't find her there."

I was nodding before he even finished what he was saying. "I know, but we might find *something*—a clue or a sign or . . ." I shook my head, holding my hands out and raising my shoulders in the international sign for *"I don't know."* I took a deep breath, then started over. "If that's where her path ends—at least, her traceable path—then I think it's where we should start."

Raiden's eyebrows climbed higher. "But that's *not* where her path ends. She went to that convenience store . . . sent you the package . . ."

I chewed on the inside of my cheek, tilting my head from side to side as I considered his point. "Then we retrace her last known steps."

Raiden inhaled deeply, like he was about to respond. Probably to argue.

I held up a hand to stop him before he could start. "Just hear me out, OK?"

Raiden blinked, and I took it for his eyes' equivalent of a nod.

"We know she made it to the store," I started. "We have the receipt, but what we don't have is any idea of where she went after that. Maybe she made it to the post office, maybe the shop owner shipped the package for her. We just don't know."

"Right," Raiden said. "But we can go there. We can ask . . ."

I acknowledged his point as valid with a sideways nod. "But

if her trail ends there, we have nowhere to go but backward," I said. "By retracing her steps, we might be able to figure out where she was headed next. Who knows—after the hidden message on the receipt and the secret passage in the house, it seems highly likely that she purposely left some other clues—clues meant just for me—along the way."

Raiden's eyes remained locked with mine for a few more seconds, then he returned to staring ahead. "Vatican City is the last place you should be going right now."

"Or," I said, "is it the *best* place for me right now? It's certainly the last place the Order will expect me to go, which means they won't be looking for me there."

Raiden blinked, but made no other response.

"Hiding in plain sight—there's a reason it's a thing," I said. "Because it works." I raised my eyebrows. "Right?"

Raiden's jaw tensed.

"I think it's worth a shot," I said. "*If* the convenience store turns out to be a dead-end . . ." If he wanted to start there, we could start there. No skin off my back.

Raiden inhaled and exhaled through his nose, then nodded once.

I blew out a breath, relieved. "All right, so . . . from what I've gathered in the journal and online"—I tapped my laptop with the tip of my index finger—" the vault is only accessible through the Apostolic Palace—the library, specifically. It looks like, for the right price, you can take a super exclusive group tour of the Vatican Palace, including a quick stop in the library. Once we're in the library, we'll lose the group—"

"Lose the group *how*, exactly?" Raiden asked.

I shrugged. "I don't know. I'll say I have to pee, or something." I waved a hand dismissively. Sneaking away was never an issue in any of my games. There was always a way. How hard could it really be? "Then we'll break into the vault—"

"Which will be locked up tight," Raiden said.

My lips spread into a broad grin. "My mom wrote the combination to the lock in her journal," I revealed. Before Raiden could voice the glaringly obvious flaw, I continued, "And the combo must still be the same, because she got in . . ."

Raiden's expression remained stony.

"So, we'll pop into the vault, look around, and get out." I dry-washed my hands. "Easy peasy."

"Right," Raiden said dryly. I chose to ignore the skepticism in his voice.

"It's a good plan," I said, the words coming out sounding more like a question than a statement.

Raiden gave me a look that wilted my optimism.

"It's not a good plan?"

"No, Cora," Raiden said, laughing derisively under his breath as he shook his head. "It's not a good plan."

I deflated, right there in my seat.

"But," he said, "it's a start."

19

I stood beside Raiden, watching the sloped belt spit suitcase after suitcase out onto the baggage carousel, thinking the whole contraption was a strange, antiquated looking thing. It was also, hands down, my favorite thing about airline travel so far.

"Hey!" I exclaimed, spotting a black duffel bag making its way down the belt. I pointed to the bag. "Is that your—"

"No," Raiden said. For the third time.

I dropped my arm and sighed.

Raiden had been a grump ever since we agreed on breaking into the Order's vault. *I* was excited. I was out of the country for the first time ever—in Rome, no less—and we had a multi-pronged plan to find my mom.

A bevy of rolling suitcases made their way down the belt, and finally I spotted my navy duffel bag—the teal piping was a dead giveaway. "Oh! There's mine," I said, stepping toward the carousel.

Raiden grabbed my arm, just above the elbow, stopping me mid-step. Even through my coat, his grip was tight, verging on painful.

"Ow . . ." I turned partway, attempting—and failing—to twist my arm out of his grasp. I speared him with a glare. "What are you—"

"We're being followed," Raiden said. "Time to go." He spun on his heel and started walking away from the baggage carousel, dragging me right along with him. His strides were long, eating up the airport's smooth tile floor, and even with my not-short legs, I practically had to jog to keep up with him.

"But my bag—"

"Leave it," he said, tone low and words clipped.

"But—"

The protests died on my tongue, and my heart leapt into my throat. I craned my neck as we hurried away, scanning the crowd scattered throughout the baggage claim area for whoever had tripped Raiden's internal defenses.

Sure enough, a pair of young men were trailing us by twenty or thirty yards. Though they wore jeans, T-shirts, and sneakers, their build and the way they moved gave them the look of trained soldiers.

I gulped and faced forward, the excitement of moments earlier replaced by mounting panic.

Ten seconds later, I spotted another pair of disguised goons making a beeline for us ahead. Once I knew what I was looking for, it was easy to pick them out of the crowd. "Raiden . . ."

"I see them," he said, veering to the left, toward the pair of sliding glass doors leading out of the airport. The sidewalk beyond was lined with a string of parked cars, gleaming in the mid-morning light.

Raiden sped up, and I was definitely jogging now. We swerved around slow-moving travelers toting their wheely bags toward the exit.

A driver dressed in a black suit flagged us down as soon as we were through the doors. "Signore, you look like you are in a hurry," he said, his Italian accent strong but his English intelligible enough. "Where can I take you?" He already had the back door to a black sedan open.

Raiden ushered me into the car, then slid in beside me. "Roma Termini, per favore," he said as the driver settled into the front seat.

"Si, prego," the driver said, turning the key in the ignition. He edged the car away from the curb.

I stared out the side window, watching for our pursuers. As the four men jogged out through the airport's sliding doors and onto the sidewalk, I locked the car door and gripped the door handle tightly.

"Sbrigati, per favore!" I told the driver, asking him to hurry. Even I could tell my accent was awful, but I didn't care. I quickly added that we were late for our train.

"Si, capisco," the driver said just a moment before stepping on the gas.

The car jerked forward, pressing me back into my seat, and we were suddenly speeding away from the airport.

The motion of the car had lulled my brain into a post-adrenaline daze as I stared out the window, watching the Roman countryside pass by. After about fifteen minutes, the agricultural fields gave way to hillsides stacked with apartment buildings. Another ten minutes, and we were leaving the highway behind for the narrower, backed-up streets of Rome.

"You leave Roma so soon?"' the driver asked, pulling me out of the motion-induced daze. "Where do you go to next?"

I glanced at Raiden.

"It's a surprise," he said.

"Ah . . . you are American?" the driver asked.

"Yeah," Raiden said. "Was my accent that bad?" he asked wryly.

I stared at him, chest heaving with each quick breath. Here he was, chit-chatting with our driver after we'd barely escaped from the airport with our lives. I, on the other hand, was practically hyperventilating.

"No," the driver said. "It was very good . . . very subtle. You have spent time in Italia?"

"Some," Raiden said. "Not enough." Surprising the hell out of me, he slung his arm over my shoulder and pulled me close.

I squeaked, my entire body going stiff. My muscles hummed with tension, and hyperventilation was suddenly no longer an issue. Now, it was an effort to take even the shallowest of breaths. There was no skin-to-skin contact, but there was still so much touching. *Too* much touching.

"Just had to bring the wife here to show her some of my favorite spots," Raiden said.

I felt hot and cold all over, totally overwhelmed by the contact.

"Ah," the driver said, smiling broadly and glancing back at us over his shoulder. "You are on honeymoon?"

"Something like that," Raiden said. "Every day feels like a honeymoon with her." He brought his lips close to my ear, making my heart skip a beat. Or three.

If breathing had been a struggle before, now it was impossible.

"Buckle up, Cora," Raiden whispered, so quiet I almost didn't hear him. "This guy is no driver." He tapped the base of the middle finger of his left hand with a fingertip as he pulled away from me.

I glanced at the driver's left hand. Sure enough, he wore a ring, the golden face displaying a shocking insignia: an eye and triple crown tucked within a monogrammed C and V.

Raiden was right. This guy was no driver. He was with the Custodes Veritatis.

I thought back to the two pairs of goons in the airport. With the way they'd come at us from opposite directions, it was almost like they'd been herding us toward the exit. Toward this car.

My eyes opened wide. It was a trap. A hastily set trap, what with the driver not thinking to remove his ring, but a trap we'd unwittingly sprung, nonetheless.

I looked at Raiden, certain the sudden burst of fear was written across my face.

Raiden smiled, expression easy. Eyes sharp. He slid his arm off my shoulders and settled in on his side of the car. He reached over his shoulder and pulled the seatbelt across his body. "I forgot how exciting driving through Rome can be," he said to the driver as the latch of his seatbelt clicked into place. How he could continue to talk to the guy with such laid-back ease was beyond me.

I followed suit, buckling my own seatbelt as I forced air in and out of my lungs, eyes locked on Raiden's face. Something was happening . . . or about to happen. I just didn't know what.

My chest constricted, and my heart seemed to be stuck in a vice. I curled my fingers around the door handle, squeezing tight. The leather of my gloves creaked against the textured plastic.

Slowly, silently, Raiden unbuckled his belt and pulled it out from his beltloops. With that same, painstaking slowness, he coiled either end of the sturdy canvas belt around his hands, careful to keep the metal d-rings from clinking against one another.

He looked at me, his gaze overflowing with a thousand unsaid things. Time seemed to slow as we stared at one another.

A heartbeat later, Raiden reached over the headrest of the driver's seat, pulling the belt tight across the driver's neck. He yanked back, hard, the effort making the veins and tendons in his neck stand out.

The car swerved as the driver clawed at the belt cutting off his air supply.

"Get his seatbelt," Raiden ground out. "Release it!"

Shock paralyzed my overactive thoughts, and I reacted instantly. I leaned forward, reaching over the center console, and pressed the button on the latch of the driver's seatbelt. As the seatbelt popped free, the car swerved violently to the left, and I was thrown against the door.

I gripped the top of the seat in front of me and looked up just in time to see a stone wall hurtling toward us.

20

My ears were ringing, my brain felt numb, and I was surrounded by darkness. The blood rushing through my veins roared like ocean waves in my ears. My neck ached—along with a dozen other parts of my body—but it dulled in comparison to the searing pain in my left forearm.

A buzzing sound was growing louder, pulling me out of my head and further into the discomfort of consciousness.

I cracked my eyes open. It was bright, and my mind was a jumble, but after a moment, I figured out where I was—the back-seat of a car.

Thoughts floated up from the murky depths of my mind.

The men chasing us at the airport.

The car.

The driver's ring.

Raiden . . .

I looked to my left. Raiden sat beside me, exactly where he'd been before the crash. He was slumped forward, his seatbelt the only thing holding him up. One end of the belt was still wrapped around his hand, propped up on the top of the driver's seatback, but his other arm hung limply, his knuckles skimming the car floor.

For a moment, I didn't think he was breathing.

My lungs froze, and my heart turned leaden, sinking into the pit of my stomach.

But then I noticed the slightest rise and fall of his shoulders with each shallow, steady breath. Relief melted away the paralyzing fear. Until I recalled how and why we ended up in the back of a crashed car in the first place.

Breath held, I shifted my focus to the driver. To our would-be kidnapper. He'd been jarred out of his seat by the crash and lay strewn over the center console, his head tucked under the glove box on the passenger side. His neck was bent at an unnatural angle.

I stared at his back for long seconds. It felt like years.

Thankfully, there was no movement. No sign of life.

After another long moment of staring and waiting and breath-holding, I finally exhaled, accepting that he wasn't going to jump up and attack me. I turned back to Raiden, reaching for him.

I froze when I caught sight of my arm. It was covered in blood.

I blinked, not really understanding what I was seeing. A deep gash ran along the back of my forearm from wrist to elbow. The arm portion of my leather glove hung below my wrist, stained red with blood. Remotely, my brain connected what I was seeing with the searing pain I'd been feeling since waking up.

Like a switch had been flipped by seeing the blood, the pain suddenly intensified, and my stomach lurched with a powerful wave of nausea. I squeezed my eyes shut and swallowed repeatedly, fighting off the urge to throw up.

Beside me, Raiden coughed.

My eyes snapped open and locked on him, throbbing, bloody arm momentarily forgotten.

Raiden groaned, and his shoulders shifted slightly. "Cora?" he said, his voice faint and raspy.

"I'm here." Using my good hand, I fumbled with latch of my seatbelt, and when I finally had it unbuckled, I scooted closer to Raiden.

He raised his head, slowly straightening in his seat, and blinked as he looked around.

I pressed the button on his seatbelt buckle, freeing him, and helped him sit up straighter. "Are you all right?" I asked.

Raiden coughed again, then winced, fingers pressing into the right side of his rib cage. "A few bruised ribs," he said. "Nothing broken." He cringed, his entire body tensing up, and he didn't move again for a few seconds. "I take that back," he said, voice tight with pain.

After a few forced and obviously uncomfortable deep breaths, he shifted his attention to me. He quickly scanned me from head to toe, stare locking on my bloody arm. "Shit, Cora . . ."

I pulled my arm in, gingerly holding it against my middle. "I'm fine," I told him. "It's just a cut."

"Like hell it is," he said gruffly. "Hold out your arm."

I stared at him, eyes opened wide. "Why?" I had the sinking feeling that he was going to do something that would hurt. A lot.

Raiden uncoiled the belt from around his hand. "We need to slow the bleeding until I can get you sewn up."

I gulped, not liking the sound of being *sewn up* one bit. But I still did as he asked and, tentatively, extended my hand toward him.

Raiden grasped my wrist, his hold gentle, and pinched the fingers of my ruined glove, gingerly pulling it off. Once my hand was free, he dropped the glove on the floor of the car. I held my breath as he wrapped the belt around my arm, just above my elbow.

I wondered if he noticed the skin-to-skin contact, like I did. I wondered if he was even aware of the fact that his skin was touching mine and the contact wasn't triggering an episode.

Once the belt was tight, Raiden coiled the tail around my arm, tucking in the end to keep it from dangling. He pulled his backpack out from between his boots and set it on the narrow seat between us. Unzipping the main pocket, he pulled out a T-shirt.

"It's clean," he promised just a moment before he tied it around my forearm, covering the wound as best he could.

Pain washed over me in waves as he knotted the T-shirt tightly around my arm. I gritted my teeth, eyes watering. Bright spots dance around the edges of my vision, and I was suddenly light-headed and cold all over. I shivered, teeth chattering.

"Breathe, Cora," Raiden said, voice calm. Distant. "Look at me."

I locked eyes with him.

"Deep breaths," he said. "In . . . and out. In . . . and out."

I forced my lungs to work in rhythm with his words. Slowly, steadiness returned, and the throbbing pain in my arm intensified. I focused on that pain, letting it sharpen my wits and hone my senses.

"Better?" Raiden asked.

Exhaling shakily, I nodded. I didn't feel good—not by a long shot—but I *did* feel better.

"Good," Raiden said. "We'll have to clean that properly and stitch you up, but first we need to get away from this crowd."

"Crowd?" I asked.

Raiden glanced past me to the window. I turned my head and looked outside, squinting as I finally registered the source of the buzzing sound.

People. Lots of them, backlit by the sun. They surrounded the car, pointing and gawking. Some even had their phones out and were holding them up like they were taking pictures, or maybe even filming the scene.

Beyond them, I could see that the wall we'd crashed into belonged to the base of a massive monument. I recognized it from my studies—the Altare della Patria. I remembered it, because I'd found it amusing that the locals had nicknamed it "the wedding cake" due to its glaring white marble and multi-tiered design. We'd hit the wall on the left side of the terraced staircase leading up to the monument head-on, just missing one of the fountains.

"Hear that?" Raiden said, and I looked at him. He held his head cocked to the side like he was listening to something.

In the distance, I could just make out the faint cry of a siren.

"That's our cue to leave. We've been here too long already, anyway." Raiden zipped up his bag and set it on his lap, then grabbed mine from its place on the floor of the car, by my feet. "Ready?" he asked, meeting my eyes.

No, I thought, even as I nodded.

Raiden shoved his door open, and using my good hand, I pulled the lever to open mine.

It didn't work.

I checked the lock, then yanked on the lever frantically, but the door wouldn't budge. It was stuck. Growling in frustration, I scooted across the bench seat toward Raiden's open door, wounded arm held close against my middle.

Raiden grabbed my good hand as soon as I was out and led me into the crowd. One backpack slung across his shoulders, the other carried under his arm like an oversized football, he pushed through the swarm of people, dragging me behind him and dodging questions of concern and curiosity from the onlookers.

Once we were free, he picked up the pace. He seemed to be favoring his left leg even more than usual. It was the same leg that had earned him an honorable discharge, and I feared he'd reinjured it.

We jogged across the busy street curving around the corner of the monument, stopping traffic and earning a barrage of shouts and honked horns. Reflexively, I started to raise my bloody hand, intending to wave apologies, but tucked it back against my middle at the sharp sting caused by the movement.

Once we were across the street, we hurried around the next block, only slowing to a walk when we reached a small parking area wedged between some ancient ruins and a church. Raiden made a beeline for the cluster of motorcycles and scooters parked together at one end. Our walk slowed further as we closed in on the bikes.

Raiden released my hand, holding out my backpack for me to take. "Put this on," he said.

I accepted the bag, gingerly easing my bound arm under the strap, then flung my good arm through the other once the first strap was settled on my shoulder.

Raiden stopped beside a flat-black motorcycle with the word "aprilia" spelled out in big, blocky letters in a deep crimson that perfectly matched the wheel rims. I was no expert in motorcycles —or vehicles of any kind—but even I could tell that this bike was far from new. I just hoped its age didn't affect its performance.

Raiden shrugged out of his backpack and set it on the motorcycle's seat. He opened the front pocket and dug out what, at first, I thought was a black, zippered day planner. That assumption died the moment he opened the case, revealing what looked like an array of dental tools tucked into individually sewn slots.

Not dental tools, I realized—lockpicks.

The case contained a couple "pages" of tools. Amazed, I watched Raiden flip the center flap and open up a Velcro pocket. He was full of surprises. He pulled out a short, coiled-up length of speaker wire, then closed the case and tucked it back into his pack.

"Anyone watching?" he asked, holding the wiring low and looking up to scan the area.

"I don't know," I said, copying him. I hadn't realized I was supposed to be paying attention to our surroundings.

There were only a few people walking along the sidewalk across the narrow street, and none seemed to be paying us any attention.

"Keep an eye out," Raiden said, crouching down by the front wheel of the motorcycle. "This should only take a second."

He was going to hotwire the bike, I realized. I choked on the dozens of questions that sprang to mind instantly—all of the whats and hows and whys—and turned away from him, frantically searching the area around us for prying eyes.

Once again, I felt like I'd been sucked into a video game. I couldn't believe this was real life. But it was, and knowing that there were no do-overs—no checkpoints or respawns were we to make a wrong move and end up dead—made it all the more thrilling. And all the more terrifying.

My heart hammered in my chest, adrenaline making me hyper-alert and ultra-focused. As I listened to the ever-louder sirens, I stared down every car that drove past. When there were no cars, I scanned the windows set into the building at the far end of the lot. The second and third floors looked like apartments to me, and I hoped that everyone was away at work. It was the middle of the morning, after all, and a Tuesday, no less.

Raiden couldn't have been working on the bike for more than a minute when the engine rumbled to life. His timing was perfect; the sound of the sirens had stopped growing louder. It wouldn't take long for some helpful onlookers to point the emergency responders in our direction. We needed to get gone, and fast.

I spun back around, watching Raiden slip his backpack on backwards so it rested against his chest.

He slung his leg over the bike's seat, then glanced at me over his shoulder. "Hop on."

Within seconds, we were flying down the street, putting

154 / LINDSEY FAIRLEIGH

some much-needed distance between ourselves and the scene of the crash. Raiden rode the motorcycle like a madman, swerving around cars and speeding through intersections. At first, I feared his crazy driving would draw attention to us. But then another bike passed us, slipping between two lanes packed with speeding cars—no helmet on the rider—and I realized Raiden's driving was mild for Rome.

We rode through the city for maybe ten minutes, finally slowing shortly after crossing the Tiber River. Raiden pulled the motorcycle into the space between two cars parked at an angle in front of a tall, pale brick building. A grocery store occupied the space on the ground floor, the entrance to the store directly in front of us.

I climbed off the bike, then stood near the back wheel while I waited for Raiden.

He flipped his backpack onto his back and reached down near the front wheel of the bike. With a quick, jerky motion, he pulled the added wire free and tucked it into his jeans pocket.

"Let's go," he said, brushing past me and heading across the street toward a six-story building constructed of brown and white stone, the exterior of the upper floors coated in a slightly orange stucco. His limp was more pronounced now, and he hugged his middle with one arm, his hand pressed against his injured ribs.

I followed him through an open, arched doorway at the center of the building and into an open-air lobby.

"Wait here," Raiden said, guiding me to a bench hidden in a small alcove just within the lobby.

I stepped into the alcove, but didn't sit. "Where are you going?" I asked, turning to face him.

"To get us a room," he said.

I opened my mouth to protest. The last thing I wanted was to be left behind, even for only a minute or two. I'd seen enough movies to know that splitting up was rarely a good idea.

"I'm not sure they'll give us one if they see you," Raiden added, shooting a meaningful look at my arm.

I glanced down. Blood had soaked through the gray T-shirt fabric and was starting to drip onto the polished floor. It struck a stark contrast against the white marble.

"Oh," I said, and backed up a step to sit on the bench. At least that way my jeans would catch the dripping blood.

Now that I was off my feet and no longer running for my life, the effects of the blood loss were more apparent. I was dizzy and felt chilled to the bone, and my whole body was shaking. I stared at the bright spot of blood staining the floor.

Raiden stood in the opening of the alcove for a long moment, watching me. I was getting the impression that he wasn't too excited about the prospect of leaving me, either.

"I'll be right back, OK?" he finally said.

Without looking up, I nodded.

"If anyone comes near you, scream."

I gave him a weak thumbs up.

He lingered a moment longer, then his boots moved away from the blood spot and out of my range of sight.

I had no idea how long I sat there, waiting for him. It could have been minutes. It could have been hours. I was beyond exhausted, awareness sliding in and out of focus, the only marker of time passing the steady throbbing in my arm.

I'd been rendered unconscious by my condition so many times over the years that I'd lost track. But I'd never passed out as a result of injury. I had a feeling I was precariously close, now. My eyelids felt heavy, my mind fuzzy. Dark spots danced around the edges of my vision, and the sound of blood rushing in my ears was thunderous.

"Hey, Cora . . ." Raiden's face was suddenly all I could see. "How are you doing?"

I blinked. "What?"

"That good, huh?"

I stared at him, taking in his strong, handsome features. Drowning in his warm, brown eyes. "Pretty eyes," I murmured.

"All right . . ." Raiden reached out, taking hold of my uninjured arm at the elbow. "Let's get you upstairs. You'll feel better once you're all patched up."

I stood, with his help, and he curled his arm around my waist and held me tight against his side, lending me his strength. I let him guide me toward a narrow, shiny elevator door. I felt like I was floating, and I actually had to look down at my feet to confirm that they were still touching the ground.

Raiden pushed the elevator's call button.

I blinked, and we were exiting the elevator.

I blinked again, and I was sitting in a chair beside a tiny, round table. Raiden was unpacking the contents of an army-green canvas case a little smaller than a football.

I blinked again, and my arm was stretched out across the wood table, resting on a folded, white terrycloth towel. The bloodied T-shirt was gone, giving me full view of the angry, oozing gash running the length of my forearm. Blood stained the skin all around the open wound.

One more blink, and Raiden was sitting in a chair right in front of me, leaning over my arm. It was cleaner now, though the towel beneath it was a different matter entirely. He held a small, curved needle between his thumb and forefinger, threaded with a stiff blue string that reminded me of dental floss.

"I'm really sorry, Cora," Raiden said, his eyes meeting mine. His brows bunched together, his face a mask of pity. "This is going to hurt . . ."

21

I sat in the chair by the little table, wound cleaned and sewn up, and arm bandaged. Raiden had already disposed of the bloody T-shirt and towel, and he'd repacked his first-aid kit and returned it to his backpack.

The only things left on the table now were a glass of water and a half-eaten chocolate chip granola bar. This was my second glass of water, and I was slowly working my way through the granola bar. I knew I needed to eat to replenish all the blood I'd lost, but I just wasn't hungry. Probably a side effect of losing all that blood . . .

Raiden stood at the room's single window, staring out through a tiny crack between the curtain and the wall. Even just standing there, he clearly favored his wounded knee.

"Why don't you sit on the bed," I suggested. "Prop your leg up . . ."

"It's fine," he said without looking away from the window. "Just a flare up." He glanced at me, offering me a half-assed smile, a faint curving of his lips that never touched his eyes, then returned to staring out the window. "It'll feel better once the ibuprofen kicks in, and it should be good as new by morning."

"Not if you don't rest, it won't," I grumbled.

Raiden either didn't hear me, or was ignoring me.

I tore off a piece of the granola bar and popped it into my mouth. *Raiden's a big boy*, I thought as I chewed; *if he says he's fine, then he's fine.*

I swallowed the bite. "I read online that the wait to get into the Vatican is super long," I said. I took a couple sips of water, then broke off another piece of the granola bar. "We should probably head over to the shop first thing so we can get in line at the Vatican before they open the gates."

"We're not going," Raiden said, voice remote.

"What?" I blurted, spitting out a tiny chunk of granola. I wiped it off the table with a quick swipe of my hand. "Of course, we're going."

Raiden turned away from the window and crossed his arms over his chest. Somehow, that gesture made his shoulders appear even broader. He already cast an imposing figure, but this only enhanced it. "No, we're not."

I opened my mouth, sitting up straighter and sucking in a breath to argue.

Before I could start, he continued, "The situation has changed, Cora—the Order knows we're here. They'll be waiting for us. They'll be *expecting* us. The second we pass through those gates, we're as good as dead." He laughed under his breath. "Well, I am, at least. You, their prize alien—" He frowned and shook his head. "Who knows what they'll do with you. Lock you up . . . dissect you . . ." He raised one eyebrow. "Nothing fun, I'm sure."

I shut my mouth, good hand balling into a fist.

"Find another way in," Raiden said. "Because there's no way I'm letting you get anywhere near those gates. If I have to tie you up to keep you away from there, I will." The hard glint in his eyes told me he meant every single word.

Shock morphed into a sickening mixture of fear and frustration as I finally came to terms with just how much danger I was in—and how much danger Raiden was in—because of me. Guilt joined the disturbing mixture of emotions. My skin felt too hot, my blood too cold. I swallowed reflexively, the spike of emotions leaving me teetering on the precipice of tears.

I was so close to finding out what happened to my mom. She was right here when she disappeared, mere blocks away from where I was sitting, *right now*. I'd come all this way, journeyed to the other side of the damn world, but I might as well have stayed back on Orcas Island for all the good it would do me.

Because Raiden was right—it was too dangerous. It would be suicide to try to pass through the public entrance to Vatican City now. This was just more evidence that I wouldn't have made it this far without Raiden. I needed him. If I drove him away, I would be lost. On my own, I was practically useless.

Before the frustration could overwhelm me to tears, I retreated into the compact bathroom. I shut the door, locking it with a shaky twist of my wrist, then leaned my back against the door. I stared at the tiled wall and focused on taking slow, even breaths.

After one last deep inhale, I crossed the bathroom and bent down to turn on the bathtub faucet. A nice long soak might soothe my frayed nerves and allow rational thought back in. I tweaked the knobs until the water was the perfect temperature, then straightened to begin undressing.

I toed off my sneakers, and awkwardly pulled my T-shirt off over my head, one-handed.

At a knock, I turned to face the bathroom door, shirt clasped to my chest with my uninjured arm. It felt like my heart rate had quadrupled in an instant.

"Cora?" It was Raiden, of course. "Are you all right?"

I swallowed roughly. "Yeah," I said, but the word was barely audible. I cleared my throat and tried again, louder this time.

"OK, well, I'm going to run across the street to pick up some food," he said, voice slightly raised. "You're going to need more than granola bars to heal up."

"All right," I said.

"I shouldn't be longer than ten minutes," he added. "I'll have eyes on the hotel the whole time, but don't let anyone in, OK? If anyone comes to the door, don't even let them know you're in here."

I nodded. "OK."

"And Cora?"

I moved closer to the door, placing my hand on the smooth, white-washed wood. "Yeah?"

"Please don't leave the room," Raiden said.

Guilt was winning the emotional battle within me, wrestling the fear and frustration into submission. Raiden was a good man —a man who didn't deserve the drama my life was throwing at him.

"I won't," I promised, resting my forehead against the bathroom door.

"Thanks," he said, voice quieter. "I'll be right back."

A moment later, I heard the door to our room open and shut.

Sighing, I pushed away from the door and moved to stand in front of the sink. I lowered the shirt, dropping it on the floor, and stared at my reflection in the mirror. I hardly recognized the woman staring back at me. My whole face was paler than usual, washed out by blood loss, and my cheeks looked gaunt, making my eyes appear too large. My irises were a brighter blue than ever before, though the latter could've been an optical illusion caused by the bloodshot whites and the dark half-moons shadowing my eyes.

My focus shifted down to the pendant dangling between my breasts. The amber-colored stone seemed to glow, even against the bright light from the bulbs overhead.

The color of the stone dredged up a memory of the necklace Demeter had been wearing in the dream from the plane. The pendants were far from the same, Demeter's appearing simpler in design, but the stone in her pendant had been the same amber color, and it, too, had seemed to glow with that strange inner light. At least, it had been the same color, *at first*, before she'd touched it and the color had drained away, leaving the stone a brilliant, diamond white.

What exactly had she done to make the stone change color? She'd been standing by the basin in the floor of that cavernous room on the spaceship, and she'd raised her hand, bringing her fingertip to the pendant.

In the mirror, I watched myself mimic Demeter's remembered movements.

She'd touched the tip of her index finger to the pendant and traced a circle around the stone. Counterclockwise, if I recalled correctly.

I gasped as the stone in my pendant changed color, suddenly burning with an electric blue light. There was no doubt about it, now—the stone was definitely glowing.

I took a step back, pulling the pendant away from my chest and staring down at the glowing blue stone. It had worked. Copying Demeter's movements *had worked*.

But, how? And more importantly, *why*? What did it mean?

My mind worked through the implications. Clearly, the dreams were more than they seemed. Not mere figments of a strained mind, but something else. Something *more*.

Were they visions of some kind? Was I seeing events from some distant future? Or was it possible that what I'd been experiencing in my dreams—what had felt like memories—were actually things that happened long ago?

Whatever it was, it had to be coming from the pendant. The dreams had only begun after I started wearing the necklace.

As crazy as it sounded—even in the privacy of my own head —I was beginning to believe that somehow, the pendant must have stored Persephone's memories, and it seemed to be feeding them to me in my sleep. It was the only thing that made any sense. And even *that* was a stretch.

Whatever was happening, I was left with a decision: continue to wear the pendant and willingly allow more of Persephone's memories to invade my dreams as I reaped the benefits of living episode-free—of actually being able to touch other people—or take the thing off and return to the way I'd been before, weak and afraid, a slave to my condition.

Like there was even a choice.

I released the pendant, letting it fall back against my skin, and turned away from the mirror. I quickly shut off the tub's faucet and opened the drain. I was so exhausted, I worried I would fall asleep in the tub. I had enough people out to get me— I didn't need to help them out by drowning myself in a bathtub.

After one last glance in the mirror, at the pendant's eerie blue glow, I switched off the bathroom lights and opened the door, leaving the bathroom and heading to the farther of the two twin beds. I fished my one clean T-shirt out of my backpack and gingerly pulled it on over my head, then settled on the bed, rolling onto my side and propping my bandaged arm on my hip, not even bothering to draw back the covers. I closed my eyes, listening to the gurgle of water draining from the tub.

Within seconds, I was out.

22

I'm walking through a deep gully, bringing up the tail end of our expedition team. Tall sandstone walls variegated with stripes of muted pink, orange, yellow, and white tower over us on either side of the narrow, twisty path. The yellow sun beats down on our backs, but my hoplon suit's built-in thermostat keeps me cool.

I trail behind Despoina, one of my spearsisters. Her hoplon suit—identical to mine in every way save for the color lighting the power channels running the length of it from fingertip to neck to toe—gleams in the sunlight, the charcoal gray fabric turning faintly prismatic. Her doru is tucked safely in its sheath on her back, the focus crystal set atop the retracted staff weapon glowing a steady coral, perfectly matching the light of her suit's power channels. The stone in the regulator hanging around her neck glows the same color.

Ahead of her, the researchers weave in and out of sight as they follow the water worn path. Two more of my spearsisters lead the way—the power channels in their hoplon suits glowing a deep emerald-green and a sunny yellow—though I only catch glimpses of them every now and again, when the path straightens enough to lengthen my line of sight.

Despoina glances back at me over her shoulder, a broad grin splitting her face. "Tell me the truth, Peri—" She holds her arms up to either side of her. "Is Atlantis living up to your expectations?"

My desire to see this new world—the only world I've known outside of the ship that carried us here—is well known among my spearsisters. This is my first time out of the Alpha site, my first time viewing the sun with the naked eye rather than through the thick sheet of ice sheltering the city since Demeter first brought me here over seventy years ago. It's been two regeneration cycles, and I am in awe. This sun-drenched land is so much more beautiful than I remember. I can't stop looking around, taking it all in.

The kiss of the sun's rays is warmer than it had been during that brief visit so long ago. And the sky—it's so open. So deep. So blue. A breeze flows through the gully, rustling the strands of hair that have escaped from my bun and carrying a woodsy, earthy scent. I've seen images and videos of Atlantis' various terrains captured during previous expeditions, but nothing could have prepared me for seeing the wonders first hand.

A slow smile spreads my lips until my grin is as broad as Despoina's. "It's so much better," I tell her.

Despoina throws her head back and laughs, and the joyous sound ricochets off the rough stone walls.

The scene shifts suddenly. I'm no longer Persephone. Now, I'm Raiden.

It's nighttime, and I'm sitting on an overturned bucket, my elbows resting on a folding table, a pair of playing cards clutched in my upraised hands. A campfire crackles nearby, the flames slowly dying.

Across from me, my buddy Kellerman throws his head back and laughs raucously. "You're too much, Raid," he says and shakes his head, his laughter dying out. "Too much . . ." He holds his cards with one hand as he takes a swig from his flask. The diamond, heart, club, and spade etched and colored in with red and black enamel on its face proclaim Kellerman's wishful status as a cardshark. One day, maybe.

I study my cards—a pair of Canadian Aces. There are two more queens in the flop, giving me four of a kind. One day, maybe, but not today.

"Just deal the final card, Killer," I say.

Kellerman is just this side of drunk, and I want to get to bed. But I want to pawn off my position as lead driver in the caravan tomorrow, more, and that's what's at stake. I like Kellerman, but not as much as I like being alive. These days, it seems like land mines are everywhere.

Kellerman narrows his eyes. He studies the four cards on the table, then shoots a hard stare at the backs of my cards. "You got a pair of bitches in your hand?"

I take a deep breath, keeping my expression blank as I return his stare. "Are you going to deal, or not?"

He knows I have the queens now, and he doesn't want to play anymore. He already knows he's lost. I can see it written all over his face.

"Man, this is bullshit," he says, throwing down his hand. He has a pair of Aces. A prime hand pretty much any time other than now. Even if the river is an Ace, his best hand is a Full House, Aces high. No match for my four queens.

I set down my cards and stand, pleased with the outcome of the game. I'm no longer lead driver tomorrow. Kellerman is. "Better luck next time, man," I tell him.

The scene shifts. I'm Persephone, once more.

Despoina pats my shoulder. "Better luck next time, Peri," she says, standing by my side on the crest of a hill.

A vast valley lies far below, and beyond it, snowcapped mountains stretch from horizon to horizon, blocking the way *west. Our expedition had several objectives, and studying and collecting samples from the anthropos living on the other side of those very mountains was only one of the objectives. I was promised people—real, live, alien people. But from the looks of the storm rolling in, nobody will be crossing those mountains for days, if not weeks, and earlier surveys told us there are no other anthropos living on this island.*

"If it makes you feel any better, they look just like us," Despoina says. She shrugs. "You've seen one kind of people, you've seen them all, right?"

I laugh dryly. "Sure, Des, whatever you say."

The scene shifts again. I'm Raiden.

I'm hopping out of the cab of my MTV on the outskirts of a dusty ghost town deep within the heart of the Syrian desert. My boots hit the ground with a crunch I've come to know and despise. I hate this place, and not only because of the dangers that lurk around every corner. I hate being so far from the sea. From the green. From the sound of crying gulls and the smell of washed-up kelp at low tide. From Cora—I hate being so far from her, most of all. This place is the antithesis of home, and I hate every damn thing about it.

I should have listened to her. I should have stayed. Once this tour is over, I'm done.

I scan the crumbling mud-brick buildings, then make my way to the front of the caravan to join Sergeant Hobbs, who's pouring over a map drawn in Sharpie atop a satellite image of the town. Kellerman and a couple other corporals stand nearby, awaiting Hobbs' orders.

"Something up?" I ask Kellerman as I approach.

He crosses his arms and shrugs. "I think Sarge is picking out a different spot to set up base."

I rub the back of my neck and glance at Hobbs. The sun is behind him, forcing me to squint. We'll be here for a few weeks, minimum, so it makes sense that he'd want to find the most secure spot to hole up. There are no hostiles here now, but that could always change.

Kellerman pulls a pack of cigarettes and a lighter out from the chest pocket of his fatigues. He opens the pack and plucks a cigarette free, placing it between his lips. "Smoke?" he asks, offering me the open pack.

I shake my head. A bunch of the guys do it—boredom, I suppose—but the habit never really caught on with me.

"Want to go again tonight?" he says, flicking the lighter so a tiny flame burst to life. "Double or nothing?"

I don't bother to tell him that double or nothing doesn't apply when the previous prize has already been spent. "Sure, man, whatever you say."

The scene shifts again. I'm Persephone.

I'm patrolling the perimeter of camp when I sense someone approaching. Not one of us, and not an animal. A person. An anthropos. He's male, and he's young. Afraid. Not of us, but of failure. Of letting his people down.

I sense others farther out. I can feel their hostility. Their hunger. Their desperation. Their minds are harder to read than those of my people, but with a little digging, I can pull what I need from their thoughts.

They crossed the mountains days ago on a hunting excursion. The game migrates over the mountains this time of the year, leaving food on the west side of the range scarce. People in their village are already dying of starvation. They can't go back empty handed. They won't. It isn't done.

After the sun set this evening, they saw the glow from the light perimeter we set up around camp. They haven't been successful in their hunt yet, and their supplies are running low. They want to raid our camp—kill us and take our food. It isn't personal; it's a matter of survival, pure and simple.

I consider alerting my spearsisters, but I fear that doing so will ensure only one outcome—bloodshed and death. I don't want to kill these men, not when all they're trying to do is provide for their people. I want to help them.

I walk deeper into the shadows and away from camp, angling toward the approaching young hunter. This is his first hunt. He must be successful in order to become a full, marriageable man in the eyes of his tribe. He promised a young woman back in the village that he would return victorious and take her as his first wife. She is carrying his child. He cannot fail.

He sees me before I see him. I can sense it in his thoughts. The channels glowing blue along the length of my hoplon suit turn me into some kind of monster to his eye.

He raises his weapon, a rudimentary bow, and knocks an arrow. I can just make out his outline now, a gray ghost in the moonlight.

"Wait," I say, slowing my approach as I pluck the correct translation from his mind. His language is harsh, guttural, and the sounds are difficult for my tongue to form. I raise my hands to show him I'm unarmed. "I mean you no harm," I tell him. I'm close enough now that I can make out his features. He's younger than I thought—younger than he sees himself.

"Demon!" he shouts and looses the arrow.

I deflect the projectile easily with a flash energy field. The burst of electric blue light flickers in and out of existence in the blink of an eye.

"Please, stop," I say, halting my approach. "I do not wish to hurt you."

The boy knocks another arrow and draws it back, loosing it deftly. He may be young, but he's adept with the bow.

I deflect that arrow just as easily as I did the last.

A sharp sting slices across my cheek. Another arrow, from one of the men farther out. Just a graze, but a few inches to the left, and it could have killed me. I was so focused on the boy that I forgot about the others.

In one smooth motion, I reach over my shoulder and draw my doru from the sheath on my back. With a thought, I extend the golden staff to its full length, nearly tripling it in size. The focus crystal set into the top burns electric blue. I slam the butt of the doru into the earth, sending out a mild shockwave. It won't hurt the approaching anthropos, but it should startle them. It's a warning; they won't win this fight.

"I do not wish to hurt you," I repeat. "Please, lower your weapons. My people will help you track the herd. We will—"

The boy unleashes another arrow, closely followed by arrows from several of his companions. I deflect them all.

"Please!" I'm all but begging now. Begging them to stop. Begging them to give me the chance to spare their lives. To save them.

But they're too afraid, and their fear deafens them to my pleas.

Without warning, an energy blast blows past me in a wave, knocking me forward onto my hands and knees. I stay there for several seconds, head hanging. I don't want to look up. I don't want to see the carnage. A blast powerful enough to knock me off my feet while protected by my hoplon suit would rip apart anyone else.

The anthropos . . . the boy . . .

"I'm sorry, Peri," Despoina says, her soft footsteps approaching me from behind. "Your heart was in the right place, but you cannot reason with people when they're desperate . . ." She stops beside me. "From the moment they first spotted our light, their fate was sealed. This was the only outcome." After a moment, she adds, "There's nothing you could have done."

The scene shifts and, once again, I'm Raiden.

I'm standing watch from the roof of a two-story mudbrick building at the edge of town. I scan the western stretch of desert through the night scope on my rifle, slowly sweeping from north to south. There's nothing to see, just like there's been nothing to see the past three hours.

When my scan takes me so far south that I'm looking at the edge of the town, I start the slow scan back north.

I catch sight of movement, maybe a hundred yards out.

At first, I think it's a large desert cat. But after it gains a few more yards, I can tell it's walking on two legs. It's a person. A small person.

I watch it for a few more seconds, then pull away from the scope.

It's a kid.

My first instinct is to put down the rifle, run out into the desert, and bring the kid in to safety—the desert is no place for a child to wander alone. But rational thought quickly shoves instinct aside. Why is a kid walking through the desert all alone in the middle of the night? I can't think of a single good reason, at least, not one that doesn't include the most terrifying word I know: ambush.

I raise the rifle and peer through the scope.

The kid is closer now, maybe sixty or seventy yards out.

I watch them for another ten yards.

The kid is carrying something, hugging the thing to its chest, but I can't tell what, exactly. From the size, I think it might be a stuffed animal or a doll.

I watch the kid slowly amble closer. Ten more yards. Twenty.

There's a blinking light on whatever they're carrying.

"Shit," I hiss.

I know what the kid is carrying now—a bomb. And depending on what it's made of, a bomb that size would be able to demolish half of this shoddily built town.

"Stop!" I shout, then repeat the word in Arabic and Kurdish when the kid doesn't slow.

But still, the kid keeps coming.

Maybe the kid speaks Turkish, or Chaldean, or Ashuri, or any other of the handful of languages spoken in this godforsaken place, but I don't know a single word from any of those languages. Hell, for all I know, the kid could be deaf.

Much closer, the bomb will be within range to take out not only my post, but our base camp a few buildings into town. Twenty-seven peoples' lives are at risk.

I make a split-second decision and pull the trigger.

The explosion throws me onto my ass, and the mudbrick structure beneath me shudders. I sling my rifle over my shoulder and race across the roof, stumbling as the tiles give way beneath my feet. I barely make it to the edge of the building and down the ladder erected earlier that day before the building collapses in on itself.

Ears ringing, I stand on the dirt road, staring at the wreckage of the place I'd been moments ago. I stare at the rubble, and all I can think is: I just killed a kid.

A kid.

The ground shakes with the force of another explosion, this one on the other side of town. Then another, closer. Smoke, sand, and chunks of mudbrick blot out the stars. I stare off in the direction of that last explosion, mouth hanging open. It was too close to base camp.

Fearing the worst, I start running, heading deeper into the town. I skid to a stop when I see that the building where we've set up camp is still standing. I can hear people yelling from within.

I duck behind a half-demolished wall two buildings over and raise my rifle, doing a quick sweep of the surrounding area, searching for other potential suicide bombers.

Without warning, the building housing our camp explodes.

"NO!" I scream, too stunned to seek cover.

Something slams into my leg, and searing pain brings me to my knees.

Suddenly, I'm not Raiden anymore. I'm not Persephone,

either. I'm me, Cora Blackthorn, and I'm aware that I'm dreaming.

Standing beside Raiden, I look at his profile. His expression is one of shock. Of disbelief. Of heartbreak. Tears streak through the dirt caked on his cheeks. I watch as he yells into the night sky, then buries his face in his hands.

"There's nothing he could have done," a woman says from behind me. Her words are foreign, though I understand their meaning, and I recognize her voice: Persephone.

I whip around, but before I can get a good look at her, she— along with Raiden and the town—is gone.

[23]

Gasping, I woke and sat bolt upright in bed, a ball of tension knotted in my gut. The room was dark, the only light the electric blue glow coming from the pendant hanging around my neck.

A word popped into my head: *regulator*. That's what the pendant was called. I knew it, because in the dream, Persephone had known it. A pattern was becoming clear; each successive time I dreamed I was Persephone, I had more access to her knowledge than I'd had the previous time.

Like knowing that when the regulator's stone was amber, it was active, creating a barrier in my mind that blocked what Persephone had thought of as *powers*. And when the stone was blue . . . I couldn't quite remember what it did, then. Everything I had known in the dream—everything Persephone had known— was slipping away, fading into the shadows at the edges of my mind.

I looked down at the pendant and touched my fingertip to the glowing blue stone. Without thinking, I traced a circle around the stone. The brighter blue faded to subtly glowing amber, and I could feel the tension oozing from my muscles. Whatever this thing was supposed to do when the stone glowed amber, I knew what it did for me—it kept me safe. It kept me sane.

Even as the latent knowledge from Persephone faded, the scenes featuring Raiden grew crisper in my mind's eye. In the dream I'd *been* Raiden. Just like I'd *been* Persephone. Both sets of dreams had felt like reliving memories, and yet they'd left me with the haunting aftertaste of an episode, just without the debilitating physical side effects.

I felt fine. Disturbed, but otherwise all right.

I heard a moan come from my left, a half-dozen feet away. I could just make out the lumpy outline of Raiden in the other bed, tossing and turning on the mattress. He'd kicked the covers off, baring his torso from the hips up. His left shoulder and arm were covered in black ink, but I couldn't tell much more than that in the darkness. The sheets were tangled around his legs, and one of the pantlegs of his sweatpants was pushed up to his knee.

"No," he murmured. "No . . . no . . ."

I blinked, eyes locked on Raiden's thrashing form. He was talking in his sleep. Was it just a coincidence that he was murmuring the same word he'd screamed to the sky in the dream? *No* wasn't exactly a rarely used word. Or was it possible that I'd somehow hijacked Raiden's dream? His nightmare? His *memory*?

Was it possible that the flashes of images I saw during my episodes were snippets of memories? *Other people's* memories, bleeding out of whoever I inadvertently touched and into me. The flashes of confusing images and sounds had always been too jumbled and muddled to make sense of before, but what if they were more than that. What if, when the stone was blue, the regulator allowed my mind to make sense of the input I was receiving from others?

Raiden let out a heart wrenching sound that was part groan, part cry.

I pushed back my covers, jumped out of bed, and crossed to

Raiden's bedside, unwilling to let him suffer any longer. If he was reliving the scene I'd seen in my dream, his emotional agony had to be crushing him. I knew first hand; I'd felt it when I'd been him.

And even if he was dreaming about some other thing, if something else was troubling him and my dream was just that—a dream—so be it. He was in pain. That much was clear enough. He'd been in pain since he first returned home, only I'd been too chickenshit to reach out to him. Too caught up in feeling sorry for myself to offer him the support he needed. I'd failed him, time and again.

Well, I wouldn't fail him, now.

I reached for Raiden with my uninjured arm, but hesitated, my hand hovering over his bare shoulder. Gritting my teeth, I deliberately lowered my hand. His skin was coated in a sheen of cold sweat.

"Raiden," I whispered, giving his shoulder a gentle jostle.

He stilled, but he didn't wake.

I waited several seconds, then shook him harder. "Raiden . . ."

He startled awake, sucking in a sharp breath. His eyes popped open, and he rolled onto his side, toward me. His hand was suddenly around my neck. His fingers tightened. He was crushing my throat, lost in some violent state of half-sleep.

I sputtered and gasped, but there was no way for me to get air in, let alone get any words out. I clawed at his hand, with both of mine, trying to wedge my fingertips between his fingers and my throat. The stitches in my forearm pulled, making the wound burn, but survival instinct shoved the pain to the back of my mind, and I struggled harder.

It was no use. Raiden's grip was a vice of flesh and bone.

I slapped at his hand, his arm, his chest—anywhere I could reach—but it didn't do any good. My throat was on fire, my lungs burning with the need to expand. I could feel myself giving up.

A switch flipped in my mind, and it was like my body suddenly knew what to do, even if my mind didn't.

I raised my arm straight up and twisted into Raiden, then bent my elbow as I jerked my arm down, slamming it against his as hard as I could.

Raiden's elbow buckled, and his fingers slipped from my neck.

Without losing momentum, I continued the twist and raised my other arm, smashing my elbow into the side of his jaw.

Raiden cried out, temporarily stunned, then lunged at me.

I lurched backward, letting him tumble off the bed.

With a grunt, he landed on his side on the floor.

I rolled Raiden onto his back with my bare foot and sat down on top of him, securing his arms to his sides with my knees and planting my left hand on the floor beside his head.

"Raiden," I said, voice harsh as I raised my hand to slap him. The strike stung my palm, and I shook out my hand before pulling it back for a second slap. "Raiden! Wake up!" The words sounded strange, like I'd suddenly acquired a foreign accent.

Raiden's face transformed, his expression going from enraged to pained.

I froze, arm still primed to strike. I wanted to lower my arm, but I couldn't. It was like I wasn't in control of my own body.

Raiden winced, closing his eyes and stretching his jaw from side to side. "Ow . . ." When he opened his eyes again, it was clear that he was really seeing me. Finally.

The switch that had flipped within me, allowing me to fight him off, switched back, and once again, I was in control of my body. I lowered my arm, planting my hand on the floor near his ear and letting my head hang down. What had just happened within me was almost as frightening as the physical struggle with Raiden had been. For a few seconds, all I did was breathe.

"You hit me," Raiden said. There was hurt in his voice—emotional, not physical.

A harsh laugh escaped from my throat. "Only because you were choking me . . ."

I peered down at him.

He looked shocked, horrified, even. His eyes traveled down to my neck, where he was bound to find an angry red mark in the shape of a hand. His hand. In a few hours, I would undoubtedly have a pretty nasty bruise.

Raiden tugged his arms free and raised his right hand, reaching for my neck.

Instinctively, my whole body tensed up, and I pulled back a few inches.

Raiden froze, his eyes meeting mine. "Cora, I didn't mean to —" He swallowed roughly, lowering his hand until both rested on his chest, almost like he was praying. "I'm so sorry," he said. "I would never hurt you."

"Not awake, maybe," I murmured, regretting the words the instant I said them.

Raiden looked crushed. Just like he'd looked in the dream. Only this time, it was because of me.

I sat up, pulling my hands from the floor. The shift in position made my precarious perch atop Raiden all too apparent. I was straddling him, my hips directly aligned with his. It was the closest I'd ever been to a man . . . or to anybody, really. But the fact that he was a man—and an attractive one, at that—made my body burn with a strange mixture of embarrassment and excitement.

I should have moved off him, I knew that. And yet, I didn't want to.

Slowly, Raiden sat up, his abdominal muscles bunching into a defined pattern. "I mean it, Cora," he said, his hands coming to rest on my hips. His eyes locked with mine, and the intensity of his dark stare paralyzed me. "Hurting you is the last thing I would ever want to do. You have to believe me."

My eyes searched his, my heart hammering in my chest.

His grip on my hips tightened. "But I did hurt you," he said, his stare dropping to my neck. "And I'm so fucking sorry." His tone alone sent cracks snaking through my heart, but it was his expression that shattered it into a million pieces. At that moment, I would've done anything to take his pain away.

"Hey," I said, raising my hands to hover on either side of his face. I hesitated, taking a deep breath, then rested my palms on his cheeks.

He winced when the fingers of my right hand touched his jaw. It looked like I wasn't the only one worse for the wear after our little wrestling match.

I shifted my right hand down to rest on his shoulder, using my left to angle his face upward so his gaze met mine, once more. "I'm all right," I said, twisting my lips into a wry smile. My arm didn't even hurt anymore, which was surprising, but I wasn't about to complain about *not* being in pain. "Turns out I can hold my own against a tough guy like you." I raised one shoulder. "Who would've thought . . ."

I ignored the part of my mind wondering how, exactly, I'd managed to fight Raiden off. How my body had, once again, done things *I* didn't actually know how to do.

Raiden's fingers began to knead my hips, pulling me closer. His gaze dropped to my lips, just for a moment, before returning to my eyes. "Cora . . ."

I was pretty sure he was about to kiss me. And I wanted him to. I really, *really* did.

But fear reared its ugly head, gripping my heart tighter than Raiden had gripped my neck just moments ago.

"I saw the explosion," I blurted.

Raiden went completely still.

I licked my lips, shifting my left hand down from the side of his face to his shoulder. "I saw what happened in the desert," I told him. "I saw the child. I saw what you did . . . what you had to do to protect your team. And I saw what happened after . . ."

Persephone's words echoed through my mind. "There's nothing you could have done," I said, and it almost felt like she was speaking through me.

Raiden's eyes searched mine. "How could you possibly know any of that?"

"I saw it," I told him. "In a dream."

Raiden moved his hands from my hips to the floor behind him and leaned back a little, his eyes slipping away from mine as his stare grew distant. When he spoke next, his voice was the faintest whisper.

"That was no dream."

24

Raiden and I sat on the edges of our respective beds, facing each other. It was just after midnight, and the lamp on the nightstand between our beds was on, bathing the room in a soft white light. I picked at a pull near my knee in the fabric of my jeans as I watched Raiden out of the corner of my eye. My arm still didn't hurt, which struck me as odd, but that was hardly the most pressing concern at the moment.

Raiden was staring at me. He'd been staring at me for the past ten minutes. Not speaking. Not moving. Just staring.

"Do you know what I'm thinking, right now?" he asked, breaking the silence but leaving the tension intact.

I shook my head. With a deep breath, I raised my hands and pulled the pendant out from inside my shirt. The stone was amber, which meant the regulator was in what I was coming to think of as safety mode.

"It's called a regulator," I told him, eyes locked on the pendant. "Well, actually, it's called something else in an alien language I don't really know, but *regulator* is the closest translation, I think." I shrugged. "When the stone is amber, like it is now, it makes me more or less normal—I can touch people without getting knocked on my ass."

"I've noticed," Raiden said, his voice a soft rumble.

I nodded, still staring at my knee. "But not when it's blue."

"It changes color?"

Again, I nodded.

"What happens then—when it's blue?"

I glanced at Raiden, just for a second, then tucked the regulator back into the neck of my T-shirt and returned to staring at my knee. "I relive your worst memories, apparently . . ."

Or, I could tear him apart with a blast of psychic energy, like Despoina had done in the dream—memory—whatever it was, but I wasn't about to tell him that. I wanted him to stay, not run for the hills, afraid I might obliterate him with an errant thought.

"Hm," Raiden murmured. "Do you have control over it? Do you make the stone turn blue, or does it just happen?"

"I control it," I told him.

He was quiet for a moment, upping the tension. "Will you show me?"

I looked at him, finally meeting his eyes. Slowly, I shook my head. "I don't think that's such a good idea."

Raiden leaned forward, resting his forearms on his thighs. "You saw inside my mind, Cora. You don't have a *condition*. You have a *gift*." He laughed softly and shook his head. "If you're telepathic, I think you should try—"

"It's more than that," I told him, standing. "It's more than telepathy." I moved to the foot of the bed, farther away from him, and started pacing the room. "I've been having these dreams—these memories of someone else's life."

"Like how you saw my memory," Raiden said.

"Yeah," I said, then shook my head, raising one hand to rub the back of my neck. "And no. This is different. *She* is different." I took a deep breath, then continued on. "Her name is Persephone, and she's not human."

Raiden sat up straighter, his eyes opening wider, but he didn't say anything.

"She's one of them—one of my people," I explained, still pacing. "She's a warrior of some kind, with amazing psychic powers. I think she lived a long time ago, and that this was hers," I said, touching the regulator. "It's like, somehow, this *device* gives me access to her memories. Every time I go to sleep, now, I relive different parts of her life."

I stopped at the door to our room and hugged my middle. "The things she could do with her mind when the stone was blue . . ." I shook my head. "It's fun to daydream about having superpowers when it's not an actual possibility, but nobody should be able to do those kinds of things." I bowed my head, clutching my sides.

Overwhelmed, I scrunched up my face, and my chest convulsed with a barely contained sob. "I don't want to read your mind, Raiden," I managed to say, voice thick with emotion, "and I don't want to accidentally tear your body apart with a thought." My shoulders shook, and I hugged my middle tighter. I was barely holding myself together.

I could hear Raiden's quiet footsteps as he approached. He stopped behind me and rested his hand on my shoulder. "All right," he said, his voice barely above a whisper. "I'm sorry. I didn't know." He squeezed my shoulder. "I can't imagine what you're going through, but I can see how scared you are. I'm here for you, Cora. Whatever you need, I'm here."

I closed my eyes, inhaling a shaky breath. "If you want to go," I said, voice tremulous, "I won't blame you. I would understand."

"I don't," Raiden said, no hesitation. "I won't. I won't leave you, Cora . . . not again." His words reminded me of the thoughts I'd witnessed in the dream. Of how much he'd missed home. Of how much he'd missed me.

His hand glided down to my elbow, and he pulled my arm

free, sliding his hand down to mine. His fingers slipped between mine, setting my nerve endings aflame.

It was the first time anyone had held my hand in for as long as I could remember, and it felt incredibly intimate. Was it always like this? Or was it so intense because of who we were to each other—because what we wanted from each other had been off limits for so long?

My chest rose and fell with each too-fast breath. I looked down at our joined hands, heat creeping up my neck, and turned partway, forcing myself to raise my eyes to meet Raiden's. I needed to know if this was all in my head. I needed to see if Raiden was feeling the same things I was feeling. The same pull. The same long-buried desire.

His gaze was intent, focused. He had never looked at me like that before. Nobody had ever looked at me like that before.

"Raiden, I—" I glanced down, brow furrowing, and shook my head. "I don't know how to—" I swallowed roughly. "I've never—" Again, I shook my head. "Obviously I . . ."

Raiden raised a hand to my chin and tilted my face up toward his. "Shut up," he whispered, his lips curving into the tiniest of smiles.

A heartbeat later, his lips were pressed against mine, and all of my thoughts and worries and fears faded away. I tensed up, just for a moment, and then I sighed, melting against him, giving in to my first real taste of passion.

Raiden's hand slipped behind my neck, his arm around my back, and never in my life had I felt so afraid and so safe at the same time. I was overwhelmed by sensation. It was too much. Not enough.

I broke the kiss, breathing hard, heart pounding in my chest. Tears streamed down my cheeks, and I buried my face against Raiden's shoulder. "I'm sorry," I sobbed. "I don't know why I'm crying . . ."

Raiden curled his arms around me, wrapping me up in my first real hug in over two decades.

"Give it time," he said, holding me tighter. "I'm not going anywhere."

25

Sitting on the foot of the bed, I stared down at my freshly bandaged arm. Now that Raiden had cleaned and redressed the wound, I knew why it hadn't bothered me much during the night —not when I'd been fighting Raiden, or later, when I'd been kissing him, or later still, when I'd been lying with him on his bed, unable to sleep so close to another person, but unwilling to move away, either.

The cut from the crash was healing better than expected. Way better, if Raiden's expression while removing the sutures had been anything to go by. The cut had fully scabbed over during the night, and it seemed to have shrunk quite a bit, leaving the skin around the wound pink, puckered, and new.

I rubbed the bandage absently. The wound itched more than it hurt now. An echo of the sharp sting remained as a dull throbbing sensation, but the itching nearly drowned out the pain.

This was the most serious injury I'd ever had, and as such, my first chance to notice anything unusual about the way my body healed. Like that I healed faster than normal. Like, scary fast. *Inhumanly* fast.

I'd had bumps, bruises, and scrapes before, of course, most

in the form of skinned knees or papercuts, and they'd all healed in a day or two—a relatively normal time frame, or so I'd thought. Now, I wondered if those wounds had all been too minor for me or my mom to notice anything unusual during the healing process. I also wondered if my mom *had* noticed but had chosen to hide my own abnormalities from me. Wouldn't want me to start thinking anything crazy like, I don't know, that I was an *alien*.

At the sound of the shower being turned on, I looked at the bathroom door. Raiden was in there, washing up before our big day of sitting in a hotel room, twiddling our thumbs. He was no longer just dead set against visiting the Vatican publicly; he was also digging in his heels about dropping by my mom's last known whereabouts—the convenience store.

His reasoning was sound. The Order knew we were here. They would have all eyes on deck, or whatever. I got it. I really did. And as much as I might enjoy daydreaming about the prospect of being locked up in a hotel room all day with Raiden, exploring my new, touchable reality, facing that same situation in real life scared the bejesus out of me. I was not looking forward to the long day of awkwardness and avoidance stretching out before me.

Besides, I'd come all this way to find out what had happened to my mom—and to get an explanation from her about why she'd lied to me about who I was for so long—and I couldn't do a damn thing toward that end. Wandering around Rome in search of her was off the table unless I wanted to sneak out on my own, and even I could admit that walking into Vatican City through the public entrance was pretty much the worst idea ever.

If only there was another way to get to the Order's vault . . .

I stopped rubbing my bandaged arm and sat up straighter. The vault was located in the Order's underground headquarters, beneath the Vatican Library. And, unless my memory was mistaken, it wasn't the only thing down there. There was a whole maze of catacombs housing the bodies of long-dead Catholic priests and even longer-dead Romans and Etruscans beneath Vatican City. And those older tunnels didn't stop at the Vatican's border. They ran all throughout the earth beneath Rome.

I sprang off the bed and rushed to the corner of the room, where I'd stowed my backpack. I unzipped the main pocket and freed my laptop, then settled in at the little round table near the window.

I knew *about* the catacombs beneath Rome—like, that they were scattered all over the city, and that they were different from the famed catacombs of Paris, having been created slowly, over two millennia, to house the remains of the deceased rather than having been created all at once, when thousands of bodies had been moved into mine tunnels to clear out overcrowded cemeteries—but I didn't know much more than that.

But, lucky me, I knew someone who did.

I quickly typed the password into my computer and logged on, opening up the internet browser and clicking on one of the bookmarked tabs beneath the search bar at the top of the window. Dark colors filled the screen—blacks and blues and purples—making the neon green text at the website's header draw the eye: *MMORPG ANONYMOUS.* The online forum was a gathering place for a very particular breed of supergeek: addicts of massive multiplayer online role-playing games. Like me.

For at least the past decade, I had spent the majority of my free time logged in to online games featuring dragons, zombies, aliens, and the like, battling the imagined beasties alongside my virtual companions. I'd joined forces with gamers from all across the globe to slay demons, avert the apocalypse, and hunt for ancient, mystical treasures. The majority of my relationships with other humans happened online, where I could connect with people I had never met in real life. Where I didn't have to worry about a pesky little thing like physical contact.

That virtual existence had seemed like enough, before. But now that I was actually out in the world, doing something *real*, it just seemed sad.

With a series of clicks on the touchpad, I navigated my way to the page listing all of my online "friends" and searched the starred favorites for the gamertag of the only one I considered a true friend: *IceQu33n*. A chat box opened in the lower right corner of the screen. My fingertips tapped on the keys.

Need to talk – 911. Meet me in Valhalla.

I hit enter, then glanced at the time. It took me a few seconds to do the time zone math. It was half past eight in the morning here in Rome, which meant it was seven thirty in Dublin. Fiona would be up. She was a daytime sleeper, choosing to align her sleep schedule with her online buddies who lived in the States.

She had a job that allowed for such flexibility, as well as a surplus of free time. It was a dream job, really, working remotely as a researcher for one of the greatest video game producers of all time, Rockville Softworks. Her current project featured a treasure hunter from the turn of the nineteenth century, the golden age of archaeology, locked in a race against time—and against an evil foe—to find the one artifact that could prevent the end of the world.

For months, Fiona had been complaining about how tedious it was to search through the never-ending historical record to map out ruins all across Europe and Asia, the setting of the first installment in what Rockville hoped would be a mega-successful new adventure RPG franchise. I was hoping so, too. The treasure hunter adventure genre had grown stale as of late, with both the long-running *Tomb Raider* and *Uncharted* franchises publicly wrapping up, and the audience—namely, *me*—was ripe for some new material.

I closed the MMORPG ANONYMOUS page and opened a new tab, typing in the address for a public chat room I used to frequent, years ago. *Valhalla* was a gathering place for players of *Thor's Hammer*, an epic one-off single-player RPG set during the time of the Norse gods. It had been released nearly a decade ago and had attained both critical acclaim and a cult following. Fans of the game, like me, were still waiting for a sequel. Online petitions had been made and signed aplenty, but so far, the collective plea for more seemed to have landed on deaf ears.

The *Valhalla* chat room was now mainly used by the most hardcore, bitterest fans of the game. I loved *Thor's Hammer*, but not enough to linger around here like a vulture circling a half-dead animal creeping through the desert. This chatroom didn't allow for direct messaging, but I hadn't logged in to *Valhalla* in years—so long that my username was a long-abandoned gamertag. If the Custodes Veritatis was looking for me online, they wouldn't be looking here.

I skimmed the lines of speculation filling the dialogue bubbles from the past hour.

SpaceGuy69 had a friend who knew a guy whose cousin's sister had worked on the original *Thor's Hammer* game, and she'd heard through the grapevine that the sequel was in development.

MisterSisterKister heard the original game's head writer had just quit his job as one of the writers for a new, secret Bethesda game franchise, which according to the five active chatters in the room, meant that now he had to be working on the *Thor's Hammer* sequel. It was *the only* explanation.

I rolled my eyes.

The laptop's speakers emitted the sound of a door creaking open, and Fiona's gamer tag, *IceQu33n*, appeared on the list of active participants in the left-side panel. She didn't waste any time, beating me to a greeting. Her words appeared in the group chat, alongside those of *SpaceGuy69* and *MisterSisterKister*, and the like.

Are you all right? It's been days! When you never logged back on, I thought . . . I don't know. Crazy things. I thought you were abducted. Or dead. But you're here, so you're all right, right? RIGHT?

I started typing a response several times, but had to delete it as Fiona continued on. Finally, when no new words appeared, I figured it was safe to reply.

*I'm fine . . . ish. Or I will be. Hopefully. *sigh* It's a long story. Listen, Fio, I need your help.*

My message appeared after two others: *WTF* and *Huh?* We were confusing the locals. Too bad.

Fiona's response was immediate.

Anything.

I smiled reflexively. Maybe I'd never met Fiona in real life, but that wasn't what made a friendship real. Dependability—being able to count on the other person, no matter what—*that* was what defined a true friendship.

. . .

Remember last month when you were telling me about mapping out parts of Rome for that game - didn't that include the tunnels beneath the city?

The other gamers piped in again, this time with more interest than confusion. They asked if Fiona was working on the *Thor's Hammer* sequel, and if this meant it would be set in ancient Rome instead of Scandinavia. Fiona ignored their chatter.

The catacombs? Yeah. Why?

My heartrate picked up speed, and I leaned in, typing fast.

Say, hypothetically, someone needed to find a way to get into the catacombs beneath the Vatican from underground - would that even be possible? Like, do the catacombs outside the Vatican and those inside ever meet up?

The chat room went quiet, all chatter stalling as we waited for Fiona's response. I could only imagine what the other gamers were thinking. Was this a staged stunt meant to build hype for the sequel? Did this mean that the Holy Roman Empire would be the antagonist of the new game? Would the premise feature an epic battle between the old gods and the new?

"It's never going to happen," I murmured. "Just let it go."

The bathroom door opened, and I looked up, watching Raiden emerge wearing nothing more than a towel wrapped around his waist. His shoulder, arm, and the left side of his chest were covered in a mass of black ink, the designs intricate and exotic. Tiny droplets of water dripped from the ends of his hair onto his muscular arms and chest. He didn't look real. He was an action figure brought to life. GI Joe's Pacific Islander buddy. He was powerful. Imposing. Deadly.

"Just let what go?" Raiden asked. Stripped of everything but *him*, he was downright beautiful.

I couldn't look away.

Oblivious, Raiden headed for his backpack tucked up against the wall on the far side of his bed, picking up the bag and setting it on the mattress.

The moment his near nakedness registered in my mind— and the realization that I was gawking—my stare snapped back to the computer screen. My neck and cheeks were on fire, and the heat was spreading. Soon, I would be a sweaty, flustered mess.

I cleared my throat. Raiden had asked me a question, though I couldn't for the life of me remember what it was. "Um, what?"

"Just let *what* go?" Raiden repeated as he dug through his backpack. He pulled out a pair of boxer briefs, some socks, and a rolled-up T-shirt, all in black.

I stared at the screen, not blinking and *not* looking at Raiden. "Just these gamers," I told him, voice coming out a little husky. I cleared my throat.

I wished Fiona would respond, already. At least then I would have something else to focus on besides all of that maleness unwittingly flaunting itself on the other side of the room.

With a faint ding, a chat bubble headed by Fiona's gamertag appeared at the tail of the string of excited chatter.

There may be a way . . . give me a sec.

I blew out a breath and sat back in my chair. That hadn't exactly been the response I'd been hoping for. But, at least it hadn't been a *no*.

Out of the corner of my eye, I watched Raiden drop his towel and pull his jeans on over his freshly donned boxer briefs. I couldn't help it. Thankfully, he didn't seem remotely aware of how his near nudity was affecting me.

Still bare from the waist up, he reached across the bed for the cell phone on the nightstand, then turned his back to me and sat on the edge of the mattress.

A deep, purplish bruise fanned up his hip and side from the waistband of his pants. It hadn't been visible when he'd been facing me, but from this angle it was impossible not to notice. The bruise looked incredibly painful, and I could only imagine how our little middle-of-the-night tumbling act had aggravated the wound. I knew he'd reinjured his leg in the crash and that his ribs had been bugging him—that he may have broken one—but this overt evidence of his injury was unexpected.

"Do you need to get that checked out?" I asked. When Raiden looked up from the phone, eyebrows raised in question, I added, "In case you're bleeding internally, or you, like, punctured a lung, or something . . ."

A crease appeared between Raiden's eyebrows, and he shook his head. "Don't worry about it," he said. "It looks worse than it is. I'll be fine."

I frowned. "Well, how's your leg?" He'd brushed his limp off as simply an aggravation of the older injury, claiming it would be better by morning. While his limp really didn't seem as pronounced as it had yesterday, it also wasn't entirely gone.

Before Raiden could answer, my eyes traveled up to his face. There was a faint, reddish-purple splotch where my elbow had connected with his jaw. That hadn't been visible during our late-night, post-fight chat. "And your face," I added. "Sorry about that."

Raiden stretched out his jaw, rubbing the joint with his

fingertips. "You got me good, I'll give you that." He set the phone back on the nightstand and grabbed the rolled-up T-shirt, gingerly pulling it on over his head. "What are you working on?"

I bit my lip, averting my gaze to the window and watching someone walk into the grocery store across the street. "I, um, maybe sorta kinda thought of a way to get into the Order's vault without actually going *into* Vatican City. At last, not the above ground part." I glanced at him sidelong, gauging his reaction. "That was the deal, right? Find another way in?"

The corners of Raiden's mouth tensed, and he grunted, his irritation palpable. "I see. And what is this other way in, exactly?"

The chill to his tone drew my eyes back to him. "Through the catacombs," I said. "My friend's been doing research for this game developer, and one of her projects was to map out the tunnels and catacombs beneath Rome."

Raiden was already shaking his head.

"If there's a way in, she can find it," I said, growing defensive.

"Reaching out to your friend is a terrible idea," Raiden said. "If the Order's monitoring her—"

"Why would they be monitoring her?" I said, interrupting him. "If my mom's journal is anything to go by, they only *just* became aware of my existence as anything more than an ancient, frozen embryo. How much could they have learned about me in the past few days? I highly doubt they would've hacked into my gamer profile and tagged all of my contacts."

"You don't know what these people are capable of."

I scoffed. "They're a bunch of *priests*, Raiden. They're not *Anonymous*," I said, blurting out the first hacking group that popped into my mind.

"Jesus, Cora!" Raiden exploded. "They're not just *a bunch of priests*." He was on his feet and striding across the room toward me, no hint of a limp.

I shrank back in my chair as he drew closer.

Raiden planted one hand on the back of my chair, the other on the table, his fingertips nudging the side of my computer. He loomed over me, enraged and menacing in a way I'd never experienced before, not with *anyone*. This was totally different from his sleep-induced fight instinct from the night before. This was Raiden fully awake. Fully aware. And fully pissed off.

"They were *your mom* and *my mom*," he ground out. "They recruit the best of the best at whatever skill they think will benefit them most." He leaned in.

I shrank back until my shoulder touched the window sill.

"We have to assume the Order is *better* than Anonymous," he said. "It's the only way to stay ahead of them. So, don't contact anyone without running it by me first. Am I clear?"

Eyes opened as wide as they would go, I gulped and nodded. "Crystal."

A faint ping alerted me to a new message from Fiona in the chat room.

My tense staredown with Raiden broke, and we both looked at the computer screen. At the six words that had the potential to change everything.

I found you a way in.

26

Fiona was waiting to send the image file to a dummy email account that took me all of thirty seconds to set up.

Kneeling behind me, Raiden watched over my shoulder as I typed the brand-spanking-new email address out for Fiona in the chat room, then clicked on the email tab and stared at the empty inbox folder.

Raiden exhaled, long, slow, and very controlled. No words necessary. He wasn't happy that I'd made contact with Fiona, but at least he wasn't going into uber-controlling lockdown mode. He was playing along. Going with the flow. For the moment . . .

Now, it was simply a matter of waiting and hoping that whatever underground route Fiona had come up with didn't just work on paper, but worked in the real world, too. The tunnels and catacombs beneath Rome were notoriously neglected, many having been reported as irrevocably damaged or flat-out collapsed over the past few decades.

For nearly a minute, I stared at the computer screen, barely breathing. Not even blinking. I didn't want to miss it.

I was so focused, that it startled me when the email appeared in the inbox. My heart gave an excited *thud-thump*, and hand trembling, I clicked on the email. I skimmed the single line of text written by Fiona.

Here you go. I don't know why you need this, but whatever the reason, be careful . . .

I took a deep breath, anticipation mounting, and clicked on the email attachment.

Within seconds, Raiden and I were staring at a black and white street map of modern Rome. The image file was multi-layered, with a second, semi-transparent layer on top of the map marked up with zigzagging lines drawn in bright colors. A key in the bottom right corner of the map denoted historical and cultural eras to each line color, following the traditional ROY G BIV rainbow scale.

Red lines belonged to the ancient times, indicating tunnels created by the Etruscans prior to the second century BC, while yellow lines indicated tunnels belonging to the first large scale excavation and construction of Roman catacombs during the second century AD. These were mostly located in the outer portion of the modern city, just beyond the outskirts of ancient Rome's walls. This didn't surprise me, as it had been against the law at the time to bury the dead within the city.

Violet indicated the most recent time period, those few tunnels scattered throughout the city belonging to the final era of Christian catacomb creation during the fifth to seventh centuries AD, with the other colors representing tunnels created at other time periods in between.

Some of the tunnels appeared to be freestanding, not connected to any others—this was most common closer to the center of the city, where the ancient Romans had never entombed any of their dead. But thankfully, Vatican City fell outside the ancient city walls, and the Romans *had* excavated tunnels underneath and around the area.

A bold, black asterisk had been drawn over a star-shaped landmark due east of Vatican City, on the western bank of the Tiber River. According to the scale beneath the key, the starred location was less than half a mile from the Vatican.

From the asterisk, Fiona had drawn a line connecting a hodgepodge of tunnel systems creating a slightly indirect route that eventually ended at a second asterisk on the southern border of Vatican City. Each transition between tunnel systems had been marked with a perpendicular line crossing through the route path. At two different transition points, about halfway along the route and about two-thirds of the way, the path split, and Fiona had drawn in an additional, dashed line. I took those to be alternate routes, should we find the main path impassable. Each detour took a longer path than the original but eventually returned to the main route before reaching the end point.

"That's Castel Sant'Angelo," Raiden said, pointing to the starting asterisk.

I glanced at him over my shoulder, throwing him some serious side eye. "How exactly do you know so much about this city, anyway?"

He shrugged, his stare never leaving the screen. "I spent some time here a few years back."

I narrowed my eyes, wanting to know more. But my curiosity about Raiden's past was quickly overshadowed by my excitement about the map. We had a way in. Or, at least, a potential way in. It was better than nothing, which was what we'd had *before* Fiona's map landed in our inbox.

Focus returning to the map, I tilted my head to the side and squinted, just a little. "Does this look familiar to you at all?" I asked Raiden.

"Well, it *is* a map of Rome . . ."

"Not that part," I said absently, ignoring the heavy dose of sarcasm Raiden had laced through those words, and continued to stare at the map. Or rather, at the randomized pattern of tunnels drawn onto the map.

Wanting to get a better look at the pattern without the distraction of all the streets and sites of modern Rome, I hid the street map layer so only the catacomb tunnels were visible.

Oh yeah, the pattern was definitely tickling my brain. I'd seen it—or something too similar to it to be a coincidence—before. I chewed on my bottom lip as I searched my memory.

On a whim, I made the image black and white.

My mouth fell open, and I sat back in my chair. "Oh my God," I breathed. I knew exactly where I'd seen this pattern before.

I tore my stare away from the screen and hunched over to dig through my backpack, searching for my mom's journal. I pulled it out of the bag and pushed the laptop back a few inches on the table to make room for the leather-bound book. I leafed through the pages until I found what I was searching for.

The unlabeled two-page spread was marked with a spider-webbed pattern of lines and symbols I hadn't been able to decipher. It was more detailed and marked with more crossing and interconnecting lines than Fiona's map, but there was no denying the similarity. I could've laid Fiona's map over the pattern drawn by my mom, and they would've matched up perfectly.

"It *is* a map," I said softly, suspicions confirmed from the first time I'd studied the two-page spread on the plane.

My mom had drawn her own map of the Roman underground—the whole thing, including the part under Vatican City. Moreover, she'd created a far more complete map of the tunnels and catacombs than Fiona had been able to construct during her months of research. This must have been the backdoor my mom had used to get to the vault. Which meant there was a way for *us* to get to the vault through the catacombs, too.

My heart rate sped up, and my foot tapped anxiously on the floor.

I found the starting point Fiona had starred on her map on my mom's counterpart. My mom had marked it with a tiny circle crossed through with an X. The location Fiona had marked as the end point of our route was marked with another crossed circle on my mom's map. My mom had drawn other tiny circles all over the map, some with X's, some with a single line crossing through them, some without any lines, along with circle-free X's.

"I wonder if a circle indicates an exit or entrance," I thought aloud. "But what about the X . . .?"

Behind me, Raiden stood and headed toward his bed on the far side of the room.

I looked up, following him with my eyes.

He reached into his open backpack and pulled out the zippered pouch that contained our cash reserve. He unzipped the pouch and pulled out a stack of American bills, quickly counting the money before returning it to the pouch, dropping the pouch on the bed, and picking up his phone. His thumbs tapped out a message, no doubt to his mom—the only other number programmed into the phone besides the number belonging to *my* temporary phone. When he was finished, he set the phone down on top of the money pouch and crossed his arms over his chest.

"I need to run a couple errands before we head to Castel Sant'Angelo," he said, his body language telling me he was expecting me to argue. I could hardly blame him. I wanted to argue that errands would be time wasted and that we should be heading out *right now*.

I stilled my foot and took a deep breath, consciously inhaling and exhaling. "What errands?" I forced myself to ask, swallowing back the protests attempting to claw their way up my throat.

Raiden relaxed a little, though his arms remained crossed and his gaze hard. "I need to go to the bank." His eyes flicked down to the pouch of money. "We need cash."

I raised my eyebrows. Money hardly seemed like our most immediate concern. "For . . .?"

"Weapons," he said grimly. "If we're going in underground, we're going in armed."

[27]

I've handled thousands of guns before, from shotguns to lasers to rocket launchers. I have badges and medals marking me as an expert sniper, and I've built pipe pistols from scratch. I have over a million kills under my belt, over two hundred thousand of those headshots.

In video games.

None of that virtual experience prepared me for the sensation of holding a real-life gun in my bare hands for the first time ever. Raiden had made me take off my gloves, claiming I would get a better feel for the pistol without them. The handgun was heavier than I'd expected. The plastic grip was cold, the texture rough against my palms. I was terrified of letting my index finger get anywhere near the trigger.

"It's a Glock 19," Raiden told me a moment after handing me the gun. "Compact, lightweight, and very reliable," he added.

"OK . . ." I held the gun awkwardly, wrist limp. It didn't feel all that lightweight to me.

Raiden had gone out to run our pre-breaking-and-entering errands on his own, having left me with specific instructions on where and how to flee should the bad guys happen to find our hotel room while he was out. Luckily, that had proved to be a non-issue.

I'd spent the hour and a half that he was gone peacefully researching both Rome's catacombs and Castel Sant'Angelo, our planned entry point to the tunnels beneath the city. Guns were powerful, but so was knowledge.

"There's no safety, and it's loaded with a full magazine," Raiden explained. "It takes 9mm rounds, in case you ever find yourself in a situation where you need more ammo and I'm not there." His shoulder brushed mine as he knelt beside my chair at the little table and gently removed the pistol from my grasp.

I flinched infinitesimally at the contact, then held my breath, hoping he hadn't noticed my reaction. I was still jumpy about being touched, even by him and even after everything that had happened between us the previous night—even more so when my gloves were off. After nearly two decades of avoiding all physical contact with people, I doubted my aversion to touch would go away anytime soon. And while I didn't technically need the gloves while wearing the regulator, I'd grown so used to wearing them that their absence distracted me.

With my next breath, I forced myself to inhale and exhale slowly, easing some of the tension in my muscles.

"All you have to do is chamber a round," Raiden said, thankfully oblivious to my flinch. "Just rack the slide"—he pulled back what I assumed to be the "slide" on the top part of the gun—"and then you're ready to fire."

He pressed a tiny button on the side of the handle that released the loaded magazine and set it on the table beside my computer, then pulled the slide back once more. A bullet popped out, landing on the table with a metallic clunk. Within seconds, he loaded the round back into the magazine and slid the whole thing back into the pistol's handle.

"There'll be some kick when you fire, so be sure to use both hands," he said, demonstrating by gripping the handle with one hand—index finger held parallel to the trigger—and cupping the butt of the handle with the palm of his other hand. "And don't stick your arms straight out in front of you, especially when going through doorways or around corners. You want to keep your weapon close." He bent his elbows, bringing the gun closer to his shoulder while keeping his overall posture strong. "Otherwise it'll be easy for your opponent to knock it out of your hands, and then you'll likely end up a statistic—shot with your own weapon."

Once Raiden was done with his spiel, I leaned away, just a little, and eyed him skeptically. "And you really think this is wise—giving *me* a gun with no safety?" I said. "What if I accidentally shoot my foot off? Or my *face*?"

The corner of Raiden's mouth quirked, like he was holding in a laugh, and he raised one eyebrow, giving me an appraising look. "Don't be an idiot, and you should be fine." Though the exchange was light-hearted, his amusement never reached his eyes. He shifted his grip so he was holding the pistol by its short barrel and held it out to me, handle first. "Don't worry—you'll get used to it."

Tentatively, I took the pistol. "Thanks," I said and placed the loaded gun on the table, pointing toward the window, away from both of us.

Raiden nodded and stood, giving my shoulder a squeeze before returning to his backpack, resting on the foot of my bed. The bag had been nearly empty when he'd left to run his errands; now, it was a lot closer to full, and the small arsenal was heavy enough to make the mattress dip significantly. I was afraid to ask what other, deadly things he'd acquired while he was out. Plenty, from the looks of it.

I was even more afraid to ask him why he thought we would need so much artillery. So, I kept my mouth shut.

Raiden pulled another pistol from the bag—this one was larger, with a barrel that widened immediately after the trigger guard, making it appear front-heavy—and popped the magazine free. He gave it a quick check, then snapped it back into the gun, glanced at something on the side—the safety, I guessed—and lifted his shirt, stuffing the gun barrel-first into the front waistband of his jeans, just behind his belt buckle. Seemed like a dangerous place to keep a loaded weapon, especially for a guy, but what did I know?

"Ready?" Raiden asked, hoisting the heavy backpack onto his shoulders.

I closed my laptop and pushed my chair back. "As I'll ever be," I said, standing. I picked up the handgun lying on the table beside my computer. "What do I do with this?" I glanced down the length of my body, giving myself a quick once over; my jeans and T-shirt were too snug to give me anywhere to conceal the weapon.

"Put it in your bag for now," Raiden said. "You can take it out once we're below ground."

My bag. Right. I would need somewhere to stow my mom's journal, anyway, and I wasn't about to leave behind the mysterious orb, even if I still had no idea what it was or why it had affected me so strangely when I touched it back on Orcas Island, what felt like an eternity ago.

I set the gun on the bed beside my bag, then pulled a hooded sweatshirt on over my head. I pushed up the sleeves, put on my gloves, then pulled the sleeves back down, just as I'd done a thousand times before.

While I loaded up my backpack, Raiden phoned the lobby, requesting a cab. The car arrived within minutes, and once Raiden spotted it pulling up in front of the hotel, we left the room and headed downstairs. I was a little dubious about climbing into another hired car after what happened the last time, but Raiden didn't seem concerned, so I kept my worry to myself.

Castel Sant'Angelo wasn't far from our hotel—maybe a mile. But I never would have guessed it was so close based on how long it took the cab driver to get us there. Either we had hit the mid-morning rush hour, or Rome had a serious traffic problem. Based on the fact that the city hadn't been designed for automobile traffic, I was betting on the latter. Really, it probably would have been faster to walk, but at least this way we were less exposed.

Our cab approached Castel Sant'Angelo from the back some twenty minutes after leaving the hotel. The impressive structure consisted of four sides of imposing stone walls surrounding a massive circular tower that had been built up over the centuries, so high that it had once been the tallest building in Rome. Even now, it stood tall among the buildings surrounding it. But then, Rome wasn't exactly a city filled with skyscrapers.

From my research that morning, I'd learned that while Castel Sant'Angelo looked like a medieval fortress, what with its high stone walls, defensive parapets, and strategic corner towers, the oldest parts of the structure had been built by the ancient Romans. Castel Sant'Angelo started its life in the second century AD as a mausoleum to house the bodies of Emperor Hadrian and his family. Centuries later, it was built up and converted into a fortress, then turned into a papal castle, and even functioned as a prison, for a time.

There was a fortified, above-ground passageway called the Passetto di Borgo that connected the fortress to Vatican City by way of Saint Peter's Basilica—a leftover from Castel Sant'Angelo's papal castle days. It would have been a perfect inroad for us if the passageway wasn't patrolled regularly or heavily guarded on the Vatican end. But, according to the internet, it was both patrolled and guarded, making it a non-viable entry point.

"I take you to the front," the cab driver said as we slowed to a stop—traffic. "You enter Castel Sant'Angelo there."

I craned my neck, taking in the endless line of cars stopped ahead of us. At this rate, it would definitely be faster to walk.

Castel Sant'Angelo was right there, directly ahead. We would only be out in the open for a few minutes.

Apparently, Raiden agreed that the brief exposure was worth the risk. He extended his hand between the front seats, a bundle of Euros pinched between his index and middle fingers. "Grazie," he said, and when the driver reluctantly accepted the bills, pushed his door open.

I fumbled with my door handle, murmured a quick thanks to the driver, and hopped out. I jogged around the rear of the car to join Raiden.

"I'm not exactly sure where to go once we're inside," I told him as we stepped onto the sidewalk that bordered the fenced-off park-like landscaping surrounding Castel Sant'Angelo.

Raiden set a fast pace, pulling ahead of me, and I sped up to rejoin him.

"I couldn't find any mention of catacombs associated with this place online," I added, not quite jogging, "unless the original mausoleum structure counts . . ."

"We go down," Raiden said, scanning everything around us.

I rolled my eyes. "Well, obviously . . ."

A street peddler started toward us, a multi-colored bundle of selfie sticks gripped in his hands like a bouquet of flowers. He plucked a blue one free as he drew near.

"No," Raiden told the guy, voice firm.

The peddler turned his attention to me, thrusting the selfie stick directly in my path and smiling while nodding. He skip-walked alongside me.

I smiled and shook my head, but the interaction only seemed to encourage him.

"No!" Raiden repeated, then grabbed the blue selfie stick, yanking it clean out of the man's grasp. Without missing a step, he chucked it over the fence.

The peddler's face fell as he tracked the arch of his now-lost selfie stick. It landed on the grass a dozen feet away, out of reach unless he wanted to buy a ticket into Castel Sant'Angelo. He stopped following us and stood at the fence line, shoulders slumped and bouquet of remaining selfie sticks drooping to the ground.

"Was that really necessary?" I asked, glancing back at the peddler as we hurried along the sidewalk.

"He deserved it."

"You don't even know him," I argued.

Raiden glanced at me sidelong. "Another couple days in Rome and you would agree with me."

I pressed my lips together and narrowed my eyes. "You know, you're sure a lot grumpier than you used to be."

"Better grumpy than naïve," he said, resuming his endless scan of our surroundings.

My mouth fell open at the unexpected dig, but I snapped it shut and huffed out a breath through my nose. I stared ahead as we continued on.

We rounded a corner, heading straight for the Tiber River. I kept my annoyance to myself, figuring tension was to blame for making us both a little snippy. There was no saying what lay ahead. We could have spent weeks researching the catacombs, but I wasn't willing to wait a minute longer than was absolutely necessary. I needed to find my mom and figure out what, exactly, was happening to me. Who was Persephone, and why was she in my head? Had my mom known this would happen? Had she *wanted* this to happen? I needed to know.

We rounded one more corner, and the road we'd been following dead-ended against a wide, vendor-lined walkway, the Tiber River on one side, the imposing stone walls of Castel Sant'Angelo on the other. Stalls offering touristy wares were set up in a long line, the sunken, murky river just visible beyond the walls lining the walkway. Pedestrians stopped here and there to examine key chains, magnets, and tiny replicas of Rome's various attractions. It wasn't bustling, exactly, but it wasn't empty, either. If this was what March looked like, I could only imagine what this place would be like in the dead of summer, when the entire city was packed to the brim with tourists from all over the globe.

We veered to the right, heading away from the consumer promenade and toward the almost hidden entrance to Castel Sant'Angelo. A minimalistic blue banner printed with *CASTEL SANT'ANGELO* hanging over an arched opening in the fortress' exterior wall pointed the way.

Once inside, we followed the walkway between the exterior wall and the central tower to a small room built within the wall, where the ticket counter was located. We purchased two entry tickets, and headed deeper into the fortress. I grabbed a self-guided tour pamphlet along the way.

"Hang on," I said, unfolding the pamphlet and slowing to skim the map marked with numbers that correlated with a key naming the various notable sites within the fortress. None mentioned Hadrian or any of the original Roman structure's elements.

Chewing on my bottom lip, I stopped and looked up, studying the central tower. The various stages of construction were visible in the different materials used to heighten the broad, circular tower. I deconstructed the tower in my mind. Thanks to the internet, I knew that, like so many of the ancient monuments in the area, the lowest, oldest portion of the tower had long since been stripped of its decorative travertine shell, exposing the ancient, structural brick underbelly.

Raiden retraced his steps back to me.

I wandered closer to the tower wall and reached out, touching the exposed brick. "This would have been part of the mausoleum," I said, sliding my fingertips along the rough, weathered brick.

I slid my backpack off one shoulder and hauled it around to the front of my body. I unzipped the main pocket and pulled out my mom's journal, flipping it open to the two-page spread mapping out Rome's underground tunnels and catacombs. The small circle marking our entry point had been drawn in the middle of a clear square of underground tunnels. I traced the faint indentation made by the head of my mom's pen with the tip of my index finger.

Raiden stopped nearby, shading me from the midday sun.

"Hadrian's mausoleum was built on a square platform," I said, raising my eyes to meet Raiden's. I patted the brick wall. "This was on top of the platform, supporting a park-like mound of earth, and the actual burial chamber would have been at the very top of that mound, but people would have entered through the base."

I looked down at the cobblestone ground and gently stomped my left foot. "I think the original base is under here. And I'd bet *that's* what these tunnels are," I said, tapping my fingertip on the small square drawn on the page. "They must dive deeper underground, connecting to the ancient catacombs."

Raiden narrowed his eyes thoughtfully. "So, we just need to find a way into the original mausoleum."

I nodded. "I'm like ninety-nine-point-five percent sure."

Raiden took the tour pamphlet from me, eyes quickly skimming the numbered map. "I don't see anything about a mausoleum on here."

"I know," I said. "We're going to have to find it the old-fashioned way."

Raiden glanced at me, one eyebrow raised in question.

I flashed him a tight smile. "By looking."

28

The self-guided tour route took us to the top of the walls of Castel Sant'Angelo, where there was an excellent view of Rome, including Vatican City, before leading us into the central tower and, eventually, down into the belly of the fortress. It was cool and damp within the central tower, all sounds reverberating off the tufa walls in a hushed echo.

As we headed down a long, broad stairway, I guessed we were nearing ground level—or, at least, modern-day ground level. In many areas, the streets of Rome had been built up over the millennia.

The stairway intersected with an arched, brick corridor that seemed to follow the outer curve of the tower. To the left, the floor of the corridor gently sloped upward. To the right, it angled downward. The way down was roped off, and a sign proclaiming "USCITA" displayed an arrow pointing to the left, telling us to follow the dimly lit corridor back up to the exit.

I frowned. If the exit was further up, maybe we had actually dropped below ground level. I shot a quick glance at the dark, roped-off corridor that led deeper into the fortress, then looked at Raiden.

A family with two young boys was descending the stairs behind us, but nobody was following them. Once they were past us, we would be in the clear to venture off the beaten track.

I grabbed Raiden's arm and pulled him off to the side, out of the way of the family. I nodded to the darker, downward-sloping corridor. "I think this must lead to the ancient entrance," I whispered, face angled up toward Raiden, but eyes on the nearing family. "Our way in must be down there."

Raiden nodded once. I could feel his gaze skimming along the lines of my face, lingering on my lips before returning to my eyes.

I wasn't used to being looked at so intently. My cheeks heated, and I was grateful for the dim lighting, hiding my blush.

I smiled to the mom and dad as the family drew nearer, nodding a quick hello. Once they'd passed, we watched them head up the opposite passageway. The seconds ticked by agonizingly slowly, and I prayed to every higher power I could think of to stop anyone else from turning the corner at the top of the stairs and delaying us further.

"All right," Raiden finally said. "They're gone." In three long steps, he was over the cord roping off the descending corridor. He waved me on, beckoning me to follow.

I gulped, nerves drying out my mouth. I was about to sneak into a forbidden part of a museum; it would be the most illegal thing I'd ever done . . . unless you counted causing the boat crash. Or assisting Raiden in incapacitating the driver attempting to kidnap us from the airport. Or being the accomplice to a motorcycle-jacking. Those were all way bigger deals, but I'd been riding waves of pure adrenaline, then. This was planned. Intentional. Not a bad guy in sight.

And despite being a relatively minor transgression, I almost couldn't bring myself to cross that roped-off line.

"Cora," Raiden hissed. "Come on!"

I could hear voices echoing from above. People were

drawing near to the top of the stairs. In a few seconds, they would round the corner and see me.

With a squeak, I turned and ran toward the rope, practically leaping over it, and rushed past Raiden, deeper into the sheltering darkness. I stopped when I could no longer see much of anything at all and figured I was just as likely to trip and break my neck as I was to find an entrance to the catacombs. More likely, probably.

"Cora," Raiden whispered, and I nearly jumped out of my skin. He was right beside me, but how he'd gotten there without me hearing him was beyond me. The man could move like a cat. A big, deadly, *manly* cat.

"Holy bejesus, Raiden!" I hissed. I huddled against the brick wall, clutching my chest and breathing hard. "How do you *do* that?"

"Do what?" he asked, voice hushed.

All I could do was shake my head. Not that he could see it.

Raiden was suddenly a lot closer. His body pressed against the side of mine, and his palm came to rest on my abdomen, holding me steady against the wall.

My stomach did a little flip flop, and my heartbeat thudded in my chest. My senses were on overload, and I was hyper-aware of everywhere Raiden was touching me. Despite the cool, damp air, I was suddenly roasting. I'd never been touched like this. Not even when we'd kissed. Not ever.

Part of me wanted to flee. It was too much. He was too close. But part of me wanted him closer. After a lifetime of going without physical contact with other people, I quickly seemed to be acquiring a taste for it. I savored it. Craved it.

"Quiet," Raiden said, his lips a hairsbreadth from my ear. His breath tickled the tiny hairs that had escaped from my ponytail, giving rise to goosebumps that started on my neck and spread down my back and chest until my whole body was covered.

I could hear footsteps on the stairs, punctuated by the rapid pounding of my heart. A burst of laughter from the passing group shattered the heavy quiet.

I jumped, heart leaping into my throat.

"Easy," Raiden breathed, his hand pressing more firmly against my abdomen.

Of course, his close proximity wasn't doing a damn thing to calm my nerves. By the time the group had passed and the sound of their footsteps had faded away, every cell in my body was awake and alert, and I was all but buzzing with nervous energy.

Raiden removed his hand and stepped away, and I had to suppress a whimper. Pathetic, I know.

I heard a gentle rustle, and felt his elbow brush mine as he unzipped his backpack. My eyes must've been adjusting to the darkness, because I was just able to make out his shadowy silhouette.

I watched him, eyes opened as wide as they would go. My breaths sounded insanely loud in my ears. I worked on slowing my breathing, making each inhale and exhale as quiet and controlled as possible.

"Here," Raiden whispered, tapping something against my arm. "It's a headlamp. Put it on, but don't turn on the light, yet."

My fingers fumbled with the device. I grabbed it by the stretchy headband and turned the whole contraption around in my hands until I found the hard, light-up part, which easily fit in my palm. Blindly, I fitted the headlamp onto my head, situating the light on my forehead, then stared at the dark shadow that was Raiden.

I wasn't positive but it looked like he was wearing something more substantial than a headlamp. Something that looked more like a mask with binoculars attached. Then my brain kicked in, and I realized what was on his head—night vision goggles. Duh.

My shoulders slumped a little. *I* wanted night vision goggles, but all I had was a lame-o headlamp.

"Come on," Raiden whispered, grabbing my arm. He tugged me deeper into the shadows.

We moved slowly, following the ramp downward. My footing wasn't very sure, and while Raiden might have been able to move as quietly as a cat at a regular pace, in my case, slow and steady meant quiet and undetected.

We weren't at it for long. It couldn't have been more than a minute before Raiden stopped, halting me alongside him. It was darker down here, and there was no longer enough light even to make out his silhouette.

I looked at him—or at least, where I sensed he was. "What is it?" I asked, voice barely audible. "What do you see?"

"A wall," Raiden said. His grip slid down my arm to my wrist, and he guided my hand out ahead.

My fingers touched cool stone. Even through the thin leather of my gloves I could tell the wall ahead was covered in a film of something that was both somewhat sticky and slightly slimy.

"Gross," I murmured, pulling my hand free and bringing my fingertips up to my nose for a sniff. The grime smelled earthy and musty. Figuring it was mold, I wiped my hand on the side of my pants.

"The walls down here are stone, but this one is brick," Raiden told me. "Looks like it was added later . . ."

I frowned. Once upon a time, this might have led up from the ancient entrance to Hadrian's mausoleum, but it wasn't a passable route any longer.

"Does the wall look new, or old?" I asked. The mold made me think old, but I wanted to be sure before I let my hopes rise too high.

"Definitely not new," Raiden said.

I smiled to myself.

"That's a good thing?"

I nodded, knowing he could see it thanks to his fancy eyewear. "My mom still marked this place as having an entrance to the underground. If this wall isn't new, then it's not blocking the entrance she used. There's another way into the tunnels."

"And by 'in,' you mean 'down,' right?" Raiden clarified.

"Yeah . . ." I narrowed my eyes. "Got something in mind?"

"Would a sewer grate qualify as a potential access point?"

My slight smile broadened to a grin. "A sewer grate would be a *perfect* access point."

The Catholic Church was notorious for co-opting ancient sacred sites and converting them to serve a purpose that benefitted them. Centuries ago, when the church first started modifying this site, they wouldn't have held much regard for the ruins of Hadrian's tomb. This ancient monument had merely been a convenient and defensible place for the pope to set up shop. If the modifications included converting the lower part of the ancient structure into something akin to a sewer, then so be it.

"All right," Raiden said. "Stay here. I'll be right back." I heard his first few retreating footsteps, then nothing.

As I waited for him to return, I quickly grew unsettled. Down here, in the absolute darkness, I felt unbalanced and paranoid. Every whisper of a sound, every gentle movement in the air—both real and imagined—intensified the feeling until I was certain I was being watched and half-convinced I would be attacked at any moment.

"All right," Raiden said, mere feet away.

I yelped, stumbling backward until my shoulder hit the sticky-slimy brick wall. I slapped my hands over my mouth just as Raiden's fingers curled around my upper arms.

"Hey," he murmured. "It's just me." He rubbed his hands up and down my arms.

I knew that—in my head—but my body wouldn't stop shaking.

Raiden pulled me away from the wall and wrapped his arms around my shoulders, hugging me close. He rested his cheek on top of my head. "I'm sorry," he whispered. "I didn't mean to scare you."

I wanted to relax, to accept the comfort he was offering me, but I was too on edge.

Raiden didn't relent. He held me more tightly against him, his hand rubbing gentle circles against my back underneath the backpack. "I'm sorry," he repeated.

Ever so slowly, the shaking subsided and instinct took over, allowing my muscles to relax and my body to ease into his.

"Are you all right?" he asked, loosening his hold so he could pull back a little. His knuckles brushed over my cheek ever so gently.

I nodded, not fully trusting my voice at the moment. My heart was pounding in my throat.

"All right." His lips brushed against mine ever so softly, and then he released me, letting one hand slide down the length of my arm until he found my hand. His fingers engulfed mine, warm even through the leather gloves. "You'll be able to turn on your light soon," he said. "Follow me."

Like I had much of a choice. I was blind as a bat down here and, thanks to Raiden, more than a little weak-kneed.

Raiden led me back up the ramp about twenty paces, then stopped once more. "It's not too far of a drop," he said, voice hushed. "I'll lower you down, and then I'll follow." He led me forward one more step. "Feel along the ground in front of you with your foot. Find the edge of the opening."

Following his instructions, I tapped my toe in a slight arch in front of me, then extended my leg out farther and started back the other way. And almost fell through the hole.

I squeezed Raiden's hand, using it to help me regain my balance. Taking a deep breath, I inched closer to the opening.

"Sit on the edge and dangle your feet into the hole," he said.

I crouched, easing down onto my butt. "What's down there?"

"Some standing water, some mold, probably rats and roaches . . . nothing too crazy." As he spoke, I could hear him moving around to the other side of the opening. "Give me your hands," he said. "I'll lower you down."

I reached out, searching for him blindly. His fingers wrapped around my wrists, gripping me tightly through the leather of my gloves. I did the same to him, though my hold didn't feel nearly as effective.

"Is this hurting your arm?" he asked.

I shook my head. "It doesn't hurt at all, anymore."

"Good," he said. "Scoot forward."

I stared at the place where he would have been could I have seen anything at all. "Please don't drop me," I whispered.

"Never," Raiden said, voice filled with conviction.

Putting all of my trust in him, I scooted forward, sliding off the edge and dropping into the dark abyss. The soles of my boots touched water first, then solid ground.

"All right," I told Raiden. "I'm down. You can let me go."

His hands slipped free from mine.

And then I heard the most terrifying sound I could think of: the clang of metal on stone as Raiden dragged the iron grate shut overhead.

He was shutting me in. Trapping me down here. Alone.

29

I stood in the mausoleum-turned-sewer, boots soaking up the drainage water and whatever other sludge was mixed in, totally stunned. My heart drummed a quick staccato, and my breathing picked up until my ragged breaths were all I could hear.

Raiden—I'd trusted him implicitly. Not once had I second-guessed his intentions or feared he would do anything that could even remotely count as a betrayal, all because we'd grown up together. Because I had feelings for him. Because he had feelings for me, or so I'd thought. The idea that I couldn't trust him had never crossed my mind.

And now I was stuck in absolute darkness in the mausoleum tunnels beneath Castel Sant'Angelo with nothing but a headlamp and a backpack full of random, useless things.

The headlamp!

Frantically, I raised a hand to my forehead and felt around the front portion of the headlamp, searching for a way to turn on the light. I found a small, soft button on the top and pressed it. The beam of light that flared to life was so bright that it blinded me for a few seconds.

As my vision returned, I squinted and looked up at the grate.

Raiden dropped down, his boots making a splash in the murky standing water.

I stared at him, utterly dumbfounded.

He was still wearing the night vision goggles, making him resemble some kind of high-tech, robo super-soldier. He extended his arms overhead, reaching for the iron grate, which covered one-third of the hole. He wasn't quite tall enough, his fingertips barely able to skim the bottom of the grate. With a heavy exhale, he lowered his arms, pressing one hand against his side and wincing slightly. All of the exertion must have aggravated his rib injury.

Raiden looked up and around, then turned his attention to me. He flinched, angling his face away from me and flipping up his night vision goggles.

"Ow . . ." He closed his eyes, rubbing his eyelids for a few seconds, then looked at me again, his eyes narrowing as he shielded his face from the light of my headlamp. "What?" he said. "What is it? What's wrong?"

I realized my mouth was hanging open, and snapped it shut. "I thought—" I shook my head.

It seemed ridiculous now. Of course he wouldn't toss me down into some underground ruins only to abandon me moments later. This was *Raiden*, after all. He would never betray me.

"Never mind," I said. "It doesn't matter."

His eyes narrowed further. "Right . . ." He didn't believe me. Probably because I was a big fat liar.

This mattered. Me doubting him mattered. After everything he'd done to keep me safe. After he'd voluntarily left behind the normal, sane world for the insanity that had become my life. What was *wrong* with me?

Raiden reached up, removing his night vision goggles completely. "So where to now?" he asked as he returned the headset to his backpack and pulled out a second headlamp, identical to mine.

I blinked a couple times, then finally snapped out of my stupor. "Oh, um . . ." I pulled one arm free from my backpack's shoulder straps and twisted the bag around to the front of my body. I unzipped the main pocket and dug out my mom's journal.

"Why don't you grab your Glock while you're in there," Raiden suggested. He fitted the headlamp around his head and turned on the light.

I looked at him for a moment, still unable to believe I'd thought he'd betrayed me. Guilt twisted in my gut, and ashamed, I returned my attention to my bag. I tucked the journal under my arm, holding it to my side with my elbow, and stuck my hand back into the bag to fish around for the handgun. I found the Glock at the very bottom of the bag and pulled it out. Gun held limply in hand, I looked at Raiden, unsure what to do with it.

"Pants," he advised. "Front or back of your waistband. Your choice. It's not chambered, so you should be safe enough from accidentally shooting yourself."

I stared at him for a moment longer. "Gee, that's super reassuring."

Raiden shrugged. "Unless you have another idea . . ."

With a breathy, exasperated laugh, I tucked the barrel of the Glock into the front waistband of my jeans, not entirely certain I wasn't about to blow off some or other necessary extremity. I zipped up my pack and resituated it on my back, then opened up the journal to the two-page spread displaying a map of the Roman underground tunnels.

"All right, if we're here," I said, pointing to the tiny circle marker drawn along the square of tunnels underneath the old fortress, "then we need to head this way"—I traced my finger along one side of the square, leading away from the circle marker—"which should be north." Brow furrowed, I looked first up the tunnel, then down the other way before focusing on Raiden. "Which way is north?"

"Good question," he said, raising his arm and turning his

wrist so he could see the face of his watch. It was one of those huge tactical watches with a million features. After a moment, he turned to the right and pointed up the tunnel. "North is that-a-way."

I glanced down at the map once more, studying the series of turns we would need to make coming up—left, then a quick right, then straight, right, left, left, right—and then we *should* be within Vatican City's borders . . . assuming this map was accurate and up-to-date. These tunnels and catacombs were ancient; there was no saying what state they were in, now, even if they'd been passable whenever my mom had drawn the map.

The only reassurance was knowing she'd made it into the vault—and back out—mere weeks ago. She must have used the underground passages, which meant there *was* a passable route.

I shut the book and tucked it back into my pack, then resettled the backpack on my shoulders. "This way it is, then," I said, heading up the passageway.

The tunnel was relatively featureless, the walls made up of large, roughly rectangular stones stacked in an offset bricklayer's pattern and curving overhead into an arched ceiling. Other than the several inches of standing water and the musty mildew smell, the nearly two-thousand-year-old passageway was in excellent condition.

I could hear Raiden following close behind me. The sound of sloshing water echoed off the ancient stone walls. Even he couldn't move silently down here. My socks were already soaked, making an additional squelching sound with each step.

As we approached the end of the tunnel, turning left was our only option. I paused at the corner and peered down the new tunnel. It looked much the same, other than the person-sized opening on the right-hand side some ten paces in. The opening itself was about six feet tall and two feet wide, supported by a red brick archway that looked out of place among the imperfect stone blocks, almost like it had been added later.

"This way," I said, shooting Raiden a quick glance over my shoulder, then heading straight for the opening in the wall.

I stopped when I reached the archway and skimmed my gloved fingertips over the brick. It was only a little slimy from whatever strain of mold favored these dank, dark tunnels. I looked back at the passageway beneath the fortress, then ahead at the narrow tunnel on the other side of the arched opening. It wasn't new, not by any definition of the word, but it was *newer* than the mausoleum passageway.

The walls were rough and uneven, with long, deep chisel marks cut into the stone, as though the route had been carved through the very bedrock.

"It's like someone added this to connect two separate tunnel systems." I looked at Raiden. "Like someone wanted to make the tunnels under Rome a usable way of getting around the city."

"It would certainly make getting around the city *unnoticed* a lot easier," Raiden said.

I nodded, thoughts wandering. My mom had known about this addition to the catacombs—known it was a viable route. Had the Custodes Veritatis done this? Were these *their* tunnels?

I touched the handle of the gun lodged in my waistband, reassuring myself that it was still there.

"We can always turn back," Raiden reminded me.

I shook my head. "No going back," I said, stepping through the archway and into the narrower passage. I was done with running. Done with hiding.

It was time to face the monsters lurking in the dark.

30

"This doesn't make any sense," I said under my breath, pausing in the middle of a long corridor lined with regular recesses for the decrepit bodies of ancient Christians.

The narrow, rectangular grave cubbies were stacked four-high, and the walls were coated in a thick layer of decaying plaster that had crumbled away in places to reveal the brick beneath, like flesh pulled open to reveal bone. The air was stale and slightly musty, but at least it didn't carry the sour taint of mildew like it had in the earlier tunnels.

We had already traversed this corridor from one end to the other and were retracing our steps on our second pass. Broken, shriveled cobwebs swayed as we passed, disturbing the air. They filled the recesses so densely, it was almost impossible to see the skeletal remains hidden within.

But we'd only broken a few webs in the corridor itself. Someone had been here recently. I was convinced that the 'someone' in question was my mom.

And yet, I couldn't figure out where to go from here. The map in the journal clearly showed a right turn near the corridor's midpoint, which would bring us into the catacombs beneath

Vatican City. I turned one way, shining my light up the corridor until I could see the place where it ended in a dead-end, then back the way we'd come originally, to the "T" where we'd taken our final left turn. I was standing as close as I would get to the midpoint without resorting to counting paces, but there was clearly no opening in the wall to my right. This was the first time the map had been wrong.

I placed my hands on my hips, one gripping the journal, the other balled into a fist, and stared at the crumbling plaster coating a pillar between two columns of recesses. Maybe there was some trick to it—some secret latch that would trigger a part of the wall to open up or . . . or *something*.

"You're sure this is the right spot?" Raiden said, the light from his headlamp joining mine on the wall.

I raised the journal and opened it to the page marked by my index finger. I retraced our route from Castel Sant'Angelo to our current location. There was a clearly marked circle right where we were standing, just like there'd been at Castel Sant'Angelo, where we had entered the tunnels through a drainage grate. That was the only other spot along our route marked by a circle. All of the other turns had been obvious.

"It's hidden," I whispered, closing the journal and tucking it under my arm as my eyes scoured the wall.

The light from Raiden's headlamp shone on me. "What do you mean?"

"Like the grate," I said. "I think that's what the circle means —the way through isn't going to be obvious. We have to find it."

I focused on the cubbies in the wall. There was no saying what was behind all of those cobwebs.

"Hold this for a sec," I said, handing Raiden the journal.

Hands freed, I squeezed between him and the wall and placed my foot on the bottom lip of the second lowest recess. Gripping the lower edge of the top recess, I hoisted myself up, coming face to face with a cobweb-coated skull. The plaster beneath my boot crunched as it crumbled under my weight, but the underlying brick held strong.

"Don't mind me," I said softly as I reached over the skeleton, pushing through the dense weave of long-abandoned spiderwebs until my fingers brushed the rough plaster wall at the very back. I was immensely grateful for the thin barrier of leather preventing me from feeling the tickle of the cobwebs against my skin. I traced my fingertips around the outer edge of the back wall, searching for any hint of a crack or opening.

I found none.

After a quick sweep across the center of the wall, I pulled my arm back and hopped down.

Raiden stared at me—or rather, at my arm—his expression a combination of sheer horror and near-vomit disgust.

I glanced down at my arm. My glove was coated in a thick layer of sticky cobwebs. I looked from my arm to Raiden and back, and grinned mischievously. "What's wrong?" I asked, reaching out with my cobwebbed hand. "Is wittle Waiden afwaid of a wittle spiderweb?"

Raiden took three skittering steps backward. "Uh uh. Do *not* touch me with that thing."

I wiggled my fingers at him and watched him shiver. Big, tough Raiden really was afraid of spiderwebs. No wonder he'd wanted me to go first through this part of the catacombs.

Laughter bubbled up my throat and burst out of my mouth. I covered my lips with my clean hand to hold it in, but the first bouts of laughter continued to echo off the walls up and down the tunnel, softening to an eerie howl that sounded so creepy it made *me* shiver. The sound continued longer than I ever would have imagined, making the hairs on my arms and the back of my neck stand on end and drowning out any remaining humor.

After a long, watchful stare down the length of the catacomb, I exchanged a quick look with Raiden, then turned back to the wall, less eager to violate the deceased's resting place than before. I quickly searched the middle two recesses just as I had the top one, then dropped to my knees to search the bottom recess.

I felt the difference immediately. The cobwebs didn't break. In fact, I was fairly certain that they weren't cobwebs at all.

The webbing here seemed to be made of some sort of ultra-thin, silken elastic material, like something someone might use for a high-end Halloween decoration. It wasn't remotely sticky, like the other cobwebs.

"It's fake!" I exclaimed quietly, craning my neck to look up at Raiden even as I reached deeper into the cubby.

Raiden knelt beside me, bowing down to look into the webbed recess.

The back wall wasn't where I'd expected it to be, and I thought I may just have found the opening. We would have to crawl through. I felt a momentary pang of pity for Raiden, but it faded quickly; at least these webs weren't genuine.

I placed my right hand on the floor of the recess to steady myself and reached further in until my entire upper body was hovering over the resident skeleton. The fingers of my left hand skimmed the back wall, and my heart sank. This wasn't the way through, after all.

I started to pull out of the recess.

Something skittered over the back of my right hand, something large enough that I could feel it through the leather glove, and I shrieked. Reflexively, I swapped hands, slamming the other down to support me as I shook out the one violated by some unknown form of creepy-crawly. My palm landed directly on the skull of the departed.

The skull gave a little under my weight. It didn't break; it sank into the floor.

I froze.

There was a faint *click*, the entire floor of the recess dropped, and I was falling.

I screamed. I couldn't help it.

The scream ended with a grunt as I hit solid ground. I landed on my shoulder and hip, the impact sending twin bursts of pain through my body and pushing the air out of my lungs. I lay there for several seconds, simply trying to regain my breath.

"Cora!" Raiden called from above. "Cora, are you all right?"

It seemed to take forever, but I finally managed to suck in a breath. Groaning, I rolled onto my back as far as I could without crushing my backpack and stared up at the opening in the ceiling maybe six feet overhead. I could see the light from Raiden's headlamp through the mass of fake cobwebs, but I couldn't make out his face. The trap door hung down from the ceiling, swinging gently, skeleton and all. Apparently that was fake as well.

"Yeah," I said, voice hoarse. "I think I'm all right." I rolled my shoulder forward and backward, then gingerly touched my hip. Both were tender, but nothing seemed to be broken. "I'm all right," I confirmed.

"Good," Raiden said. "Let me see if I can figure out how to reset the trap door. I'll be down in a minute."

"No prob," I said as I shifted onto my hands and knees. I grabbed the handle of the Glock, resituating the gun in my waistband, then stood and took a few cautious steps, staring down at the floor as I checked the stability of my hip. It had taken the brunt of the fall and was definitely sore, but my leg still felt sturdy enough. I had no doubt that, in a few hours, the bruise would be magnificent.

I tried to wipe the spiderwebs off my gloves, but the webbing was too sticky. Sighing, I pulled off the gloves and tucked them into my back pocket, then turned my attention to the new tunnel.

It was a long corridor, which was nothing new, but the walls were covered in brightly colored frescoes depicting what, at first, I thought were various biblical scenes, what with all of the saintly figures standing with golden halos behind their heads. But I didn't recognize a single scene from either the Old or New

Testaments. I frowned, figuring these were scenes honoring some long-dead saint or martyr.

My fingertips skimmed over a gold-leafed halo that glimmered in the light from my headlamp. Only the Catholic Church could have protected these frescoes from damage or the gold inlay from looters over the centuries. I was no expert on Christian art, but even I could tell these frescoes were ancient and priceless. We *had* to be within the Vatican's territory now.

I didn't recognize any of the artwork from the research I'd done on the catacombs beneath Vatican City, so I figured we were in the secret portion, beneath the Vatican Library, the part that belonged to the Custodes Veritatis, exclusively.

I moved down the corridor slowly, studying the elaborate friezes painted on the walls. The bright, cheerful colors and luminous gold leafing felt out of place in this secret, underground space. The images were so beautiful—so intricate—it was a shame that they were hidden down here, where so few could appreciate them.

Every ten yards or so, unlit torches rested in wrought iron wall sconces straight out of the middle ages, and I wondered when they'd been lit last. The stone behind and above the torches was black with soot from frequent burning, a sign that these passages were still in regular use by the Order.

Up ahead, the corridor ended with a sharp right corner maybe sixty yards away. I'd memorized the map my mom had drawn of the Order's secret underground lair, and I was fairly certain I would find the vault door at the end of the next corridor, just around the corner ahead.

I glanced over my shoulder, peering back at the hole in the ceiling. Raiden was still up in the catacombs, messing with the trap door.

I chewed the inside of my cheek. Surely it couldn't hurt to just take a peek around the corner, just to get a glimpse of the vault door. I would be doing my due diligence, really. How else would I be able to make sure we were alone down here?

Taking a deep breath, I drew the Glock from my waistband. My palms were sweaty, making my grip on the gun feel slick and slippery. I wiped first one hand on my jeans, then swapped gun hands and wiped the other.

As I made my way farther up the corridor, I imitated Raiden's cat-like prowl as best I could, though my pace was half as fast as his—and half as quiet. I paused to study the wall sconce for a moment—the torch appeared to be of the genuine, fire-burning variety and smelled of kerosene—and then I continued on my way.

I was nearing the end of the corridor, not more than a half-dozen paces from the corner, when I heard it—the distinctive beep of a two-way radio.

I froze, heart pounding.

And then I heard the beep again, followed by a low, masculine voice. It had come from up ahead. *Around* the corner.

A guard.

He was making his way up the passageway, toward me. He was speaking in Italian, and it took my brain a few seconds to translate his words.

"Seriously, guys, stop playing around. Who's down here?" After another radio beep, he continued, "I can see your light . . ."

Instinctively, I covered my headlamp with my hand, fingers frantically searching for the button to turn it off. A few seconds later, I found the button and pressed it firmly. The lamp went dark. Belatedly, I realized that single move probably gave me away as an intruder. Not that the guard wouldn't have figured out my shouldn't-be-here status soon enough, anyway . . .

The guard fell silent. Now that my headlamp wasn't flooding the corridor with artificial light, I could see the beam from his flashlight reflecting off the wall up ahead. It bobbed with each of his steady steps.

I inched backward, afraid to move any faster for fear of making noise. Which was stupid, because the guard already knew someone else was down here. Someone who very clearly didn't belong.

I shot a quick glance over my shoulder, looking for Raiden. But the trap door was still open, the corridor still empty.

My heart pounded, and my brain was screaming for me to turn and run as fast as I could. But something held me in place. Not fear. Something else. Something that made my heart pump faster and my breaths come quicker.

It took me a moment to recognize exactly what I was feeling —anticipation.

Thoughts that weren't my own flitted through my mind.

. . . stand your ground . . .

. . . take him out . . .

. . . shut him up before he has a chance to alert the others . . .

. . . you know what to do . . .

. . . do *it . . .*

. . . do it now *. . .*

I recognized the voice from my dreams. It was Persephone.

Feeling strangely out of body, I moved closer to the wall. Closer to the corner. It was like I was an avatar in a video game and someone else was dictating my movements through a controller. I couldn't do anything to stop myself. I wasn't sure I wanted to. I felt drunk with adrenaline, and the sensation was intoxicating. I wanted *more*.

I crouched down, setting the pistol on the floor behind me, then leaned forward, planting my hands on the cool stone. Muscles coiled and veins humming with tension, I waited. My lungs pulled air in, fueling my blood with oxygen. My senses sharpened, becoming laser-focused. I closed my eyes, listening to the guard's slow approach.

His breathing was harsh in the stillness of this place. The

sound of boots scuffing the stone floor was grating to my ears. I had a vivid mental picture of him creeping along the adjoining corridor. He was almost to the corner. Almost to me. Almost . . .

I opened my eyes. The instant the nozzle of his rifle peeked around the corner, I struck.

My hand shot out, and my fingers curled around the barrel of his rifle. I yanked on the gun, twisting it sharply.

The guard yelped as I pulled the rifle out of his grasp, tugging him around the corner in the process. Like it was second nature, I flipped the gun in my hands and smashed the butt into the guard's face.

His surprised expression went slack as his legs gave out, and he collapsed onto the floor, twisting slightly on his way down.

I flipped the rifle back around so the butt was tucked under my armpit, right where it belonged, and aimed the business end at the guard's forehead. My index finger hovered over the trigger, but I didn't squeeze.

I couldn't shoot him. It would give us away to the rest of the guards.

Slowly, I raised the nozzle of the rifle and shifted the gun so I was holding it across my body, eyes narrowing in thought. I needed to move the guard. To restrain and hide him. But *where*?

"Cora?"

I spun around, easily shifting the rifle back into the ready position.

Illuminated by the beam from the rifle's flashlight, Raiden stood directly beneath the trap door, one foot in front of the other, frozen mid-step. He raised his hands defensively. "Whoa . . . whoa . . ."

I blinked, my lips parting, arms locked and rifle aimed at Raiden's head. I was still in that strange, out-of-body state of mind. Not in control. For three long heartbeats, I was paralyzed, unable to lower the rifle, no matter how badly I wanted to.

I started trembling. The breath whooshed from my lungs, and

the tension drained from my muscles. I crouched down and practically dropped the rifle on the floor. I couldn't get it out of my
hands fast enough.

I stood and backed up a step, nearly tripping over the unconscious guard. I glanced down at him as I stumbled to the side,
hugging my middle.

Raiden closed the distance between us in a matter of seconds.
"For a moment there, I thought you were going to shoot me," he
said, stopping just out of arm's reach. He hesitated for only a
second before reaching out, gripping my shoulder, and pulling
me against him. His arms wrapped around me, engulfing me in a
snug embrace.

I felt tiny all of a sudden. Tiny, and safe.

I let out a breathy sound against his shirt that was part laugh,
part cry and curled my arms around his back. How was I
supposed to tell him that, for a second there, I'd thought I was
going to shoot him, too? How was I supposed to tell him I didn't
think I'd been the one holding the gun? That it had been my
hands, but it hadn't been *me*?

"You took down that guard?" Raiden said, more of a statement than a question.

I nodded against his shoulder. If he asked me how, I wouldn't
have an answer.

The same way I'd taken out the baddies on the boat and the
same way I'd bested him in the hotel room—in the mental
backseat, while someone else controlled my body. I'd heard
Persephone's voice; that had been a first. And it left me
wondering if she was the one who had been sliding into the
driver's seat, allowing me to do things I shouldn't have been
able to do.

"Are you all right?" Raiden asked, his arms loosening. He
stepped back, hands settling on my upper arms, and gave me a
quick, assessing once over.

I nodded. Physically, I was fine. Mentally and emotionally, I wasn't so sure. But we didn't have time to dissect what was happening to me right now.

I glanced down at the still unconscious guard. He wouldn't stay out forever.

The guard's radio beeped, startling me, and a tinny voice filled the corridor. "Matteo, check in, now," another guard demanded in Italian. "What is your status?"

I gulped and looked at Raiden.

"Do you know where to go from here?" he asked.

I nodded, not trusting my voice to work just yet, and shakily pointed to the corner ahead.

"All right, let's get moving," he said, releasing me and moving toward the guard. "Can you grab the guns?"

Raiden squatted, reaching for the guard's arm and thigh, and with a grunt, hoisted the not-so-small man onto his back in a fireman's carry. With another grunt, Raiden stood, making the whole thing look way too easy. He took a moment to adjust the guard's position on his shoulders, then shot a pointed look at the rifle on the floor before raising his gaze to meet mine.

I scurried to scoop up the Glock and stuffed it into the front waistband of my jeans, then headed for the rifle. It felt cold and heavy, and completely unfamiliar, and I held it awkwardly with both hands.

When I turned back to Raiden, he was already making his way up the passageway.

I hugged the rifle diagonally across my body, freeing one hand, and reached up to turn on the light on my headlamp, then followed Raiden.

"What are we going to do with him?" I asked, voice hushed. I glanced over my shoulder. Where there was one guard, there were sure to be more. Much as I hated the idea, it was time to consider abandoning the mission.

"Bring him into the vault with us," Raiden said. "Assuming we can even get in."

"Oh, right—the vault." Purpose rekindled, I rushed ahead, passing Raiden. I rounded the corner and skidded to a halt.

There it was. Right there. The door to the Order's vault.

It was nothing like I'd imagined. It was neither ancient nor ornate. It was plain and practical gray steel. The door looked out of place among all of the gold and bright colors painted on the walls.

A chill crept up my spine. My mom had been here mere weeks ago. I was moments from finding out if following my instinct to come here had been the right call.

Raiden rounded the corner and headed straight for the door, moving quickly despite his heavy burden, and I followed close on his heels. He stopped a few steps from the steel barrier and motioned to the door. "Be my guest, Cora."

I flashed him a nervous grin and stepped forward. The lock was strange, unlike anything I'd ever seen before. It reminded me of a puzzle from one of my games. It looked like a cryptex, made up of six steel inch-wide rings that spun around a horizontal axis, each ring marked by a series of ancient symbols. They were similar to the letters in the ancient Greek alphabet, but with some Cuneiform patterns mixed in, as well as some of the stylistic elements of Japanese characters. I recognized them both from my mom's journal and from my dreams. These symbols belonged to the Atlantean alphabet. *My people's* alphabet.

My fingers hovered over the rings. All I needed to do was line up the correct series of symbols.

"The journal," I said, glancing back at Raiden. "Where is it?"

"In my bag—the front pocket," he said, turning partway to give me access to his backpack.

I quickly unzipped the pocket and pulled out the journal, then flipped to the page displaying my mom's smaller map of these tunnels as well as the six-digit code. The steel dials clicked faintly as I spun them, the internal mechanism offering up more resistance than I'd expected. It took a few minutes, but finally I rolled the final symbol into place. It clicked quietly, and I held my breath.

A deep *clang* sounded from within the door, and a moment later, it cracked opened. I inhaled deeply and curled my fingers around the edge of the door.

I was seconds from entering the vault where my mom had found the regulator and the crystal orb.

And hopefully, where I would find some answers.

31

The vault door was incredibly heavy, opening slowly and silently. I stopped pulling when I had it a third of the way open, and I slipped through the opening into the vault. The beam of light from my headlamp cut through the darkness, a sweeping spotlight illuminating only where I looked.

The vault itself was as surprising as it was simple. The room was perfectly round, and smaller than I'd expected, maybe twenty feet in diameter. The single, curved wall was built of travertine bricks about the same size and shape as the standard cinder block. The only break in the stone wall was directly opposite the door, where a tall, narrow archway was built into the wall. It had the look of a doorway, but a single, heavy slab of stone blocked the way.

The floor, too, was travertine, though slabs of some darker stone had been inlaid into the floor in a series of concentric semicircles. The pattern tickled my mind, though I didn't know why.

Six stone pedestals stood around the periphery of the room, three on either side, each a perfect cylinder—none of the frills or embellishments typical to Roman construction. From the looks of it, each pedestal was a solid, seamless piece of travertine.

I set down the rifle, propping it against the wall directly to my right and moved closer to the nearest pedestal. I dropped to one knee and leaned in to get a closer look.

I raised my hand and ran my fingers over the surface of the pillar. The stone had been smoothed and polished to perfection, and markings had been carved in neat columns, a precise string of alien symbols running from the top edge of the pedestal all the way down to the floor. The symbols were clean and simple, like the pedestal itself.

As I stared at the writing, it started to make sense to my mind. What had been gibberish just a moment ago was suddenly clear as day.

. . . a doru can only be wielded by an empowered warrior from the Order of the Amazons. In the hands of anyone else, a doru is little more than a sturdy staff. The weapon is constructed of a collapsible shaft of orichalcum, rendering it nearly indestructible. The focus crystal at the top of the doru concentrates the Amazon's psychic energy, turning the doru into the most dangerous, powerful weapon ever created by the Olympians. The first doru was created by accident, when—

The sound of the door clanging shut interrupted my examination of the writing on the pillar. I twisted on my knee and watched Raiden set the guard on the floor, gently laying the man on his side.

Raiden shrugged out of his back pack and crouched down to fish around in the bag. After a few seconds, he pulled out a couple of long zip ties—military grade, no doubt. He proceeded to tie the guard's wrists together, then moved on to his ankles.

Placing a hand on my knee, I pushed up to my feet and turned back to the pedestal. A two-foot-long, golden rod no thicker than the circle made by my thumb and forefinger rested on the top of the pedestal in a groove that must have been carved just for it. I recognized it from the sketch in my mom's journal. A gracefully intricate pattern of curling and swirling lines had been carved along the length of the golden rod. A smooth, clear stone approximately the size and shape of an egg had been set into one end. With all of the decoration, the rod looked more like something a monarch would wield on the day of their coronation than any kind of weapon.

But this *was* a weapon—a *doru*, according to the writing on the side of the pedestal. An incredibly powerful weapon, but only when wielded by an *empowered* warrior of the Order of Amazons. I wasn't sure what "empowered" meant, but remnants of Persephone's memories from my dreams told me that was what she had been—an Amazon warrior.

And in my gut, I knew that this wasn't just any doru. This doru was *hers*. The same doru I—she—had wielded in the dream of her disastrous first contact with humans.

I reached out with one hand, running my fingertip along the length of the doru. It felt warm to the touch, and the clear stone —the focus crystal—slowly filled with an amber glow. When I pulled my hand away, the color faded from the stone. My frown deepened.

"That looks familiar," Raiden said, coming to stand beside me. He recognized it from my mom's journal. "Any idea of what it is?"

I glanced at him, then returned my stare to the doru. "It's a weapon," I told him.

"It doesn't look like a weapon."

"No," I agreed, "it doesn't." I finally managed to tear my stare away from the doru, curious about the items on display on the five other pedestals.

Planting my hands on my hips, I looked around the room, illuminating each pedestal with the beam from my headlamp.

Three of the pedestals were empty, including the remaining two on this side of the room.

As I made my way to the next pedestal, I could sense Raiden's stare following me, though he stayed put. A small depression had been carved into the top of this pedestal, just the right size and shape to fit my pendant. A pleased smile curved my lips. I was staring at the first bit of evidence confirming that I had put the puzzle pieces together correctly and that my mom really had come here, to this vault hidden beneath Vatican City.

I shrugged off my backpack and set it on the floor, crouching down beside it as I unzipped the smaller front pouch. I fished out the cell phone Raiden had given me, flipped it open, and selected the camera app. The phone was pretty basic, but it wasn't featureless.

Standing partway, I slowly moved around the pedestal, snapping pictures of the writing as I moved. We didn't have loads of time to lollygag in here. The quicker we looked around and got out—far away from both Vatican City and the Custodes Veritatis —the better. I could translate the writing later.

I finished with the pendant's pedestal, then moved on to the next. A perfectly round depression had been carved into the top, just the right size to fit the crystal sphere. I recorded the text written around that pedestal as well. I was about to move on again, when a phrase popped out from the mass of symbols: *consciousness orb*.

I straightened, phone hand dropping down to my side. "Of course," I breathed.

How had I missed it? I'd assumed Persephone's memories were being filtered into my mind from the regulator because the dreams had only started once I was wearing it. But I hadn't considered another possible source—the crystal sphere. When I first touched it, right before it knocked me unconscious, I would have sworn it had been filled with a swirling, incandescent blue mass. *Just* the first time. After that, the sphere had appeared empty, and touching it had been harmless.

Because Persephone's consciousness had already been downloaded into my mind.

"What is it?" Raiden asked, making his way across the vault toward me.

I blinked, looking at him. "It's . . ." I shook my head. "It's complicated. I'll fill you in once we're out of here."

Shaking off the shock, I hurried across the room to examine the three other pedestals.

One displayed a folded-up garment. Another displayed a perfectly smooth, six-by-six cube that seemed to be made of solid obsidian, or maybe onyx. The final was empty, only a three-inch-wide, disk-like depression remaining of whatever had been displayed there.

I photographed the pedestal displaying the garment from every angle as quickly as possible, then retrieved my bag from the other side of the vault.

Though I felt certain that the garment was ancient—as ancient as this chamber—the fabric felt soft and supple against my fingertips. I paused, garment in hand and brow furrowed, then shook my head and carefully folded it smaller before putting it in my bag.

I moved on to the pedestal displaying the cube, gently compressing the items in my backpack to make room. I set the bag down on the floor at the base of the pillar, made a quick circle around the pedestal, snapping pictures with my phone, then tucked the phone into my pocket and reached for the cube. The instant my fingertips made contact with the cube, it started to glow. A subtle, silvery light backlit intricate grooves carved into the stone, invisible to the eye until now.

I pulled my hands back a few inches, afraid to move more than that, and watched the cube glow brighter and brighter. And as it brightened, it started to hum.

"What did you do?" Raiden asked, rushing across the room toward me.

I shook my head, unable to look away from the glowing, humming stone cube.

The light was changing—shifting. It was bleeding away from the grooves, forming a very distinct, solid line that ran all the way around the artifact.

"Get back," Raiden hissed, grabbing my arm and pulling me away from the pedestal.

We made it three steps before the glowing and humming reached a crescendo. And then, abruptly, it stopped.

The cube went dark. Quiet.

We froze, staring at the cube, afraid to move.

With a click, followed by the distinctive hiss of a vacuum releasing, the stone cube split in half and opened.

I jumped, just a little.

"What the hell?" Raiden said, voice little more than a whisper.

Lips parting, I took a step toward the pedestal. This wasn't just a cube of stone. It was a *box*. And like Pandora, I felt compelled to find out what was inside.

Raiden stopped my forward momentum with the tight grip he had on my arm. "I don't know if that's smart . . ."

Behind us, came the very distinct metal clang of a heavy, steel lock disengaging.

Heart hammering, I spun around just as artificial lights flared on overhead and the vault door started to swing outward.

In the blink of an eye, Raiden had his handgun out and trained on the door.

A tall, lean man stepped through the doorway and into the vault. He had thinning blond hair, and pale skin lightly lined with age. He wore a tailored, slate-gray suit and had a distinctive air of confidence and authority. His expression was placid—serene, even—like he wasn't remotely surprised to find intruders in the vault. Like he'd been expecting us.

He stepped to the side, and four armored guards filed into the vault through the doorway, each armed, handguns trained on us. Or rather, on *me*.

For all intents and purposes, Raiden should have been the one drawing their potential fire. He was the one pointing a gun at them. He *should* have been the bigger perceived threat. And yet, all four guards were targeting me. I swallowed roughly, and licked my lips.

The man in the suit stepped forward, drawing my attention back to him. He opened his arms wide in the universal gesture of *welcome*, which struck me as odd. And then he smiled.

"An honor, truly, ancient one," he said, bowing his head. When he raised it again, his eyes fixed on me. "I've been waiting a very long time to meet you."

32

I was struck dumb, eyes opened wide and brow furrowed. Getting caught had always been a possibility, but being *welcomed*—that threw me off guard.

The man in the suit brought his hands together in front of his chest, fingertip to fingertip. "Did you know, I found Diana in much the same position just a few weeks ago . . ." It was clear that English wasn't his native tongue, but his accent was hard to pinpoint; it had a lilting, almost sing-song quality that made me think of Scandinavia.

I sucked in a breath to demand that he tell me where my mom was, right now.

"She managed to get away," the man said, cutting off my demands before I could utter a single word. "For a time . . ." He turned away from me slightly, clasping his hands behind his back, and made his leisurely way along the perimeter of the vault.

I turned with him, breaths slow and steady despite my pounding heart. I could feel Persephone in my mind, alert and ready. It was the most aware of her I'd ever been, and I knew that if she felt that she needed to take over, she would. And I wasn't sure I could stop her. At the moment, I wasn't sure I would want to stop her.

"We caught up with Diana later, of course," the man in the suit said, pausing at the pedestal displaying the doru, then glanced across the room to the garment's empty pedestal. He stared for a few seconds longer. I was blocking his view of the box, or I'd have bet he would have checked on it, as well.

"She, too, was a thief," he said, not even sparing me a glance as he continued his slow journey around the room. "Though I dare say, a better one than you."

I glanced at Raiden, but his attention was locked on the four guards spread out near the door. I spotted the rifle propped up against the wall, wishing I'd never put it down. A moment later, I remembered the pistol tucked into my waistband, hidden by my sweatshirt so long as I didn't move much. But it was as good as useless; by the time I drew it, one of the goons would put a bullet in me.

My gaze drifted to the doru.

According to the notes in my mom's journal, my people's alphabet had yet to be deciphered by the Order. Which meant that they hadn't been able to translate the writing on the pillars. It was unlikely that anyone would have guessed that the inconspicuous, ornate rod was actually a weapon. The guards likely wouldn't shoot me on the spot for reaching for a stick when they were armed with guns.

I knew first hand just how powerful the doru could be when wielded by the right hands. What I didn't know was whether *my* hands counted as the right hands.

I returned to watching the man in the suit, taking one tiny, test step toward the doru. Nobody seemed to notice my movement. Or, at least, they didn't seem to care. So, I took another step.

"Such a strange relationship, yours and Diana's," the man in the suit said. "She clearly views you as her daughter, and yet the two of you share no DNA. You aren't even of the same species." Brow furrowed, he shook his head, chuckling softly, like my relationship with my mom was some amusing curiosity. "*And yet,*" he said, "she would give her life for you."

I froze, breath held in my lungs, barely a quarter of the way to the doru. What was he implying? Was he saying that my mom was *dead*?

He sighed. "Diana will be glad to hear that you are all right . . . though less glad, I think, to learn that you are here."

I exhaled shakily. Relief flooded my body. I'd been preparing for the worst, but now I knew there was hope that she—that *we* —would make it out of this situation alive.

I was desperate to demand that the man in the suit tell me where my mom was, but I was fearful of drawing attention to myself. He seemed perfectly content to continue his bad-guy monologue while making his slow journey around the vault. How cliché. But, so long as it kept him distracted, I wasn't about to interrupt him.

I was mere steps from the doru when he stopped. He was almost directly across the room from me, his stare locked on the cube.

"It's a box," he said. "And you opened it." He looked at me suddenly, eyes widened by shock. "I'd long suspected there was more to the artifact, but now . . ." He shook his head. "How did you open it?" His eyes narrowed, stare going hard. "Tell me."

I opened my mouth, but I wasn't sure what to say—all I'd done was touch the thing—so I simply shook my head, shoulders rising in the slightest of shrugs. Until I had the chance to translate the writing on its pedestal, I would be as clueless as the Order was about the nature of the box.

"Unless it is not something you did," he said, thinking aloud. "It is who you are—or *what* you are. You are the key." He laughed, a feverish glint to his gray eyes. "I knew it! It will work

. . ." He glanced at the arched doorway blocked by a slab of stone, and let out another, shriller laugh. "It *will* work."

I had no idea what he was talking about. More than a little unsettled, I took another step toward the doru, bringing the weapon within arm's reach.

"You have been holding back on me," the man in the suit said. He wasn't talking to me, not anymore.

He was looking at Raiden—talking to Raiden. Like he *knew* him. And based on his words, it sounded a lot like Raiden had been feeding him information. Information about *me*.

I couldn't believe it. I wouldn't believe it. It couldn't be true. This was Raiden, after all.

My brows drew together, dread coiling in my gut. I shifted my gaze to the man I'd entrusted with my life. "What does he mean?"

Raiden's jaw was clenched, his shoulders stiff. For several long seconds, he didn't move. He didn't even breathe. But then he exhaled, and his shoulders drooped. He lowered his gun and bowed his head.

"Look at me," I said, voice cracking.

He closed his eyes.

"Look at me, Raiden," I demanded. "Look at me and tell me you're not working for them." My chin trembled as an invisible knife slid into my chest, puncturing my heart. "Raiden, please . . ."

Ever so slowly, Raiden shook his head. "I'm sorry, Cora," he said, finally opening his eyes and meeting mine. "I didn't have a choice."

"Oops," the man in the suit said. "I guess the cat is out of the bag now . . ."

So it was true. Raiden was working with the Order.

The knife in my chest twisted, shredding bits of my heart. I had no words. No breath. I was frozen in that moment, paralyzed by this revelation. By Raiden's betrayal.

Had Persephone suspected this? Was that why I'd initially thought he had trapped me under Castel Sant'Angelo, and why I'd had such a hard time lowering the rifle when it had been aimed at him? Had she seen the truth, where I'd been blind?

"Look in my head, Cora," Raiden said, taking a step toward me. "Like you did with the dream . . ."

"Not so fast," the man in the suit said, pulling a silver revolver out from a shoulder holster hidden within his jacket.

Raiden's only acknowledgement of the revolver was to stop moving, but his attention was still locked on me. "I know you can, Cora, so just do it. Then you'll see . . . you'll know . . ." There was desperation in his voice. "Do it, Cora," he begged. "Please!"

I stared at Raiden, tears streaking down my cheeks.

"What is Mr. Cross talking about?" the man in the suit said. "What does he mean?" But his demands went in one ear and out the other. He didn't matter, not right now. Not when faced with the reality of Raiden's betrayal.

Numbly, I pulled the regulator out from my T-shirt by the chain and traced my fingers around the amber stone, knowing that by the time I completed the circle, it would be glowing a brilliant, electric blue. And with the change in the stone's color, there would be a change within me, as well.

I just had no idea how extreme that change would be.

The instant my fingertip traced all the way around the stone, the mental floodgates opened. I was inundated with voices in my head, with thoughts and memories that weren't my own. I squeezed my eyes shut and clutched the sides of my head, knocking the headlamp clean off. One voice stood out above the others, the voice that had been there all along: Persephone.

. . . *surrender* . . .

I felt like I'd been fighting the current of invading thoughts, emotions, and memories for hours. For days. In reality, it had probably only been a matter of seconds. A matter of seconds, and in some ways, an entire lifetime.

Persephone's voice cut through the miasma, a lifeline yanking me out of the grip of deadly psychic undertow.

. . . surrender . . .

"I can't!" I wailed. Was she crazy? What was she thinking? If I stopped fighting the flood of thoughts and memories, they would drown me.

. . . surrender, and you'll be free . . .

I shook my head, hunching over and gasping for breath.

. . . surrender, and you'll regain control . . .

"How?" I gasped. I was desperate, fighting a losing battle and quickly running out of time, and Persephone's words weren't making any sense.

. . . stop fighting . . .

. . . let it in . . .

. . . let it all in . . .

She wanted me to stop fighting? Easier said than done. I'd been fighting my "condition" my whole life, to the point that preventing another "episode" had become my main goal. Fighting this—this *whatever it was*—had become second nature. It was more than habit; it was an obsession. The worst thing about my life had *become* my reason for being.

It was sad. And disturbing. And above all else, really damn pathetic.

I hated that fear had overtaken my life. That I had let it.

So, I listened to Persephone. On my next exhale, I relaxed my mental guards. I stopped fighting the foreign input inundating my mind. I let it in—the thoughts, the emotions, the memories. I let it *all* in.

And in doing so, I realized that it wasn't foreign at all. At least, not any more than the light my eyes processed or the sounds picked up by my ears. Like sight and hearing and touch, my "condition" was the furthest thing from the accursed illness

I'd always thought it to be—it was just another sensory inroad allowing me to perceive more about the world around me. Just another way for external data to enter my brain and be processed into something comprehensible. Just another sense. That was it. That was all it was.

And just like that, by surrendering for a single moment, something that had been a struggle my whole life became easy. It became natural.

I could feel anger and confusion, annoyance and heartbreak. And fear. So damn much fear. It saturated the room, thick and suffocating. Everyone was afraid. The goons were afraid of me, as was the man in the suit, though he was also intrigued by me, as well as slightly peeved. His name was Henry, and he was the head of the Custodes Veritatis—the Primicerius—and his carefully laid out plans were being derailed. He'd accounted for all the factors, or so he'd thought.

But he hadn't accounted for me. For Persephone. For what I —we—could do.

And then there was Raiden. He was the only one who wasn't afraid of me; he was afraid *for* me. He wanted to come to me, to hold me and to keep me safe, but he didn't want to die. I could sense that he wasn't afraid of death; rather, he was afraid of dying without purpose. He would welcome the quiet, the peace, but only if it came as a result of a worthy sacrifice. Dying to save his mom was first and foremost in his mind.

That thought struck a chord within me, and I followed it. I could sense that Emi was the reason for his betrayal. Henry had approached Raiden while he was on his way back from the bank, earlier this morning. Henry had shown Raiden a video of his mom, tied to a chair in the kitchen of Blackthorn Manor. In the video, she was bruised and bloody from hours of torture. Beaten and broken. But she was still alive, and she would remain that way, Henry had promised Raiden, so long as he delivered me to the Order.

Raiden had said no, at first. Refusing was what his mom would've wanted him to do. It was what he had been trained to do in the Army. No negotiating with terrorists. Never bargain with the bad guys, because they rarely held up their end of the deal.

But Henry had told him things—about me. About what he wanted from me. About what he wanted me *to do* for the Order. He had convinced Raiden that the Order didn't want to hurt me. That they didn't want to hurt his mom, or mine. That they didn't want any more pain or bloodshed. That he was sorry for it, but that it had all been necessary. That there was a bigger picture. That the safety of humanity—of the world—was at stake.

Henry had made Raiden believe. He'd had to; it was the only way to convince Raiden to help him. Because there was one other person in this world besides his mom who Raiden would die to protect.

Me.

Despite the betrayal, the knowledge that Raiden cared so deeply about me—as deeply as I cared about him—soothed the ache in my heart. I could see that he had wanted to confess the truth to me the whole time we were in the catacombs, but that he had been afraid doing so would trigger the alter-ego that had been emerging more and more frequently—the alien warrior woman who had taken him down in the hotel room. If he had tripped her survival instinct, he never would have gotten me here, and his mom's life would have been forfeit.

I understood why he did it—why he had been willing to trade my freedom for his mom's life. In his shoes, I probably would have done the same thing. His betrayal still hurt, but not like before. I had already forgiven him.

I straightened and lowered my hands, and when I opened my eyes, I sought out Raiden's face.

Except, he wasn't where I expected him to be. The situation had changed while I was wading through his mind.

Raiden was lying face-down on the floor, two of the guards holding him down. Henry stood just a few steps away from him, gun pointed at his head. The other two guards remained near the open door, handguns still trained on me.

"Here's what's going to happen," Henry said, glancing at me. "You are going to walk through that doorway"—he nodded toward the blocked stone archway—"and find your way through the labyrinth that lies beyond. And once you are through, you are going to bring me whatever you find at the end, or every single person you care about will die."

His threat triggered something within me. Within Persephone. In the moment between heartbeats, she took over, balling my hands into fists and gritting my teeth.

"No man gives me orders," I said, my voice sounding foreign to my own ears.

I grabbed the doru off the stone pedestal. The instant my fingers closed around the weapon, the ridges carved along its golden surface flared with the same electric blue light as the regulator's stone. I flipped the doru over the back of my hand, and when it was once again in my palm with my fingers curled around it, it was three times as long as it had been before. Now, it looked much more the weapon it was.

I twisted the doru around so one end was tucked under my arm, snug against my body, and aimed the glowing focus crystal at one of the guards restraining Raiden. A bolt of blinding, deadly energy shot out of the staff, blasting into the guard's chest. He flew back, slamming against the wall just a moment before a second burst of energy struck Raiden's other detainer.

I shifted my aim, locking on Henry.

But before I could get off another shot, the deafening crack of gunfire filled the room. A bullet struck the doru, knocking it out of my grasp, and the staff flew several yards away. It hit the wall with a clang, then clattered to the floor.

"Stop!" Henry shouted.

Ears ringing, I froze, very aware of the fact that the tide of the battle had turned against me. Against Persephone. Against *us*.

Raiden now knelt on the floor where he'd been laying before, hands raised as he stared down the barrel of the revolver.

The remaining guards still had their pistols aimed at me.

Persephone returned control to me, and ever so slowly, I raised my hands in surrender.

"If you have to shoot her," Henry said, "aim for a leg or an arm. We need her alive." He glanced my way, just for a fraction of a second, a tight, humorless smile curving his lips. "Now, ancient one, here is what is going to happen. You will enter the labyrinth. You will find your way through to the end, and you will bring me whatever you find in the final chamber. If you fail, you will die in the labyrinth—none who have entered the labyrinth have ever returned—and out here, Diana, Emiko, and Raiden will meet the same end."

I held in the hundreds of caustic remarks dancing on my tongue.

"But," Henry continued, "if you are successful, you will have earned my gratitude, as well as my mercy. Nobody else has to die today."

I cleared my throat. "What if there's nothing at the end of the labyrinth?"

Henry's cheek twitched. "That would be unfortunate, for all involved."

I pressed my lips together, reading his meaning loud and clear. If I reemerged from the labyrinth empty handed, my mom, Emi, and Raiden were as good as dead.

An errant thought slipped from Henry's mind to mine. He fully intended to follow through on his threat to kill my mom and Raiden, should I fail to comply, but not to kill Emi.

My eyes opened wide. Henry wasn't planning on killing Emi, because he didn't have her. The woman Raiden had seen on the video—the woman tied to a chair in the kitchen of Blackthorn Manor—wasn't Emi. It was a charade, a performance, convincing but *fake*. Emi had evaded the Order. They hadn't captured her. She was still out there, and they didn't know where.

"Raiden, they don't have your mom," I said in a rush. "It wasn't her on the video. It was a—"

"Shut up!" Henry shouted, punctuating his words by shifting his aim down to Raiden's thigh. He squeezed the trigger.

Once again, the crack of gunfire was deafening.

I slapped my hands over my ears even as I screamed, "NO!"

Raiden shouted out in pain and rolled onto his side, hands clamping down over the gunshot wound in his thigh.

I took a lurching step toward Raiden, but Henry turned his gun on me, halting me mid-step. He made a tutting sound with his tongue, then shifted his aim back to Raiden. "No medical attention for your friend, here, until you've returned from the labyrinth."

My eyes bulged. "He could bleed out!"

"Maybe," Henry said, "but that is entirely up to you . . ." He gave a sideways nod toward the impeded archway. "Best hurry, ancient one."

I glared at him for a long moment, then crossed the room to retrieve my bag. Out of spite, I pushed down on the lid of the cube until it clicked and was, once again, sealed shut.

When my eyes returned to Henry's, he was mirroring my glare.

I hoisted my backpack onto my shoulder, then raised my other hand, flipping up my middle finger.

Raiden made a choking noise, and I glanced down at him. His face was taut with pain, but when I met his eyes, and saw the grim humor dancing in their depths, I realized he was suppressing laughter. I could feel the amusement wafting off of him. And the relief at knowing his mom was all right. And the pain radiating out from the gunshot wound in his thigh. It hurt like hell, but he was certain nothing vital had been struck, and he already knew the bullet had gone clean through his leg. He wasn't the least bit worried about bleeding out; his biggest concern was about infection. And about me.

"Hold on, Raiden," I told him and, with a nod—a silent promise—I turned my back to him and headed for the archway.

Henry claimed that no person to enter the labyrinth had ever made it back out.

Well, all evidence pointed to the fact that *I* wasn't a person, at least, not in the human sense. I would succeed where all before me failed. For Raiden, and for my mom.

I had to.

33

Very aware of the four sets of eyes staring at my back, I approached the archway, sliding my left arm through the other strap of my backpack and settling the bag on my shoulders. When I reached the stone slab blocking my way, I paused and gave the archway a quick scan from floor to keystone and back down.

The top of the arch was constructed of seven larger stone blocks, the largest being the keystone. Smaller stone blocks were stacked one upon another on either side all the way down to the floor. A single word had been inscribed into the keystone, the Latin word for *truth*: Veritas.

Interesting. It seemed the Order's name—translated to "Guardians of the Truth"—was more literal than I'd thought.

I scanned the stone slab next, from keystone to floor and back up. I stopped halfway, eyes landing on a line of writing carved across the center of the massive stone. This, too, was in Latin.

THE ONLY WAY IN IS THROUGH

. . .

Through the archway? That seemed too obvious.

I narrowed my eyes.

Or through the *stone*?

Tilting my head to the side, I leaned in closer to the stone slab and raised my hand. I hesitated only for a moment before pressing my palm to the smooth surface.

My hand passed straight through, like the barrier was no more substantial than air. Air charged with static electricity, but air, nonetheless.

Pulling my hand back, I scanned the stone slab again, brows drawing together. It looked solid, but clearly it wasn't.

"It's a hologram," I said softly, voice filled with awe.

It was perfect. So perfect, that I never would have believed the stone wasn't really there if my own hand hadn't just passed right through the thing. The ancient Romans never could have created this. I wasn't sure even modern people could create such a realistic, believable hologram. Which meant it wasn't human-made, but alien-made. Atlantean-made.

I turned partway, meeting Raiden's eyes one last time. "I'll come back," I told him. "Just stay alive." And then I turned back to the archway and walked through the slab of stone.

Energy tingled over my skin as I passed through the hologram, making the tiny hairs all over my body stand on end. When I came out through the other side, I found myself in near complete darkness. Only patches of faintly glowing green iridescence stretching out in a long, uneven line overhead broke up my dark surroundings, and glimmering specks of that same eerie neon green floated all around me.

I reached up to switch on the headlamp.

"Crap," I hissed when my fingertips touched my bare forehead. The headlamp had fallen off when I'd been overwhelmed by all of the psychic input.

I pulled the cell phone from my back pocket, intending to use its built-in light. But it wouldn't turn on. No matter how hard or long I pressed down the power button, nothing happened. It didn't matter that the battery had been nearly full just a few minutes earlier; now, the phone was dead.

Growling under my breath, I turned on my heel, intending to pop back out to the vault to grab the headlamp.

And walked straight into a wall of stone—not the holographic kind.

"Damn it," I muttered, slapping the stone wall with both hands. No wonder nobody had ever returned—the archway only allowed passage one-way.

At the unmistakable whoosh of fire igniting, I spun around. Two torches had flared to life about twenty paces ahead, illuminating either side of a high-ceilinged stone passageway. A few seconds later, two more torches auto-ignited some fifty paces down, followed by two more after that. I stopped counting after the eighth set of torches flared to life.

The passageway was nearly twice my height and just wide enough that I couldn't touch both sides at once with my arms fully extended, and it seemed to go on forever. The pairs of torches were placed opposite one another in archways that broke up the seemingly never-ending corridor into shorter sections.

I looked up at the ceiling. The glowing iridescence had faded to a pale green in the torchlight. It appeared to be a thick blanket of some sort of mold covering the stone overhead, the slightly florescent color making it look almost like it had been irradiated.

There was a strangely sweet, musty scent in the air. It must have been coming from the mold, I realized, and wrinkled my nose.

I started up the corridor, slowing when I neared the first set of torches. After the archway, the corridor was bisected by another, perpendicular to this one.

At the sound of a metallic clatter behind me, I spun around, hands clutching my chest.

The doru lay on the floor a few yards in from the hologram.

I frowned, eyes narrowing. If Henry had been willing to lose the ancient weapon to the labyrinth, he really must have been rooting for me to make it all the way through. I wondered what had been hidden in the labyrinth that he was so desperate to get his hands on. Not that it really mattered to me. Nothing was more valuable than the lives of my mom and Raiden.

I jogged back to the hologram, scooped up the doru, then turned and headed up the corridor once more. I stopped in the intersection between passageways and planted the butt of the doru on the floor before first looking down the corridor on the left, then down the one on the right. The torch-archway pattern continued on in both directions until the torchlight blended into one solid glow. It was like I'd stepped into Daedalus' fabled labyrinth, only this one wasn't a prison for a savage minotaur. It was a prison for *me*.

My heart plummeted as I returned to looking up the seemingly endless corridor stretching out ahead of me. I hadn't thought this would be easy—nobody had ever made it out alive, after all. But *this* was impossible.

I rubbed the back of my neck. A dull throbbing was settling in at the base of my skull. Clearly, the stress of the situation was getting to me.

A growl rumbled up the opposite corridor, making me jump. I spun to the left, fully expecting to see some kind of monster watching me from farther in.

But there was nothing there.

The growl faded, replaced by a forceful exhale that brought to mind a bull preparing to charge and the unmistakable sound of hooves on stone. The clopping lasted several seconds before fading along with the growl. Those were exactly the kinds of sounds I might expect a minotaur to make.

Except minotaurs weren't real. They were mythical beasts. Remnants from stories of the ancients.

My heart gave a heavy *thud-thump*. I was afraid to move. Afraid to breathe. I stood in the intersection between corridors, frozen in place. I stood there for so long, and the silence grew so heavy, that I started to think I had imagined the whole thing.

Until the growl rumbled up the passageway again, louder this time.

Without thinking, I turned in the opposite direction and sprinted up the corridor. I skidded around the corner two archways down, slowing to a jog as I headed deeper into the labyrinth. Each step sent dizzying reverberations through my skull, making me increasingly unsteady.

I had just rounded another corner when my steps faltered, and I stopped, planting one hand on the wall. I blinked, shaking my head to clear it, but that only made the dizzying headache worse.

This wasn't just stress; this was something more. Something in the labyrinth was messing with my head, and fast.

That growl came again, rolling up the passageway behind me. My whole body tensed up, and fear gripped my heart. Fear for Raiden and my mom. Fear for me, too.

I pushed off the wall and continued on in a stumbling jog, reaching out to steady myself with a hand on the wall every few steps. I had a pretty good rhythm going by the time I reached the next intersection of passageways. I rounded the corner, expecting to find yet another empty corridor.

A corpse sat curled up against the wall on the left, just before the next archway. It wore priest's robes, the heavy black fabric hanging loosely on the desecrated frame. I was no expert, but even I could tell that this guy had been dead for years.

The hairs on the back of my neck stood on end, and my mouth was suddenly a desert. I licked my lips with my tacky tongue, swallowing roughly.

I approached the body slowly. Cautiously. If this were one of my video games, the dead priest very well could've been lying in wait to jump up and attack me.

My hazy brain started filling in the gaps of what was happening down here. Had the growling, roaring creature that seemed to be stalking me killed the priest? Would this be my fate, too? Would I end up a shriveled corpse curled up against a wall, forever trapped in this labyrinth?

I paused about ten paces from the corpse. So close, I could see that the priest's skin had dried out and darkened as it thinned, giving him a mummified look. His eyes had long since rotted away, and his lips had retracted as they'd dried, leaving him with a ghastly grin. His left arm draped down to the floor, his hand resting on a thick book bound in black leather.

At first, I thought it was a bible. But then, I spotted the pen clipped to the cover, partially concealed by the priest's decrepit hand. Maybe it wasn't a bible, but a journal. And if it was a journal *and* the priest had been writing in it, maybe he had recorded some of what he found down here. Maybe he knew what the growling creature was. Or even better yet, maybe he knew the way out. Or, based on the fact that he'd died down here, which ways *didn't* lead out.

I moved closer and held the doru up defensively, keeping a close eye on the corpse's grisly face. At the first hint of movement, I was fully committed to smashing his skull to smithereens. This labyrinth was too creepy, and I had seen too many zombie movies and played too many video games to expect the dead to stay that way.

But the priest didn't move, thankfully. I reached him and nudged his hand off the cover of the book, cringing at the brittle, crunching sound his arm made. I bent down and scooped up the book, backing away even before I had fully straightened my legs.

Keeping one eye on the priest, I moved farther down the corridor. I pressed my backpack to the wall to ensure that nobody

—and no*thing*—could sneak up on me while I was distracted, and looked down at the book.

The symbol of the Custodes Veritatis had been stamped into the front cover. I ran my fingertips over the depression in the black leather, then opened the book. It wasn't a bible, that much was clear. But it also wasn't a journal. The first page was blank, but the second had two words printed onto the page in bold, black type: *LIBER VERITATIS.* This was the missing book mentioned in my mom's journal.

I fanned through the pages, searching for anything that might help me. The pages in the first two-thirds of the book were filled with neat, black type, but the remaining third was handwritten, the last several dozen pages completely blank.

I paused when I reached the inside of the back cover. The thick white paper was covered in a dense-packed grid.

I felt a surge of adrenaline when I realized what I was looking at, and my mind cleared up a bit.

It was a map—of the labyrinth. And based on the solid, unbroken line bordering the map, there was no exit. No way out. No end to this madness.

"You're not trying to get out." That voice—I would have recognized it anywhere.

Startled, I dropped the book, and it hit the stone floor with a *thunk*.

Persephone—she was right there, her back to me as she stood in the intersection between corridors just fifty paces ahead, dead center of all four arches. Her dark hair was pulled up into a neat bun atop her head. She wore a tight-fitting black suit with channels of electric blue glowing in a distinctive pattern from neck to fingertip to toe. It was the same thing Demeter and the other Amazons had been wearing in my dreams—in her memories. The same garment I had tucked into my backpack in the vault.

My leaden heart was suddenly galloping in my chest. How

was she *here*? I thought she was dead—how could she be down here, when just minutes ago, she was in my head?

Was it possible that she worked for the Order? Or had she, by some strange coincidence, broken into the vault immediately before me and snuck into the labyrinth?

"Hey!" I called out, wincing as the sound of my voice reverberated inside my skull, magnifying the headache. Dead priest forgotten, I snatched the *Liber Veritatis* off the floor and started toward Persephone. "What are you doing in here?" I demanded. "And what do you mean I'm not trying to get out?"

Persephone turned, just a little, enough to acknowledge that she heard me, but not enough to show me more than a hint of her profile. "You're trying to get *in*," she said, and it was as though I could hear her voice both with my ears and in my mind.

I shook my head, ignoring the dizzying effect. "No, I—"

"This way," Persephone said and stepped to the left, disappearing around another corner.

"Wait!" I shouted. The sound was like a gong inside my head, throwing me off balance. I missed a step and stumbled to the side, my shoulder just grazing the wall. I rested my forehead against the cool stone and took deep, measured breaths.

With one last breath, I pushed away from the wall and continued after Persephone, moving as quickly as I could manage. I stopped in the archway, turning to follow her, and found myself staring down a long, empty corridor.

She couldn't have slipped around another corner that fast. There hadn't been enough time.

But that didn't change the fact that she was gone. Vanished. Like she'd never even been here to begin with.

Maybe she hadn't. Maybe she was a ghost. Or maybe she was a figment of my imagination, and I was losing my mind. Maybe it didn't matter.

What had she said before disappearing around the corner?

You're not trying to get out.

I squeezed my eyes shut, rubbing my temples with my thumb and middle finger as I tried to remember the rest. My head was pounding, and coherent thought was growing slipperier by the second.

And then Persephone's second statement coalesced in my mind.

You're trying to get in.

My eyes popped open, and I looked down at the book, flipping to the map in the back. There was a small, triangular open area in the center of the map. At first glance, I'd assumed the blank spot meant the priest hadn't quite finished mapping the labyrinth before he'd died. But now that I was looking for it, I could see that the open area was almost entirely enclosed, surrounded by a warren of dead-end tunnels. All dead-ends, save for one.

A single corridor led into the open space at the heart of the maze.

I couldn't imagine how long it must have taken the priest to map the whole labyrinth. Days, maybe weeks, from the looks of all of the twists, turns, and dead-ends. How he had managed to do such a thorough, meticulous job while also evading the beast that was down here was beyond me.

Something else tickled my brain, and an image of the dead priest flitted before my mind's eye. He didn't look mauled or ravaged or anything like how I would've expected the victim of a captive, savage beast to look. Rather, he looked like was resting. Like he had run out of energy and had gotten comfortable while he waited to die.

I narrowed my eyes. What if there was no beast down here at all? What if it was a trick of the mind?

I glanced up at the ceiling. The thick blanket of irradiated-looking mold continued here. No doubt the floating spores filled the air, invisible in the torchlight, but still there.

A few years back, I read about mold having psychoactive effects. I was going through a phase where I spent days on end binge-watching nearly every ghost-hunting show out there, only to be disappointed when my own independent research suggested that mold containing neurotoxins was likely responsible for alleged ghost sightings, especially those that happened in older, "haunted" buildings. Older, meaning more time for mold to spread. More time for spores to saturate the walls and floors . . . to linger in the air.

Was that what was happening here? Was mold responsible for my hazy, aching head? Was it poisoning my brain, making me hallucinate?

I frowned. Was the mold the reason I was suddenly not just hearing Persephone's voice in my head, but seeing full-fledged apparitions of her, too?

The ghost of a whisper floated up the passageway toward me, giving rise to a sudden bout of goose bumps. I shivered, swallowing roughly.

It's not real, I told myself. Not that thinking that made the next whisper any less creepy.

Taking a deep breath, then wrinkling my nose as I considered what I'd just inhaled, I refocused on the map. I tried to recall the turns I had made when first fleeing deeper into the labyrinth, then later, when chasing Persephone. I tracked different routes on the map, but none of the combinations I tried worked—either ending in dead-ends or impossible turns.

I was lost. I felt the color drain from my face as I realized the truth. The map wouldn't do me any good. Unlike in my games, there was no little beacon marking my position.

"This way."

My head snapped up, and I barely caught a glimpse of Persephone before she disappeared around a corner up ahead.

I stared after her, frozen by indecision. I had no idea where I was on the map, and any way I tried to go would likely just get me more lost. But, then, so would following an imaginary woman.

Unless she wasn't imaginary.

Persephone had been in my head for days, helping me work my way out of difficult situations. Helping me cope with the sudden insanity that had invaded my life. Helping me do things I shouldn't have been able to do. I had to accept that there was a very real possibility that this apparition of her wasn't a figment of my imagination. A very real, very small possibility. Which made following her a better alternative to the crapshoot of me trying to find my own way through the labyrinth.

I laughed under my breath. It was a hopeless, mania-tinged laugh. A desperate laugh. A resigned laugh. I was still laughing as I stashed the priest's book in my backpack and took my first step to follow Persephone.

At this point, what did I have to lose?

34

I passed more corpses as I delved deeper into the labyrinth, chasing after Persephone. They grew more concentrated the deeper we went.

Some were huddled in groups of two or three, while others were alone. Some were on the fresher—and riper—side, while others were little more than skeletons. Some wore priests' robes, others black or camo tactical clothing, while others still were bedecked in full suits of armor. Some wore little more than brittle scraps, the ancient fabric of their clothing having dissolved over the centuries.

I didn't stop to examine their remains or look for any more goodies like the priest's book. My time was limited. Add on the fact that, with each rounded corner, my mind felt hazier and I was more light-headed. I feared I might drop within the hour.

The growls had been replaced by haunting whispers and moans almost the moment I realized the mold was likely the hallucinogenic variety. Despite being pretty damn certain it was all in my head, the sounds were still eerie as hell and distracting enough that I had to consciously try to ignore them.

I lost track of the twists and turns almost immediately, going on faith that around each corner, I would find Persephone waiting at the next bend. She would linger just long enough for me to catch sight of her before slipping around the next corner, once again disappearing from sight.

My run soon slowed to a jog, my jog to a walk, until even calling my forward movement walking was being generous. At best, I was hobbling, head hanging as I leaned heavily on the doru. I had no clue how the priest had managed to map this place; it was all I could do to drag one foot in front of the other, and I had probably only been down here for twenty or thirty minutes.

"Hang on," I mumbled to Persephone as I rounded the next corner, fingers curled around the edge of the stone wall. "I just need a sec . . ."

I leaned my right shoulder against the wall, resting my cheek on the cool stone, wishing the floor would stop tilting back and forth. I closed my eyes, dragging in deep breaths of the poisoned air.

When I finally raised my eyelids to look for Persephone, icy dread washed over me. This passage ended with a solid stone wall, and the corridor was littered with the bodies of the dead—more than I'd seen anywhere else in the labyrinth. But Persephone was nowhere to be seen.

I stumbled forward a few steps, then paused to look back the way I'd come. The last intersection only had one other corridor. Maybe I mixed up which way she had gone.

Brow furrowing, I shook my head, like that might dispel some of the cobwebs tangling my thoughts. The jarring motion was a mistake, only making my head spin more.

"Cora . . ."

I stiffened, going absolutely still. Up until now, the whispering, disembodied voices had been unrecognizable, their words indiscernible. But that had very clearly been my name, and there was no mistaking my mom's voice drifting up the corridor behind me.

"Come here, Cora," she said, her voice faint and wispy. She sounded weak, pained. "I need your help." Her words were accompanied by the sound of shuffling feet slowly drawing nearer.

I held my breath.

"Help me . . ." The two words devolved into a throaty gurgle. It was a sound nothing living would make, and it sent shivers cascading down my spine.

Instinct took over, and I pushed off the wall, stumble-running farther down the corridor. It didn't matter that I didn't know where to go from here; all that mattered was getting away from the thing creeping up the last passageway, pretending to be my mom. I ran until I reached the end of the corridor, then turned, looking for the next passageway.

But the wall to the left was solid stone, no arched opening to pass through, just a torch in a bronze sconce.

I spun around.

The wall to the right was just as solid.

I glanced over my shoulder, looking back the way I'd come.

The long corridor was empty, save for the dead. And, thankfully, it was quiet . . . for the moment.

I turned back to the wall at the end of the passage. This was the first dead-end Persephone had led me to. I had spotted others down untraveled corridors, but this was the first one I had come to, personally.

Which made me think that it had to be more. That it wasn't a dead-end at all. That maybe, just maybe, it was a door—the door to the triangular room at the heart of the labyrinth.

I ran my hands over the cool stone, eyes scanning from ceiling to floor. An arch had been built into the wall, framing what appeared to be a walled-off passage, much like the entrance to the labyrinth. Except this archway wasn't blocked by a holographic stone slab. This one was blocked by a very real, very solid wall of stacked stone blocks.

And while the walls throughout the labyrinth were relatively smooth to the touch, this one was pocked with perfectly round, dime-sized divots, gouged out of the stone blocks in clean, symmetrical patterns. Clearly, the holes had been carved into the faces of the blocks purposely.

Some of the stone blocks had more divots; some had less. Just one, chest-high near the center of the wall, had a single divot carved into its face.

I traced my fingertip around the lone divot, then dipped my finger into the shallow hole. Just the white crescent at the base of my nail was visible, making the hole about half an inch deep.

The faintest hint of whispering touched my ears, and I bowed my head and closed my eyes, taking a moment to gather myself.

It wasn't real. It was all in my head. It had to be.

The stone shifted slightly under the pressure from my finger, and my eyes popped open. Frowning, I pulled my finger out of the hole and pushed on the stone with my whole hand.

With the sound of stone grinding on stone, the block depressed about an inch, until there was a metallic click.

A second later, fire exploded in my hand and then in my shoulder as a needle-thin silver spike speared through me.

I shrieked, staring wide eyed at the spike, following it from the back of my hand to the place where it disappeared into my shoulder.

Almost as quickly as the spike shot out of the wall, it retracted.

Shaking, I pulled my hand away from the wall and turned it around to stare at my palm. Blood seeped out of the wound and streamed down my forearm. I could feel the warmth of more blood soaking into my T-shirt, as well. But despite the intensity of the pain a moment ago, I almost couldn't feel it, now.

Shock, I realized. As a defense mechanism, my brain must have turned off the pain receptors in this part of my body. I wasn't sure if this reaction to pain was normal or if it was just another part of my increasingly obvious other-ness, but I was glad for it, nonetheless.

I was even more glad for the momentary silence. The burst of adrenaline must have been enough to clear my head of some of the neurotoxin, giving me respite from the relentless whispers. I doubted the quiet would last, but I savored the silence while it was there.

Holding my wounded hand to my chest, I took a couple unsteady steps backward, putting some distance between myself and the booby-trapped wall.

My gut—and years of gaming experience—told me this wasn't just a senseless booby trap. It was a puzzle. It had to be, and I felt certain that depressing the right stone would reveal a passage. But press on the wrong stone, and another trap would be triggered.

I wondered if all of the stones released spikes, or if there were a variety of deadly options. I supposed there was only one way to find out.

Narrowing my eyes, I focused on the wall as a whole.

Only some of the stone blocks in the wall were pocked with holes. The rest were smooth, like those throughout the rest of labyrinth. The marked blocks were arranged in a diamond pattern, starting one row up from the floor and reaching almost to the top of the wall. The stone blocks near the center of the diamond arrangement had a lower concentration of holes—with the block that housed the spike that had impaled my hand residing at dead center—and it looked like the number of holes on any given block generally increased the farther it was from the center. That was as much of a pattern as my mold-muddled mind could spot.

The whispers, silenced by the shot of pain-induced adrenaline, were starting up again. As they grew louder, it became harder and harder to concentrate.

Blowing out a breath, I shifted my focus to the individual stones. The diamond arrangement was made up of twenty-five stone blocks, and so far as I could tell, there were also twenty-five holes in the most pock-marked block. That led me to believe that each stone block had a different number of holes, ranging from one to twenty-five. I just had to figure out which number was the right number.

Math was far from my strong suit. But the history of mathematics—and mathematical discoveries—was something I knew a little more about.

I ran through the various famous or significant numbers in my head. There was Pi—3.1415 . . .—which represented the relationship between a circle's diameter and its circumference. And then there was Phi, or the "Golden Ratio"—1.618 . . .—which represented the relationship between two specific shapes, as seen in naturally occurring spirals. There was also Euler's number—2.718 . . .—which related to exponential growth.

I frowned. None of those were whole numbers, which seemed to be my only options.

A few other significant numbers came to mind, like the speed of light and sound, but those numbers were way too big.

No single whole number between one and twenty-five stood out in my mind as being all that significant—other than one, and I'd already tried the one-hole stone block. Oh no, one was definitely *not* the winning number.

My eyes opened wide as an idea popped into my head. "What if it's not a single number?" I thought aloud. What if it was a *sequence* of numbers?

Two incredibly important sequences came to mind—the Fibonacci Sequence, and the sequence of prime numbers. The Fibonacci Sequence started with *one*, which ruled it out. But the first prime number was *two*. Neither of the divots in the two-hole stone block had stabbed me, yet, and I didn't have any other ideas so I figured it was worth a shot.

Taking a couple more steps back, I raised the doru and tucked one end of the staff under my arm, pressing the other end against the middle of the stone block with two holes drilled into its surface. It was one of the blocks directly below the lethal *one* block.

I stepped to the side so I wasn't in line with the pair of holes. If this wasn't the right choice, I really didn't want to be shot with poisoned darts or impaled by any more ancient spikes.

The initial shock that had numbed the pain in my hand and shoulder was wearing off, and both were beginning to throb. The pain no longer had a clarifying effect on my mind. It combined with the increasingly loud whispers and moans filling the corridor, further muddling my thoughts.

I took a deep breath, focusing my ever-diminishing mental capacity on the task that would hopefully get me out of this mess. Once I was through this wall, I would grab whatever artifacts had been locked away in the center of the labyrinth and find a way out.

Closing my eyes, I leaned into the doru. The stone block resisted for a fraction of a second, and then it sank into the wall.

I held my breath, waiting for the click that would signal another trap triggered or the deep rumble I imagined I would hear as the wall opened up to let me pass.

For a solid ten seconds, I stood there, eyes closed and breath held, doru pressed into the stone block, waiting.

Nothing happened.

I blew out my breath and opened my eyes. Lowering the doru, I scanned the wall ahead of me, then glanced at the walls on either side.

A doorway hadn't opened up, at least, not anywhere I could see. The only change was that the stone block with two holes was still sunken into the wall. It was more than a little disappointing.

But on the plus side, I wasn't dead. So, there was that.

Eyes narrowed, I raised the doru again and pressed the end against the stone block with three small holes drilled into the surface. Three was the next prime number. Maybe the barrier to entry wasn't selecting the right stone, but selecting the right *series of stones.* Maybe, in order to pass, I needed to prove that I knew the sequence of prime numbers, not just the first number in the sequence.

It made sense, from a wheedling-out standpoint; anyone could randomly select the right single stone block. In fact, there was a one in twenty-five chance of randomly picking the right number. Which meant that, statistically speaking, one out of every twenty-five of the yahoos who had attempted to solve the puzzle would have found a way through the wall. There were well over twenty-five dead guys in the labyrinth—well over three times that many—and according to Henry, not a single person had ever made it out. That meant there had to be more to the puzzle.

Tensing my core muscles, I leaned into the doru and pushed the next stone block into the wall.

Again, I held my breath. Again, I waited for the click that would signal a trap triggered. And again, nothing happened.

I lowered the doru and stared at the wall. Now, two stone blocks were depressed, and I still hadn't triggered another booby trap. Looked like I was on the right track.

I repeated the process five more times, pressing in and locking into place the stones blocks with five, seven, eleven, thirteen, and seventeen holes drilled into their surfaces.

The whispers had grown louder—so loud that they were nearly deafening in the corridor. My thoughts were a jumble, and my hand and shoulder throbbed in sync with my heartbeat, the pain no longer dull, but sharp and dizzying. Each successive prime number was more difficult to remember, each stone block harder to push in.

I pressed the end of the doru against a block several feet above my head, this one with twenty-three holes drilled into its surface. It was the largest prime number on the wall.

The instant the stone was fully pushed in, the other stones slid back to their original places.

I froze, staring at the wall, waiting for something else to happen.

But nothing did.

I lowered the doru and looked around. Nothing had changed. There were no new openings in the walls. There was no new passageway. It was just me and the dead, and the voices in my head.

Figuring I must have missed something, I turned back to the wall, running through the sequence of prime numbers out loud. "Two, three, five, seven . . . seven . . . seven . . ." With all of the whispering and moaning, I couldn't think of the next number.

"Cora . . ."

I stiffened.

"Cora, help me." It was Raiden. He was behind me. Not in some other corridor, about to round the corner. I could hear his shuffling steps. He was *right* behind me.

I squeezed my eyes shut. I may have been hearing Raiden's voice, but I knew he wasn't *really* behind me. There was no way Henry would have let Raiden slip from his grasp. This was just another trick of the mind. A hallucination caused by the toxic mold.

I refocused on the task at hand, listing prime numbers in my head.

Two . . . three . . . five . . . seven . . .

"Cora . . ."

"Shut up!" I hissed, restarting the sequence.

Two . . . three . . . five . . . seven . . .

"Eleven," I whispered, eyes popping open.

I raised the doru, pressing the butt of the staff against the first stone block. I pushed the block in, locking it into place, then did the same with *three, five, seven, eleven, thirteen,* and *seventeen.* I was raising the end of the doru to the stone block with twenty-three drilled into the surface again, when I paused.

Twenty-three wasn't the next prime number; nineteen was. I'd skipped nineteen the first time. That must have been the reason it didn't work.

I lowered the end of the doru, pressing it against a chest-high stone block with nineteen perfect little holes gouged into its surface. I pushed it in, locking it into place, then did the same with the final stone block high above.

As the block locked into place, a deep gonging sounded within the wall, charging the air and echoing down the corridor.

Not a second later, the wall shifted, slowly sinking into the floor with a deafening rumble. The whole corridor trembled, the vibrations seeping into my body as anticipation took hold within me.

I'd done it. I'd solved the puzzle. I'd beaten the labyrinth.

Finally, it was over.

35

As I passed under the archway, my excitement was replaced by confusion, quickly followed by a wash of disappointment. A skeletal corpse blocked my way, curled up on its side in the fetal position. Whoever it was had made it past the booby-trapped wall, but they hadn't made it out of the labyrinth.

Which meant I hadn't reached the end. It *wasn't* over.

Numbly, I stepped over the corpse and looked around. The dead priest's map had been accurate about the shape of the chamber at the heart of the labyrinth.

It was triangular, and small, each side no longer than a dozen feet. The space was completely enclosed, save for the opening in the wall behind me, and a single torch burned in a sconce on either of the walls ahead. The walls, ceiling, and floor were stone, like the rest of the labyrinth, but in here, the ceiling was free of the thick carpeting of mold. A triangular stone pedestal stood in the center of the chamber, its foot-long sides parallel to the walls. It was topped with a shallow basin, maybe two inches deep and four inches across. The floor was made of long, narrow wedges of stone fanning out around the pedestal, stretching all the way to the walls.

I crinkled my nose. There was a sharp bitterness to the air, making me think of menthol and bleach. The smell wasn't unpleasant, exactly—preferable to the musty sweetness pervading the rest of the labyrinth. But it was extremely pungent. So strong, that it took me a few seconds to realize that the whispers and moans had fallen silent. I couldn't hear a single shuffling footstep, and Raiden's voice no longer taunted me.

And the headache—it was fading, and fast.

I stretched my neck, tilting my head first one way, then the other. Whatever the source of the medicinal odor, it was doing a damn good job of clearing the effects of the mold from my head. I inhaled and exhaled deeply, appreciating the cleansing scent more and more with each successive lungful of air.

As my mind cleared and my awareness sharpened, the pain in my hand and shoulder intensified. My eyes watered, and for the briefest moment, I missed the dulling effect of the mold-induced haze.

I squeezed my eyes shut, gave myself three deep breaths to gather my wits about me, then opened my eyes and turned my attention to the pedestal at the center of the room. I reached it in three steps.

Around the shallow basin, narrow grooves divided the surface of the pedestal into nine sections, three on each side. They extended out from the basin like the rays of the sun, each ending with a small depression about the size of a quarter. At the bottom of the basin, a handful of marble-sized gemstones glittered in the dancing torchlight.

I leaned over the pedestal to get a better look at the gemstones. They were huge, spanning a range of vibrant colors from yellow to violet. I had no doubt that any single gemstone would be priceless. At least, they would be priceless out in the world; in here, each gemstone was just another puzzle piece.

Cautiously, I reached into the basin and picked up a gleaming, deep-blue sapphire.

The sound of stone grinding on stone made me spin around. The wall between the labyrinth and this chamber was slowly rising up from the floor, sliding back into place.

My fingers closed around the sapphire, and my heartbeat stumbled as it sped up. I lunged toward the closing wall, but froze after taking just the one step. Retreating into the labyrinth wouldn't do me any good. Out there, I would end up just like the dozens upon dozens of bodies scattered about the maze.

I turned around, eyes locking on the triangular pedestal. "And I agree to that," I said, reciting Robert Frost under my breath, "or in so far as I can see no way out but through."

I squared my shoulders, held my head high, and returned my focus to the new puzzle. After dropping the sapphire back into the basin, I glanced over my shoulder, curious to see if returning the stone would open the wall again.

It didn't.

Exhaling a sigh, I studied the pedestal's surface. It seemed obvious to me that the solution to this puzzle required placement of each gemstone in the appropriate depression. There were nine holes in total, which meant there were well over a hundred thousand possible arrangements, maybe even *hundreds* of thousands. But there would be just one solution.

There had to be a pattern. Based on the last puzzle, I couldn't imagine the builder of the labyrinth picking a random arrangement of the gemstones as the solution for this one. Then it wouldn't be a puzzle at all, but more of a combination lock. And I was getting the impression that these puzzles meant something; they were tests, and only the worthiest—the one who could pass all of the tests—would reach the prize at the end.

I was tempted to just start arranging the stones, hazarding a guess at what the pattern might be. I glanced around the room. There was no saying what kind of traps lay in wait, ready to be triggered by even a single wrong move.

I narrowed my eyes.

The chamber itself was trap enough. Would the builder really have booby-trapped this space further? He or she—whoever they were—clearly wanted someone to make their way through the labyrinth. If that wasn't the desired outcome, the builder would have nixed the puzzles altogether and made the prize at the end impossible to reach.

But this wasn't impossible. It was extremely difficult and even more dangerous, but it was *not* impossible.

I stared down at the surface of the pedestal for a long time, weighing my options. I really only had one—to place a gemstone in a depression and see what happened. I would have to do it eventually, or resign myself to slow death by dehydration.

Before I could talk myself out of it, I reached into the basin, grabbed a gemstone at random—an emerald, this time—and dropped it into one of the holes.

I held my breath, waiting for spikes to shoot out of the floor or for the ceiling to start lowering.

But nothing happened.

It looked like I wouldn't be impaled or crushed today—at least, not here, and not for attempting to falsely solve this puzzle.

Empowered by my newborn freedom to experiment, I scooped the rest of the gemstones out of the bowl and began arranging them in the divots in order by color, starting with the old rainbow-based standard: ROY G BIV. I placed the eighth gemstone, a deep violet amethyst, then stared at the ninth hole.

It was empty. So was my hand.

I looked at the basin, hoping I had missed a gemstone when scooping out the rest. But it was empty, too.

Had I dropped a gemstone in my haste to solve the puzzle?

I drew my bottom lip between my teeth, chewing on it as I slowly scanned the floor. I assumed the ninth gemstone would be about the same size as the others; they were all a little larger than the standard marble. And though I didn't want to fall prey to a trap built of assumptions, I was thinking this last gemstone had to be a diamond—it was the only major gemstone that was missing from the set.

My slow scan of the floor faltered when I reached the corpse curled up near the wall, where the opening from the labyrinth had been. I felt the blood drain from my face and a chill settle into my bones. Looking up at the ceiling, I took a deep breath, closed my eyes, and swallowed roughly, searching for some other solution.

The last thing I wanted to do was search a decrepit corpse for the missing gemstone. Sure, looting dead guys was a major part of most of the video games I played—it was one of the main ways players stocked up on pretty much everything from armor and weapons to ammo and first-aid supplies in virtually all RPGs and action-adventure games—but the prospect of digging through a dead man's pockets *in real life* made my stomach turn.

Groaning, low and slow, I opened my eyes and returned my gaze to the corpse. It was neither the most decomposed nor the freshest of the bodies I'd crossed paths with in the labyrinth so far. In a way, it was better preserved than the other bodies I'd come across—almost looking mummified—probably because, until now, it had been sealed in this chamber, untouched by even the movement of air. Despite Rome being a high humidity area, down here, it was cool and dry.

The corpse's skin had thinned and, I guessed based on its straw-colored hair, darkened until it looked like tanned leather stretched over his skeleton. And I guessed the corpse to be male based on the short hair.

He lay face-down, thankfully, so I'd yet to catch a glimpse of his no-doubt grisly face. Based on his clothing—typical turn-of-the-century archaeologist fashion with khaki trousers, a linen shirt that was still off-white-ish in the places not directly touching the body, a leather satchel, a matching canteen, and a brown fedora befitting of good old Indiana Jones—I placed the man as at least a century dead.

His lack of stink was a pretty good indicator. And his clothing had a brittle quality to it that marked it as predating the modern era of pop-culture; the outfit hadn't been influenced by our current notion of what a tomb-raiding adventurer should wear. This guy was the genuine article, not an imitation. Not that it had done him any good in the end.

I inhaled and exhaled deeply, shoulders rising and falling, then moved closer to the corpse. The chamber wasn't large, and after two steps, I was nearly on top of him.

I slipped my backpack off my shoulders and set it on the floor beside me, then crouched down, reaching for the dead man's bag with my uninjured hand. I turned it over and, with a flick of my fingers, flipped the leather flap open. I leaned forward to peer inside.

There was a book—one more to add to my rapidly growing collection—and a rolled-up leather case about as thick as my wrist, as well as a green, rectangular tin no larger than a standard bible.

I pulled out all three items, placing them on the floor before peeking into the bag to see what might be hiding at the bottom. I reached into the satchel again, grabbing a shiny brass compass and a collapsible telescope. I stared at the compass for a moment, watching the needle spin around and around. Brow furrowing, I set it down and stuck my hand back into the bag, scraping the bottom with my fingertips.

But that was it. No gemstone.

Resting my forearm on my knee, I took a quick breather, attempting to bolster my corpse-looting resolve with a series of deep breaths and a couple silent affirmations.

I am strong.

I am brave.

I ran through a mental list of all the strong, brave things I had done lately. Even if it felt like I had just been a passenger in my own body and Persephone had been in control, I had still done those things.

And I could do this.

I gulped and leaned forward, planting my knees on the floor, then reached for the dead man's trousers, hand trembling. Whatever I told myself, I wasn't really sure I could do this. At this point, I was an old pro at seeing dead bodies, but other than the skeletons I'd brushed against while searching for the trap door in the catacombs, I'd never touched a dead person. I really didn't want to start now.

And I didn't have to, I realized.

I pulled my trusty leather gloves out from my back pocket. Wincing, I tugged the left glove onto my uninjured hand, then stuffed the other glove back into my pocket and returned my attention to the corpse.

I inhaled deeply, held my breath, and slid my fingers into the dead man's trouser pocket. The fabric was as stiff and brittle as it looked, and the front of the pocket tore on either side as I searched.

I blew out a breath and pulled my hand out. The pocket was empty.

I quickly checked the other pocket, but it was empty, too.

Sitting back on my heels, I stared at the corpse. The only thing left to do now was to turn him over to make sure he wasn't lying on the missing gemstone. I shivered as I considered the possibility that if this guy had died on top of the gemstone, and over the decades his body had been in here, slowly decaying and mummifying, the gemstone could very well have sunken into his flesh.

After a quick repeating of my strong-brave affirmation, I reached across the dead man and gripped his far arm through his shirt sleeve. He felt petrified, almost like he had been carved of wood. I frowned, eyebrows rising. Surprisingly, this wasn't as gross as I'd expected.

With a grunt and a tug, I awkwardly rolled the dead man onto his back. He was far from heavy, but considering his leathery, mummified state, I supposed that made sense. All of the moisture had probably long since left his body.

His face was about what I had imagined—dry, thin lips pulled back into a death grin and mouth surrounded by a short, scraggly beard. His eye sockets were vacant, and his nose stopped at the bone.

I tried—and failed—not to envision what his final days of life must have been like. I imagined the loneliness he must have felt. The panic. The fear and the sadness. I thought about his family, if he'd had one, and how they must have felt when he never come home. And I couldn't help but wonder if this man had been in the same position I was currently in—if lives had been depending on his successful return.

The faint sting of welling tears tingled in my eyes, and I blinked a few times. I cleared my throat and took a deep breath. Now was not the time to commiserate with a dead man.

I laughed under my breath and shook my head. For all I knew, this guy could have been just as bad as psycho-Henry back in the vault.

I set aside sentiment and scanned the corpse carefully, from head to toe, then examined the floor where he'd been lying just a moment ago. No gemstone.

There was one last place to look.

Gritting my teeth, I pried the fingers of one of his hands open, snapping a few digits at the joints, then checked the other hand. Both were empty.

Exhaling heavily, I sat back on my heels and pulled off my glove. It was coated in dusty, dead man residue. I stuffed the glove back into my pocket with its partner, then added the dead man's things to my backpack, keeping only the journal out.

The journal's cover was soft and suede-like. I flipped it open, then thumbed through the pages, finding the last page of writing.

I figured any clues pointing me in the right direction—or in the *wrong* one, considering the man's state of deadness—would be at the end. The journal didn't disappoint.

. . . I know Jack didn't intend any harm. He was frightened, as was I. He panicked. I cannot blame him for fleeing when the wall started to close up again. And yet, the boy sealed my fate when he took the diamond. I shall not make it any further into the labyrinth without the ninth stone. A pity, truly. We made a good go at it.

Nina told me this would be the adventure that did me in. She called me Icarus, and told me I was trying to fly too close to the sun. I kissed her and told her not to worry. I told her I would return. In my heart, though, I, too, knew this expedition would be my last.

Should anyone find this journal and make it through the labyrinth, it is my last wish to have this book returned to my family . . .

"Well, shit," I said, snapping the journal shut with one hand.

Some long-dead guy named Jack had run off with the diamond, leaving me one gemstone short and making the puzzle unsolvable.

After everything, this was it. The end.

I bowed my head over the journal. My death sentence—and my mom's and Raiden's—had been delivered in the words of a dead man, written over a century ago. It was almost laughable.

Or at least it might have been, if it wasn't so damn sad.

36

"The regulator . . ."

At the sound of Persephone's voice whispering through my mind, I snapped my head up and looked for her. But she wasn't here, not like she was before.

I chalked up her earlier appearance to the mold. It had messed with my head, making me hear terrifying things, but maybe it had helped me, too.

"Try the regulator . . ."

"The regulator?" I repeated aloud, touching my fingertips to the pendant hanging around my neck. Did Persephone think it could serve as a stand-in for the puzzle's missing piece?

I waited to see if she would give me any further direction, but it seemed she'd fallen silent once more. I was back to being on my own.

I considered my options and figured the couldn't-be-that-simple solution was the first one to try.

Gripping the regulator, I pulled the necklace off over my head, gently shaking my ponytail free from the chain. I held the necklace up, letting the regulator dangle in front of my face. The stone still glowed that electric blue, but I remembered how it had

looked when Emi had held it in her hand. Colorless and clear—
like a diamond.

I pursed my lips and shook my head. There was no way the
stone in the regulator was a diamond. For one, it was *huge*. And
while blue and yellow diamonds did exist, last I checked,
diamonds didn't change color. Or glow.

Brimming with disbelief, I lowered the regulator down to the
pedestal. I set it over the empty depression, stone-side down,
then let go of the chain. I held my breath, counting my thudding
heartbeats.

One . . . two . . . three . . . four . . .

The sound started as a low rumble, but within seconds, it was
a roar. The whole chamber shook, and I clutched the pedestal for
balance.

Gemstones bounced out of their depressions. I just barely
managed to snag the regulator by the chain before it fell.

Without warning, the stone beneath my feet dropped out of
the floor.

And I dropped with it.

37

I dropped ten or fifteen feet. Far and fast enough to bruise, but not to break.

For long seconds, I lay on my back, just trying to breathe. The wind had been knocked clean out of me for the second time that day, and it was like my lungs had forgotten how to draw in air. I tried again and again to inhale, but all I managed was to gasp as my lungs spasmed. Bright spots danced around in the darkness encroaching on the edges of my vision as the threat of unconsciousness closed in.

I finally managed a lungful of air, and it was like I had been underwater and was just now breaking through the surface. I had been drowning, but now I could breathe.

Once I had put some distance between myself and unconsciousness, I propped myself up on my elbows and stretched out my neck. I winced, cringing. My hand and shoulder were still the brightest spots of pain, but I hurt pretty much everywhere now. I could only imagine how I would feel in an hour or two.

I sat up all the way, then looked around. On my left, the floor was about six inches above my landing spot; on my right, it was six inches below. Again, I looked one way, then the other, brain processing what I was seeing.

A stairway. I'd landed on stairs.

I studied the shape of the next stair up; it was a long, narrow wedge. Had the floor of the chamber *become* the stairs?

I looked up. Sure enough, the triangular pedestal was there, high overhead. Now that the stairs had settled in place around it, I could see that the pedestal was just the top part of a long pillar making up the axis of a spiral staircase.

I looked to the right again, craning my neck to see around the pillar. The stairs descended until well out of sight.

With a sigh, I planted my uninjured hand on the higher stair on my left and pushed myself up to my feet. I groaned as I stood.

Once I was up, I secured the regulator around my neck once more. I glanced down, watching as the stone filled with a subtle amber glow. Apparently, it returned to the active, psychic-input-blocking state if I put it down. Good to know.

My backpack was a few steps up, along with my dead companion. Most of him, at least. He'd lost his head during the fall; it was nowhere to be seen, and I figured I would find it at the bottom of the stairway. I could see the end of the doru just poking around the pillar, back up near the top.

Feeling like my feet weighed a thousand pounds each, I lugged my sore body up the stairs. I gathered the handful of gemstones I passed, tucking away a ruby, sapphire, amethyst, moonstone, and a black gem I didn't have a name for in the front pocket of my jeans.

I retrieved the doru, then started back down the stairs. When I reached my bag, I paused to stuff the dead man's journal into the main pocket before hoisting the bag onto my back and continuing on down the stairs.

The farther I descended, the darker it grew, until I reached the final stair and the way ahead was pitch black. I was just starting to turn around to head back up to retrieve one of the torches when a spotlight flared, illuminating a three-foot circle about a dozen paces beyond the bottom stair. A moment later, a man flickered into existence in the center of the lighted area.

I staggered back. My heel caught on the edge of a step, and I lost my balance, landing on my butt a couple stairs up. Even as I fell, I raised the doru, aiming it at the man.

He flickered again, going completely transparent for a few seconds, like he might vanish into thin air. Like he wasn't really there at all.

I straightened, planting the butt of the doru on the floor and standing. Tilting my head to the side, I studied the man standing maybe twenty feet away. It had to be a hologram.

He appeared somehow larger than life—taller than any man I had ever met, not that I'd met all that many, and exotic looking in an otherworldly way. He was fair, with alabaster skin and ashy, almost silver blond hair that had been pulled back into a low ponytail. His eyes straddled the line between blue and green. There was an unearthly beauty about him, set off by an overwhelming air of power, both physical and intellectual.

He was dressed monochromatically, his tailored pants, knee-high boots, and long, fitted coat that buttoned up from waist to collar all the same silvery shade. All he needed were a couple of pointy ears, and he would have fit right in on the set of a Tolkien movie.

There was something familiar about him, besides his general elvish-ness. I figured I must have seen him in one of Persephone's memories, but I couldn't quite place him.

He wasn't just a still image projected in 3D. He blinked. He breathed. He stared off into the distance, hands clasped behind his back, like he was waiting for something. Or someone.

I took a single step closer, and that strange sense of familiarity multiplied. I could have sworn that I knew this man. And *not* just from the scattering of Persephone's memories I had seen while dreaming. I felt like *I* knew him. Like *I,* Cora Blackthorn, had a connection with him.

I felt unexpected emotions when I looked at him—sadness and longing. A hint of bitterness and betrayal, but also respect. So much respect. And so much desire.

I swallowed roughly. It had to be coming from Persephone. *She* had to know him. And based on the things I was feeling, she knew him well.

I took another step toward the hologram of the man, not sure I had intended to move at all. It was like the emotional gravity between us was drawing me to him against my will.

The man's stare shifted, his striking aqua eyes locking on me. I froze.

"Congratulations," he said, bowing his head slightly. He spoke Latin, and it took my mind a moment to switch over into translation mode. "You have proven your worth by successfully passing all of my challenges and reaching the end of the labyrinth."

I blinked, and suddenly I was somewhere else. Someone else. I was Persephone.

"I'm sorry," I say, voice breaking. A tear sneaks free from between my lashes and slides down my cheek. "I wish . . ." Hades' knuckles brush over my cheekbone, stealing another stray tear, and my voice fades away, the words losing their meaning.

"I know," he says softly. "Me too."

I clear my throat and open my eyes, my gaze locking with his. My heart pounds against my sternum. "What are we going to do?"

With the pad of his thumb, Hades traces the line of my jaw from earlobe to chin before lowering his hand. "The only thing we can do," he says.

. . .

I blinked again, and I was back in the labyrinth with the hologram of the same man—Hades—utterly disoriented. Persephone's flashback of Hades had felt absolutely real to me, as if I
had really been there. Really lived her life. Really loved
this man.

"Your reward awaits you," Hades said, "but first you must
choose."

He turned his head to the left, and another archway illuminated in the wall. "Eternal life," he said, then looked to the right
and said, "priceless treasure," as another archway lit up in the
opposite wall. He stepped to the side, turning to look over his
shoulder as a third archway glowed in the wall behind him. "Or
the knowledge of the ages."

Hades returned his attention to me. "The choice is yours."

I blinked, and once again, I was transported into one of
Persephone's memories.

*"Was it all a trick?" I stop within arm's reach of Hades, fully
connected to his mind. "Was I just a tool you needed to fix our
broken society?"*

*I'm both looking at Hades and looking into him. I can see his
face, the tension hardening his handsome features, but I can also
see flashes of his past playing out right before my eyes. He can
feel it, all of the information I'm pulling from him. He knows
what I'm learning, and he can react to it, but he can't do a damn
thing to stop it from happening.*

*"Yes, Peri," Hades says, well before I've reached the parts of
his mind I'm seeking. "I was using you."*

*I take a step back, jolted out of his mind by the unexpected
confession. I feel like he just punched me in the gut, and I stare
into his eyes, sensing the truth in his words.*

The scene shifts abruptly.

Now, I'm on my knees on rough ground, Hades kneeling in front of me. I hurt. Everywhere. And I'm not mad at him anymore. All I want is for him to hold me in his arms and tell me everything is going to be all right. I'm desperate for him to lie to me.

"Peri," Hades says, placing his hand on the side of my head and tilting my face up toward his. "Are you all right?"

My chin trembles, but I can't bring myself to tell him the truth. To tell him I'm dying. "Yeah," I say faintly, feeling short of breath and knowing it will only get worse. "I'm fine."

"Pathetic," Demeter shouts, marching toward us.

The Amazons who are still able to stand after the battle form a wall blocking her path.

"Let her through," I say. She can't hurt me now, not when I'm already half-dead.

The line of Amazons splits apart, and Demeter slides through, a sneer on her face.

"All of this trouble, and for what?" Demeter says, stopping a few paces behind Hades.

He turns on his knees partway, but he doesn't move out from between us. It takes me a few irregular heartbeats to realize that he's protecting me from her. A useless gesture, but sweet, all the same.

"You failed," Demeter says, her tone full of condescension, "and now we'll all die at the hands of the Tsakali." She sniffs. "Well, except for you. You'll die here, and soon, from the looks of it."

Within me, the laugh starts small and choking. It travels up from my chest, making its way up my throat until it bursts out of my mouth, dry and thready.

"What?" Demeter says, narrowing her eyes.

"The chaos fragments," I say, coughing.

Hades grips my elbow, helping me stay more or less upright.

"They weren't . . . on the ship," I tell Demeter, then take a shuddering breath.

My heartbeat isn't just irregular now, it's weakening, too. The dark spots dancing around my vision close in, until Demeter and Hades are all I can see. A tear breaks free, streaking down my cheek.

Hades' grip on my elbow tightens.

"What are you talking about?" Demeter snaps. "I saw Hades take them onto the ship . . ."

"Escape pod," I say, voice breathy. The ship may never have left this planet's atmosphere, but the chaos fragments had. "Long . . . gone . . . now . . ."

Demeter's stunned expression is the last thing I see before my vision goes black. My heart seizes, and I collapse forward.

Hades catches me, pulling me onto his lap. He brushes the hair out of my face, his touch gentle, and strokes my cheek. The sensation remains long after my awareness of who he is or why he's touching me has faded away.

Until even that, too, is gone.

Until there's nothing.

Gasping, I sucked in a shuddering breath. I was trembling from head to toe. The montage of memories ended almost as soon as it started, lasting no longer than a heartbeat but leaving behind a lifetime's worth of emotions. I had felt Persephone's love for Hades. And I had felt her death. I had died with her.

I took a step forward, only it wasn't me moving my legs. "Hades!" I said, no more control over my lips and tongue and voice than I had over my feet. "Where are you projecting from?" I spoke in a language I'd only ever heard in Persephone's memories.

Unable to stop my legs, I took four more steps toward Hades, until I was standing within arm's reach.

He stared at me—at us—but didn't say anything more.

I could feel Persephone's frustration. My hands balled into fists, and my trembling intensified to full-fledged shaking, though I wasn't sure if that last was because *I* was trying to take back control.

"Hades, it's me—it's Peri." My—our—eyes scoured his face, searching for some hint that he could hear me. "It worked. Whatever you did—it worked. I'm back. I'm alive."

Without warning, Hades vanished.

I felt it the moment Persephone realized what had seemed obvious to me—the hologram of Hades wasn't a live projection, but a recording. Hades hadn't responded to her, because he hadn't been able to hear her. As impossible as it seemed, the hologram of him must have been recorded hundreds, maybe thousands of years ago.

Persephone's excitement turned to sorrow, and my heart drooped under the weight of her despair. I—she—hung my head. "You brought me back," I said—she said—softer this time.

Most of Persephone's emotions felt foreign to me. I felt them like they were my own, but I didn't have the background or experiences to root them, leaving them baseless and somehow hollow. But the sense of extreme loneliness that washed over me as she spoke those final words was all too familiar.

I felt it the moment Persephone relinquished control. She let go, then pulled away, withdrawing to some dark, shadowy place within my mind.

"You're not alone," I whispered, a tear streaking down my cheek.

But she was already gone, hidden away, only the barest hint of her despair spilling over into me.

I took a step back, closing my eyes and inhaling deeply to clear the last vestiges of her emotions from my heart. I exhaled, then opened my eyes, focusing on the place where the hologram of Hades had been. A moment later, I switched my attention to the three glowing archways.

It was a test. Whatever Hades had claimed in his little speech, I felt certain that the gauntlet wasn't over; this choice was the final test. Eternal life, priceless treasure, or the knowledge of the ages—the correct choice seemed obvious to me.

I looked at the archway on the left. Eternal life would be great, at first. But what about in a thousand years? In a million? A billion? I would be all alone—more so than I had ever been in my life, and there would be no end to the loneliness in sight. Eternal life would become eternal damnation.

I shifted my attention to the archway on the right. Priceless treasure just seemed like such a heavy-handed option. The prospect of having everything you ever wanted—who would ever turn that down? Which, I figured, was the point. It was a tempting misdirection playing off one of the most basic and prevalent human characteristics: greed. But treasure wouldn't help me now. It wouldn't help my mom or Raiden.

I looked straight ahead, focusing on the middle archway. I narrowed my eyes. Knowledge of the ages—it was the least glamorous option, but easily the most valuable. It had to be the right choice.

I started toward the center archway, but paused when I was two steps away. The glow filling the archway was bright and uniform, blocking my view of whatever lay beyond. I took it to be another hologram, and I wondered if, like the hologram at the entrance to the labyrinth, this one would only allow a one-way trip.

I would be able to pass through, but I wouldn't be able to return. If I chose wrong, this would be it. Game over. No respawns. No second chances. I would either be right, or I would be dead.

I took a step toward the archway. My boots felt like they

weighed a thousand pounds, and I wasn't sure I could take that final step.

I gritted my teeth. I was dead if I chose wrong. But I was also dead if I did nothing.

"Grow a pair," I murmured. And took the final step.

My skin tingled as I passed through the glowing hologram filling the archway, just as had happened when I first entered the labyrinth. Only this time, brilliant, golden light drowned out the world, fading along with the tingle as I took another step and cleared the archway.

I blinked, processing what I was seeing. I looked back at the archway I'd passed through, then peered around the new space. I was instantly struck by a sense of déjà vu.

The chamber was round and about the same size as the vault, and that same pattern of three concentric circles was inlaid into the floor, darker stone breaking up the light. And, like the vault, this chamber had two doorways—the one I had passed through to enter, and another, seemingly blocked by a solid slab of stone.

But *unlike* the vault, there was just one pedestal, standing alone at the center of the room. No writing had been carved into the sides of the pedestal, leaving the jet-black stone polished and smooth. A stone cube was on display atop the pedestal, looking to my eyes like an exact replica of the one in the vault.

I approached the pedestal. I assumed the cube wasn't simply a chunk of stone, but another box. Was this where Hades had stored the "knowledge of the ages?" Or did it contain some ancient, advanced weapon that would incinerate me the moment I touched it?

Only one way to find out.

I took one last step and stopped, resting the doru against the side of the pedestal. Taking a deep breath, I reached out my uninjured hand and touched my fingertips to the top of the cube.

Almost instantly, a glowing line encircled the box. A second later, there was a click, and the glowing line became a crack.

I straightened, not moving. Barely breathing.

Ever so carefully, I lifted the top half of the cube. It raised about an inch, but wouldn't budge any further.

I bent down to look inside.

Two crystalline disks about the size of silver dollars were secured vertically by shallow grooves within the inside of the box. There were more grooves, like the box had been made to hold more of the disks, maybe a dozen. I had no idea what the disks were—some sort of advanced data storage, I hoped. I needed something of value to offer Henry when I returned.

I reached into the box with thumb and middle finger and pinched one of the disks. Pulling gently, I slid it out of the box and set it on my open palm.

Without warning, a glowing ball of light sprang out from the surface of the disk, hovering over my hand.

I froze.

After the initial burst, the light faded to a softly glowing, opaque image. It was another hologram, this one a perfect sphere about eight inches in diameter. It was mostly blue and brownish-green, with patches of white at the top and bottom. And there was no mistaking the familiar shapes breaking up the brilliant blue—continents. I was looking at Africa and Europe dead-on.

I raised my other hand to run my fingertips along the surface of the holographic globe. The moment I touched the hologram, there was a flash of light, and a faint tingle traveled up the length of my finger, like the shock from the buildup of too much static electricity.

I moved my finger to the side, and the surface of the hologram moved with it.

"Huh," I said, moving my finger again. And again, the hologram shifted. Now I was looking at the Middle East.

Frowning, I flicked my finger to the left.

The holographic globe spun, the motion blurring the image, until it slowed and eventually stopped, settling with South America facing me.

I narrowed my eyes and leaned in a little.

A small, white light blinked in the dark green patch that had to represent the Amazon rainforest. Without delineated borders, I couldn't be certain, but I thought it was marking a place in Brazil.

It wasn't lost on me that my mom's original expedition had been to Brazil. Was it just a coincidence? Or was it more than that?

Frowning, I touched the blinking beacon.

A series of symbols popped up, like they were being projected from the beacon. It only took my mind a second to translate them. They were numbers. A very specific series of numbers, written in a very specific way—geographic coordinates.

I repeated the series of numbers over and over, out loud and in my head, memorizing them. Once I was sure I wouldn't forget them, I returned the first disk to the box and fished out the second. The holograph of earth vanished the moment the edge of the disk entered the opening of the box, almost like the box itself was the off switch.

I pulled the second disk out of the box, fully expecting another holographic globe to pop up over my hand. I was surprised when, instead, I was faced with a waterfall of shimmering, golden symbols hovering above my open hand. The writing streamed into and out of focus too quickly for me to read any of it.

Brow furrowed, I shook my head. I wanted to know what marvels the disk contained, but I didn't have time to read any of it right now. I slid the disk back into the box and pushed down on the top, until the box appeared, once more, to be a simple stone cube. I would have to make a deal with Henry—offer to translate the writing for him in exchange for something. I couldn't think of what, at the moment.

It was time to get out of here. Past time.

I stowed the cube in my backpack and resettled the bag on my shoulders, picked up the doru, and rounded the pedestal. And froze.

I had been wrong. The sides of the pedestal weren't bare. At least, not all of them. A thick column of writing had been carved into the backside.

I pulled my phone out of my pocket, intending to photograph the writing, but remembered it was dead before I even flipped it open. With a sigh, I tucked it back into my pocket and removed my backpack, setting it on the floor once more. I retrieved my mom's journal and tore a few blank pages out from the back of the book, then pulled a pencil from the front pouch. Holding a sheet of paper up against the writing carved into the stone, I lightly shaded over it like I was doing a grave rubbing.

The symbols quickly took shape on the paper. I swapped out the first sheet for the second, then the second for the third. I was working on the fourth sheet, recording the lowest portion of the column of writing, when the string of symbols taking shape on the paper caught my attention.

PERSEPHONE

I froze, then started shading even faster. Key phrases stood out, and the gears in my mind slowly rotated, one by one clicking into place.

. . . cloned embryo . . .

. . . stasis egg . . .

. . . surrogate mother . . .

. . . resurrection . . .

"Oh my God," I breathed, the sheet of paper shaking as I pulled away from the pedestal.

"The sphere of consciousness was supposed to be introduced to the child upon birth," Persephone said.

From directly behind me.

I spun around, sheet of paper slipping from my limp grasp and eyes opened as wide as they would go. "What—how—" I stumbled over my words, head slowly shaking back and forth.

The woman standing just a half-dozen steps away wore a form-fitting suit, black with electric blue piping running from her neck out to her fingertips and down to her toes. A doru was strapped to her back, tucked into a sleek harness. Her dark hair was pulled up and twisted into a bun. Her skin was pale, her features strong but feminine, her build athletic. And her eyes were a deep sapphire blue.

The same shade of blue I saw every time I looked in the mirror.

"It's protocol," Persephone said, eyes locking with mine. "To prevent a fractured consciousness."

I swallowed roughly, feeling like I was staring into a funhouse mirror, one that reflected back a warped, idealized version of myself.

"You—" I couldn't get the words out. My jaw trembled, and I licked my lips. "You're *me*."

39

"Actually, if you want to get technical about it," Persephone said, smiling wryly, "*you're* me."

Ever so slowly, I shook my head. "I've lost my mind."

"No," Persephone said, shaking her head, too. She took a step toward me. "Well, yes, actually, but just for a moment—just long enough for us to talk, face to face." She took another step.

I held up my hand, not sure I could handle this better version of myself getting any closer.

Persephone nodded, acquiescing. "Your shock gave me an opening."

"Oh," was all I could manage to say.

"We don't have much time, Cora, and I need you to listen to me." Persephone's voice was filled with vehemence. "Return to the vault and take the other cube, but leave your bag down here. You can retrieve it later, but this is the only place it will be safe from *them*."

"But what about my mom and Raiden?" I asked. "I have to give Henry something . . ."

"Don't you see?" Persephone said, shaking her head. "Once you've returned to him, the only one to have ever made it through the labyrinth alive, the balance of power between the two of you will have shifted . . . in your favor."

I blinked, lips parting and eyes widening.

"No matter what, we cannot let them get their hands on the cubes. Better the holodisks contained within remain lost down here forever than end up in their hands."

Numbly, I nodded. "What do they want?"

"I don't know," she said. "Much has changed since I died."

Again, I nodded. Much had changed since Persephone died. And I was her clone. Sure. That made perfect sense.

"You need to translate everything written on the pillars and stored in the holodisk to figure out what exactly Hades is planning." Her brow furrowed. "It must have something to do with saving our people, but . . ." She shook her head. "There's no way to know without more information."

Half of what she said slipped past me. I was still stuck on her comment about Hades, particularly on the tense she had used—present, not past.

"What Hades *is* planning?" I said, brows drawing together. This place was old—crazy advanced technologically, but ancient nonetheless. And Hades had *built* it. "But isn't he, you know, *dead*? And not just a little dead . . . like, way dead."

Persephone tilted her head to the side. "Maybe, but probably not," she said. "He's too smart . . . too stubborn. It's complicated." Before I could ask her to explain more, she continued, "go to the place marked by the beacon. See what else Hades wants us to find. And try not to let the Order know what you're up to."

I gulped, then nodded once.

This was really happening. I was really *her*.

Persephone was fading, like the ghost she was. "And be careful, Cora. I'm always with you, but I can't always help."

Again, I nodded.

Persephone was fully transparent, now. "If you die, we both

die," she said. "Forever . . ." Her final word was spoken in my head, and her apparition was gone.

I stood there, dumbfounded, staring at the place where Persephone had been. I finally had some answers, but they only spawned more questions. About a million of them. Maybe the answers were written somewhere, recorded by the camera in my phone or the sheets of paper on the floor, or maybe they were contained within the cubes, but I didn't have time to figure that out right now.

Raiden . . . my mom . . .

Thoughts of the people who were relying on me snapped me out of my stunned state and into action. I gathered the sheets of paper off the floor and tucked them between the pages of the journal, then stowed the book in my backpack. Straightening, I leaned the doru against the wall beside the archway. I couldn't risk having it confiscated the second I stepped foot in Vatican territory.

After a moment, I crouched down, unzipped the bag, and dug out the hoplon suit. I would look more formidable in Henry's eyes wearing the ancient armor than my mundane jeans and sweatshirt. But even more importantly, I would *feel* more formidable.

"I hope you're right about this," I murmured to Persephone, as I set my folded-up clothes on the floor beside my backpack.

I wasn't entirely convinced that leaving the bag and all of the artifacts contained within it down here in the labyrinth was the best plan. But I agreed with Persephone on one thing—it would be better to lose the ancient, alien technology forever than to hand it over to the Custodes Veritatis.

Taking a deep breath, I squared my shoulders and, once again, stepped through a wall of stone.

40

I was surrounded by cold water. Flowing water. It swept me away, disorienting me, and I struggled to differentiate up from down.

On sheer, dumb luck alone, my toe dragged across a rocky surface—the bottom, I hoped. I pushed off with all my strength.

Seconds later, I broke through the surface. I sputtered for breath as I flailed with arms and legs, attempting to keep my head above the water.

My injured shoulder slammed into a huge rock jutting out of the water, and searing pain whited out my vision as I spun around. Gasping, I reached for the rock with clawed fingers, barely managing to get a good grip before I was swept past it.

Luckily, the hoplon suit's gloves afforded me excellent grip, and I dug my fingers into a crevice a few inches above my hand-hold as I hacked up a lungful of water. Once I reached the point where I could take long, deep breaths without choking, I was finally able to take in my surroundings.

I was in the middle of the Tiber River, directly beneath a massive stone arch. At this point, if I never saw another stone arch it would be too soon. The rock I was clinging to wasn't just a rock, but the base of a pillar supporting a bridge, and the crevice that had become my handhold was the crack between two immense stone blocks.

The arch curved high overhead, dropping back down to the river about fifty yards away. The murky water of the Tiber River flowed lazily between the two pillars, barely a ripple in the surface save for the wake created by my disturbance. If it hadn't been for my injuries and the disorientation of being dumped out of the labyrinth ten feet underwater, I doubted I would have struggled at all.

Squinting, I looked beyond the bridge. The sky was clear but for a few wispy clouds, and the noon sun shone high overhead. I spotted the tower of Castel Sant'Angelo peeking over the high retaining wall beyond the west bank of the river. The five-arched Ponte Sant'Angelo crossed the Tiber a short way up river.

I dragged myself to the end of the pillar to see how far away I was from the river's west bank. This bridge was constructed of three arches, with two massive pillars planted in the river itself. My pillar held up half of the central and western arches. I estimated the riverbank to be about forty yards away, slightly closer than the other pillar.

Forty yards—that was shorter than the length of an Olympic swimming pool. I could handle that, even swimming with one lame arm across the river's current. It was far from raging, and though I wasn't an expert swimmer, I could manage a decent breaststroke. And considering that all of my swimming experience had taken place in the frigid Puget Sound, the chill to this water didn't bother me one bit. In fact, I could barely feel it through the hoplon suit.

I pulled my way around the base of the pillar to the other side and planted the soles of both feet against the wall of stone underwater. Taking a deep breath, I pushed off as hard as I could and swam my way toward the riverbank.

When I was about five yards out, my knee struck a stone

lodged in the mucky riverbed. "Ouch," I muttered, pulling my head out of the water and holding myself up with one hand.

I crawled the rest of the way to the water's edge, my good hand sinking into the silty sediment each time I planted it on the riverbed. I headed for a set of stairs handily built into the paved walkway running along the bank of the river, pausing for a moment with my elbows on the paving stones and my knees in the water.

I crawled the rest of the way onto the paved landing and, on hands and feet, clambered up the six stone steps to the walkway. At the top, I turned so I was sitting, then laid back and stared up at the sky, chest rising and falling rapidly from the exertion. Clearly, I needed to get more exercise.

While I lay there, I worked out my next moves. I would give myself a minute to catch my breath, and then I would run back to Vatican City, cut to the front of the public admittance line, and demand to be taken to see the Primicerius of the Custodes Veritatis. I figured those three words would do the trick.

"Stai bene?" The face of a middle-aged man appeared over me, blocking my view of the sun. "Signorina?"

I blinked in surprise. A laugh bubbled up from my chest and burst out of my mouth. I covered my mouth with one hand, giving the concerned man a thumbs up with the other. I was good. Or, as good as I could be, considering all of the *everything* I was dealing with right now. I just hoped the gesture translated.

The man didn't look convinced, but he did leave me alone, which was all that really mattered.

Once he was out of sight, I flopped my arms out to either side, inhaled deeply, and smiled.

Maybe I was crazy. Maybe I was an alien clone. Maybe I would die tomorrow in the search for the ancient Greek god of the dead.

But today, I was alive. Today, I had the means to save my mom and Raiden.

Today, for once, my life had a purpose.

Which meant that *today* was the best day of my life.

I was right, dropping the three magic words—*Primicerius* and *Custodes Veritatis*—worked like a charm.

Ten minutes after shoving my way to the front of the line in Saint Peter's Square, I was being escorted by a couple of heavily armed guards down a marble stairway to the passages beneath the library in the Apostolic Palace. And my guards didn't look like members of the Italian Carabinieri or the Pontifical Swiss Guard. These men didn't wear police gear or old-timey uniforms like I would have expected of members of those organizations, respectively; they wore black and gray camo, black body armor, and an array of weaponry that would've impressed even Raiden.

All of this muscle for little old me, and I wasn't even armed. Not that a trifling thing like weaponry really mattered. I felt fairly confident that, should push come to shove, Persephone would be able to take down both guards without making me break a sweat, no weapons needed. These guys were badasses, there was no mistaking that, but Persephone was next level. She was something else entirely. She was an Amazon warrior, and when it came to combat, no man—or woman—was her equal, save for another Amazon.

The guards must have been told not to touch me, because they were making an art of keeping their distance while simultaneously crowding me. I wondered what, exactly, they had been told. Henry had seen me read Raiden's mind, plus I had put on a fun little display with the doru. And there was no saying what kind of information Raiden had fed them on me. I hadn't gleaned those details from his mind.

Regardless, it was clear that a hands-off policy was in place.

The stairs gave way to a wide passage with a low ceiling, the polished marble transitioning to less shiny travertine. The dim lighting and pale stone lent the place the feel of a mausoleum.

Intricate cast iron gates blocked evenly spaced openings on either side of the passage. I peered through the first opening as we passed. Through the gate, I could see a small alcove filled with wine racks loaded up with wine bottles covered in a heavy coating of dust. Not a mausoleum, I realized, but a wine cellar.

After passing three more wine alcoves on either side, we reached an intersecting corridor and took a right. About ten yards in, another stairway delved deeper under the library.

When we reached the bottom of that second stairway and turned the corner, I recognized where we were—the torch-lined passage that led to the vault. One more corner up ahead, and the vault door would be within sight.

The guards stopped when we reached the final corner, taking up posts on either side. The vault door was shut, another guard posted there. Waiting for me.

I marched past my escorts and started down the final corridor, reviewing my plan in my head.

I wanted to get this over with and to get both Raiden and my mom out of here and into the labyrinth as quickly as possible. Once we were through, we would need to flee the city and hole up somewhere remote, where we could regroup and plot our next steps.

I was certain Persephone could've come up with something

better, but she had been quiet since exiting the labyrinth. Maybe she exhausted herself by appearing to me like she had. I didn't know.

What I *did* know was that my lame-o, vague plan was the only plan I had.

Both my mom and Raiden were expert plotters, so I was very comfortable with putting all of my eggs in their baskets, once we'd flown the coop, so to speak.

I was about halfway down the corridor when the guard at the door turned to lock and started rotating the dials, entering the six-digit code. There was a deep *clang*, and the lock disengaged, the reinforced door cracking open a few inches. The guard stepped across the corridor and pulled the door open the rest of the way.

Henry came into view first, standing with his left side to the doorway and his arms crossed over his chest. He looked my way as the door opened. His eyes locked with mine, and a pleased grin spread across his face.

A moment later, I spotted Raiden, sitting with his back leaned against the pedestal displaying the cube. The muscles and tendons in his neck were taught with pain, but the grin that spread his lips was bright and earnest, and when his eyes met mine, his whole body seemed to relax a little.

His and mine, both.

His injured leg was stretched out on the floor in front of him, a swath of white bandages wrapped around his thigh. Henry must have changed his mind about withholding medical attention. Maybe he wasn't as dickish as I had originally thought.

Raiden started to stand, but only made it halfway up.

A guard within the vault stepped into the doorway, blocking Raiden's path before he was even on his feet.

Raiden eased back down to the floor, his hands balling into fists.

When I was ten steps from the doorway, I touched the regulator, tracing the tip of my index finger around the stone, changing it from amber to electric blue. The narrow channels running the length of the hoplon suit glowed the same, vibrant color. I sucked in a breath at the sudden influx of psychic input, like dozens of voices shouting in my head, but the foreign thoughts quieted to whispers by the time I exhaled the breath.

"So the labyrinth exits elsewhere," Henry said, turning to face me fully as I entered the vault. He scanned me from the feet up, raising an eyebrow when his eyes returned to mine. My wardrobe change was noted.

I shot a quick glance around the vault. Two guards were posted on either side of the door within the vault, and another two stood on either side of the arched entrance to the labyrinth.

"Yes," I said, my attention settling on Henry, once more. "It exits *elsewhere*."

The hoplon suit had dried almost as soon as I was out of the river, and I had twisted my hair up in a tight bun after letting it dry partway, mimicking Persephone's standard hairstyle, in the hopes that Henry wouldn't be able to tell it was damp. I couldn't risk him figuring out where the labyrinth exited.

"How unexpected," Henry said.

I could sense in his thoughts that he was already formulating a plan to force me to reveal the exit point. There was no hint that he had noticed my hair wasn't completely dry.

"It would seem that you've returned empty handed," he said, uncrossing his arms. In his mind, he was shuffling through his next moves. "I thought I made myself clear—or does your friend's life mean so little to you?"

I took a slow step toward Henry. Then another. And another.

The guards raised their automatic rifles, training them on me.

I stopped, just out of arm's reach of Henry.

He didn't move, but I could sense the shift in his confidence. He fought the urge to take a step back, to put more distance between us. I was different, now, in his eyes. Before, he had feared me as one would fear a downed powerline—my power was wild and uncontrolled. Now, he feared me as one would fear a trained warrior. I had shifted out of the role of pawn and into the role of opponent. His priority was no longer forcing me to do his bidding, but making it out of the vault alive.

Persephone had been right. Henry wasn't in control of the situation anymore.

I was.

I smiled. "Here's what's going to happen, Henry," I said, repeating the same words he had used when giving me orders earlier. Now, I was the one giving the orders. "I'm going back into the labyrinth, and I'm taking Raiden and my mom with me."

I paused, surprise widening my eyes as an unexpected thought drifted from Henry's mind to mine: he didn't have my mom, not anymore. She had escaped while I was in the labyrinth. Emi must have snuck into the Apostolic Palace and sprung her. A laugh bubbled up from my chest, and I didn't bother holding it in.

Henry eyed me warily.

I almost couldn't believe how much the tides had turned since I'd last faced him in this room. Today was just not his day.

"I take that back," I told him. "I'm going to take *Raiden* into the labyrinth, and you're going to let me, because you want what I left in there, and the only way you have any chance of getting your hands on that special, secret prize is by letting me go." I took one more step toward Henry, bringing me well within his personal bubble. "Do we have deal?"

His breaths were deep, controlled. Within his mind, his thoughts spun as he worked through all of the possible scenarios, ranging from killing me here and now to letting me go with Raiden. To get what he wanted, he only saw one option: let us go.

"Good call," I said, stepping past him.

In three steps, I was standing in front of Raiden. I held my hand out to him, pulling him up to his feet.

"Are you up for this?" I asked him.

Raiden nodded, which was a relief, because after my little showdown with Henry, we didn't really have much of a choice.

"Good," I said, flashing Raiden a quick smile. I reached past him and snatched the storage cube off the pedestal behind him.

"What—what are you doing?" Henry sputtered as Raiden and I walked toward the entrance to the labyrinth. "You can't take that! It wasn't part of the deal!"

Raiden passed through first, not hesitating for even the briefest moment.

I paused, eyeing each of the four guards posted around the room, then glanced back at Henry over my shoulder. "What are you going to do—shoot me?"

I held his stare, waiting until his outrage gave way to cool-headed logic and just the barest hint of admiration. Waiting until he saw that, once again, he didn't have a choice.

The corner of his mouth lifted, forming the shadow of a smile, and he bowed his head infinitesimally. "I'll see you again, ancient one."

I returned his faint smile. "I'm counting on it."

———

Thanks for reading! You've reached the end of Legacy of the Lost, *but the story continues in* Fate of the Fallen.

Go to lindseyfairleigh.com/sacrifice to grab a free copy of Sacrifice of the Sinners, *the Atlantis Legacy prequel.*

MORE BOOKS BY LINDSEY FAIRLEIGH

ATLANTIS LEGACY

Sacrifice of the Sinners

Legacy of the Lost

Fate of the Fallen

ECHO TRILOGY

Echo in Time

Resonance

Time Anomaly

Dissonance

Ricochet Through Time

KAT DUBOIS CHRONICLES

Ink Witch

Outcast

Underground

Soul Eater

Judgement

Afterlife

THE ENDING SERIES

The Ending Beginnings: Omnibus Edition

After The Ending

Into The Fire

Out Of The Ashes

Before The Dawn

World Before

For more information on Lindsey and her books:

www.lindseyfairleigh.com

Join Lindsey's mailing list to stay up to date on releases AND to get a FREE copy of *Sacrifice of the Sinners.*

www.lindseyfairleigh.com/sacrifice

ABOUT THE AUTHOR

 Lindsey Fairleigh is a bestselling Science Fiction and Fantasy author who lives her life with one foot in a book—so long as that book transports her to a magical world or bends the rules of science. Her novels, from Post-apocalyptic to Time Travel Romance, always offer up a hearty dose of unreality, along with plenty of history, mystery, adventure, and romance. When she's not working on her next novel, Lindsey spends her time walking around the foothills surrounding her home with her dogs, playing video games, and trying out new recipes on her husband. She lives in the Pacific Northwest with her family and their small pack of dogs and cats.

www.lindseyfairleigh.com

Facebook: www.facebook.com/lindsey.fairleigh
Instagram: @authorlindseyfairleigh
Pinterest: www.pinterest.com/lindsfairleigh
Newsletter: www.lindseyfairleigh.com/join-newsletter